A
Deceptive
Bargain

A Deceptive Bargain

Laura Beers

MORE ROMANCE BY LAURA BEERS

ENGLAND, 1814

MARTHA RUSHED EAGERLY DOWN THE LONG, EXPANSIVE HALLS OF Chatswich Manor towards the nursery. If there were windows in the hallway, she knew she'd see the sun barely peeking over the horizon, but every morning it was the same routine. She would relieve the nursemaid and take over watching Caroline until Lady Lansdowne rose for the day.

Her employer and dear friend, Eliza, the Marchioness of Lansdowne, spent most of her day with her child, which made her an oddity to the elite of London society. The ton couldn't comprehend such loving, devoted parents as Lord and Lady Lansdowne. They doted on their eight-month-old baby, the Lady Caroline Kate Beckett, with a fierceness that she had never seen.

As she walked into the nursery, Caroline made cooing noises in her crib, expressing her desire to be picked up. Sarah, the nursemaid, started to rise from her chair but stopped when she saw Martha approach.

"You are late," Sarah chided gently with a smile. "I'd nearly decided to start her morning routine, but I know how much you love picking Lady Caroline up from the crib."

"It is true," Martha replied, returning her smile as she

approached the crib. "It is my favorite part of the day." Placing her hands on the crib rail, she leaned forward and smiled warmly at the precious child. "How are you this fine morning?"

In response, Caroline beamed and reached out for Martha. Scooping the baby up in her arms, she hugged her tightly. "I am in love," she murmured softly, kissing Caroline's soft cheek.

A pleasant baritone chuckle came from the doorway. Turning her head, she saw Benedict, the Marquess of Lansdowne, leaning against the wall, dressed in his riding attire. "No matter how hard I try, you always seem to beat me to the nursery in the mornings," he remarked in a teasing tone.

She dropped into a polite curtsy. "You made the mistake of going riding, my lord."

"Ah, I see where I strayed," he joked with a twinkle in his eye.

Walking closer to Lord Lansdowne, she asked, "Would you like to hold your daughter, sir?"

Benedict gave a slight shake of his head. "I am only teasing you, Martha." With a sweep of his hand, he indicated she should walk ahead of him. "Although, I daresay my wife will not be as tolerant."

Martha laughed, snuggling the infant closer. "If only you were like the other vain and pompous lords and ladies who only see their children in the nursery. Then I would be free to hold Lady Caroline to my heart's content."

As they walked towards Eliza's bedchamber, Benedict clasped his hands behind his back. He glanced at her, curiosity in his expression. "Have you considered my wife's request to become her companion? You would have more time to spend with Caroline."

"I am happy with my position as Lady Lansdowne's lady's maid," Martha assured him as she shifted Caroline to her other hip, eager to end this futile conversation.

Turning his gaze straight ahead and keeping his tone neutral,

Benedict observed, "You were born into nobility and are worth far more than a lady's maid."

"I may have been born into nobility, but my father was a lowly vicar, making me merely a country bumpkin," she replied dismissively.

Stopping in the hall, Benedict turned to face her, his brow furrowed. "We both know your uncle is Lord Waterford, and you are not just a country bumpkin."

"Need I remind you that I haven't seen my uncle in over seven years," she said, making silly faces at Caroline. She was promptly rewarded with the baby's giggles. "Besides, that is not my life anymore."

Benedict regarded her with a kindness in his eyes that allowed her to feel safe enough to trust his intentions. "My point being, you are Eliza's friend and confidante. You are completely qualified to act as her companion."

"Typically, companions are reserved for unmarried women or widows, and Eliza is neither," Martha pointed out. "Plus, she has *you*." She softened her words with a smile.

"That is true, but we want to elevate your status in our household, especially since you are Caroline's godmother."

Martha met his gaze, considering her words carefully, being mindful that Lord Lansdowne was still her employer. As she rocked Caroline on her hip, she asserted, "I am grateful for your kind words, but I have no desire to be a companion. I prefer being a lady's maid, because I enjoy serving Lady Lansdowne."

Benedict sighed. "I wish you would open…"

A feminine voice cut him off. "That is rubbish," Eliza declared, walking towards them. "You may continue hiding out, but it is time you became my companion."

Even in the morning, Lady Lansdowne looked beautiful in her green wrapper, her auburn hair pulled back into a loose chignon, her olive skin and high cheekbones glowing with good health.

As she saw her mother approach, Caroline clapped with glee and tried to lunge out of Martha's arms. Laughing, she handed the baby to Eliza. "We were on our way to wake you."

With a loving glance at her husband, Eliza explained, "I can't sleep without Benedict, and he rose early to go riding… without me." A small frown came to her lips, but Martha detected no hint of censure in her voice.

Benedict put his arm over his wife's shoulder, pulling her close. "You looked so peaceful this morning. I didn't dare disturb you." Grinning, he leaned in and whispered, "Besides, I kept you up very late last night."

Lowering her gaze, Eliza blushed as her husband kissed her cheek. "Well, I suppose you had a good reason."

Watching the undeniable love between Eliza and Benedict, Martha felt overwhelming happiness that these two kindred spirits had found each other. Lowering her gaze to grant them some privacy, Martha knew that she would never feel passion such as theirs. Suppressing the yearning in her heart, she reminded herself that she wasn't worthy of love, for she was ruined, body and soul. Her innocence had been snatched from her and replaced with distrust and fear.

"Now," Eliza's voice broke through her thoughts, "I thought we could go shopping today in the village."

"I am sure Mr. Larson will be pleased to accompany you," Martha replied, looking up again. "After all, he mentioned he has a passing fancy for bonnet shopping."

Benedict chuckled as Eliza said, "I allowed you to be my lady's maid for two years, but I am in desperate need of a companion now."

"No…"

"…thank you," Eliza blurted, finishing Martha's sentence. "I know you are happy being a lady's maid, but you were born to do so much more."

Martha sighed at her friend's enthusiasm, despite knowing

that they were about to have the same conversation they always did. "I appreciate what you are trying to do, but I have a deep mistrust of men in general. That alone would make me a horrible companion."

"You like me," Benedict teased.

"I do now. But it took months before I could even speak to you," Martha reminded him. "Besides you, I only trust Mr. Larson, Lord Jonathon, and Lord Camden. That is not a wide selection of men. You must understand that I have no desire to socialize with men ever again."

"Excellent," Eliza proclaimed with a victorious smile. "A companion is not required to mingle with gentlemen."

"I would prefer to play with Lady Caroline all day," Martha said, watching the baby lunge for her father.

Benedict lifted Caroline from Eliza's arms. "This precious rascal already has a nursemaid," Benedict maintained as he tossed his daughter in the air, her laughter echoing in the hall. "I will entertain this lovely lady up in the nursery while you prepare to break your fast."

Eliza arched an eyebrow. "Did you just call our daughter a rascal?"

"I did," he admitted, amused. "She managed to win over my heart, just as easily as you did." Leaning in, he kissed Eliza's cheek before he turned to walk back to the nursery.

Eliza looped her arm through hers. "Come, my dear companion."

As they walked towards Eliza's bedchamber, Martha was grateful for this dear friend, who was the one constant in her life. Without Eliza, she would still be at the mercy of those men who only wanted her for one vile purpose. She closed her eyes against a flood of painful emotions. They always came back to haunt her at the most inopportune moments, despite her best effort to keep them buried deep inside.

Shuddering, the vivid memory of India took her back to a

time she would rather forget. The smell of the musty tent, the dry straw on the floor digging into her legs, and the men bartering for her as though she was merely an animal for sale.

"Martha," Eliza's voice came from far away, "you are safe."

Slowly, she opened her eyes and saw the concern on Eliza's face. She offered a weak, reassuring smile before saying, "I know I am safe here at Chatswich Manor, but I am not safe from the memories that plague me. I will never be free of those."

"You will be," Eliza assured her. "It will just take more time."

Martha shook her head, not believing her friend's words. "It has been two years since you saved me, and I still relive those memories as if they were yesterday. I spend most nights in the nursery because I can't sleep. When I close my eyes, those years of slavery come back to haunt me with such a vengeance that I wish I could slip into oblivion."

Reaching out, Eliza hugged her tightly, providing her with much-needed comfort. "You are always welcome to stay here, either as my lady's maid or as my companion. You will never need to fear for your safety again," she expressed as she took a step back.

"Thank you," Martha murmured.

"You should really stop thanking me. You thank me every day."

Swallowing hard, Martha replied, "I'm afraid I can't stop. I am still just as grateful as I was the moment Mr. Larson walked me over to you, and you removed my bindings, declaring me free."

"If you really want to thank me," Eliza said deliberately, "then live your life as you see fit. Be happy."

Martha smiled broadly. "If that is your wish for me, then please know that I am happy being your lady's maid at Chatswich Manor. Now, may we drop this companion nonsense?"

"We'll see," Eliza agreed quickly, making it clear that she did not intend to let the matter drop.

She sat down at the dressing room table, handing Martha the hairbrush. As Martha brushed Eliza's hair, a loud knock came from the door. "Enter," Eliza ordered.

The door opened, and Mr. Larson walked into the room, his usual confident demeanor replaced by an aura of reluctance. "There is a visitor for Miss Martha downstairs."

A feeling of dread washed over Martha, and she tensed. Trepidation in her voice, she asked, "Who is the caller?"

Frowning deeper, Mr. Larson cleared his throat. "He claims that he is your father."

Martha gasped, dropping the brush onto the floor. "No, no, no, no..." she muttered in disbelief. Without thinking, she backed up until her legs hit the four-poster bed. "How did he find me?"

Tentatively, Eliza rose and placed her hands on the back of the chair. "I have a confession," she stated warily. "Every year since we brought you here, I have sent a letter to your father and mother to let them know you were safe."

Eyes wide with disbelief, Martha exclaimed, "Why would you do that? I did not grant you permission to do so!"

"They are your parents, and I assumed they were worried about you," Eliza explained.

Martha scoffed. "I guarantee that they were not. You had no right!" She hesitated, then tentatively asked, "Did they ever write back?"

Eliza shook her head. "No, they did not. But your father did come all the way to Chatswich Manor to call on you. Perhaps he has a good reason."

"I don't care," she asserted, pushing away from the bed to pace the room. "Did you ever wonder why I never spoke of my father? My father is a tyrant. He never cared for me."

"Maybe time has softened his manner?" Eliza proposed, hopefully.

Martha stopped pacing, knowing she needed to express her feelings adequately. "I owe you my life, Eliza, and respect you dearly, but you can't presume to know the complexities of my father. There is a reason I ran away from him. At times, I wondered what was worse," she hesitated, "living under his thumb or being subjected to slavery."

Eliza cast a worried glance towards Mr. Larson. "Surely, it could not have been that bad."

"It was," she assured them, her voice firm.

Mr. Larson stepped closer, his tone compassionate. "If I may, your father isn't in a position to hurt you now. Not only are you employed by Lady Lansdowne, but I would never let another person lay a hand on you ever again."

"Thank you," she responded, touched that his expression was so caring and sincere. How she wished she had a father like Mr. Larson, a man who had always treated her with kindness and respect.

"If it would help, I will escort you downstairs and remain in the room as you meet with your father," Mr. Larson encouraged.

Martha ran her hand down her black servant's frock. "I haven't agreed to meet with him, yet," she reminded them, her resolve weakening.

"But you will," Eliza stated, knowingly. "Mr. Larson and I have nothing to do all day *but* convince you to meet with your father."

She sighed, knowing it was inevitable. Her friends were just as stubborn as she was. "I will go, assuming both of you will remain in the room with me."

"Yes, I would be honored," Eliza confirmed. "Since you are seeing your father for the first time in years, let's dress you in one of my gowns."

Martha shook her head. "I will meet with him as I am."

AFTER SHE TUCKED THE LAST PIN INTO HER BLONDE HAIR, Martha placed her hand on her stomach, which churned with dread. She stood outside of the drawing room, knowing that only one wall separated her from her father.

Eliza reached down and grasped her hand. Leaning closer, she whispered, "You can do this."

Nodding her head, Martha took a few steps and entered the room, drawing strength from Eliza and Mr. Larson behind her.

When she walked into the drawing room, her father stood, his eyes narrowing dangerously as they took in her black servant's frock. "You work as a servant?" he shouted.

"Father," she responded with a tip of her head, ignoring his outburst. Gesturing towards her friends, she acknowledged, "May I introduce Lady Lansdowne and Mr. Larson, the steward of Chatswich Manor?"

With a wave of his hand, her father dismissed them. "I would like a moment alone with my daughter."

"I would prefer that they stay," Martha said, attempting to keep her voice steady.

Her father's expression hardened, but he nodded his acceptance.

Eliza gently nudged her towards the settee, opposite her father. As they sat down, her father kept his steely gaze on her, making her even more uncomfortable. Smoothing out her skirt, she cast a furtive glance at Mr. Larson, who stood back near the wall.

Taking in a slow, deep breath, Martha turned to face her father, taking a moment to study his features. Time had been kind to him. His handsome looks had not diminished much, although his brown hair had begun to fade. The creases around his mouth had deepened, giving the only real indication of his age. He was impeccably dressed in a very fine, dark blue tail-coat, buff trousers, and Hessian boots.

She remembered that he'd always insisted on presenting himself well, even to the detriment of others. He may look the part of an English gentleman, but she knew his cold, tainted heart all too well.

Breaking the silence, her father declared, "I have come to take you home."

"I am home," she replied without hesitation.

"You are not home," he scoffed as his eyes darted around the room. "You are working as a servant..." he turned his gaze towards Eliza, "which was somehow omitted in both of Lady Lansdowne's letters."

The epitome of grace, Eliza simply smiled at the harsh words. "Mr. Haskett..."

"You do not need to justify your actions, my lady," Martha interrupted, then answered her father firmly. "Lady Lansdowne originally offered me a position as her companion, but I choose to work as her lady's maid."

"A fitting position for a fallen lady," her father mumbled under his breath.

Mr. Larson took a step forward, his expression matching the warning in his words. "You will be civil to Miss Martha, or I will escort you out."

After only a moment's hesitation, her father tipped his head in acknowledgement before he turned his gaze back towards her. He cleared his throat. "I did not come to fight with you, Martha. I want you to move back home..." he hesitated before adding, "...with me."

"No, absolutely not!" she exclaimed, jumping up.

Her father sat back in his seat, completely unaffected by her outburst. "Your uncle, Lord Waterford, passed away seven months ago, and I inherited his earldom."

"But what about my cousin, Daniel?" she asked, dreading his response.

"He died, as well," her father replied with no hint of emotion. "As my daughter, you are now a titled lady."

Slowly, she lowered herself onto the settee. "I have no desire for a title."

Dismissively, her father made a show of picking some lint off his sleeve. "And yet, you have one."

Martha felt Eliza's hand cover hers, and she felt strengthened by her friend. Returning her father's gaze, she said, "Thank you for coming in person to inform me, but this changes nothing."

"This changes everything!" her father proclaimed. "You are a lady."

She shook her head. "It doesn't matter. I have no wish to leave Lady Lansdowne's employ."

"Come home with me and allow me to prepare you for the social Season," her father urged. "We will buy you gowns and find a suitable match for you."

Martha shook her head. "No, I have no desire to ever be married."

He eyed her with contempt. "That is ironic, is it not, since you ran away to elope with the merchant's son?"

"Lord Waterford…" Mr. Larson began in a low growl.

Martha put her hand up to stop her protector. She turned to face her father. Her voice shook, but she pressed forward with determination on her face. "No, Mr. Larson. He asks a fair question. I made a foolish mistake, and it was a mistake that I have paid for dearly. Not a day goes by that I do not regret my naïve actions. But that is in the past, and I must look towards my future; a future that is not conducive to having a husband."

Lord Waterford sat forward in his seat, his voice somewhat

pleading. She had never witnessed that before. "At least hear me out… for your mother's sake."

"My mother?" she asked, confused.

His eyes grew sad, reflective. "Your mother passed away five months ago."

Martha's hand flew to her mouth, her eyes filling with tears. "Mother is dead," she murmured in disbelief. After a long moment, she whispered, "How?"

"As you may recall, your mother was prone to headaches and became increasingly addicted to laudanum. The doctor said her heart eventually gave out." The admission seemed to have affected him deeply. He now appeared tired, and the hard lines in his face had softened.

Martha blinked back the tears threatening to slide down her cheeks. Even though she hadn't seen her mother in over seven years, the finality of her death made Martha question her resolve to not attempt a reconciliation. It may not have been her mother's fault that she married a tyrant, but she had never shielded Martha from her father's brutal treatment or heavy hand.

"I have made many mistakes in the past, ones that I regret every day, but I am begging you for another chance," her father pleaded softly, appearing sorrowful.

"I don't know…" Martha replied, her voice trailing off.

"Please, just give me one Season. Your mother made me promise to give you a Season." He hesitated, then swallowed slowly. "I hope we can reconcile our fragile relationship."

"We don't have a relationship, Father," she remarked dryly.

Lord Waterford dropped his head and sighed. "You are my daughter."

"In blood, yes, but our paths parted ways long ago," Martha replied, knowing her words were harsh. She was not going to pretend to be a kind, loving daughter to a father that was anything but kind and loving.

With a tight frown, Lord Waterford reached over to the table and picked up his top hat, standing slowly. "Reside with me and give me one Season to prove to you that I have changed. After that, if you have not selected a husband, then I will release your dowry to you and gift you with one of my estates. And, if you desire, I will leave you be."

Martha eyed her father suspiciously. He had never been known for his selfless service. "What do you hope to gain from this?"

Fidgeting with the hat in his hands, her father looked forlorn. "Nothing but the chance to prove to my daughter that I still love her." His fingers stilled, and his gaze grew insistent. "If you won't do it for me, then do it for your mother. It was her last wish."

"But I am ruined since I ran away to elope with Simeon," Martha reminded him.

Lord Waterford shook his head. "We suppressed those rumors by explaining you were residing with your uncle in London."

"But I have been gone for more than seven years," she pressed. "How is it possible that no one has wondered why I have been gone for so long?"

"Our town is full of simple people that do not comprehend the complexities of how nobility lives," he attempted to explain. "As far as the town was concerned, you were being prepared for Society."

"I see," she acknowledged softly, still not convinced.

Lord Waterford grimaced, appearing uncomfortable. "I know Lady Lansdowne informed me that you never wed the merchant's son, but were you... uh... intimate with him?"

"No, I was not," she informed him. "He deceived me in many ways, but that was not one of them."

His smile showed his relief. "Thank goodness for that. A gentleman does not like sharing a wife with another."

Martha stifled a groan. Apparently, he thought she was still an innocent. He must not know of her past. Regardless, she had no intention of marrying anyone. "Father, I have no desire..." she started.

He put his hand up to stop her. "The Season starts in a month, and I will be residing at our townhouse in London. Send me a note regarding your decision."

Lord Waterford nodded his farewell to Lady Lansdowne. Before taking a step, he turned his gaze back towards her. "We may have had our differences in the past, but I wish to start a new chapter in our lives; one that includes each other."

Offering her a smile, Lord Waterford turned and walked out the door.

Martha's heart grieved the loss of her mother, but she knew she'd be glad if she never saw her father again. No good had ever or would ever come from associating with him. She determined in that very moment to never see or speak with him again.

2

As Martha breathed a sigh of relief, Eliza said the most ludicrous thing. "I think your father is right. You should go to London and have a Season."

Martha's jaw dropped, utterly shocked by her friend's words. "Are you mad?"

Ignoring her ire, Eliza pressed, "Just hear me out..."

"No, I will not," she declared. "You don't know him like I do. He is callous, unfeeling, cruel..." Her voice trailed off as her chest heaved with fury. "I do not trust him."

"Nor do I," Mr. Larson agreed, walking closer to them.

Benedict entered the room with Lady Caroline in his arms. "Did I hear shouting?" His eyes held concern. "I was up in the nursery when I saw a coach driving away."

Grinning, Eliza announced, "Martha's father came to visit her."

"Interesting," Benedict remarked as his eyes shifted towards her.

"That is not the best part," Eliza shared, her eyes twinkling with merriment. "Our dear, sweet Martha is now a titled lady."

Benedict smiled widely. "Is she now?"

"Please stop this madness," Martha begged. "I have no intention of making use of the title."

Stepping closer to his wife, Benedict inquired, "Why ever not?"

Martha put her fingertips on her temples as she formulated her thoughts. "I am not a lady."

Mr. Larson smirked. "I beg to differ."

With a huff, Martha chose to overlook Mr. Larson's teasing and dropped her hands. "I will not go back and live with my father. You can't possibly understand what it was like to live under his oppressive rule."

Eliza laughed. "I believe I might have an idea, Lady Martha."

"Don't call me that," she stated.

"Why not?" Eliza teased. "It is your name."

Moving to the drawing room door, Martha peered out into the hall, confirming no one had overheard their conversation. She closed the door, granting them additional privacy.

Returning to the settee, she explained, "I made the mistake of being born a girl."

"That is a common mistake," Benedict mocked as he kissed his daughter on the top of her head.

With a soft chuckle, Martha sat on the settee. Then, all traces of humor disappeared. "My parents tried for years to have an heir and were devastated when I was born. I was forgotten, left to my nursemaids, until my father needed to act like a devoted father to his parish. As I got older, his expectations became unrealistic, and he punished me for any indiscretion."

Tears welled in her eyes as she admitted, "To our parish, he was a kind but firm vicar, and he played the part very well. But it was just an act. He only cared about himself." She wiped a tear off her cheek.

Eliza sat next to her and handed her a handkerchief. "Maybe he changed?"

"I highly doubt that," she responded, her voice terse, almost expressionless.

Mr. Larson moved to sit in a chair across from her. "Is that why you ran away?"

Martha's hands gripped the handkerchief tightly, wondering how to answer. She had only revealed the sordid details of her past to Eliza, but perhaps it was time to trust Mr. Larson and Lord Lansdowne with part of her story.

She started with a shaky breath. "I fell in love with Simeon. He was everything my father was not; attentive and kind." Her voice broke off as she gathered strength to continue. "He was the son of a wealthy merchant in our village, and we grew up together. However, my father did not approve of someone working in a trade, and as I got older, I was forbidden to spend time with him."

Leaning down, Benedict sat Caroline on the carpet and watched as she clapped with glee. "Ah, forbidden love," he quipped.

Watching Caroline reminded Martha that she would never have a family of her own. With a tense smile, she rose and said in a clipped voice, "And we all know how that ended."

Dipping her head, she started to leave, but Eliza's hand reached out and touched her arm. "We do, but we also know that your story is not done yet. You have your whole life ahead of you. It is time for you to stop hiding."

"I am not hiding," she protested. "This is my life, and I am happy."

"You are most definitely hiding, Lady Martha," Mr. Larson affirmed.

"Do not call me that," she demanded. "Besides, you all seem to forget that I have been in that world, and it was not kind to me."

Dropping her hand, Eliza rose and eyed her with compassion.

"I feel it is in your best interest to go to London with your father and have a Season."

"No," she argued, shaking her head, "it is not."

"Hear me out," Eliza pressed. "Your father is trying to make amends with you and wants to give you a Season. Furthermore, if you don't marry by the end of the Season, then he will release your dowry and gift you an estate."

Martha crossed her arms over her chest and walked to the window, peering out. "Then what? Live in a huge estate, alone and afraid?" she questioned. How could she make them understand that she did not want that life?

"Martha," Eliza's cautious voice came from behind her, "you are my dear friend, and I love you."

"I feel the same way," she expressed as she turned around to face Eliza.

"You have every reason to be hesitant of this world, but it is time for you to start living again," Eliza encouraged.

"By living, you mean trusting others again," she corrected.

Eliza nodded. "That is exactly what I mean."

Martha huffed and tilted her head defiantly. "Those years at a brothel cannot be undone. They robbed me of my past and future, and I refuse to go back into the world as if nothing happened."

"If I may…" Benedict started from across the room.

"No, you may not," Martha interrupted sternly. "I am grateful for all the kindness that you have bestowed upon me, but this is *my* choice." Recognizing the inappropriateness of her tone, she dropped into a curtsy. "I apologize for my harsh words, my lord," she mumbled.

Deciding that she was finished with this conversation, she started to walk past Eliza, but her friend put her hand on her sleeve once again. "Please don't be angry. We just want what's best for you."

Martha's anger dissipated at the sight of Eliza's crestfallen expression. "I am sorry as well. I have no right to speak to you that way," she said, offering an apologetic smile.

"You have every right, especially when you are not wrong," Eliza admitted as she squeezed her arm, then dropped her hand. "You are a grown woman and are free to make your own choices."

Wincing, Martha recalled, "I believe the words you used after you bought my freedom were 'no one will ever own you again'."

Mr. Larson's voice was tender as he observed, "You are not the same woman that we found on the floor in India."

Tightening her resolve, Martha lifted her chin, determination straightening her spine. "You are right. I am not the same woman, and I made my choice. I will remain as I am."

A WEEK LATER, DR. EMMETT MADDIX EXITED THE COACH IN front of Chatswich Manor, his black leather bag tucked securely under his arm. He had been summoned by Lady Lansdowne because her daughter, Caroline, was sick and needed immediate medical attention.

As his eyes roamed the lavish, three-level, stately structure, he admired the wide, evenly spaced, embellished columns and pilasters. Two towers extended high above the flat roof, but the carved stonework above the main door drew his attention. Adding to the grandeur of the estate was a large river winding through wooded, rocky foothills dancing between large boulders on its way towards the valley.

The main door opened, and Lady Lansdowne rushed out onto

the circular, cobblestone drive to greet him, relief evident on her face. "Emmett, you are finally here!"

"I came as soon as I could," he replied, not bothering to reveal that they had only stopped to swap out the horses. "Your note said that Caroline was horribly sick with influenza, and the village doctor was trying to kill her."

Taking a moment to study Eliza, he took in her wrinkled dress and disheveled appearance. Her auburn hair was pulled into a low chignon, with errant strands falling down the sides of her face. He was most concerned by the dark circles under her eyes, which testified to her exhaustion.

"We are beside ourselves right now. Caroline grew sick about six days ago and doesn't appear to be getting any better. We called for the village doctor who informed us that she had influenza. He recommended we treat her with *leeches*," she explained urgently, displaying an unease which was at odds with her usually confident demeanor.

Following her into the estate, his steps faltered at that announcement. "And did you?"

Eliza stopped and turned to face him. "No, I did as you instructed me to do."

"Which was?"

"I promptly removed him from our home."

"And?" he pressed.

Eliza sighed, "I told him he was a quack."

He nodded his approval. "That is right. I have found in my experience that leeches do more harm than good. It is a medieval practice that I wish we would stop."

Eliza looked worried. "I have never been so afraid."

Walking over to a side table, Emmett put his bag down then turned back towards her. "I will go examine Caroline in a minute, but first," he paused, "how are you?" His eyes roamed her face, attempting to see if fatigue was the only concern for Eliza.

She waved her hand dismissively. "Do not concern yourself with me. I am perfectly healthy."

"No, you are not. You look exhausted, your wrinkled gown tells me you slept in it, and your hair is coming out of its pins." Ignoring the narrowing of her eyes, he added, "I assume you have not eaten or been outside in days."

Her lips formed a tight, white line. "Emmett, you don't need to fuss over me."

"I am your doctor, as well."

"I am not in need of any doctoring," Eliza insisted.

Sighing in response, he leaned back against the wall. "Eliza, you are very stubborn."

Chuckling came from the other end of the hall as Benedict walked closer. "You are fighting a losing battle, my friend."

Emmett shook his head when he saw Benedict mirrored Eliza's haggard appearance. "Are either of you resting or taking care of yourselves?"

Benedict approached Eliza and put his arm around her shoulders. "I was just coming to find my wife, so I could escort her up to our bedchamber for a nap." He yawned. "It has been a long night."

Lifting a skeptical brow, Emmett asked, "Don't you have hundreds of servants who could look after Caroline while you rest?"

Eliza's lower lip trembled for a moment before she shared, "I am worried that every breath might be her last, and I dare not leave her side."

Emmett winced as he straightened from the wall, hoping her words weren't true. In a soft voice, he inquired, "Who is with Caroline now?"

"Martha," Benedict revealed. "She insisted that Eliza and I sleep for a few hours."

Emmett bobbed his head in understanding. "If I have your permission, I will go to the nursery and examine Caroline."

"Of course," Eliza affirmed, leaning against Benedict. "Please wake me if anything changes."

Attempting to lighten the mood, Emmett asked, "We have been in worse scrapes than this, have we not?"

To his surprise, Benedict's tough exterior crumbled. "Not I." Anguish and heartache filled those simple words.

Picking up his bag, Emmett started for the nursery. After fighting side-by-side against a French invasion in Scotland, he had stayed close with Eliza and Benedict and considered them dear friends. Furthermore, he had helped deliver Caroline and even had the honor of becoming one of her godfathers.

The image of Miss Martha came to his mind. She was one of Caroline's godmothers and a most perplexing woman. He had witnessed her speaking on only a few occasions to Lady Lansdowne. She had a stony demeanor and appeared entirely unapproachable. She seemed an odd choice for a godmother, especially since she was only a lady's maid. But who was he to judge?

As he neared the nursery, he heard the most beautiful singing drifting down the hall. The door was opened wide enough that he could see Martha sitting on a chair with Caroline sleeping in her arms. She was singing a French lullaby that he was unfamiliar with.

Not wanting to interrupt the beautiful melody, he took the time to admire her undeniable beauty. She had soft, delicate features, blonde hair that glowed in the sunlight from the window, and full lips that drew his attention. The look of love on her face as she stared at the infant tugged on his heartstrings, but behind it lay anguish and sorrow that was palpable. What had happened in her life to cause her to be so wary of others?

As the song ended, he waited a few moments before he cleared his throat. Her eyes darted up to him, and a flash of annoyance crossed her face. In one smooth motion, she rose, placed Caroline in her crib and took a few steps back, obviously putting more distance between them.

Wanting to set her at ease, Emmett asked gently, "What were you singing?" Slowly, he moved to place his bag down on a small table.

"It is a lullaby that my nursemaid used to sing to me," she revealed, her tone flat.

"It is beautiful. Are you fluent in French?"

Martha eyed him suspiciously as he waited patiently for her answer, allowing him to examine her more closely. Her cheeks were pink, her shoulders slumped, and sunken eyes confirmed her exhaustion. Finally, she answered, "I am."

He grinned, hoping to relieve some of her tension. "You are full of surprises, Miss Martha."

Not acknowledging his words, she muttered, "If you will excuse me, Doctor Maddix. I will step outside as you examine Lady Caroline."

"Before you go," he hesitated, attempting to find a reason to extend their conversation, "can you describe Caroline's condition?"

Sadness lined her features as her eyes strayed back towards the child. "Six days ago, I noticed that Caroline had become lethargic, and she was hot to the touch. We fought to bring the fever down, but it hasn't broken yet."

"Does she have a cough?"

"Yes."

Eliza had informed him of Caroline's condition in her letter, but he still wanted to examine her. Walking up to the crib, he noticed that Martha was slowly inching towards the door. Leaning over, Emmett placed his ear on Caroline's chest and listened to her haggard breathing. Next, he confirmed her pulse to be peculiarly quick and irregular.

Reaching into his pocket, he pulled out an ivory tool and placed it in Caroline's mouth. Tucking his finger under her chin, he tilted her head to examine her mouth and throat. He noticed her skin tone was good, and the color of her throat confirmed she didn't have scarlet fever. If any child could fight off influenza, it was this infant.

"What is that?" Martha asked as she took a few steps closer to him.

Stepping back from the crib, Emmett held up the thin tool for her examination. "It is called a tongue depressor. I use this tool to press on a patient's tongue, which allows me to examine their throat." He held it out to her. "Would you like to look at it?"

Tentatively, she reached out and accepted the tongue depressor, fingering the rounded edges on each side. "Where did you get this?"

"It was a gift from my father," he admitted, proudly. "It is made from the tusk of a narwhal."

Martha looked perplexed. "What is a narwhal?"

"It is a whale that has a large tusk protruding out of its mouth."

"Oh," she mumbled as she extended the tongue depressor back to him.

Emmett accepted the tool and returned it to his pocket. Reaching into his bag, he pulled out several small, glass bottles and placed them on the table.

"Can you save Caroline?" she asked weakly before she began coughing.

Turning to face her, he picked up one of the glass bottles and nodded. "I am going to try. I plan to treat her with a syrup of squills, which is an extract from a bulb that grows in the Mediterranean area, as an expectorant to help with her cough. For her pain, I will also give her a small dose of laudanum."

Martha's face grew serious. "If you will write down the dosage, I will ensure the medicine is given to her."

"No, that is not necessary. I will stay and administer the

medicine," Emmett said. "I want to ensure the powders are dosed accurately."

"I assure you that I am completely capable of following your written instructions," Martha insisted with a tightness in her voice.

"I have no doubt," he responded quickly. "However, I will stay until Caroline makes a full recovery." He glanced fondly over at the infant. "Because she *will* recover."

Martha covered her mouth as another raspy cough erupted. "How can you be so sure?"

"Because she is a lot like her mother," he jested with a small smirk. "She is too stubborn to die."

"Dr. Maddix…" Her words were stilled by another cough.

Taking a step closer, his eyes roamed her face with concern. "How long have you had that cough?"

"Only a few days," she stated, taking two steps back.

Hesitantly, he ventured, "I would like your permission to examine you."

"No, you may not," she responded forcefully.

Wanting to help, he took a step closer to her, and Martha shrank back, her eyes filled with panic. Calmly putting his hands up in front of him, he observed in a soothing voice, "Your cheeks are pink, your eyes betray your fatigue, and you have a rattling cough. I fear that you may have influenza as well."

Martha coughed again but attempted to stifle it. "I am well. Please concern yourself only with Lady Caroline's condition."

A pitiful whimper came from the crib, and Martha brushed past him to check on the baby, who remained asleep. As she leaned over the crib, her hand tenderly rubbed the top of the child's head.

Turning to retrieve the bottles, he saw Martha sway slightly. Instinctively, he reached out to keep her from falling. The moment he placed his hand on her elbow, she gasped and punched him in the throat.

3

THE MOMENT DR. MADDIX'S HAND LEFT HER SLEEVE, MARTHA ran out into the hall and didn't stop until she reached her bedchamber. She opened her door, slammed it, and locked it in one fluid motion. Turning around, she rested her back against the door, sliding down until she was sitting on the floor.

Burying her face in her arms, Martha sobbed. No man had touched her since she was auctioned off in India. As the memories of those men touching her, forcing her to do horrific acts, overwhelmed her, she succumbed to an unrestrained wail of grief.

After a few moments, she struggled to regain control. No, she thought, shaking her head, I will not dwell on those ever again. She had buried those memories deep within her soul, and there they remained, for the most part. Periodically, however, they tried to surface, forcing her to remember the hell she had endured.

When Dr. Maddix touched her, she'd panicked, jabbing him in the throat, just as Eliza had taught her. Horror filled her mind. What if she had killed him? She was warned to only hit someone in their throat in self-defense, because it could crush the windpipe, causing the airway to close. Her eyes widened as she realized she had left him to die while she was sobbing in her bedchamber, feeling sorry for herself. What was the matter with her?

Dr. Maddix didn't deserve to die for her thoughtless actions. He was not like the cruel men in her past. He had kind eyes and spoke with gentle purpose. Martha sobbed again. It was her fault that she had hurt him. She had been so incredibly tired and started feeling light-headed, which caused her to sway. He had reached out only to steady her, but she had punched his throat, most likely killing him.

Giving herself a firm shake, she tried to dispel the paralyzing fear that held her. No, she had to save the doctor. She needed to go find Mr. Larson. He could fix this. He would save Dr. Maddix. As she rose to her feet, she heard a soft knock on her door and heard Lady Lansdowne say, "Martha, it's me. May I come in?"

Martha wiped her tear-stained cheeks with her hand and flung open the door. "I think I may have killed Dr. Maddix," she announced. "You need to help him."

"That is impossible," Eliza replied. "I just saw Dr. Maddix holding Caroline in his arms."

With a deep sigh, Martha closed her eyes and held her hand to her breast, unable to verbally express her relief.

With a worried look, Eliza explained, "I couldn't sleep, and I heard a door slam shut. When I went into the hall to investigate, I heard sobbing."

"I am sorry for disturbing you," Martha apologized, leaning her head against the side of the door. "Please do not concern yourself with me."

Eliza brushed past her into the room. "Now, why did you believe you killed Dr. Maddix?"

"I punched him in the throat," she confessed.

Eliza pressed her lips together. "Were you trying to kill him?"

"No!" Martha shouted in surprise. "Of course not! I didn't plan to hit him." She closed the door and turned to face Eliza. "After I hit him, I fled. When I was thinking clearly again, I feared I could have collapsed his windpipe."

Slowly, Martha walked over to her four-poster bed and sat down. Not every lady's maid slept in a large bedchamber, but Lady Lansdowne had insisted that she sleep in a room near her own. Eliza had cited practical reasons, but Martha knew it was more than that.

"It takes a hard punch to damage the windpipe," she explained, eyeing her warily. "Why did you hit Dr. Maddix?"

Martha lowered her gaze, embarrassed. "He touched my arm."

"Was he too familiar with you?" Eliza asked with understanding in her tone.

She shook her head, placing her hands up to her cheeks, vaguely noting that they felt hot. "It was not like that at all. Dr. Maddix reached out to steady me, and I simply reacted. I jabbed him in the throat and fled."

Eliza's lips twitched. "I see that our self-defense sessions have paid off."

Martha's shoulder slumped even more as she admitted, "I didn't mean to hurt him. He was the first man to have touched me since..." Her voice trailed off.

"Your reaction is understandable," her friend reassured her. "Would you like Mr. Larson to accompany you to the nursery as long as Dr. Maddix is here?"

Martha shook her head. "No. That is not necessary. I have never had a reason to fear Dr. Maddix."

"He is a good man. Furthermore, he is a proficient doctor, so please avoid killing him." Eliza smiled. "At least until Caroline is healthy again."

Attempting to concentrate on Lady Lansdowne's words, Martha yawned as she felt her eyes getting heavy. Perhaps she needed to lie down for a moment.

Walking closer to the bed, Eliza looked concerned. "You look flushed, Martha. Are you feeling all right?"

"I am well enough." Her statement might have been more convincing if she hadn't started coughing uncontrollably for the next few moments.

"I am going to get Dr. Maddix," Eliza declared, turning towards the door.

"No, I am fine," Martha rushed to assure her. "I just need to rest my eyes for a moment, and I will be up soon to see to my duties."

"It has been a trying week. Why don't you take a nap until dinner?"

"I don't plan to sleep. My eyes are heavy, and I just need to close them for a moment," Martha explained drowsily, as her head drifted towards her soft pillow.

"I think you are unwell," Eliza pressed.

"I love you, too," Martha mumbled as she closed her eyes and let sleep overtake her.

GENTLY LAYING A SLEEPING LADY CAROLINE INTO THE CRIB, Emmett stepped back as Eliza walked into the nursery and, in a hushed voice, announced, "Martha is unwell."

He turned to face her. "I suspected as much, but she refused to let me examine her." Absently, he rubbed his throat where it was still sore from Martha's jab. Luckily, she had hit the side of his neck, and not his windpipe. It had shocked more than hurt him.

"You can go examine her now," Eliza insisted.

Emmett frowned. "I cannot examine a patient without their permission."

"Please," she pleaded. "She fell asleep and is delirious."

Furrowing his brow, he replied, "Miss Martha appeared exhausted, but she did not exhibit any signs of delirium."

"She told me that she loved me."

Emmett chuckled. "I daresay my valet has never expressed such tender feelings."

A whimper came from the crib, and Eliza walked closer, keeping her loving gaze on her daughter. Her eyes filled with sorrow, and she swiped at the tears as they slid down her cheeks. "How is Caroline faring?" The question came out soft and reluctant.

"I have good news," he declared, waiting for Eliza to turn to face him. Rarely was he able to provide patients with such great news, so he took a moment to smile. "I am confident she is on the road to recovery."

Her eyes grew wide in astonishment. "Truly?"

Emmett nodded, glancing down at the sleeping infant. "Truly. Her fever responded immediately to the medicine, and her pulse has slowed. Most likely, she was already on the mend before you sent for me."

"I am so pleased," she replied with unshed tears in her eyes.

"As am I," he expressed softly. "I will remain here for a few days to ensure she suffered no permanent damage from the influenza." He hesitated, then continued, "Assuming that is acceptable to you and Lord Lansdowne."

Eliza's eyes filled with gratitude. "You are always welcome in our home, Emmett."

"Thank you." He walked over to his doctor's bag.

After another glance at her sleeping baby, Eliza looked back at him. "I apologize for taking you away from London."

Emmett reached for a glass vial and placed it in his bag. "Don't be. My uncle, Lord Exeter, has kept me busy for the past year, instructing me on the various aspects of running a profitable estate." He sighed. "If I have to balance one more ledger or handle another tenant dispute, I fear that I might literally go mad."

She grinned, as he hoped she would. "Have you stopped working as a doctor?"

Emmett grinned. "No, much to the dismay of my uncle and parents. Instead of attending soirées and balls, I go to the hospitals and assist in surgeries or minister to the sick in the rookeries."

"That is very admirable of you," Eliza acknowledged.

In response, he shook his head and sighed. "No, it is a meager contribution, but it is all I can find time to do at the moment. I have found being related to a powerful earl can be quite time-consuming."

"Imagine that," came her teasing response.

Emmett took a moment to organize his bag. "I have instructed Sarah, the nursemaid, to bathe Caroline in room-temperature water every three hours, and I will continue distributing the medicine. Since I am giving her opium, I want to ensure the correct dosage, because too much would prove fatal," he explained in his no-nonsense tone.

Eliza stepped closer to him. "I cannot express our gratitude for all that you have done to help Caroline."

"I didn't do much." His eyes drifted towards the crib. "Your daughter is an incredible fighter."

Sarah walked into the room with a pitcher in her hands. After placing it on the table near the window, she curtsied to Lady Lansdowne. "My lady," she murmured respectfully. "I was preparing to bathe Lady Caroline."

Eliza nodded. "Excellent." She turned towards Emmett with clasped hands. "This will give you time to examine Martha."

He frowned. "I dare not touch her again."

Sarah gasped loudly as she stared at him. "You must never touch Martha."

Raising his hands in front of him, he tried to explain, "I put my hand out to steady her, and she responded by hitting me in the throat."

Picking up a nearby basin, Sarah repositioned it near the pitcher. "Having a jab to your throat is better than being stabbed with her dagger," she stated dryly.

"Dagger?" he asked Lady Lansdowne with raised eyebrows.

Eliza's lips twitched as she shared, "I have been teaching Martha how to defend herself. One of those lessons might have included a dagger."

"Ah," Emmett replied. "Did you teach her how to shoot a pistol as well?"

"Perhaps." Eliza grinned mischievously.

Emmett shook his head, but a smile played on his lips. He would never criticize a woman for learning how to defend herself, but he had not been prepared to be attacked for lending a helping hand.

Benedict rushed into the room with a panicked look on his face. "Emmett, it is Martha. She is shouting nonsense and thrashing about in her bed."

Eliza rushed over to her husband. "I left Martha only a few moments ago."

"I was walking down the hall, and I heard shouting," Benedict explained. "I opened her door and saw her thrashing around on the bed."

Picking up his medical bag, Emmett brushed past Benedict and ran towards Martha's room. It was easy to find because of her shouting. Running into the room, he raced to the bed. Martha's face was blotchy and coated with sweat.

"No, don't touch me! Get off me!" Martha shouted as she twisted and tossed in her bed.

Turning towards a maid that was in the room, he ordered, "I need a basin of cold water and a cloth."

As the maid left the room, Martha yelled, "I am friends with *Shadow*! She will kill you for this!"

Peering over his shoulder, he saw Eliza's eyes widen. Emmett had already assumed that Eliza was *Shadow*, but it mattered not. Confirming the identity of England's top spy was not important right now, his focus was on saving Martha.

He reached out and felt her hot, clammy skin. She was burning up! Emmett opened his bag and pulled out the laudanum. Tilting his head towards Eliza, he instructed, "I need some assistance removing Martha's clothes and putting on her nightshirt." Then, he turned his focus on Benedict. "I need a glass of water and honey to dilute the laudanum."

As Eliza retrieved the nightshirt from the dressing table, Benedict excused himself from the room. Sitting Martha up, he was able to remove her frock, but she was tossing about so wildly, he was unable to loosen her stays. Reaching into his boot, he pulled out a dagger and cut the strings of her stays, allowing her to take in deeper breaths.

Before he placed the nightshirt over Martha's chemise, he wanted to listen to her heart. Turning her so he could put his ear to her back, he was rendered speechless by the terrible scars that ran along the length of her bare spine. Gaping, he turned his outraged gaze to Eliza, and she responded with a sad, knowing look.

Shaking off his shock, he placed his ear to her hot back and listened to her uneven heartbeat. If they didn't bring her fever down fast, then she would die. Quickly dressing her, he laid her down and heard a soft knock at the door. In two strides, he opened the door and accepted the basin and cloth. He dipped the fabric in the cool water and placed it on her forehead.

"Do you have any ice?" he asked hopefully.

Eliza nodded. "We do."

"Bring as much as you can. We are going to wrap her in ice. The cold of the ice will help bring down her fever faster," he explained hastily.

Eliza immediately ran out to do his bidding, and he was left alone with Martha ranting incoherent phrases. The only recurring, anguish-filled demand was for no one to touch her. Her hair was wet, and the sweat glistened off her skin. Soon, her nightshirt would be soaked through.

Arching her back, Martha let out a wail of pain as she shouted, "Do not call me Lady Martha!"

Lady Martha, he thought to himself. Was she a titled woman? Regardless, if he didn't save her, soon she wouldn't be anything.

Benedict ran into the room with a glass, and Eliza followed him with two footmen holding chunks of ice.

"Place the ice on the bed," he directed. Once the footmen dropped the ice, he tucked the pieces next to Martha and wrapped the sheet around her.

Benedict handed him the glass, and he quickly stirred in the laudanum powder. Tilting Martha's head, he poured the medicine down her throat slowly. Not a drop was to be wasted.

As Emmett laid her back onto her pillow, he knew he had done all that he could for now. The rest was up to her.

Eliza stepped closer. "Now what?"

He looked up at her, sadness filling his eyes. "Now we wait."

❦ 4 ❦

It had been four long days since Martha had taken ill, and she still laid in bed, alternating between moaning, thrashing about, and sleeping restlessly. Emmett yawned as he sat in a chair beside her bed, a medical book in his hand. Between caring for Lady Caroline and Martha, he was exhausted.

Down the hall, he could hear Caroline laughing and playing with her nursemaid. She had made a full recovery, and there appeared to be no lingering effects from the influenza.

Rubbing the back of his neck with his hand, Emmett watched the rise and fall of Martha's chest. Her fever had broken yesterday, but still, she slept. He feared that she might never awaken.

"How is she?" Eliza asked from the doorway.

Tilting his head towards her, Emmett replied, "Alive, for now."

Eliza kept her eyes trained on Martha as she walked into the room. "You can go rest if you would like," she said. "I can stay with Martha and alert you of any changes."

"I think that is a grand idea." He closed the book and took a moment to stretch his back.

Standing next to the bed, Eliza leaned over and brushed

strands of hair off Martha's face. "I fear my friend doesn't have the will to live."

Emmett had similar thoughts but hadn't had time to voice his concerns to Eliza. As he placed his book on the table, he asked the question that had been plaguing him for days. "How did Miss Martha get all of those scars?"

A frown played on Eliza's lips, and she waited so long to respond that Emmett thought she wouldn't answer. Finally, she said softly, "It's not my story to tell."

"She must have been through hell."

Sadness saturated her voice as she admitted, "You could never imagine the squalor and torment she had to endure. It would have broken a lesser woman." There was a slight pause, and in a barely discernable voice, she added, "It would have broken me."

What did Martha have to overcome to become friends with Eliza? It had not escaped his notice that they shared a unique bond rarely seen between a lady and her lady's maid. Beginning with the fact that Martha had a bedchamber on the same floor as the rest of the family.

Silence descended upon the room as they both watched Martha sleeping. Benedict's voice came from the doorway, dragging their gaze away. "Any change?"

Eliza shook her head disappointedly. "No."

Benedict walked into the room and closed the door behind him. "Emmett, if you don't mind, we need to speak privately with you."

Running a hand through his tousled hair, a knowing grin came to his lips. "I assume you want to discuss Miss Martha's outburst."

Leaning against the wall, Benedict folded his arms over his chest. "We had never anticipated…"

His words were cut off by a soft knock. Mr. Larson stepped

into the room, closing the door behind him. "Did I miss the talk?" he asked Benedict.

Benedict shook his head. "I had just started when you so rudely interrupted us." His lips twitched at the corners as they did when he was teasing, but his face remained stoic.

Mr. Larson shrugged. "I was rushing down the hall but had to stop by the nursery and toss Lady Caroline up in the air."

Benedict turned his attention back towards Emmett. "As I was saying, we had not planned to reveal *Shadow's* identity to you." His gaze was as firm and unrelenting as his words.

Leaning forward in his seat, Emmett admitted, "I daresay I was surprised when Martha blurted out *Shadow* was a woman, but it was not hard to assume who *Shadow* was." His eyes shifted knowingly towards Eliza.

"It's not that we don't trust you," Eliza assured him as she sat on the edge of the bed, "but you must understand the paramount importance of keeping *Shadow's* identity tucked away." Her tone was light, but there was a warning in those words.

"I don't trust you," Mr. Larson growled. "We should just kill him."

Trying not to roll his eyes, Emmett asked, "Have you ever considered an intervention without resorting to threats?"

Benedict chuckled. "I just informed Larson that he is becoming too predictable."

Mr. Larson glared unrepentantly at him. "I have found threats to be quite effective in ensuring cooperation."

"Yes, but have you considered smiling to soften the blow?" Benedict inquired. "For example," he focused on Emmett, "if you reveal *Shadow's* identity, then we will be forced to draw and quarter you." His lips turned up into a forced smile. "Understood?"

"That was an empty threat," Mr. Larson responded. "Everyone knows that only the king can order someone to be drawn and quartered."

Benedict rubbed his chin thoughtfully. "Good point. What about…"

"Enough," Emmett exclaimed, not the least bit amused. "Did you forget that I fought side-by-side with you on the shores of Scotland to prevent a French invasion, and I saw Eliza wielding her black longbow?" He turned his focus to Mr. Larson. "And did you forget that you already threatened me in Lord Downshire's drawing room about revealing the Beckett's family association to the Crown?"

"What these ninnies are attempting to say… and failing miserably, I might add," Eliza chastised, casting a disappointed look at Benedict and Larson, "is that we are entrusting you with this secret."

Emmett's tone softened as he spoke to Eliza. "I understand. I consider you family, and I would no more betray you than I would my king and country."

Smiling, Benedict's next words only held humor. "Good, because you are one of Caroline's godfathers, and I really don't want a reason to kill you."

Mr. Larson never blinked, continuing his unrelenting stare at Emmett. "If you betray Eliza, then I will saw you in half, transversely, through the central body mass, while I force you to watch."

Benedict started slowly clapping. "That was much better," he teased. "I really felt the intensity of that threat. But, pray tell, where are you going to find a medieval saw long enough to make good on it?"

"And who will hold me down?" Emmett pressed, morbid curiosity compelling the question. "Perhaps that is not the most effective way to kill someone."

"I disagree," Mr. Larson argued. "After the fire of Moscow in 1812, the Russian peasants hated the French with such a ferocity that whenever they captured French soldiers in the woods, they sawed them in half."

"I stand corrected." Emmett tipped his head graciously. "However, you have nothing to fear from me."

Benedict's smile was genuine. "Good. Now, if you will excuse me, I am off to play with my daughter before her naptime."

Eliza jumped up from the bed. "I will join you." She hesitated, then turned back to Emmett. "Assuming it is all right with you."

Emmett sat back in his seat. "Please go," he urged. "I can rest my eyes here just as easily."

As Eliza walked across the room, she asked, "Will you alert me if there is any change?"

"I will," he promised. "Now, go enjoy your daughter before naptime."

After the door was closed, Emmett leaned his head back against the wall and closed his eyes. He wondered when Martha would wake up, or if she would wake up at all.

A BALDING INDIAN MAN STOOD IN FRONT OF A GROUP OF GODLESS men as Martha huddled on the ground, her hands bound with twine. He shouted, "Who wants to take this girl off my hands? Be warned she is useless, lacks all emotion, and refuses to give her customers any type of enthusiasm or pleasure. However, I have no doubt that the right man could convince her of the error of her ways."

A few of the men in the group chuckled and howled in amusement.

A paltry sum began the auction. Men bid on her as if she was livestock. As the price rose, she vowed to never let another man touch her. If her life was forfeit because of that, then so be it. She was prepared to die. She had nothing left to live for anyway.

The auction concluded, the winner announced, and a tall man stepped out of the crowd. He held his hand out to assist her off the ground, but she shrank back. Kindness crept into his eyes as he leaned forward and whispered, "You are safe."

She scoffed. This man certainly had a different definition of safe, but she slowly rose and followed him out of the tent. He led her into an alley, where a shadowy figure waited, cloaked in a cape. As they approached, a delicate hand emerged from the cape and slid the hood back, revealing a beautiful lady with auburn hair. Compassion filled her eyes as she cut the twine from her hands and spoke softly, "You are free."

Gasping, Martha's eyes shot open. It only took her a moment to recognize she was in her bedchamber. Turning her head, she saw Dr. Maddix sitting next to the bed, just a few feet away. He had a book opened in his hand, but it appeared forgotten. Instead, he was staring out the window with a look of regret, his eyes betraying his mental anguish.

For a moment, unobserved, she studied him. Dr. Maddix was a handsome man with dark brown hair and broad shoulders. The firm set of his jaw bespoke authority. However, his eyes seemed to mirror her soul, and she wondered what caused him to carry such pain. Suddenly realizing how close she was to the man, she felt the urge to flee from his presence but was surprised to feel her body was too weak to do her bidding.

"You are finally awake," Dr. Maddix observed with an unconvincing smile. He closed the book and placed it on the table. He started to rise, then hesitated. "Do you mind if I check your pulse?"

In response, she shook her head and curled her fingers inward.

He leaned back in his seat. "You were a lot more agreeable when you were asleep," he teased lightly.

She opened her mouth to ask a question and was surprised by her raspy voice. "Where is Lady Lansdowne?"

Glancing at the open door, he replied, "You just missed her. Apparently, she wanted to spend time with her daughter. Probably because my chess skills did not impress her." He grinned.

Shifting her gaze towards the chess board, Martha just nodded her understanding. She felt her eyes drift closed again.

"Before you go back to sleep," Dr. Maddix said, "are you in any pain?"

She opened her eyes and acknowledged his question. "No, I am just tired."

"Good, good," he murmured. "I found that laudanum does not agree with you."

Despite the fatigue she felt, her curious gaze found him. "Why do you say that?"

Dr. Maddix took his hand and rubbed the back of his neck. "You were having horrific hallucinations. That is a known side effect of opium. We informed the staff you were delirious and to give your words no heed."

"What was I screaming about?"

He dropped his hand and sighed. "To start with, you were shouting about being sold to a brothel, demanding that no one touch you, and insisted that Lady Lansdowne bought your freedom."

"Oh," she mumbled, casting her eyes to the floor. What could she say to that?

Glancing over at the open door, he lowered his voice. "You also announced that you were friends with *Shadow* and that the notorious spy was actually a woman."

Closing her eyes in mortification, Martha could not believe that she had made that mistake, laudanum or no laudanum. How could Lady Lansdowne ever forgive her for breaking her trust?

"I, for one, already suspected the truth," Dr. Maddix continued, seeming oblivious to her pain. "It wasn't hard to deduce when I saw Eliza with a longbow in her hand in Scotland or the way she braved the French army."

Continuing with his one-sided conversation, his words were laced with compassion. "You should know that Eliza is not angry with you, nor is anyone else in the household."

Keeping her eyes closed, she couldn't will herself to believe his words. What would she do without Eliza's friendship? She would be alone.

Fear gripped her heart when Dr. Maddix's calm, almost soothing, voice stated, "I don't know what happened to you, but I would like to help."

Opening her eyes, she responded with a shaky breath, "If you had truly wanted to help, you would have let me die."

"You cannot mean that," he objected, his eyes full of sympathy.

Martha turned her head, so she wouldn't see the pity on his face as she admitted, "I wholeheartedly mean that. I have wanted to die since the moment I was sol..." Her voice broke off. She had no intention of trusting Dr. Maddix with her torment and pain.

A deafening silence descended over the room, and Martha determined to make no more effort at conversation with this man, even if he was a doctor.

The silence continued for so long that she turned her head to see if he was still in the room. To her surprise, he was reading his book, or at least pretending to.

Dr. Maddix glanced up, gave her a slight head bob, closed the book, and smiled. "Oh, good. You are looking at me again."

Confused by his words and tone, she stayed silent and stared at him.

Placing the book back on the table, he leaned forward in his seat. "As I was saying before, I want to help you, Lady Martha."

"Do not call me that," she insisted, her voice rising.

"Fair enough." He grinned playfully. "I will not call you Lady Martha, but only if you start talking to me."

"I am talking to you."

Dr. Maddix shook his head. "I am not talking about useless chatter. I am referring to your past trauma."

Looking up at the ceiling, she murmured, "I do not know what you are referring to."

"I think you do," he replied in an understanding tone. "My medical diagnosis leads me to believe that your dreams were repressed memories brought to the surface as your body fought your high fever."

She kept her eyes trained on the ceiling. She would not talk to him about this. Only Eliza knew the full truth and comprehended her shame.

"Miss Martha," Dr. Maddix coaxed gently, "there is nothing more important to me at this moment than helping you in any way that I can."

"You can help me by leaving this room," she admonished. She did not want his help or his pity. No! She didn't want anything to do with Dr. Maddix.

Again, silence descended upon the room as Martha attempted to control her growing frustration at this bold, irritating man. At no point had she asked for his help.

She must have drifted off to sleep, because she woke up to a darkened room, with only a small fire in the hearth to provide light. Shifting her head, she was expecting to see an empty chair, but to her surprise and horror, Dr. Maddix smiled back at her.

"Go away," Martha groaned.

Ignoring her aggravation, but remembering that she was wary of men, Emmett responded cheerfully, "Good, you are awake. With your permission, I would like to bring you a bowl of broth and feed you."

He waited patiently for her response, knowing he would accomplish nothing by rushing her. After a long pause, she said, "If you bring me the bowl, I can feed myself."

"As you wish." He rose and reached for the bowl from the table next to him. Being mindful to approach her slowly, he kept the broth in front of him and took the few steps towards the bed. "May I help you sit up?"

"No, you may not," she snapped.

Emmett waited as Martha maneuvered into a sitting position, then leaned back until she rested against the wall. When she was ready, he gently lowered the bowl into her reach, carefully avoiding touching her delicate hands.

"There is no spoon," she observed, looking at him expectantly.

"It is only broth. Just bring the bowl to your lips."

Martha frowned. "That is very uncivilized."

"I won't tell anyone, if you won't," he teased.

With a small sigh, she brought the bowl to her lips and took a tentative sip. Her eyes widened with pleasure, and she quickly drank the broth. As she lowered the bowl, she asked, "May I have some more?"

He shook his head. "I am afraid not. First, let's see how your stomach reacts to the broth. If it is favorable, then we will add in some heartier food tomorrow. Perhaps some bread and eggs."

Emmett tried not to smile when he heard Martha's stomach growl.

She glared at him and admonished, "It is not funny. I am starving."

He dipped his head in acknowledgement. "I have no doubt. You have not eaten real food in almost a week."

"A week?" she repeated, bewildered.

Watching her carefully, he asked, "Do you remember the day I arrived?" She nodded, and he continued, "After I examined Caroline, I noticed you were showing symptoms of influenza, but you refused to let me examine you."

"I remember."

"Do you remember hitting me?" He grinned.

She lowered her gaze. "I do, and I am sorry for that."

"Don't be," he urged. "It was my fault for touching you. Although, I was only trying to help."

Looking up at him, Martha's eyes shone with sadness. "I am afraid I am not used to gentlemen showing me kindness."

Compassion swelled in his heart. Noticing the empty bowl in her hands, he pointed at it. "If you hand me the bowl, I can put it on the table for you."

She bobbed her head and extended it towards him. Emmett placed it on the table and sat down, edging his seat forward slightly.

He was curious about one thing. "May I ask how old you are?"

"I am twenty-four."

"I thought you were younger."

"I feel much older," she murmured.

Nodding at her comment, he decided to shift the conversation to a safer subject. "After our first attempt at bringing your fever down, we had to keep the rest of the household staff away."

Martha frowned. "That was wise. We wouldn't want the influenza to spread to the rest of the staff."

Smiling gently, Emmett shook his head. "No, mainly because we didn't know what you might blurt out."

Noting the look of shock and devastation on her face, he rushed to clarify, "Your reaction was no fault of your own. It was the sickness and medication."

She pursed her lips together and lowered her gaze, clearly not believing him. He wanted to smack himself for upsetting her when she was already in such a delicate condition. He tried a different approach.

"For the past seven days, Eliza, Benedict, Mr. Larson, and I took turns sitting by your bedside and caring for you."

"But what about Lady Caroline?" she asked, looking back at him.

Emmett genuinely smiled. "She has made a full recovery and has made up for lost time. She runs this household ragged."

"I adore that little girl." Her words were full of love.

With deliberate movements, he reached for the pitcher of water, pouring some into a glass. He extended it towards Martha, who graciously accepted it. "I know. I do, too, which is why I always took the night shift, to allow Eliza and Benedict plenty of sleep."

"When do you sleep?" she asked, watching him closely.

"I don't."

She took a long sip of water, appearing to consider her next words. "And why is that, Dr. Maddix?"

Emmett turned his gaze towards the window as he debated how to answer. "When I close my eyes at night, memories surface." He hesitated a moment before saying, "And I prefer they stay buried."

"Oh," came her sad reply. "I can relate."

"I know you can. During the day, I try to stay busy, or else the banished thoughts come to my mind and can bring me to my knees." He kept his voice calm, struggling to suppress his overwhelming feelings of guilt.

Martha took another sip and lowered the glass to her lap. "At times, I feel the burden of my memories are too great for me to bear."

"I used to feel the same way, but it changed when my meddlesome cousin tried to help me," he said thoughtfully.

"Lady Downshire?"

Emmett nodded and chuckled. "My cousin, Rachel, showed up in Scotland and demanded that I let her help me. At first, I refused, but then she almost died..." His voice trailed off at the painful memory.

"I know the story has a happy ending, because Rachel lived and married Lord Downshire," Martha observed.

A wide smile spread across Emmett's face. "It is true that Rachel lived, but she made sure that I continued living as well."

"How?"

"After school, I worked as a physician, but I got tired of helping the same aristocratic families. Every time I tried to lobby for the poor and their deplorable lack of medical attention, I was chastised by my colleagues for being too radical. After a few years, I bought a commission in the Royal Navy to work as a surgeon, providing proper medical care to the seamen aboard the warships. I was excited at the prospect of helping king and country, and it started off just as I intended." He stopped as his memories began to resurface, and he fought the too-familiar anger.

Martha leaned over and placed the glass on the table. As she sat back against the wall, she asked, "Why are you so angry?"

He looked at her in surprise. "Why do you think I am upset?"

"I recognize the look in your eyes," she answered as crinkles formed between her brows. "You don't have to finish your story. It is all right."

"But I do," he insisted, determination in his eyes. "The more I share my story, the less hold it has on me."

"I disagree," Martha argued. "Why relive the horrors of your past when you can banish them deep in your soul?"

"Because banished memories don't always stay buried," he contended with empathy in his voice.

Martha's eyes grew reflective. "Well, by all means, please finish. I am not going anywhere."

He poured himself a glass of water, took a sip, and began. "Originally, I was assigned to a frigate responsible for fighting off French ships in the channel, but when another surgeon died in battle, I was reassigned to fight the Americans."

Emmett placed his glass on the table, stood up, and walked closer to the fireplace with his head hanging low. He placed his hands on the mantle and leaned in, watching the flames flicker in the hearth.

"What I quickly learned was that we were no better than looting pirates. We would board privateer ships, impress their crew into service, and confiscate their vessels. And we did it all in the name of the Crown."

He pushed off the mantle and turned away. "After Rachel nearly died, I realized how lost I truly was. Then I stood on the shoreline of Rockcliffe as the French army advanced towards shore, and my life flashed before my eyes. I vowed, if I made it out alive, I would start living again." He leveled his gaze towards her. "Especially since I realized that my purpose was bigger than my own life."

Martha offered him the tiniest of smiles. "It is true, you will be an earl one day."

"No, being an earl has nothing to do with it," he asserted. "I am a doctor, and the people in the rookeries are dying every day from diseases that the wealthy have treatments for."

"An earl has substantial pull in Parliament to effect change," she reasoned.

"That is true as well," he confirmed. "During the day, I am learning about my uncle's vast holdings for my father, but in the evenings, I go into the rookeries and help those poor people."

"When do you sleep?"

"As I admitted before, I don't," he reminded her. "There are too many people that need help, and I find sleep to be intolerable."

Martha's eyes roamed his face before she replied, "It is admirable of you for being willing to help others in need."

Emmett shook his head. "There is nothing admirable about it."

Her lips tightened at his sharp words. "I disagree."

Tossing back his head, his eyes stared at the ceiling before he shared, "I have done some horrible things in defense of the Crown, things that I cannot undo…" His voice hitched, and he took a shuddering breath to reign in his emotions. "I hope only to atone for my sins."

"I find it hard to believe that you could have done something despicable enough to cause such deep pain," she said.

Meeting her gaze, he kept his voice steady as he admitted, "I killed a girl."

MARTHA REARED BACK IN SURPRISE. DR. MADDIX'S ADMISSION may have unnerved her, but she did not believe the man intended to harm her. "You killed a girl?" she repeated back.

"Not by my own hands, but I allowed it to happen," he admitted, his voice full of anguish.

Knowing there was more to the story, she pressed, "During the war?"

His eyes became pained as he dropped down into his chair. "Yes, but she was not a casualty of war."

"Did you love her?" Martha prodded.

He nodded. "I did, as I would a sister." Leaning forward in his seat, he put his face in his hands but then dropped them. "We are one and the same, you and I," he said to her surprise.

Martha opened her mouth to declare that they were not the same, but he continued, "We both have a valid reason to give up, but that is the very reason why we must press forward."

"You cannot presume you know me," she admonished, "my trials, my experiences."

"It is true," he conceded, "but just because you are alive, doesn't mean you are living."

Her eyes widened as she tried to formulate an argument to his ridiculous statement.

Dr. Maddix lifted his brow. "Can you honestly tell me that you are truly living, opening yourself up to new experiences? Just like me, you have hardened your heart against the world."

Stalling for time, Martha reached for her glass on the table, then took a sip before asking, "Why would I want to live in a world that has shown me such cruelty?"

"If that is the case, then I encourage you to look past yourself and find ways to ease others' suffering," he encouraged.

Martha huffed. "And who tried to ease my burdens as I was being beaten and tortured?"

Dr. Maddix placed his elbow onto the table and rested his chin onto his hand. "It is clear you went through trauma, but I feel…"

"No!" she exclaimed, her chest heaving with fury. "You do not get a say in my life. For five years, I endured hell at the hands of others."

"What happened to you?"

His eyes reflected pity, and she bristled. She didn't want his sympathy. She felt every beat of her heart as the anger brewed inside of her. "You have no right to question me about my past. I can never forget the betrayal of being sold by my…" Realizing what she had almost revealed, she closed her mouth, looked away from him, and attempted to calm her breathing.

Scooting his chair closer to the bed, Dr. Maddix spoke in a soothing tone. "I have seen your scars."

Her eyes grew wide at his admission, but she countered with, "You have only seen my visible scars."

"I do not doubt that," he replied. "However, mental scars can heal, just as physical scars do."

"What is it that you want of me, Dr. Maddix?" she asked, returning her vexed gaze to him.

"I want you to rejoin Society."

"Leave me be." Who was he to suggest such a ridiculous notion?

Dr. Maddix leaned back in his seat. "I understand you are a titled woman now and your father wants you to return to London for the Season."

"Leave. Me. Be!" she demanded.

"I could," he murmured. "Or, I could help you."

Was he daft? Rolling her eyes, she stated flatly, "I don't need your help."

"I disagree."

"Go away."

"No."

"Leave me."

"No."

"Are you a simpleton?"

Drumming his fingers on the table, he smirked. "I daresay that my years of schooling answers that question."

She crossed her arms over her chest. "I don't want your help."

Dr. Maddix's eyes held humor. "I know, but I am giving it to you freely."

"You are wasting your time," she insisted. "I will never accept your help."

"It is my time to waste," was his obnoxious reply.

Knowing this conversation was going in circles, she lowered herself down and placed her head on her pillow. "Good night, Dr. Maddix."

"Good night, Lady Martha."

Removing her pillow, she tossed it at him and was gratified to see it hit him in his face. "Thank you," was all that he said as he placed it behind his head. Leaning back, he closed his eyes. "I will see you tomorrow."

6

MARTHA OPENED HER EYES AS THE DRAPES WERE OPENED, allowing bright sunlight into the room. She blinked until her sight cleared. Lifting her head from the pillow, she realized Dr. Maddix must have returned it while she slept. Refusing to think kind thoughts about him, she started to voice her objections to him for opening the drapes when Eliza appeared in front of her.

"Good morning," Lady Lansdowne announced cheerfully, sitting on the chair next to the bed. "I have ordered you breakfast. When Dr. Maddix informed me that you woke up yesterday, I accused him of lying. But here you are... alive." She smiled.

Sitting up, Martha placed the pillow behind her before leaning back. "Trust me, I am not pleased with the outcome."

"You are too dramatic."

Adjusting the sleeves on her nightshirt, Martha announced, "After breakfast, I will rise and go about my duties."

"Dr. Maddix has ordered you to stay in bed for at least three days."

Her lips parted in surprise. "Three days? But who will help get you dressed and style your hair?"

Eliza arched an eyebrow. "I am not useless."

LAURA BEERS

"Of course, I did not mean to imply..." she started to explain.

"Besides, I have hired a new lady's maid," Eliza informed her.

"You are firing me?" Martha didn't think this day could have started any worse.

Smoothing out the net overlay on her pomona green gown, Eliza smiled smugly at her. "I am."

Martha pursed her lips. "I know what you are doing, and it will not work."

"I don't know what you are referring to," she replied with an innocent expression.

Pulling her blonde hair to one side, Martha braided it with quick, practiced movement. "You are trying to force me to become your companion."

"No," Eliza revealed with a shake of her head. "I previously offered you the position as my companion, but I have decided not to have a companion at this time."

Staring at Eliza with narrowed eyes, Martha tried to remain calm. She knew that Lady Lansdowne was used to getting her way, but this was different. This was her life! She had no intention of going to London to reside with her father.

As they stared at each other in stubborn silence, Benedict walked into the room and asked, "Has Lady Martha agreed to travel to London with us for the Season?"

"Not yet," Eliza stated with a tight smile.

Benedict stepped closer to his wife and whispered loudly, "Did you inform her that she is relieved of her duties as your lady's maid?"

"I did." Eliza nodded, tilting her head towards him. "We had just begun our conversation when you walked in."

Claiming the seat next to his wife, Benedict smiled at Martha. "How are you faring?"

She returned his smile. "Much better. Thank you, my..."

"Do not finish that sentence," Benedict ordered. "No more 'my lord' for you, at least not in private."

Martha sighed. "Lord Lansdowne, I appreciate what you are trying to do, but I will not be going to London as Lady Martha."

Benedict furrowed his brow and leaned closer to Eliza. "What do you suggest we do now?"

With a twinkle in her eye, his wife responded, "We have only just begun the war."

Before she could comment on Eliza's ridiculous statement, Dr. Maddix walked into the room with Lady Caroline in his arms. She clapped her hands with glee. When Caroline saw Martha on the bed, she reached for her.

Dr. Maddix's steps faltered as he asked, "May I approach your bed? It appears Caroline is quite eager to see you this morning."

"You may," Martha replied, immensely pleased by his simple request.

Stepping closer, Dr. Maddix barely made it to the side of the bed when Caroline lunged for her. Martha caught her and pulled her tight against her chest. How she loved this baby!

Caroline patted her cheeks and tugged at her hair, but Martha did not care. Turning her head towards Eliza, she saw her friend's knowing smile. Martha frowned and tried to look stern.

"Please stop smiling."

"I can't help it." Eliza's smile grew wider.

"I am not doing your bidding," Martha stated, her tone exasperated, but immediately turned her attention back to Caroline.

Dr. Maddix cleared his throat, drawing her attention before asking, "Lady Martha, with your permission, may I check your pulse and examine your throat?"

She nodded tentatively as Benedict reached over and collected Caroline.

Looking pleased, Dr. Maddix slowly reached for her right wrist, pressing down with his thumb. He gave a knowing bob of his head and slid his free hand into the pocket of his waistcoat, pulling out a tongue depressor. Bringing it close to her mouth, he asked, "Will you open your mouth for me?"

In response, she opened wide and was surprised when he pressed the flat ivory blade down onto her tongue. Again, he gave a knowing nod. "Just as I thought," he said with a smile, "everything appears to be in order."

Emmett stepped back as he tucked his tongue depressor back into his pocket. Leaning his hand against the back of Benedict's chair, he advised, "When you travel to London, I will request you stop every two hours to stretch your legs and breathe in the fresh country air."

Martha rolled her eyes. "I am a servant and will sit on the exterior of the coach."

"You are a lady," Eliza countered, "and will sit inside the coach with Benedict, Caroline, and myself."

Opening her mouth to argue, she was surprised when Benedict advised, "It is no use fighting the inevitable."

Frustrated with this futile conversation, Martha glanced around the room for her black servant's frock. "Where is my dress?"

"Burned," Eliza said.

"Burned?" she repeated. "What am I going to wear?"

"Your new gowns, of course," Eliza replied with an aura of innocence.

"My new gowns?" Confused, she looked at Benedict who was tossing Caroline in the air.

"My wife has been very busy preparing your new wardrobe," Benedict informed her, catching the baby and grinning at her giggles.

"You were just lying in bed for almost a week," Eliza teased, "and I took advantage of it. I had a seamstress take your measurements."

Martha stared at her with disbelief. "I was not just lying

down. I had influenza." She turned her fury towards Dr. Maddix. "How could you allow Lady Lansdowne to do this to me?"

Dr. Maddix gave her a perplexing look. "Most women would be pleased to receive a new wardrobe."

"I am not like most women," she retorted. "I don't need fancy gowns."

"But you do," Eliza assured her. "You also needed gloves, a riding habit, boots, slippers, and multiple ball gowns."

"Eliza..." Martha growled, but Dr. Maddix interjected. "Before you get too angry at Lady Lansdowne, you should know that I encouraged her."

"Why would you do that?" she demanded.

He crossed his arms in front of his chest. "I believe I made my thoughts known on the subject last night."

"And I told you that I was content being a lady's maid," she argued back.

"You say you are content," he said, glancing at Benedict and Eliza, "but, *we* believe you are hiding."

"You don't even know me," she shot back, her anger rising. "I will not be coerced."

Eliza's face softened at her words, even though her words were sharp. "Martha, you are like a sister to me and helped me when I was at the depths of despair. Now it is my turn to help you."

"I never asked for your help," she replied. "Why won't you let me stay as I am?"

"Because it is time for you to become who *you* are meant to be," Eliza assured firmly, then leaned closer to the bed, placing her hand over Martha's. "Do you remember when I was struggling, and you encouraged me to trust Benedict with my heart?"

"I do, but that was completely different," Martha stated flatly.

"You may provide excellent advice, but you are horrible at following your own," Eliza teased, smiling as she arose. "You have been fired as my lady's maid, and I do not require your services as my companion. If you wish to ride with us to London, then we will escort you to your father's townhouse."

"And if I choose not to go to London?" she pressed.

Her expression turning stern, Eliza placed her hands on her hips. "If you won't go willingly, then I will force you."

"You wouldn't dare," Martha challenged with narrowed eyes.

"Try me." The two women stared at each other, neither willing to back down.

"Eliza," Benedict's voice broke their trance, "why don't we give Lady Martha some time to ponder this?" With Caroline on his hip, he reached for his wife's arm and began gently leading her from the room.

Martha could hear Eliza mutter, "Why must she be so stubborn?"

When Benedict and Eliza were gone, Martha turned towards Dr. Maddix, ordering, "Leave me."

He bowed. "As you wish, my lady."

Reaching for the pillow from behind her, she tossed it at him. "I told you not to call me that."

Catching the pillow, he looked amused as he took three slow strides towards her, maintaining eye contact. "You are not the same woman that I saw a week ago."

"That is not true."

Emmett placed the pillow on the side of the bed. "I disagree. After all, you do not flinch when I am near you anymore."

"I don't flinch around Lord Lansdowne or Mr. Larson either," she observed.

"True, but they aren't forced to examine you medically," he pointed out. "A week ago, you wouldn't even let me near you."

Glancing up at him, Martha realized how close he was but felt no anxiousness. "I am not going to let Eliza drag me to London," she mumbled. She had no other response to his comments.

Dr. Maddix's eyes grew fearful. "Please do not make Eliza angry," he teased. "She can be quite frightening."

Stifling a smile, Martha was surprised when she yawned instead. "I apologize, I must be more tired than I realized."

With tenderness in his eyes, Dr. Maddix responded, "Nearly dying can have that effect."

Closing her eyes, Martha decided to take advantage of having nothing to do but recover.

FOUR DAYS LATER, MARTHA SAT ON A BENCH BEHIND CHATSWICH Manor, dressed in a white gown and a rich blue spencer. She was watching the birch trees sway in the wind and listening to the river flow towards the village.

Attempting to keep her irritation in check, she kept her lips pressed together, but anger stirred inside of her. Eliza had burned all her servant's frocks and underclothing, replacing them with muslin gowns and silk stays. She had no choice but to dress in the clothes that Eliza had provided for her, but she refused to let Eliza's new lady's maid style her hair. She was not a lady. She did not deserve this.

Why couldn't Eliza see that she was content serving her? She didn't want to go live with her father. She did not trust his intentions. Besides, she was safe with Eliza, tucked away upstairs and far from the demons of Society. Why did Eliza want to take away her life, her home?

Martha sighed. She owed Eliza her life, but she did not want to step out of her shadow. She couldn't. She was too afraid. In fact, it had taken her months to even leave the security of Chatswich Manor and walk outside. Mr. Larson had been kind enough to place a bench next to the estate, so she had a place to sit and listen to the beautiful sounds of nature. How could she go to London and be expected to go into balls, soirées, and house parties? The thought of meeting so many people seemed overwhelming and terrifying.

Her breathing started to increase, and she looked at the ground. She could not endure it. What if a gentleman asked her to dance and tried to touch her? No, she could not do that.

A calm, soothing male voice broke through her thoughts. "Lady Martha," Dr. Maddix addressed her from a few yards away.

Martha lifted her eyes towards him, a sense of relief washing through her. Dr. Maddix had become her friend over these past few days, and he was always a welcome part of her day. Even though he was vexing at times, he had the most amusing stories, and she found herself relaxing around him.

"Lady Martha," he repeated, only this time his eyes shone with concern. "Are you all right?"

As she calmed her labored breathing, she tried to explain, "I was just thinking about dancing."

He nodded. "Ah. Would it help you to know that I also panic at the thought of dancing with another? It is quite frightening." He shuddered dramatically.

She laughed a bit at his reaction. "I am sure that ladies vie to get your attention at balls."

"I wouldn't know," he replied, "because I don't attend any social events."

"You do not attend any?"

"I go only to the events that my uncle forces me to attend."

"Why?" She was attempting to understand his logic.

Dr. Maddix put out his hand, palm up. "May I approach you?"

With a tilt of her head, she answered, "Yes, please." It pleased her that he always asked her permission.

Dropping his hand, he stepped closer, but still maintained a comfortable distance. He shifted his gaze towards the hills. "I have no interest in the frivolity of the ton, whose lives are devoted only to amusement. It was a façade that I could not maintain."

Martha could hear the pain in his voice even though he tried to hide it. "Do you not wish to get married, Dr. Maddix?"

He shook his head. "I do not."

"Why not?" she pressed.

Dr. Maddix returned his tormented gaze back to her. "I highly doubt any woman would want to marry a physician that ministers to the poor."

His response surprised her, but she pressed, "I imagine many women are willing to marry a man who will one day inherit an earldom."

He nodded slowly, then shifted his gaze away from her. "True, but that is not the type of woman that I want. I want a woman who shares my passion for helping others."

"There must be some ladies that lobby for the poor?" she asked softly.

"I have yet to find one."

"Perhaps you are not looking in the right places."

Staring off in the distance, he didn't respond for a long moment. Turning to face her, he pointed at the bench and asked, "May I?"

"Did Eliza send you to talk some sense into me?" she asked warily.

He grinned. "She did."

Sighing, she scooted to the far side of the bench. As Emmett sat down, he leaned forward and placed his elbows on his knees, resting his forehead on his hand. "I understand your need for solitude, I truly do... but if you don't go to London, I doubt you will ever open your heart to trust again."

"I have no desire to trust others," she said firmly.

Dropping his arms, he turned his knowing gaze onto her. "Therein lies the problem, Lady Martha. You would deny the world of your talents because you are too afraid to live."

"I have no talents that the world would be interested in." She shifted her gaze towards the foothills.

"That is not true," he insisted. "You are kind and compassionate."

Frowning, she asked, "How would you know that?"

Emmett leaned his back against the bench and smiled. "I am a doctor and have the power of observation. From the moment I met you at Caroline's christening, I knew you were a woman of great compassion, but you have managed to stay hidden."

"Now you sound like Eliza," she mumbled.

"Eliza is very wise." He chuckled, then grew serious, turning his dark green eyes towards her. "Do you recall when I told you that I killed a girl?"

She nodded.

"There is more to the story," he admitted softly.

She tilted her head, curious about what great burden Dr. Maddix bore.

He offered her a faint smile before sharing, "When I served as the surgeon aboard the *Regulus,* we were sent to fight against the Americans. One of our assignments was to board Yankees' privateer ships, under the premise of looking for deserters from the Royal Navy. It soon became clear that my captain, Captain Allister, impressed American men on a whim, with no care for their situation."

Dr. Maddix hesitated, his voice becoming strained. "On my last mission, Captain Allister decided he needed a cabin boy and selected the son of the privateer ship's captain. When the captain refused to let the boy go, Captain Allister shot him dead, in front of his crew, for mutiny." His voice grew pensive.

Not knowing what else to say, Martha spoke honestly, "I am sorry you had to witness that."

"That is not the worst part," he admitted, wincing. "Upon a physical exam of the lad, I discovered a young woman who had bound her chest with bandages and cut her hair in hopes of disguising her gender from the Royal Navy."

Martha shuddered, knowing what men did to vulnerable women.

Dr. Maddix continued his story, his voice tight. "I did my best to hide Eleanora. I even convinced the captain to let the lad work alongside me, but eventually, the captain discovered her gender. I had wrongfully assumed that Captain Allister held a glimmer of honor."

Rising quickly, Dr. Maddix walked a few paces away and clasped his hands behind his back. After a moment, he turned back around, anguish visible on his face. "A few nights later, I was called to the captain's quarters, and his cabin was in shambles. Eleanora lay dead in the middle of the room, with a pool of blood under her head. Her shirt was ripped open, scratches were all over her body, and her face had visible bruising."

Emmett's voice dropped away. His hands were balled into fists at his sides, and his knuckles were white. "As I rushed to her, the captain ordered me to examine him first. He even dared to imply the girl was mad and attacked him."

Martha's face paled at the sight she imagined. "That poor girl," she breathed. "What happened next?"

He clenched his jaw. "I picked up the pistol from the table and shot him in the leg. I wanted Captain Allister to feel pain. I wanted to kill him with my bare hands, but I was restrained by the other soldiers. I wanted..." His voice hitched. "I wanted revenge for Eleanora."

"Why?" she asked curiously. "Why did you throw your military career away for a girl you just met?"

Dr. Maddix just stared at her with a shocked expression. "Because Eleanora did nothing wrong and did not deserve her fate. She was innocent in all of this."

Touched by his words, Martha pressed, "Most men would not care as deeply as you."

His eyes softened, filling with compassion. "I wish I had been there to save you, Lady Martha. I would have fought with my last breath to prevent the depravities that fell upon you."

Touched beyond words at the kindness in his tone and gestures, she hastily wiped away a tear that slid onto her cheek. Somehow, Dr. Maddix had managed to break through her barriers, and she found herself beginning to trust him. When did that happen, she wondered.

"I had a fiancé who was supposed to protect me," she admitted with pain, "but he was the one who sold me into slavery."

"Your fiancé sold you into that life?" he growled. His tone would have normally frightened her, but she found it oddly comforting, considering the circumstances.

"Yes," she said. "He promised me a life of love, and instead sold me to a vile merchant named Mr. Wade."

"Mr. Wade?" he repeated back with disbelief in his voice. "The merchant who abducted the ladies of Society and was killed by *Shadow*?"

"That is the one," her voice cracked with emotion. "She saved my life, then went after Wade."

Emmett took a step forward but stopped. "How long did you have to endure?"

Her face fell as her emotions threatened to be released. "Five years," she painfully uttered.

Within a moment, Emmett was sitting next to her, his eyes roaming her face. His tone had the unmistakable ring of sincere, heartfelt earnestness. "I wish I could wipe away your pain, but I am powerless to do so. What I can promise is that no one will ever harm you again."

Staring deep into his eyes, she asked skeptically, "Why do you care so? I am practically a stranger."

In slow motion, he reached over and gently placed his hand over hers, giving her ample time to protest. When she did not withdraw her hand, his eyes filled with tears. "I failed Eleanora, and in doing so, I have spent the past year and a half searching for a purpose in my life. I cannot sleep for fear of her memory, and I cannot stop working for fear of seeing her lifeless body. My life is consumed with atoning for my wrongs. I know you are not Eleanora, but you remind me so much of her." Tenderly, he encompassed her hand.

"Dr. Maddix," she ventured, hesitantly, "I am beyond redeeming."

"You are wrong. You are worth far more than you have led yourself to believe." A small smile formed on his lips as he urged, "Come to London and become the lady you were destined to be."

Knowing she was powerless to deny his plea, she murmured, "I can't do this alone."

"I will be there to help you," he assured her, "as will Eliza and Benedict."

She frowned as she glanced at their hands, surprised she did not feel panicked by his touch. "Most likely I will disappoint everyone."

He shook his head. "I doubt that."

"I am afraid, Dr. Maddix," she admitted painfully, her words growing softer. "I am so afraid."

Kindness laced his features as he replied, "It is all right to be afraid. Life can be trying at times, but you have endured more than most, and I am confident you can take on the ton."

"And if I cannot?"

With a twinkle in his eye, he responded, "Your father only asked for one Season. After that, you can take your dowry, move to your small estate, and embroider to your heart's content."

"I don't embroider," she said dryly.

"Do you play the pianoforte?"

"I do."

He smiled widely. "Then you can play the pianoforte to your heart's content."

Rolling her eyes, Martha asked wryly, "You have it all figured out then, Dr. Maddix?"

"I do, Lady Martha."

Removing her hand from his, she admonished, "Do not call me that."

"What would you like me to call you?" Dr. Maddix inquired as he rose from the bench.

"Martha," she said.

Wiping off his buff trousers, he replied, "I will do as you ask, but only if you call me Emmett." He must have sensed her hesitation because he added, "It is a fair trade."

"I suppose... Emmett," she uttered softly.

Looking pleased, he held out his hand to her. Without withdrawing his hand, he expressed, "I will always offer to assist you, but I am not offended if you decline. I understand you do not like to be touched." His eyes crinkled at the corner as he offered her a minute smile. "And there is nothing wrong with that emotion."

"Thank you for understanding," she replied. Glancing at Emmett's hand, she knew she had to make a choice. Should she reject him and stand up on her own? Or should she allow him to assist her as she rose? Gazing into his warm green eyes, Martha knew she had nothing to fear from Emmett. He may be a man, but he meant her no harm, and although she couldn't yet trust him completely, she was starting to believe that he wouldn't betray her.

With a swift motion, she placed her gloved hand into his and allowed him to help her rise. Once she was standing, she took a step to the side to provide herself with more space between them. He gave her an understanding nod. "May I escort you to the drawing room?" he asked.

"I would like that very much."

Emmett offered his arm, but she shook her head. In response, he lowered his arm, appearing utterly unphased by her rejection. As they walked back into Chatswich Manor, Martha realized she was going to London to face her father. However, she was not sure which one she feared more; him, or the ton.

7

APPROACHING THE DRAWING ROOM, EMMETT STEPPED ASIDE AS Martha walked into the room. Following behind, he saw Eliza, cradling a drowsy Caroline in her lap, reading a book. Putting the book aside, she rang the bell and Sarah, the nursemaid, appeared from the other room.

Sarah curtsied. "Is Lady Caroline ready for her nap now, my lady?"

"She is," Eliza replied as she kissed the top of her daughter's head.

Sarah walked closer and reached down, picking up Caroline into her arms. As she neared Martha, she stopped. Leaning down, Martha kissed Caroline's cheek and whispered, "Have a good nap, dearest."

Once Martha and Eliza were situated, Emmett tugged on his waistcoat as he sat on the chair next to Martha.

"Are all of your trunks packed?" Eliza asked him.

He nodded. "They are. I plan to depart within the hour."

"You are leaving?" Martha asked, surprised.

Emmett gave her a smug grin. "Careful Martha, it almost sounds like you will miss me."

"Could anyone miss a thorn in their side?" she huffed. But despite the strong words, he detected a hint of wistfulness in her tone.

He chuckled. "I daresay you know how to keep a man humble." His smile dimmed. "It is true that I am leaving, but I will call upon you when you arrive at your father's townhouse."

"Do not fret," Eliza assured her, "we will be departing tomorrow morning."

Emmett noted Martha was again wringing her hands in her lap, her eyes downcast.

"Martha," he prodded. Her fingers stilled, and she looked up to meet his gaze. He detected the slightest glimmer of panic in her eyes before she blinked it away. Knowing that she would not share her fears willingly, he felt a surge of protectiveness. "If you would prefer, I can delay my journey till tomorrow. It would not be a bother." He failed to mention he had received a letter from his uncle demanding his immediate return.

"Would you mind?" She nibbled her lower lip hopefully.

"That settles it, I shall depart tomorrow," he confirmed, smiling.

Relief washed over her face as Martha nodded gratefully at him. "Thank you," she murmured softly. Her next question was directed to Eliza. "Are you positive I cannot reside with you for the Season?"

Eliza shook her head, causing the ringlets near her face to sway back and forth. "If you want your dowry at the end of the Season, you will need to reside with your father. You have nothing to fear," she stated, her voice firm, unyielding.

With a shaky voice, Martha declared, "You may trust my father, but I don't."

Eliza arched an eyebrow. "Who said I trust your father?"

"Then why are you insisting I reside with him?" she asked in disbelief.

Eliza lowered her brow as her eyes softened, but they

remained intense. "I have no reason to distrust your father, but I trust you. So, if you don't trust him, then neither do I."

"Why don't you trust your father? Surely, he only has the best intentions for you?" Emmett queried.

For a moment Martha was silent, pursing her lips. "Sadly, that is not the case. My father was the second son of an earl and was ordered by his father to become a vicar. He had no desire to serve others or God. Frankly, he finds poor people beneath him, in station and in mind."

"He did not appear that way. Perhaps he has changed?" Eliza asked.

"He is vain and pompous, no matter what he says or how he appears," Martha asserted. "The leopard cannot change its spots."

Furrowing her brow, Eliza shot Emmett a worried glance before saying, "Have you considered that your mother's death may have changed his heart?"

Martha stood and walked to the window. As she gazed out, she sighed, "Contrary to what my father claimed, he did not love my mother. It was a forced marriage."

"You mean an arranged marriage," Emmett corrected.

She turned around to face them. "No, it was a forced marriage. My grandfather threatened to disinherit my father if he didn't marry my mother and my mother came into the marriage under similar circumstances. They were both unhappy about it but could only show their displeasure in private."

Shifting in his seat, Emmett questioned, "Why would your mother agree to the marriage then?"

"She is only a woman and had no choice in the matter," Martha explained, her words dripping with sarcasm. "Her father sold her off just as my father tried to do to me."

"Is that why you ran away?" Eliza's gentle voice prodded from the settee.

Martha frowned, creating deep lines in her forehead. "It was.

I was destined to marry Baron Whitehall, who was equally as horrible as my father and was years older. In addition, they indulged in similar vile practices." Walking back to her chair, she slowly lowered herself down. "I did not want that path, so I eloped with Simeon."

"Were you in love with him?" Emmett asked.

A haunted look came over Martha's face and tears came to her eyes, but she blinked them away just as fast. "Desperately, or at least I thought I was. I was young, naïve, and besotted." She lowered her gaze, adding in a pained whisper, "And foolish."

An awkward silence descended between them as Eliza shot Emmett a helpless glance. He leaned forward, sitting on the edge of his seat. His eyes scanned Martha's face as she kept her gaze fixed on the carpet. "What Simeon did to you was inexcusable, but you can't let your past define who you are. You have to keep fighting."

Martha's eyes shot up towards him. "Fight for what?" she demanded. "What do I have to live for?"

"You have us," Eliza chastised gently.

"And I am grateful for that," she replied. "That is why going to London is pointless. Everything I want is right here."

"What about marriage?" Emmett asked.

Martha shook her head. "I will never get married."

Eliza sighed softly. "What about children of your own?"

She squeezed her eyes shut, but not before he saw a pain far deeper than anything he had witnessed before. "I am content with being a godmother to Caroline."

"Will you at least attempt to open yourself up to love when we arrive in London?" Eliza pressed.

"No, I will not. You must understand that love is not possible," she stated, her eyes flickering towards Emmett, "at least not for me."

"Martha has been wonderful at giving advice, but she is horrible at living it," Eliza informed Emmett.

Martha's eyes grew downcast. Her words were hardened, cynical. "You both seem to forget that I am ruined. Even if I wanted to get married," she paused, frowning, "no one would want me."

Emmett furrowed his brow. "Why do you believe that?"

Meeting his gaze, her eyes grew guarded. "It is the truth."

Gently, he replied, "I disagree. That is your perception of yourself. I don't believe you are ruined."

Martha gave him a weak smile. "I know what you are trying to do, but it won't work. My reality has poisoned my heart, and I walk in darkness, for it is all that I deserve." Abruptly standing, she announced, "Now, if you will excuse me, I will need to pack the plethora of dresses that Eliza ordered for me." Without another word, she walked out of the room, leaving Emmett and Eliza staring at her retreating figure.

Eliza broke the silence first, her tone pleading. "We have to find a way to help Martha."

He turned to face her. "Martha has experienced a trauma that affects her deeply." Regretfully, he added, "Some people can't recover from that."

"Martha can," Eliza confirmed with a bob of her head. "She has changed so much since she has come to live with me."

"I can only imagine."

"After I learned the truth about Wade and what he did to Martha and the other girls," Eliza started, hesitantly, "I made it my mission to stop him. However, it nearly destroyed me." Her voice filled with emotion as she admitted, "Martha saved me from myself. How can I not do the same for her?"

"Sometimes a friend needs to offer a gentle nudge in the right direction, but in your case, a giant shove was needed," Emmett teased.

"I truly believe that going to London will help her achieve the life that she deserves." A mischievous glint sparkled in

Eliza's eyes. "Furthermore, I have already devised a plan for keeping Martha safe."

He chuckled. "Why am I not surprised?"

Standing, she replied, "Trust me." Her words were simple but powerful.

"I do," he confessed, rising as well. "Now, let's help Martha."

THE POUNDING OF THE RAIN WAS RELENTLESS ON THE COACH AS they traveled through the English countryside. They were still a few hours outside of London. The windows of the coach were closed to keep out the rain, but that created an uncomfortably muggy environment for travelling. For two days, Martha had been confined with only Eliza and Caroline to converse with.

The men had decided to ride, and Martha had envied their decision, at least until the rain started. For most of the morning, she had watched Emmett on his horse. He was quite the impressive rider and had trained his horse well. She huffed at that thought. Emmett probably had harassed his horse until it started to do his bidding.

Why did she find him so irritating, yet his presence so reassuring? His voice seemed to penetrate her senses, and she found herself becoming exceedingly comfortable in his presence. Banishing her wayward thoughts, she glanced over and saw Eliza still had her eyes closed, with Caroline sleeping cradled in her arms.

Turning her gaze back towards the window, she couldn't see even a few feet in front of her because of the downpour. A bright flash lit the sky, followed by a loud, crashing boom. Eliza's eyes shot open at the noise. "Was that thunder?" she asked softly, glancing down at her still-sleeping baby.

Martha nodded. "It was."

Unexpectedly, the carriage jerked to a stop and the door was flung open. A drenched Benedict held the door open as he tenderly gazed at his wife and child. "We cannot journey any farther today. The weather…" Another bright light lit up the sky and the nearly simultaneous roar of the thunder interrupted him. "We've stopped at an inn. Unfortunately, it is not our usual inn, but rather one of lesser repute."

"I understand," Eliza murmured. "We will eat our meals in our rooms and avoid the common hall."

Benedict nodded approvingly. "My thoughts exactly. Emmett and Larson have gone to secure a section of rooms." He offered his hand to assist his wife.

Martha quickly draped a blanket over the sleeping babe as Eliza exited the carriage. Benedict reached his hand back to assist her and she stared at it.

He smiled reassuringly. "It is all right, Martha."

As the rain poured onto his face, Benedict waited as she tentatively placed her hand into his. Stepping onto the step, she started to yank her hand back, but Benedict encompassed her hand. "The ground is slick. Let me assist you until you are on firm ground."

Accepting his help, she was immediately grateful for his assistance as her feet slid a bit on the wet dirt. When she stepped onto the old, broken cobblestone, he released her hand and went to escort Eliza into the dilapidated inn. As she walked on the soaked cobblestone, she started slipping but was stopped by a hand on her elbow.

Before she even had time to react to the touch, the supportive hand was gone. Tilting her head at a slight angle so she could see around her bonnet, she saw Emmett standing next to her. His brown hair was wet and clinging to his forehead. Water droplets flowed down his face and clothes. He gave her a one-sided grin as he offered her his arm. "Careful, cobblestones can be treacherous when wet. May I assist you into the inn?"

Martha pursed her lips and glanced at the offered arm. "No, thank you." Turning back towards the inn, she took two steps and stepped into a large puddle, soaking her kid boots. "Great," she mumbled under her breath.

Without warning, she was scooped up into Emmett's arms as he ran towards the inn. Her breath quickened at his firm hold on her, and she tried to wiggle free.

"It will be all right, Martha. Just relax," he instructed her.

Once they were under the eaves, Emmett gently placed her on her feet and stepped back.

"How dare you pick me up," she chastised. "You had no right."

Glancing over her shoulder, she saw the water pouring unceasingly over the eaves. He ran his hand through his wet hair, sending water droplets into the air. "You left me little choice. I didn't dare leave you unassisted on the slippery cobblestone, nor did I have any desire to follow behind you slowly. In case you haven't noticed, I am completely soaked."

Frustrated that his logic was sound, Martha grumbled, "Regardless, you could have at least warned me."

"I believe I already politely offered to assist you," he pointed out.

Mr. Larson came up from behind her. "Lady Martha, why are you not in the warmth of the inn?"

Untying the ribbon of her bonnet, Martha carefully took it off and shook off the excess water. "I was just voicing my displeasure at Dr. Maddix for picking me up without my permission."

Taking a step closer to the inn, Mr. Larson surprised her by saying, "Forgive me, but if Dr. Maddix hadn't picked you up, I would have."

Emmett smiled, but quickly wiped it off his face when she

narrowed her eyes. "I apologize. Now, can we please get you inside before you catch a cold? After all, I just nursed you back to life from influenza."

Opening the door, he stepped aside as she walked into the hall. One look at the room and her steps faltered. It was filled with men who turned to gaze at her lewdly. Her initial reaction was to flee, so she turned to run.

Before she could take a step, Emmett placed his hand on the small of her back and leaned closer. "You have nothing to fear, Martha."

The men continued to gawk at her as if she were the last biscuit. The room was filled with long, rickety wooden tables littered with empty tankards. A scantily clad woman roamed the room, filling the empty cups with more amber-colored liquid.

A large, bulky man rose from a bench in the back and approached them, his lecherous, dark eyes perusing her blue traveling gown. Shrinking back against Emmett's hand, she couldn't seem to speak for the fear that held her captive.

Dropping his hand, Emmett moved to stand in front of her, blocking her from the man's unsavory glances. The man walked closer and stopped a few feet from them. "Welcome," he said, his tone anything but inviting. "We were hoping the lady would join us for supper."

Emmett shook his head. "Unfortunately, she is tired and would like to retire to her room."

The man glanced over his shoulder at the rough-looking men before he returned his gaze to Emmett. He straightened to his full height, his words slurred by too much strong drink. "It was not a request."

Fearful, Martha clutched the back of Emmett's tailcoat so tightly that her fingers began to hurt. Emmett made a clucking noise. "You are not in a position to make a request of us."

The man chuckled dryly as he crossed his arms over his

chest, scoffing, "We are in the perfect position. There are only two of you… and twenty of us."

Emmett turned to speak to Mr. Larson. "I count eighteen including this ruffian."

The man dropped his arms as he roared, "How dare you!"

Mr. Larson nodded. "I am not sure if we should even count him, considering he doesn't know how to count."

The ruffian in question took a threatening step towards Mr. Larson. "I know how to count to two," he growled.

"Yes, but there are three of us," Mr. Larson pointed out, completely unphased by the man's anger.

Daring a glance, Martha saw Benedict standing at the base of the stairs, and he did not look pleased. Advancing towards the leader, he narrowed his eyes. "You are being rude. I suggest you back away and return to your drink."

Instead of backing down, the bulky, ignorant man turned his ire on Benedict. "We just wanted the lady to eat supper with us."

Benedict stood his ground. "And the lady has declined your invitation."

Lacing his hands together, the man cracked his knuckles and said, "I think not."

Frowning, Benedict shrugged out of his tailcoat and dropped it to the ground. "This is your last warning. Let the lady pass."

The men in the room roared with laughter as they stood up from the long, wooden benches. Once the laughter died down, the leader smirked. "We don't want you to eat with us. Just the lady." He reached for her, but Emmett knocked his hand aside.

"Don't put your filthy hands on the lady," Emmett ordered with such an intensity that Martha was momentarily stunned. Normally, his words were smooth and comforting.

"I will do as I please," the man sneered.

Ignoring him, Emmett turned around slowly, and she let go of his tailcoat. He tenderly looked at her, his eyes filled with compassion. "Unfortunately, these men are being discourteous, and it appears we need to teach them a lesson."

With wide, fearful eyes she replied in a worried tone, "But there are so many of them."

He smirked. "There are eighteen of them but three of us. If you ask me, they are vastly outnumbered."

Martha looked over the men in the room, and she swallowed slowly. If Emmett and her friends were not successful, she feared her fate. Her hand slid into her reticule to retrieve her pistol, but Emmett encompassed her hand.

"Don't reach for your pistol just yet," he said gently. "You have nothing to fear."

"But…"

"No buts," Emmett responded, cutting her off. "We will keep you safe."

The man's rage-filled voice came from behind him. "You and…"

Emmett turned his head and growled, "Do you mind?"

The man closed his mouth, his eyes sparking with fury.

Shifting his gaze back to her, Emmett suggested, "Why don't you stand over there? This will only take a minute." He pointed towards the corner of the room and gave her an encouraging nod.

All the men watched her walk to the corner and turn so her back rested against the wall for support. Emmett removed his coat, tossing it aside. Mr. Larson stood next to him and jested, "You can't fight in a riding coat?"

"I prefer not to," he said, smiling.

Suddenly, a loud grunt echoed in the room, and the leader pulled his arm back to hit Emmett. Turning his body so the punch did not land, Emmett grabbed his wrist, twisted it, and elbowed the man in the jaw. The man fell back, stunned.

Another man ran towards Emmett, and he tucked his shoulder, causing the man to flip over his back. Over and over, men approached her friends and they fought off each attacker with the same intensity. Martha had never seen men fight with such valor. What was more, they appeared to be enjoying themselves, their smiles growing broader with each successful blow.

Most of the men were smart enough only to approach Emmett, Mr. Larson, or Benedict once, but a few were not as bright. As the last man fell, Martha's eyes took in the damages caused by the fighting. Tables were overturned, benches broken, spilled ale on the straw, and men sprawled out on the floor, many unconscious.

Emmett picked up his coat and cautiously approached her. "May I take you to your room, Lady Martha?" He offered her his arm.

Nodding, she eagerly reached for his arm as they stepped over the bodies on the ground. At the top of the stairs, he took a key out from his waistcoat as they walked. Stopping at a door at the end of the hall, he quickly unlocked it. His critical eyes scanned the small room before he handed her the key and gave her a reassuring nod. "You will be safe here tonight."

"Thank you," she replied gratefully as she dropped his arm.

Stepping into the room, she closed the door and moved to sit on the bed. She could hear scraping in the hall, and she went back to the door. Hesitantly, she opened it and peered out. To her surprise, Emmett was sitting on a chair next to her door.

"What are you doing?" she whispered.

Leaning his head back against the wall, he winked at her and teased, "I thought it was rather obvious. I am protecting you."

"You don't need to sit outside my door," she assured him. "I will keep the door locked."

His expression grew serious. "Locks can be broken."

"You are most kind," she expressed, touched by his thoughtfulness.

"There is nothing kind about it, Martha," he replied in a serious voice. "No one will ever hurt you again."

Offering him an appreciative smile, she started to close the door when she heard Mr. Larson say from down the hall, "If that is the case, you might want to work on your fighting skills."

Emmett chuckled. "My fighting skills are exemplary. I am confident that I dispatched more men than you did down there."

Not waiting to hear Mr. Larson's response, Martha closed the door and latched it. Walking over to the bed, she laid down and soon found she was quite drowsy. But this time, she wasn't afraid to close her eyes. Her protector was keeping her safe.

8

MARTHA'S EYES FLEW OPEN AS THE CARRIAGE JERKED TO A STOP. Momentarily frightened, she peered out the window. They'd stopped at Lady Camden's country home. She frowned, perplexed. "I thought we were going to London."

Shifting Caroline in her arms, Eliza just smiled. "You didn't think I would send you to your father's townhouse without protection?"

Martha eyed her friend suspiciously. "What do you have planned?"

"You shall see."

The carriage door opened, and Benedict's hand reached in to help Eliza out of the carriage. After she stepped out, he offered his hand to Martha and waited patiently for her. With far less hesitation than before, she placed her gloved hand into his and allowed him to assist her.

As soon as her feet were on solid ground, she pulled her hand back and clasped her hands together. Glancing over at Emmett, she saw him handing off his horse to a waiting groom. A smile lit his face when he saw her, causing her breath to hitch.

Emmett closed the distance between them in a few strides. "Do you know why we are here?"

She shook her head in response. "No, but Eliza told me she had a plan."

"Ah," he responded in amusement. "I hope it is a good plan."

"Of course, it is a good plan," Eliza declared.

Before anyone could respond, the door of the country home swung open and a very pregnant Lady Camden waddled out. She stopped after only a couple of steps, placed a hand on her stomach and exclaimed, "Eliza, you are here! Please come inside and have some refreshment."

Emmett offered Martha his arm, but she shook her head. In response, he gave her a crooked smile and gestured that she should lead the way.

"Thank you," she acknowledged gratefully.

His eyes crinkled at the edges as he walked beside her. "We are friends, and friends accept each other for who they are, quirks and all."

"Quirks?"

"Did I say 'quirks'?" he teased. "I meant endearing quirks."

Feeling a need to defend herself, she asserted, "You know why I don't like to be touched."

"I do, but…"

He was cut off by Adrien, the Earl of Camden, approaching them. He stopped and bowed. "Lady Martha. Emmett. You two have failed to notice that Eliza and Benedict have moved inside." He grinned, easing the formality of his greeting.

"Lord Camden." She curtsied respectfully. As her eyes met his, she said, "I would prefer if you would call me Martha."

His eyes shone with approval. "And you must call me Adrien."

She shook her head. "No, sir, that is too informal."

Smiling gently, he turned his gaze to Emmett. "How did you get tricked into traveling with Eliza and Benedict?"

"Eliza summoned me when Caroline was sick with influenza. Then Lady Martha became ill, so I stayed on," he replied.

"Do not call me Lady Martha," she muttered under her breath.

Emmett shifted to face her. "Pray tell, how will I address you in the ballrooms or opera houses?"

"That is simple. I won't be attending any balls, operas, soirées, or anything of that nature. Besides, I already have it on good authority that you don't attend those frivolous parties, either." She offered him a private smile.

Emmett grinned. "Your father requested one Season. How do you suppose you will avoid all the social aspects when you are in London?"

Martha recognized his point, reluctantly. Thinking quickly but speaking slowly, she said, "If I do go to balls, I will enjoy the company of the older ladies who no longer dance."

With a bemused look, Emmett stated, "I find it humorous that you truly believe you could blend in, even in a room filled to the rafters."

Ignoring his words, she pressed, "If gentlemen do approach me, then I will just decline their invitations to dance."

"That plan sounds flawless," he quipped. "And how do you propose you will be introduced if you don't want to be called Lady Martha?"

"I will just have to hide in the library."

They looked at Adrien when he chuckled. "This argument appears to be going nowhere. Shall we adjourn to the drawing room?"

Adrien offered his arm to Martha, and she felt her face pale. She couldn't turn down Lord Camden's offer to escort her to the drawing room. Before she could react, Emmett informed him, "Martha prefers to walk unescorted."

Dropping his arm, Adrien gave her a smile. "Then after you, my lady."

Feeling grateful for Emmett's intervention, she started walking towards the main door, listening to the men chatting merrily behind her. A few moments later, she walked into the drawing room and sat down on an armchair near Eliza and Benedict. Sitting opposite was Lady Camden, her husband claiming the seat next to her. Emmett pulled a chair closer to create a small circle.

"Where is Caroline?" Martha asked curiously.

Kate smiled. "Cosette has her. Eliza thought it was best for Caroline not to be here."

Before she could ask why, the men in the room rose almost in unison. Curious, Martha looked towards the door. A young woman, with brown hair and wide, expressive green eyes, walked demurely into the room. Her hair was pinned tightly at the base of her neck, and she wore men's clothing. Even more surprisingly, there was a pistol tucked into her trousers, and a dagger was strapped to her leg.

When the young woman saw Eliza, she curtsied, gracefully, as if she were in a ballroom. "Lady Lansdowne, it is a pleasure to see you again."

"You are looking well, Josette," Eliza responded. "Did you get the books that I sent over?"

A smile brightened her face. "I did, thank you."

Eliza pointed towards a chair. "Please join us."

With a nervous glance at Kate, Josette sat in the proffered chair. Her back remained rigid as her eyes scanned the room.

"Josette, I would like to introduce you to my dear friends, Lady Martha and Dr. Emmett Maddix," Eliza said.

The men sat down after the introductions were made.

Josette graciously acknowledged her with a tip of her head. "It is a pleasure to meet you."

Martha smiled, then turned to Eliza when she began to speak.

"I am going to get right to the point," Eliza stated as she smiled at the young woman. "My sister, Kate, has informed me that you continue to excel not only in your studies, but you have surpassed Adrien's expectations in weapons training."

"It's true," Adrien agreed, with a bob of his head. "Josette is proficient with a dagger and can shoot a pistol with deadly accuracy."

Josette kept her expression guarded. "I am grateful for Lady Camden's large library and the opportunities that have been offered to me here."

Eyeing her closely, Eliza asked, "Did you have weapons training prior to coming to the country home?"

"No, ma'am."

"You are a remarkable young woman, Josette," Eliza expressed, her eyes filling with approval.

"I am not," came her quick reply.

"But you are," Kate interjected, smiling with pride at the young woman. "You help run the estate, tutor the other girls in their studies, and train with the guards. I must admit I have not discovered one thing that you cannot do well."

Tugging at the sleeves of her white shirt, Josette lowered her gaze to the floor. "I am not deserving of such praise, my lady."

Eliza sat back in her seat, studying her. "Where are you from?"

"I am an orphan," the girl mumbled.

"Where were you raised?" Eliza pressed.

"Nowhere of consequence," she replied cryptically.

"Were you sent to boarding school or tutored by a governess?" Benedict asked.

"I am self-taught, my lord," Josette responded.

Benedict rose from his seat and walked to the drink cart. As he poured himself a drink, he acknowledged, "It is apparent that you are hiding from something... or someone."

Josette's eyes shot up in alarm. She turned her gaze towards Kate. "May I please be excused?"

Kate's face softened as she regarded Josette. Her words held no censure. "For the past year, you have been a wonderful addition to the refuge, but you have never once shared any details about your past. Despite this, it is obvious that you were taught good breeding and are well educated. It leads us to assume that you were born into privilege."

Josette's lips tightened into a straight line, her hands clasped tightly together.

Clearly not expecting an answer to her statement, Kate continued, "This country home is a refuge for women, and will always be so, but I can't help but wonder if you are stifling yourself by remaining here."

"Are you throwing me out?" Josette questioned weakly, fear in her voice.

"Heavens no," Kate rushed to assure her. "You will always be welcome here."

Eliza accepted a glass of water from Benedict. After taking a sip, she lowered the glass and stated, "I have a proposition for you."

"No, thank you," Josette answered promptly.

Eliza arched an eyebrow. "But you haven't heard the proposal."

"If your proposition would require me to leave this country home, then I am not interested," Josette replied flatly.

Eliza's lips twisted in amusement. "Even if it means a settlement of £5,000 and a chance to run a school for girls in the rookery?"

Josette's eyes widened. "What is your proposition?"

"Lady Martha is in desperate need of a companion who is trained in a variety of weapons," Eliza informed her.

Looking at Martha sharply, Josette observed, "It sounds like you are looking for someone to protect Lady Martha, only the guard is to be disguised as a companion."

Eliza nodded her approval. "That is precisely what I am looking for." She smiled. "In exchange for acting as a companion for the Season, you will be compensated £5,000 and will become the headmistress of The Beckett School for Girls on the East side."

Josette frowned. "Why would you ask me to run a boarding school? I am not yet nineteen."

"Age may be a number, but our experiences determine how old we truly are," Adrien stated.

With an encouraging smile, Kate added, "There is more to you than what you have shown to us here."

"It is true," Eliza agreed with a bob of her head. "I recognized it from the moment I saw you on our last visit."

Playing with the sleeves of her shirt, Josette ventured, "Assuming I went along with this charade, why would Lady Martha need a companion?"

All eyes shifted towards Martha as she shared, "My father has requested my presence in London for the Season, and I don't trust his intentions."

"Has your father made threats against you?" Josette inquired of her.

Martha shook her head. "No, he has not."

"Then why do you fear your father?" she asked.

A sad smile came to her lips. "It is a long, painful story."

"I understand," Josette responded. "If I act as your companion, then I would like to stay in the shadows at social events."

"If Martha has her way, she will be right alongside you," Emmett teased.

Josette turned her attention to Eliza. "I must beg the question, why ask me?"

An understanding look came to Eliza's face. "That is an easy question. My siblings and I plan to open a boarding school for girls on the East side. We intend to educate girls, thus enhancing their prospects for the future." Leaning forward in her seat, she continued, "We were waiting for a strong female to fill the position as the headmistress, someone who would not be afraid to live in the rookery. This woman had to be educated and in a position to defend herself."

Josette shook her head sadly. "As much as I would like to accept the position of headmistress, I am afraid I don't have the necessary wardrobe to act as a companion."

A lady's voice came from the doorway. "I have already made all the necessary articles of clothing required, including multiple ballgowns," Cosette confessed, holding Caroline in her arms.

As Cosette walked further into the room, Martha took a moment to admire the beautiful woman with black hair and creamy white skin. She was dressed in a long-sleeved green dress with intricate floral designs sewn into the net overlay of the dress.

"How is that possible?" Martha whispered to Eliza. She knew that Cosette's fingers had been broken while she was in Newgate as a condemned spy.

Cosette smiled and held up one of her hands. "Lord Camden arranged for a surgeon to reset my fingers, which has allowed me to sew again."

"That is wonderful news," Eliza said, smiling. "I am so glad that they healed properly."

"Thank you, Lady Lansdowne," Cosette replied with a curtsy.

Eliza gave her a disapproving shake of her head. "How many times have I told you to call me Eliza?"

Cosette smiled unrepentantly. "About a hundred."

Adrien chuckled. "She still refuses to call me Adrien."

"She calls me Kate." Lady Camden smiled smugly.

Placing his arm around his wife's shoulders, Adrien said, "That is because you are sisters."

Cosette turned her attention back to Josette. "Two weeks ago, Lady Lansdowne sent a missive, commissioning a whole new wardrobe for you."

When Martha's eyes shot to Eliza, she just shrugged. "It is good to be prepared."

Smiling mischievously, Cosette stated, "And I have a team of seamstresses available for an emergency such as this."

"This is a far cry from a real emergency," Josette argued.

Cosette raised a brow. "I disagree. I have been pleading with you to dress like the lady we know you are."

"That life is over," Josette declared forcefully.

Silence descended over the group, and Martha found her heart constricting for Josette. "Josette, I too was raised in privilege, but I made a choice that altered my entire course. I don't belong in my father's world anymore, but I have agreed to one Season." She hesitated, before adding, "I need a friend more than a companion."

A sly smile came to Josette's lips. "A friend that is trained in weapons."

"Exactly." Martha laughed.

Josette sat back in her seat. "If you don't trust your father's intentions, then why not just live with Lady Lansdowne for the Season?"

"I have asked that very question," Martha said with a smile.

Benedict reached over and placed his hand over Eliza's, and a look of love passed between them. "Martha's father is requesting one Season from her. If she completes the Season without getting married, then he will release her dowry and gift her a small estate." He glanced over at Martha. "But the condition is that Martha resides with her father for the Season."

Eliza's eyes grew intense. "Your job would be to ensure Martha is safe at all times. If anything of suspect happens, then you will immediately seek us out."

"What do you think may happen to Martha?" Kate inquired. "Do you believe he may strike her?"

Martha shook her head. "My father may have been brutish in my youth, but I doubt he will hit me now."

"Then why a guard?" Josette asked Eliza. "Why not just visit her every day?"

"I am still hopeful that Martha's father wants to make amends, especially since he seemed so sincere earlier," Eliza admitted. "But one is always prepared for the worst-case scenario, are they not?"

Josette winced. "I wasn't," she murmured under her breath. Tilting her head, she turned to Martha. "It appears I will be your companion for the Season."

Martha nodded, feeling both relief and dread. She now had a protector in the shape of a pistol-and-dagger-wielding young woman. What could her father possibly gain from her? She had nothing, was nothing. Maybe Eliza was right. What if her father did want to reconcile and had no hidden agenda?

A soft, baritone voice broke through her thoughts. "You can do this, Martha. It is only one Season."

Looking at Emmett, she felt grateful for his friendship. He made her feel safe and protected. "One Season," she repeated.

❧ 9 ❧

As they neared her father's townhouse, Martha began tugging on the ends of her gloves. Why did she agree to this madness? What was she trying to prove?

Why hadn't she taken Emmett up on his offer to ride into town with her? She now regretted her hasty decision and wished that he was sitting next to her in the coach, teasing her and making her laugh. She found she greatly enjoyed spending time with the contrary doctor. At least he promised that he would call on her tomorrow.

Josette's voice broke through her thoughts. "What has you so upset, Lady Martha?"

"Do not call me Lady Martha," she admonished harshly. Realizing her tone was inappropriate, she offered a nervous smile. "I apologize for my sharpness. I fear that I am more anxious than I thought."

Dressed in a white, high-waisted dress adorned with a plum ribbon, Josette eyed her carefully. "And why is that?"

Lowering her gaze, Martha replied quietly, "I am worried about seeing my father again."

Josette remained silent, waiting for her to continue.

Unsure how to begin, Martha attempted to skirt the truth. "I ran away from home when I was sixteen, and I haven't been on speaking terms with my father for more than seven years."

"Did you run away to elope?"

Martha pursed her lips. "I did."

"Were you married?"

She shook her head. "No."

"Where have you been living for the past seven years?"

Ignoring her companion's question, she turned her head to look out the window. She was not ready to share what she had to endure during that time or discuss the trauma she experienced.

After a moment, she turned her attention back to Josette. Her eyes widened in surprise to see her companion fingering a knife in her hand. Looking into her face, she saw that Josette's eyes were hard, reflecting bitterness. "I recognize that look. Someone hurt you deeply," she ventured.

"Yes, someone did," Josette confirmed. "Which is why I know that you were hurt as well."

"I was." Martha's heart softened as she realized they were not so different after all. "I am truly sorry."

"Don't be." Josette clenched the handle of the knife, her eyes growing harder. "I was sent away at sixteen as well."

Martha smiled weakly. "If we can endure one Season, then both our lots in life will be vastly improved." Even as she spoke the words, she knew it didn't matter what her station was in life. She wouldn't ever be free from her memories.

The carriage jerked to a stop in front of a large, three-story townhouse with cream-colored stucco. Pilasters framed both sides of the entrance, and a fanlight window sat over the door.

When the carriage door opened, the footman reached in his hand to assist her. Shaking her head, she placed her hand on the door for support and carefully stepped out of the carriage. Before she took another step, her father rushed out of the house with a welcoming smile on his face.

"My dear, you are finally here," Lord Waterford proclaimed with his arms wide open.

"I am," she mumbled, partially because she was unsure how to proceed. Her father acted as if he was delighted to see her.

Glancing over her shoulder, he saw Josette exiting the carriage. "And you brought a friend?"

"Miss Josette is my companion," she informed him.

He tipped his head graciously. "You are most welcome here."

Josette cast her a confused look before she dropped into a curtsy. "Thank you, my lord."

Her father took a moment to peruse her blossom-colored gown with puffy sleeves. "I see that you have an appropriate wardrobe fitting your station."

"I do," she replied, "thanks to Lady Lansdowne."

Lord Waterford nodded his head approvingly. "That was most kind of her." He held out his arm to her. "Shall we go inside?"

Tentatively placing her hand on her father's arm, Martha allowed herself to be escorted inside. It had been more than eight years since she last set foot in this townhouse, and she was surprised at all the changes that had been made. Her uncle had always been a man of simple taste, and his décor had reflected that. But now, it was different.

"When did Uncle Theodore redecorate?"

Puffing out his chest in pride, her father responded, "I redecorated after he passed away. What do you think?"

Her eyes took in the bright red wall-paper with gold floral designs, bold Persian rugs, and ostentatious furniture. Not sure how to respond without insulting him, she mumbled, "It is... unique."

"It is," he agreed. "My brother was a spendthrift and never appreciated the value of money." He looked down at her knowingly. "Your mother was the same way."

Trying not to roll her eyes, she attempted to keep her face

expressionless. Although her father used to be a vicar, it appeared that he had not changed his views on spending.

Moving away from the door, Martha glanced over her shoulder to see if Josette had followed them, but she was nowhere to be found. Stepping into the drawing room, her father escorted her to the settee and assisted her as she sat down. Once she was situated, he sat down next to her.

He smiled. "I am so pleased that you are here."

"I am here only for the Season," she reminded him.

Much to her annoyance, his smile grew wider as he leaned back in his seat. "My dear Martha, you may find you enjoy the benefits of being the daughter of an earl. Or, you may find a handsome suitor and marry."

She shook her head. "I have no intention of ever marrying."

Lord Waterford chuckled. "Playing hard to get, I see. Men like a challenge."

Frowning, she admonished, "This is not a game, Father. I wish to live my life without a husband."

Her father's smile faded as he watched her. "I apologize for teasing you. I just want what's best for you."

"Since when?" she huffed.

Sorrow etched Lord Waterford's face as he admitted, "I haven't been the best father, have I? I know I was hard on you, but I thought you needed a firm hand to guide you. Unfortunately, I pushed you away, and I apologize."

Shocked by her father's humble apology, she found herself staring at him, unable to formulate her thoughts. He appeared sincere, and she wanted to believe him.

"I understand that you don't trust me, and that is all right. I hope to spend the rest of my life making up for lost time. After losing my wife, brother, and nephew so close together, I realize how important family is in our lives."

"How did my uncle and cousin die?"

Lord Waterford sighed, and the melancholy, plainly written

on his face, deepened. "They were traveling to their country estate, and the carriage overturned when the driver turned a corner too fast. It was a horrible accident."

Wringing her hands together, Martha couldn't understand her father's behavior. He was trying to reconcile with her, and she didn't know how to feel about that. For so long, she had hated him, but perhaps he had changed?

Her father's voice drew her back into the conversation. "Lady Lansdowne has graciously offered to host a ball in your honor later this week."

"A ball in my honor?" Martha's eyes grew wide, feeling horror wash over her. Impossible! She couldn't attend a ball and be the guest of honor.

Her father nodded. "I don't blame you for being excited. She has invited only the finest families and is sparing no expense." He glanced at her inquisitively. "If Lady Lansdowne is so fond of you, why did she force you to be her lady's maid?"

"When I first met Eliza, I was a guest in her home for months," she ventured, carefully avoiding the truth. "Later, she did offer me a position as her companion, but I declined."

"Why would you stoop so low as to become a lady's maid when you could have been a companion and held some dignity?" he grunted disapprovingly.

Now this is the father that I am familiar with, she thought. "I owed Lady Lansdowne a great debt, and I wanted to show my gratitude by serving her."

"You were not raised to be a servant." His voice was harsh.

"True," she admitted, "but I ran away from that life."

Lord Waterford's face fell. He reached out and grabbed her hands. "That was my fault. Promise me you will never run away again."

Martha tilted her chin up. "I can promise I will never run away from you again. Next time, I will walk away and never look back."

"I understand, but I hope that you will not find that necessary," he conceded.

Martha returned his gaze and decided that Eliza was right. It was time to let her father back into her life.

EMMETT RUBBED THE BACK OF HIS NECK AS HE SAT DOWN AT HIS desk. For hours, he had gone through the ledgers and meeting reports from his uncle's tenants.

"Are you taking a break?" his uncle asked from across the room.

"No, uncle," he replied. "I just can't believe how much work is associated with running two households, dealing with tenants, and maintaining a thriving farm."

Lord Exeter chuckled as he sat on an upholstered armchair with a file on his lap. "That is why I have a man of business, two stewards, and five foremen. However, it is vital that we always review the ledgers and ensure our tenant's complaints are being heard."

"I can see why my father insisted I should come to London," he muttered.

Placing the file on the table in front of him, his uncle remarked, "Your father is my heir and does not seem interested in inheriting the title."

Leaning back in his chair, Emmett shook his head. "My father has made no secret that he has no desire to be an earl." He hesitated, anxious about his uncle's reaction. "And frankly, neither do I."

Rising, Lord Exeter walked to the drink tray and poured himself a drink. "I have suspected as much. You seem to care more for doctoring the poor than balancing the ledger or making your voice heard in Parliament."

"I know you are a staunch Tory," Emmett began, "but I do not feel the same about politics."

After taking a sip, Lord Exeter lowered the glass. "The war changed you. I can see it in your eyes."

"More precisely, the war gave me clarity."

"Which is?"

Looking down at the open ledger, Emmett sighed. "I am not happy with the path laid before me."

His uncle's brows drew together. "You are a rich young man, and God willing, will one day inherit an earldom. What is not to be happy about?"

Leaning forward, Emmett closed the ledger and tapped the cover. How could he put into words the anguish he felt? He met his uncle's gaze. "I have respected and admired you since I was a little boy. I wanted to grow up to be just like you... a rich, powerful earl." He frowned. "Now, I do not care for titles, wealth, or prestige. I just want to be a doctor and minister to others."

A long moment of silence followed his remarks. Finally, his uncle replied, "Then go. Follow what your conscience dictates."

Emmett's eyebrows rose in surprise. Did his uncle just encourage him to pursue his doctoring pursuits? "Pardon?"

His uncle put his glass on the tray and walked closer to the desk. Placing his hands on top, he leaned in. "I care for you as a son, and I want you to be happy. These ledgers will be here tomorrow, the following weeks, or years from now. If you want to take a step back to pursue your passion, then go. I will not stand in your way."

Standing up from his seat, Emmett adjusted his waistcoat. "Thank you, uncle."

Pushing off from the table, his uncle took a step back. "I hope you will eventually see the benefits of being an earl. Along with the title, you will have wealth and estates, powerful friends, and you will be able to enact change in Parliament. Furthermore, you must understand my estates employ almost two hundred servants who rely on the income that you supply them."

"I understand what a great responsibility it is," Emmett replied. "I will not let you down."

Lord Exeter looked worried. "Can I at least persuade you to take footmen to act as guards when you go into the rookery?"

"There is no need," Emmett explained with a smirk. "I can take care of myself on the east side."

"There are dangerous…" Lord Exeter's words trailed off when Lord Beckett and Benedict walked into the room. He smiled broadly as he acknowledged the two men. "Gentlemen, what a delightful surprise."

"I daresay your butler will let anyone through your doors," Lord Beckett remarked.

Emmett had long admired Lord Beckett, whose stance radiated confidence, reminding all that he was not a man to be trifled with.

Benedict chuckled. "Your tone was quite threatening when you demanded to see Lord Exeter right away."

"You both are always welcome in my home," Lord Exeter said, approaching the drink tray. After pouring two drinks, he turned and handed one to each of the men. "Now, what can I do for you?"

Lord Beckett adjusted the large file in his hands before he took a sip of his drink. As he lowered the snifter, he revealed, "I was hoping to speak privately to Dr. Maddix for a moment."

His uncle turned to give him a pointed look before turning his attention back to Lord Beckett. "Of course, but you must say good-bye before you leave."

Once his uncle had exited the room, closing the door behind him, Lord Beckett sat on a chair in front of the desk. "I will get straight to the point. I would like to recruit you as an agent of the Crown."

Emmett's eyes grew wide at those unexpected words. Sitting, he wondered, how does one respond to such a ludicrous request?

Gulping his drink, Lord Beckett placed his empty glass on the desk and leaned back. "I heard about your heroic actions in Rockcliffe. You managed to impress my most hardened agent."

"I impressed you?" he asked, shifting his gaze to Benedict.

He shook his head. "Not me. Larson."

Emmett lifted his brows in surprise. "I take that as a compliment."

"You should," Lord Beckett stated. "I understand our prince regent offered to make you the Viscount of Berkeley for your courageous actions in Scotland, but you turned it down."

"I did," Emmett confirmed. "What I did in Rockcliffe, I did for king and country, not for praise or titles."

Lord Beckett's eyes reflected approval. "We are now in a situation where we need your particular skills."

"Which are?" he prodded.

"We need a physician," Benedict admitted.

Glancing between them suspiciously, Emmett asked, "Pray tell, why would you need a doctor?"

The frown lines around Lord Beckett's mouth deepened as he explained, "On the banks of the River Thames, a small town called Gravesend has been a known paradise for smugglers for centuries. It relies heavily on watermen as their source of income. But recently, press gangs have impressed many of the men into service, leaving their women and children vulnerable to a more deplorable element, known as The Cursed Lot."

Benedict took a sip of his drink. "There is a pub in Gravesend called The Cloven Hoof. It is rumored to be the hangout for The Cursed Lot and is the center of illegal activities in the area."

Leaning forward in his seat, Emmett rested his forearms on

the desk. "Are we discussing illegal card games like hazard or faro? If so…"

"No, that is not what we are referring to," Benedict insisted, cutting him off. "We are talking about a sophisticated smuggling ring."

"Again, why would you need a doctor?"

Lord Beckett's brow dipped inward. "The Cloven Hoof is situated in an industrial area, near a sulphur mill. We believe that is where the smuggled goods are stored, but every time the revenue men raid the building, it turns up empty."

Emmett leaned back. "Smuggling is not new, especially during times of war."

"True," Lord Beckett agreed, "but The Cursed Lot have managed to smuggle contraband out right from under the custom officials' noses, eliminate their competition, and have taken over the entire town, leaving many dead in the process."

"How has this gang acquired so much power?" Emmett questioned.

Benedict took the last sip of his drink. "That is what you will need to discover."

Adjusting the file in his hand, Lord Beckett frowned. "The Bow Street Runners were hired to run this investigation, but every time they convinced someone to come forward, that witness ended up floating in the River Thames. After a Runner was murdered, Sir Conant, the chief magistrate of Bow Street, came to me directly and asked for the Crown's assistance in the investigation."

"This is indeed horrible, but why would the Crown need a doctor? Why not a seasoned agent?" Emmett questioned as he glanced over at Benedict.

Benedict grinned. "We feel that a physician would not arouse suspicion if you came in under the ruse of providing Gravesend with medical care." He glanced at Lord Beckett before adding,

"Besides, you have already made a name for yourself by visiting the rookeries and doctoring the needy."

Lord Beckett opened the file, pulled out a sheet of paper, and extended it towards him. "An endowment has opened up a charitable hospital for the people of St. George's parish. We have you listed as the physician that will run the hospital and oversee the day-to-day operations. A small building near the church has already been converted into a suitable space for you to minister to your patients."

Emmett's eyes scanned the paper looking for the generous benefactor. The name Mr. George Larson caught his eye. He lifted a brow as he lowered the paper. "The benefactor is Eliza's protector?"

"On paper, yes," Lord Beckett confirmed.

As Benedict leaned forward to place his empty glass on the desk, he revealed, "A local convent will provide sisters to rotate as volunteer nurses. One sister is even trained as a midwife." He leaned back in his seat.

Emmett mulled over their words. "To clarify, you are asking me to go into a small town, minister to them, and get them to trust me, all with the intention of betraying them."

Lord Beckett shook his head at his words. "No, we are asking you to help a small town that could not afford a physician and help root out smugglers that are killing innocent people to ensure their silence."

Running a hand through his hair, Emmett knew he couldn't deny medical attention to the poor. The more he served, the more he felt like he was atoning for his past sins. "I will do it," he said firmly, "but I have a few conditions."

Lord Beckett's lips twitched slightly, appearing amused. "I am listening."

He abruptly stood up from his chair. "I will need supplies, medication, bandages, and other basics to help care for the people." His gaze returned to Benedict. "And I would like an agent to be tasked with following Lady Martha to ensure she is protected at all times."

"That is already done. Eliza requested a guard to be assigned to Martha before we departed for London," Benedict informed him, smugly. "Furthermore, you might be interested to know that we have requested a detailed investigation on Lord Waterford."

Nodding, Lord Beckett confirmed, "It is true. We should have that report shortly."

"Thank you," Emmett responded gratefully. "I will sleep better knowing that Martha is safe."

"Martha is it?" Lord Beckett teased. "She must be a special lady to warrant so much concern for her safety."

An image of Martha came to his mind, and he smiled to himself. "She is a remarkable woman."

"Just as I thought," Lord Beckett said as he rose. "I will look forward to meeting her at the ball."

"Ball?" Emmett asked, confused.

Benedict chuckled. "The invitation was sent to your aunt, and she responded that you would be attending."

"I will ask my aunt for more details," Emmett replied with enthusiasm. He wondered briefly why attending a ball with Martha excited him so much.

Lord Beckett handed him the large file. "All the information you need is in here, including the location of the hospital at St. George's. Since this will be a joint operation, I am assigning you a Bow Street Runner as a partner on this assignment. His name is Mr. Simeon Martin, and he will act as your head nurse."

Emmett lifted his brow as he placed the file on the desk. "Does Mr. Martin have any training as a nurse?"

"None," Benedict replied, "but he is a phenomenal Runner and can be trusted."

"Expect him to make contact sooner rather than later," Lord Beckett added.

The two men moved towards the door, but Lord Beckett spun

back around. "Be careful traveling to Gravesend. The main road crosses Blackheath, which is notorious for highwaymen."

Opening the top drawer of his desk, Emmett pulled out a pistol and tucked it into the waistband of his trousers. "Thank you for the warning, but I am always prepared."

"Is that your only weapon?" Benedict asked in concern.

Emmett shook his head, feigning annoyance. "Do you think I am so cavalier about my safety that I would only carry one weapon on my person?" He smirked. "I have an overcoat pistol in my right boot, a sheathed dagger in my left boot, and my doctor's bag holds another spare pistol."

Nodding their approval, the men said their goodbyes. After they'd departed, Emmett dropped into his chair, pondering what he had just agreed to. He was going to work for the Crown to track down a group of smugglers. Well, that was the downside. The upside was that he was going to help a small town, providing them with medical care.

Well, he didn't have time to sit around and dwell on it. Rising, he requested that his uncle's crested post-chaise be brought around, grabbed his medical bag, and walked to the door. He would go to Gravesend and see what he was up against.

❧ 10 ❧

RUSHING DOWN THE STEPS OF HIS UNCLE'S TOWNHOUSE, EMMETT started to step into the coach when he heard his name.

"Dr. Maddix, may I have a moment of your time?"

Removing his foot from the carriage step, he turned around and was surprised to see a man of similar age leaning up against the iron fence holding a large, wooden chest in his hands.

"How may I help you?" Emmett asked curiously.

The man straightened from the fence, but his gaze never left the ground. "May we speak privately in your coach?"

"For what purpose?"

Taking a few steps closer, he replied in a hushed but urgent tone, "My name is Mr. Simeon Martin. I believe you are expecting me."

"Would you prefer to have this conversation in my townhouse?"

"No, I would prefer to have this conversation on the way to Gravesend," Mr. Martin replied firmly.

Emmett nodded his acceptance. Stepping into the carriage, he sat across from Mr. Martin and closed the door.

Glancing at the chest on the bench next to Mr. Martin, Emmett asked, "Now, what do you wish to discuss with me?"

"I presume that Lord Beckett informed you that we would be working as partners," Mr. Martin stated.

Emmett noted the man's sarcastic undertone. He adjusted his coat before answering. "He did. However, I did not expect you to make contact so soon."

A flicker of annoyance flashed on Mr. Martin's face. "Did Lord Beckett not divulge the seriousness of this mission?"

Emmett eyed his traveling companion. "Are you always this intense, Mr. Martin?"

"I am," he declared flatly, "when the lives of innocent women and children are at stake."

"I understand." The stench of the rookeries drifted into the carriage and Emmett reached to close the window. "I was told that I will be running the charity hospital at St. George's in Gravesend, in hopes the patients will trust me enough to share what they know."

"That is correct," Mr. Martin replied with a decisive bob of his head. "Do you think you can handle the complexity of your assignment?"

Emmett tried to keep his tone civil despite his new partner's obvious hostility. "I will manage. Do you think you can manage the ruse of being a nurse?"

"I will manage," Mr. Martin mimicked his exact words, then he leaned back in his seat, maintaining his hardened gaze. "It is rubbish that I need a partner at all, much less someone like you."

"Can you be more specific?" Emmett asked in annoyance.

Mr. Martin scoffed, "I don't have time to babysit an entitled gentleman who pretends to care about the people in the rookeries."

Ignoring the Runner's direct insult, Emmett grunted, "Are you always this addled when you meet someone new?"

Resting his arm on the top of the chest, Mr. Martin pursed his lips. After a few tense moments, he spoke again, clearly as irritated as before. "When I was told I would be assigned an agent of the Crown to partner with, I expected to work with someone like…"

"*Shadow?*"

"No, more like *Hawk.*"

Emmett smirked. "I am sorry to disappoint you. If it helps, I worked an assignment with them in Scotland."

"So I was told," Mr. Martin replied dryly. "I did my own research and discovered you have quite an impressive medical background."

"Was that an insult or a compliment, Mr. …"

Mr. Martin cut him off, his eyes reflecting contempt. "You studied at Cambridge and are licensed by the Royal College of Physicians. Furthermore, you had an apprenticeship under Mr. James Parkinson to train as a surgeon, which is highly irregular for a doctor of your status. Why would you throw that all away to become a lowly ship's surgeon?"

"I threw nothing away," Emmett asserted. "I had an immense desire to serve my king and country which allowed me to gain valuable insight and experience in the medical field."

Mr. Martin rubbed his chin before asking, "Then why were you court-martialed for shooting your captain in the leg?"

Emmett humphed at the question. "If you truly dug into my background, then you should be able to tell me."

Mr. Martin's eyes grew wary. "Those files were supposedly destroyed in a fire."

"There you have it," he declared vaguely.

"I was hoping you would tell me."

Emmett smiled, but there was no warmth behind it. "I don't have to tell you anything."

Mr. Martin's jaw tensed. "Rumor has it that you and your captain fought over the affections of a woman," he paused, his eyes fixed on him, "and you were a sore loser."

Running his hand through his hair, Emmett attempted to control his temper. "I have not determined what to make of you yet, Mr. Martin. However, I find your company to be less than tolerable right now."

"Just so you are aware, my focus is only on bringing down a smuggling ring and capturing the leader of The Cursed Lot. You handle the hospital, and I will do the real investigative work." He scoffed as he rolled his eyes. "I doubt a gentleman of your social standing could even handle this assignment."

Emmett banged on the side of the carriage with his fist, alerting the driver to stop. When the carriage jerked to a standstill, he pushed open the door. "I have reached my quota of insults for today, and I don't intend to spend three hours traveling with you in a confined space. Get out. Find your own transportation to Gravesend."

Mr. Martin looked smug as he crossed his arms over his broad chest. "No. I am not going anywhere."

"This is your last warning."

Mr. Martin chuckled dryly. "As if you can stop me..."

Before the offending man finished his sentence, Emmett punched him in the jaw, knocking him unconscious. Grabbing a handful of his shirt, he tossed him into the arms of a waiting footman. "Place him against the building," he ordered, closing the door. He again banged on the carriage.

Bracing his legs for the expected lurch forward, he reached for the chest on the seat. Opening the lid, he was pleased to find the medical supplies that Lord Beckett had promised. One section was filled with lancets, scalpels, syringes, bleeding cups, mixing bowls, and an ornate jar filled with leeches. The other side held over twenty-nine bottles of medical concoctions, some labeled as quinine, calamine, peppermint water, exotic spices, and laudanum. He shook his head in wonder, realizing that Lord Beckett had anticipated that he would accept the assignment.

Leaning his head back against the plush carriage seat, he let his eyes drift closed. If he was lucky, he wouldn't fall asleep deeply enough to dream.

THE CARRIAGE JERKED TO A STOP, WAKING EMMETT FROM HIS restless nap. Forcing back a yawn, he reached for the chest as the footman opened the door and stood aside. "St. George's Church, as you directed, sir."

"Thank you," he replied, stepping out of the carriage onto a worn cobblestone street. "Wait for me here."

The footman tipped his head. "As you wish, Dr. Maddix."

Emmett shifted the chest in his arms as he admired St. George's Church. The classical building had yellow bricks and stone dressings, topped with a Stonewold concrete tile roof. A tall, four-stage tower dominated the west side, and narrow, round-headed windows were evenly spaced around the nave.

On the south side of the church, separated by a lush garden, sat a small, square building with narrow windows and a thatched roof. The door was open, and smoke rose from the chimney. This looks like an excellent place to ask for directions, he thought.

As he approached the open door, he heard loud murmurings coming from inside and a woman's voice admonishing them to be patient. He knocked on the door, pushing it fully open, and was surprised to find the room filled with people of all ages, turning to look at him with dirtied, expectant faces. An older woman, dressed in a simple, black tunic with matching veil, gently pushed her way through the people.

Stopping in front of him, the woman wore a frustrated expression. "Dr. Maddix, we were expecting you hours ago." Her eyes shifted towards the chest. "Medical supplies were delivered this morning, but I am pleased to see that you brought your own medical chest."

"Pardon?" How could they be expecting him when he only just learned about the assignment? And when did Lord Beckett arrange for all these medical supplies to be delivered?

Turning abruptly, she bade him follow her further into the room. Pointing to the left, she informed him, "These people have been here since early this morning and refused to leave even to eat." She sighed. "They were afraid to lose their places in line."

Pointing to her right, she explained, "Everyone else I gave a number based upon the severity of their symptoms."

Assuming she was one of the nuns from the convent, he said, "You seem quite competent with diagnoses, sister. If I may inquire, how is that possible?"

"You may call me Sister Mary, and I am a trained midwife."

"Excellent, I have immense respect for midwifery," he replied quickly. "However, it appears that you have had some medical training as well."

She turned to walk further into the room, speaking over her shoulder. "My father was a physician, and he spent considerable time educating me in medicine."

She stopped at a closed door and clasped her hands in front of her. "This is the back room. You can examine patients here."

"Have you been responsible for ministering to the sick in the parish?" Emmett asked.

A sad, wearisome look came into her eyes. "It is a significant role to fill, and we have lacked adequate supplies for so long. It is too much for us to handle. Between the press gangs and smugglers, we..." Her mouth snapped shut as she blinked away her emotions. "I will send in your first patient as soon as you get situated."

Recognizing the dismissal, Emmett shifted the chest in his hands and opened the crude door that offered minimal privacy.

Once inside the room, he noted a straw mattress on an iron frame, a writing table, and a chair.

He placed the chest on the ground and opened the lid. Before removing any items, he ran his finger along the table and was pleased to see that it was not covered in grime.

Sister Mary knocked as she pushed open the door but kept her hold on the handle. "Your first patient," she announced.

A woman dressed in a faded brown dress with a brown cap covering her hair walked into the room holding hands with a young child. The boy's clothes were held together by twine. The knees of his trousers boasted gaping tears. His shoes had visible holes, and it was apparent that they would not last much longer.

Emmett plastered on a smile as he greeted them. "What ails you today?"

Urging the boy forward, the mother explained, "Johnny has had a cough for over a month now, and it is getting worse."

The boy looked fearful, so Emmett decided to sit on the chair to appear less dominating. As he sat down, the chair legs broke, and he tumbled to the floor. Shaking his head at his misfortune, he heard Johnny giggle.

Looking up at the boy peeking out from behind his mother's skirts, Emmett chuckled. "I admit that I have had better days."

The boy came out from behind his mom and tentatively took a few steps closer to him. "Are you really a doctor?"

"I am." Emmett stood and wiped off his trousers.

"My mama made me wait all day to see you," Johnny informed him.

"Did she?"

The boy nodded his head. "Do you have any food?"

"Hush, Johnny," the mother admonished. "We will eat after the doctor examines you."

Turning his head back towards his mother, Johnny asked hopefully, "Does that mean you got money to buy food?"

"No, Johnny. I don't have any money," she answered softly,

her tone sad. "Mind your manners and show respect to the doctor."

The boy looked dejectedly at the floor. "Yes, mama."

Frowning, Emmett leaned back against the table. "You have no money for food?"

The woman placed her hand on Johnny's shoulder. "We are normally given two meals a day at the parish workhouse, but Johnny's cough is getting worse, so we decided to wait in line to see you."

His eyes widened in surprise as they darted towards Johnny. "You are both employed at the workhouse?"

"Yes, we are fortunate to live there," the mother confirmed.

Emmett frowned as his eyes scanned their worn clothing, dirtied faces, and sunken eyes. "Are you paid for your work?"

Glancing down at her son, she replied, "We are given a bed to sleep in, food in our bellies, and two-pence a week."

"For each of you?"

She shook her head. "No, for both of us."

He made a note to check on the parish workhouse at his first opportunity. "Have you managed to save any money?"

The woman's face paled. "We were informed that you would be helping us at no cost."

He gave her an understanding smile. "Make no mistake of that." Addressing the boy, he asked, "How old are you?"

Glancing at his mom for permission, he replied, "Five."

"Ah," Emmett said, rubbing his chin thoughtfully. "That is the age when boys are typically given a pet dragon."

Johnny's eyes grew wide in wonder. "A pet dragon? Like a fire-breathing dragon?"

Emmett grinned. "I know of no other kind, do you?"

"No, mister," he responded with excitement in his eyes. His smile faded as he turned back to his mom. "What do dragons eat? If they eat human food, then we don't have any."

Emmett pointed his finger towards the ceiling as if he just

came up with a brilliant plan. "I have an idea," he exclaimed. "I will buy your pet dragon from you for..." he paused, reaching into the pocket of his waistcoat and pulling out a handful of coins, "... ten shillings."

The boy's mouth dropped open. "Ten shillings?" he repeated in awe. "But I don't have a pet dragon."

"Not yet," he said with a smile. "I will intercept the man who delivers dragons and claim your pet." He held out the coins in his hands. "And you get ten shillings."

As the boy reached for the coins, the mother grabbed the boy by the arm. "No, sir, we do not take charity."

"But mama, it's not charity. I am giving him my dragon," the boy explained innocently.

Crouching down low, the mother put her hand on his chin and forced the boy to look at her. "Nothing comes free in this world, and we will not be indebted to the doctor."

Johnny turned his head, his eyes reflecting sadness. At that moment, the boy's stomach rumbled loudly, and his mother put on a brave face. "If we hurry, we can eat supper."

The boy's face dropped even lower. "The food is always covered in dust."

Knowing he needed to act, Emmett reached into his waistcoat and exchanged the coins with two different ones. Extending them to the mother, he said, "If you will not accept the money for yourself, please accept it for your son. His boots have holes, his clothes do not provide any warmth, and I can see the bones on his shoulders."

The woman's eyes strayed toward his hand, and she gasped. "Doctor, you grabbed the wrong coins."

He shook his head. "No, I did not," he insisted. "I intentionally grabbed two gold coins."

There was a knock at the door, and Sister Mary poked her head in. "Dr. Maddix, you are spending entirely too much time with your first patient." She lifted a brow. "You have almost fifty people waiting to see you and the line is growing."

Reaching for the woman's hand, he gently placed the coins in her hand. "Thank you," he said.

"Thank you?" she repeated in confusion. "You are the one giving us coins."

He took a step back. "Now, let me examine Johnny."

Johnny looked up at him with admiration. "You are nice. I hope the bad men don't kill you like they did my dad."

The woman's eyes grew fearful as she placed a hand over her son's mouth. Her voice trembled as she claimed, "Johnny has the wildest imagination."

Emmett just gave her a nod as he went to examine Johnny. It was clear that the woman was hiding something, but he would deal with that later.

MARTHA HAD JUST FINISHED PINNING BACK HER HAIR INTO A neat, low-slung chignon when a knock came at her door. As she rose to open the door, it opened barely wide enough for Josette to slip in before closing the door behind her.

She smiled at her companion. "You do realize that it is perfectly normal for us to be seen together."

With a laugh, Josette smoothed out her lavender gown while saying, "I do, but I am attempting to avoid a specific footman. I may have inadvertently given the impression that I was flirting with him."

"And were you?"

Josette scrunched her nose. "Perhaps."

Noticing that her companion's hair was haphazardly pinned back, Martha patted the dressing table chair. "Come sit and let me fix your hair."

"How do you know how to fix hair?"

"I haven't always been a lady," she informed her.

Walking over to the chair, Josette lowered herself gracefully. "You look like a lady to me."

"Looks can be deceiving," Martha replied earnestly. After

removing the pins from Josette's long, brown hair, she began brushing it. "Now, back to the footman. Why were you flirting with him?"

"So I could retrieve this," Josette answered as she reached into the pocket of her dress and pulled out a key.

"You flirted with a footman to obtain a key?"

"Yes."

Placing the brush down, Martha prodded, "For what purpose?"

"After we arrived, I took the opportunity to tour the entire townhouse, but the door to your father's study was locked, and I was unable to pick the lock." Josette tucked the key back into her pocket. "I initiated a conversation with a footman, during which I slipped the key out of his pocket."

While twisting her companion's hair into a chignon, Martha said, "I had wondered where you ran off to last night."

"Your father was not too keen on me joining you for supper."

"That is not true."

Josette laughed. "After I took my last bite of dessert, he summarily dismissed me for the evening. Remember?"

Martha gave her an apologetic look. "I did notice that. I'm sorry."

With a flick of her wrist, Josette replied, "You have no reason to apologize. It gave me time to talk with the household staff."

"And did the staff reveal anything?" Martha asked as she placed the long pins in her companion's hair.

Josette shook her head. "No, they are loyal to your father."

"Perhaps my father has changed his ways, and he isn't hiding anything," Martha suggested. There was a small part of her that wanted to believe that he was telling the truth.

"After everyone retired for bed, I snuck into your father's study."

Reaching for a long yellow ribbon, Martha weaved the ribbon through Josette's hair. "And did you discover anything?"

Turning in her seat, Josette placed her hands on the back of the chair. "I did," she answered, her eyes holding concern. "I am afraid it is not the best news."

Martha sighed and sat down on the settee. "Go ahead."

Shifting more in her seat, Josette shared, "Your father is heavily in debt to a pub called The Cloven Hoof."

Martha pursed her lips as frustration poured over her. It appeared that her father had not changed as much as he claimed. "A pub? Why would he be in debt to a pub?"

Josette rose and joined her on the settee and explained. "Pubs are notorious for harboring gambling dens."

"I did not know that," she admitted. "How much debt has my father accrued?"

"If I had to guess, I would say roughly £20,000 worth of unpaid notes." Josette gave her a faint smile. "There is more."

"More?" Did she want to know more?

"There were also bills for a house of ill-repute."

Sighing again, Martha felt only disgust at her father's actions. It was obvious that he still had his vices. What else was he lying about?

How could her father go to such a place? How could he do that? Didn't he know that not all women were there by choice? That some were forced, beaten and tied to their beds to keep them from escaping?

Martha felt raw rage building up inside of her; rage against her father; rage against her lot in life. Simeon may have sold her into slavery, but all those men she encountered were guilty as well. Her heart pounded wildly as she clenched and unclenched her hands. Jumping up from her seat, she felt her spirit darkening.

"Martha, are you all right?" Josette asked with concern.

She glared down at her companion with narrowed eyes. "No, I am not all right!" she exclaimed. "My own father robs women of their virtue. He casts them aside, without a thought to their welfare."

Pacing back and forth, she railed, "How can men be so loathsome, so revolting, so…" Her voice trailed off as angry tears flowed down her cheeks.

Glancing at Josette, she saw that her eyes were filled with pity, and that was her undoing. Not bothering to wipe away her tears, Martha raced out of her room and down the hall, intending to escape to the solitude of their private garden. At the top of the stairs, she saw Emmett standing in the entry hall, handing his hat to the butler.

As she rushed down the stairs to meet him, Emmett raised his head and greeted her with a smile. But then it disappeared, and his eyes shone with worry. In a few strides, he closed the distance between them. "What is wrong, Lady Martha?"

She could not accurately portray the anger coursing through her body, so she just tightly pressed her lips together. Emmett wouldn't understand. How could he?

"I brought my barouche," he informed her softly. "Would you like to go for a ride?"

Martha nodded weakly.

Emmett offered his arm, and she found herself reaching for it. His gaze traveled over her shoulder and gave a quick nod. Turning her head, she saw Josette behind her, watching her with sympathy.

Without saying a word, Emmett escorted her out the door and assisted her into his barouche. Once she was situated, he turned and helped Josette onto the driver's bench. Climbing into the carriage, he sat across from her, watching her, but she refused to look him in the eyes.

Finally, he leaned forward and broke the silence by asking, "Did your father strike you?" His voice sounded controlled, but she could hear the underlying anger in the question.

"No," she answered in a low quivering voice.

"Did your father say something to offend you?"

"No."

"Then what has you so upset?"

Martha scoffed and glared at him. "You don't understand. No one understands. I was happy being a lady's maid." Fortunately, the sound of the bustling street and the clattering of the horse's hooves on the cobblestone allowed their conversation to remain private even from the driver.

"You were happy hiding."

"Yes!" she exclaimed, throwing up her hands. "I was safe."

"Are you not safe in your father's home?"

Clenching her hands, she wanted to hit Emmett's handsome face. Why was he so difficult? "I am not safe from my memories," she declared furiously. "As a lady's maid, I only interacted with the select few people I trusted, knowing they would not betray me."

Tilting his head towards her, Emmett started, "If I may…"

"No, you may not!" she shouted.

A few women on the street turned, shaking their heads in disapproval.

Arriving at Hyde Park, Emmett turned and instructed the driver to veer off the dirt path and away from prying eyes. Once they stopped, he hopped out and helped her step down. After they walked away from the barouche, he asked deliberately, "Now, what has you so angry?"

Her hands balled into fists by her sides. "I discovered that my own father frequents brothels."

Emmett winced apologetically. "I can't imagine the betrayal that you must feel…"

She put her hands up to stop his words and spat out, "Do not presume to know my emotions."

"Martha…"

"Stop! Just stop!" Martha stormed off.

Once she reached a small stream, she stopped and crossed

her arms over her chest, huffing. Why was she so angry? She wasn't angry at Emmett per se, she was just angry with everything and everyone. She'd had a difficult childhood, a despicable fiancé, five years of hell, and now she was tired. She couldn't do it anymore. Her emotions were refusing to stay buried. Why couldn't she push them back down?

Emmett's voice came from behind her. "If you are truly unhappy, then I will drive you over to Eliza's townhouse."

Ignoring his concern, she stood rigid, her back to him. "Did you know she has arranged a ball in my honor?"

"I did," he replied. "Benedict and Lord Beckett called on me yesterday."

"I will be expected to dance," she informed him.

She could hear Emmett's boots crunch on the dry leaves as he took a few steps closer to her. "Is that why you are upset?"

Spinning around, Martha glared at him through narrowed eyes. "No, I am angry that I went along with this mad ruse."

"And what ruse is that?"

She threw her hands up in the air. "The one where I pretend to be a lady."

He frowned. "That is not a ruse."

"I did not ask to become a lady," she countered.

"And yet, you are."

Her eyes scanned the trees. "No, this is not my life... not anymore."

"Then what do you want?"

"I want to return to my role as Eliza's lady's maid."

He eyed her for a moment before dipping his head in defeat. "If that is what will make you happy."

Tilting her chin, she declared, "It will."

"All right."

"All right," she repeated.

Emmett stood watching her, disappointment clearly on his

features. After a long moment, his face became expressionless. "Allow me to escort you to Eliza's townhouse."

"Thank you," she replied as she took a few steps towards the barouche.

As she passed Emmett, he surprised her by saying, "I didn't think you would quit without a fight."

"Pardon?"

He shook his head and took a step closer to her. "You are deceiving yourself, Martha. You are not just giving up on this life; you are giving up on yourself."

"I am not!" she exclaimed. "I am protecting myself."

"From whom?"

"From everyone!" She closed the distance between them and poked him in the chest. "You are not allowed to stand there and judge my choices."

His lips tightened before saying, "I understand your anger…"

"No, you don't," she interjected. "No one understands what I have been through, the hell that I endured."

"Fine," he mocked. "You are the only person in the history of the world that had something horrible happen to them." He looked heavenward. "If everyone that experienced their own personal hell gave up, then where would we be?"

Her mouth gaped at his sarcastic tone, and she opened her mouth to defend her position.

Before she could speak, he added, "I have an idea of what happened to you, and I am truly sorry. But you are giving up too easily." His words were sincere and heartfelt, and almost affected her resolve… almost.

"And I told you that I have nothing left to fight for," she insisted.

Emmett reared his head back in surprise. "You don't have anything left to fight for? Fight for your friends; fight for your goddaughter, Caroline; but more importantly, fight for yourself."

"Why? What's the point?" she asked, searching his eyes.

Slowly, he raised his hands and gently placed them on her shoulders. "Because if you don't, you are depriving the world of a remarkable woman."

"I daresay that you need spectacles."

Offering a grin at her attempt at humor, he urged, "It is time for you to let go of all that has been brewing inside of you. It is time for you to move on."

Lowering her gaze to his lapels, she pressed her lips together. How could she let go of the hate that she had been harboring for so long? "I don't think I can. At times, it has been the only thing that has kept me going."

Raising her gaze, she saw a hollow expression in Emmett's eyes as he shared, "After Eleanora's death, I was numb to what was going on around me. When I started to get feeling back, hate, anger, and self-loathing consumed me." His eyes softened as he gazed at her. "I even plotted Colonel Allister's downfall. I was going to rob him of all the joy he had surrounding him and replace it with misery and despair."

"What happened?"

He dropped his hands and stood back. "After my cousin helped me feel other emotions again, I started picking up the shattered remnants of my life, piece by piece. I focused on my passion, being a doctor and helping people."

Taking a good look at Emmett, she noticed that he had dark circles under his eyes. "Did you sleep at all last night?"

"No. Remember, you are not the only one with nightmares that plague you when you close your eyes."

She frowned at his response. "You must sleep, Emmett."

He shifted his gaze away from her. "I will, but I promised to call on you today."

"Did you go into the rookeries last night?"

"No, I was ministering to patients at a charity hospital in Gravesend." He waggled his brow. "Are you keeping tabs on me, Martha?"

She rolled her eyes, ignoring his last comment and asking a question of her own. "May I join you next time you go to the charity hospital or the rookeries?"

He shook his head. "No. It is not safe for you."

"I could bring food to pass out or..."

Emmett interrupted her. "Get that ludicrous notion out of your head. It is not safe for you to travel to Gravesend or even to walk near the rookeries."

"But you go?" she asked with a furrowed brow. "Why is it safe for you?"

"It's not." He hung his head in shame. "But you are not the only one that welcomes death."

Her mouth gaped, finally recognizing that Emmett truly understood her plight. When she could speak, she pleaded, "You can't die on me. Promise that you won't die."

Emmett looked puzzled. "I promise."

With tear-filled eyes, she tried to explain her feelings, surprising even herself with the passion she felt. "Without you, I would not be standing here. I would never have been strong enough to take my first step." She swiped at the tears running down her cheeks. "Although I keep faltering, I know you will be there to strengthen me."

With a smug grin, he teased, "I thought you despised me."

"I do. At times, I find you to be the most maddening man, but..." she paused, her voice hitching, "you have always been kind to me. You are my friend." She smiled up at him.

He dropped the smugness, offering a genuine smile in its place. "You are my friend, as well."

Turning her head, she took a moment to listen to the stream as she pondered Emmett's words. Was it possible to start over and pick up the shattered pieces of her life? Could she learn to trust as she had once before? It seemed like a tremendous feat, but her soul seemed lighter by the mere thought of it.

"Where do you suppose we go from here?" she asked as the wind billowed her dress around her.

"Anywhere we want," he replied as he stood next to her.

She gave him a side-long glance. "I may flounder."

"Then you would be human."

They stood in comfortable silence listening to the flowing stream, the rush of the wind through the trees and the mourning doves calling out. After a few moments, she turned to face Emmett.

"I would like to go yell at Eliza now."

He chuckled. "Lead the way, my lady."

❧ 12 ❧

WALKING PURPOSEFULLY TOWARDS ELIZA'S DRAWING ROOM, Martha had not waited for Emmett to escort her. Her companion, Josette, had come into the townhouse with her but had gone in a different direction. As she entered the room, her steps faltered when she saw Lady Camden sitting and chatting merrily to Eliza. Drat! She couldn't yell at Eliza with her sister present.

Both women turned their heads at her arrival, and Eliza jumped up. "Martha, what a pleasant surprise," she gushed as she came over to give her a hug.

Returning the embrace, she waited until Eliza took a step back before she admonished in a hushed tone, "I am mad at you."

"Whatever for?" Eliza asked innocently.

She frowned. "How could you host a ball in my honor?"

Kate chuckled at her words. "Most people would be pleased to be introduced into Society by the Marchioness of Lansdowne."

"I planned to hide in the crowd," she explained. "I can't hide if I am the guest of honor."

Emmett's voice came from the doorway. "How many times

do I have to tell you that you are too beautiful to remain hidden?"

Feeling flattered, warmth crept into her cheeks. She turned back towards Emmett. "You've never told me I was beautiful."

"I didn't realize I needed to," he replied unapologetically. "You must be prepared. Gentlemen will line up to dance with you."

"I haven't danced since I was a girl," she admitted sadly.

"Why?" he asked, walking closer to her.

Martha sighed despairingly. "Those carefree days are gone."

Eliza spoke up, "Do you know how to dance?"

She nodded. "I was trained by a dance master, along with the other daughters of the gentry in our town."

Glancing over at her sister, Eliza smiled playfully. "Shall we practice now?"

Smiling, Kate stood slowly and walked to the pianoforte. As she sat on the bench, she suggested, "Let's practice the waltz."

Emmett offered his hand. "As the only gentleman in the room, I would be honored to dance with you."

Shrinking back from his hand, Martha shook her head. "No," she stated emphatically. "I am not going to dance."

Before anyone could react, Josette entered with a paper in her hand. "The prince regent is coming to Lady Martha's ball?" she asked loudly.

Eliza beamed in approval. "Excellent. I see that you have mastered picking locks." Turning towards Kate, she explained, "I have been teaching Josette how to pick locks, and to give her additional practice, I lock specific rooms."

Reaching for the letter in Josette's hand, Eliza chastised lightly, "However, from now on, kindly refrain from reading *my* personal correspondence."

Josette extended the letter towards her. "I apologize, my lady."

As she folded the note, Eliza instructed, "You must ensure

that every item you touch appears as if it was never disturbed. You cannot leave evidence that you were there. It is much too dangerous."

Vaguely acknowledging Eliza's espionage advice to Josette, Martha sat on a nearby chair, sighing in disbelief. "Prinny is coming to the ball? He mustn't come. If the prince regent ever learned of my past, he would be disgraced for attending."

"That will not matter to Prinny," Eliza assured her.

Wringing her hands together, Martha asked, "How can you be so sure?"

"Trust me," Eliza answered, her eyes twinkling with mischief. "Also, Prinny informed me that he wishes to dance with you."

She attempted to keep her wits about her, although she felt the color drain from her face. "I have no desire to dance with the prince regent." Her voice was surprisingly steady, considering the circumstances.

Grabbing a chair, Emmett relocated it next to hers. "It would be a grave insult to not dance with Prinny."

Martha sat straight up, her back rigid, but she was unable to keep the trepidation out of her voice. "I understand. I will dance with the prince regent, assuming he asks."

Eliza smirked. "Oh, have no doubt."

Emmett stood and offered his hand again. "Do you know how to waltz?"

"No," she answered.

He playfully wiggled his fingers. "Trust me." His words were simple but no less valid. She did trust him, wholeheartedly.

Tentatively, she brought her hand up and allowed him to assist her as she rose. He led her closer to the pianoforte as Kate began playing, and the beautiful music filled the room.

Standing in front of her, he explained gently, "I am going to place my left hand on your waist."

Her breath hitched in anticipation as he slowly moved his

hand till it rested on her waist, feeling the warmth of his palm and fingers through her gown. An unfamiliar tingle coursed through her body at his touch. Not trusting herself to say anything, she remained silent, blinking up at him.

"Now, I am going to take your left hand into mine." He encompassed their gloved hands and raised them up. He stared deeply into her eyes. "How are you faring?" he asked, his tone betraying his concern. "Would you like me to stop?"

The expression in his green eyes, so warm and intimate, held her captive. She felt his hand loosen around her waist. Recognizing that he had misconstrued her silence for apprehension, she murmured, "Don't let go." Her cheeks burned with embarrassment as she rushed to clarify. "I want to learn how to waltz."

Martha watched as he smiled that achingly sweet smile that somehow managed to penetrate through all her defenses. "Allow me to lead," he said softly as he started swaying her to the music.

AS HE DANCED WITH MARTHA, EMMETT FELT SOMETHING SHIFT between them. Her body molded perfectly into his arms, and he suddenly had the desire to never let her go.

Neither of them spoke as he led her to the music, and they continued to stare deeply into each other's eyes. From the very beginning, he'd had a fierce desire to protect her, to help her, but maybe she was helping him. Perhaps she was providing a new sense of purpose and direction in his bleak, sometimes dreary, life.

Without thinking, he pulled her closer. In response, her eyes widened in surprise, and her back became rigid. Realizing his mistake, he started to loosen his grip but stopped when she relaxed back into his arms.

Hesitantly, he broke the silence. "How are you faring?"

"I am faring well, thank you," she admitted. "You are an excellent dance partner."

If he wasn't mistaken, Martha actually blushed. He grinned impishly. "Careful, my lady, it almost sounds as if you are enjoying yourself."

Martha tilted her head and smiled so brightly that her eyes lit up. "I believe I am. My previous dance partner was a fourteen-year-old girl."

"Ah," he replied. "Well, I am glad to be of service."

Taking advantage of his nearness, Emmett took a moment to admire his beautiful dance partner. Her face was flawless, notwithstanding the little frown that furrowed her brow as she gazed over his shoulder. "What is it?" he asked.

She looked into his face, and her eyes reflected vulnerability. "Why are you helping me?"

"Do I need a reason?" he asked, surprised by her question.

Her frown deepened. "I have done nothing to deserve your friendship, but you continually support me, even praise me. Why?"

It was his turn to shift his gaze as he pondered her question. For a long moment, he didn't say anything. Finally, he responded, "To be honest, I feel that we are kindred souls. And for the first time, I don't feel alone."

"You have never been alone, Emmett," she asserted in a wistful tone. "You are surrounded by family and friends that love you."

"As are you."

She shook her head as she looked away. "No, I don't."

He didn't speak until she peered up at him. "Family isn't always blood, and I would say that your family is fiercely loyal to you." He grinned.

Her face softened, and her eyes reflected gratitude. "You are…"

"Do they realize the music stopped a while ago?" Benedict's voice interrupted from across the room.

"Hush, dearest," Eliza admonished.

Martha dropped her hands and stepped back, her cheeks flushed. Emmett immediately felt the loss of her contact and wanted to pull her back into his arms. Instead, he turned to face Benedict and was surprised to see Kate, Adrien, Eliza, and Josette standing there, watching them, and they all wore bright, obnoxious smiles.

Not knowing what to say and feeling a bit awkward, he turned his attention back to Martha. "May I escort you home?"

Her hands covered her pinkish cheeks. "I would appreciate that."

Ignoring the group's knowing grins, Emmett offered Martha his arm and was happy when she accepted it. As they walked towards his barouche, he realized the dance had unearthed his feelings for Martha. But he also knew in his heart that he could never act on them. She trusted him, and he would never betray that trust by pursuing his feelings. He couldn't. He wouldn't. Should he?

❧ 13 ❧

THE BAROUCHE HAD BARELY COME TO A STOP IN FRONT OF HER townhouse when Lord Waterford came rushing down the steps and opened the small door, helping Martha out. Once her feet were on solid ground, he pulled her into a tight embrace. Unfamiliar with such affection from her father, she did not return the embrace.

Seeming not to notice her reticence, he leaned back, his hands rising to cup her cheeks. "Child, I have been so worried." Frowning, he glanced towards Emmett, who was assisting Josette out of the barouche. "Come, we will discuss this inside."

Reaching for her arm, her father escorted her up the steps and into the house. Once inside, he steered her towards the drawing room, where he dropped her arm and walked straight to the drink tray.

Martha sat on an upholstered settee, waiting for her father to explain his unusual behavior. Emmett had followed them in and sat in an armchair near her, but Josette failed to join them.

After her father had thrown back a drink, he slammed the glass down on the drink tray. Turning to face her, her father's face held a mixture of emotions. Dare she assume concern was one of them? "Where have you been?" he demanded.

"Dr. Maddix invited me for a carriage ride, and we stopped at Lady Lansdowne's townhouse," she explained after sparing Emmett a glance.

Her father's heated gaze turned towards Emmett. "Am I to assume that you are Dr. Maddix?"

"Yes, Lord Waterford," Emmett responded.

He humphed. "Do you normally fraternize with your patients, Doctor?"

In response, Emmett's jaw clenched tightly. "Sir, I promised your daughter that I would call on her today, and I am a man of my word."

"Just not a man of honor," Lord Waterford huffed.

Emmett jumped up, enraged. "How dare you make such an outrageous statement! We did nothing suspect, and Lady Martha was properly chaperoned by her companion, Miss Josette, at all times."

Her father grimaced, looking away. "Despite that, I came home from a meeting, only to discover that my daughter had fled my home in a frenzy, and with a man that had just come to call." His face grew pensive. "I thought," he hesitated, "you had run away again."

As all apprehension drained from her, Martha felt compassion towards him for the first time. "No, Father, I had just heard some distressing news, and I found I needed air."

Walking over to her, Lord Waterford sat down on the settee and reached for her hands. "What news caused you to be so upset, my dear?"

Realizing she shouldn't have shared that detail, she thought quickly, then lied. "I realized I had not packed one of my favorite gowns."

Her father smiled indulgently at her, seeming to believe her ridiculous explanation. "I understand. Women have such delicate constitutions, especially when it comes to such trivial matters." He tightened his grip on their entwined hands. "But, we have a lovely garden in the back, and I would prefer you to use that when you feel hysteria coming on."

Her mouth gaped a little at his blatant insults, and she found she had no words to respond.

Mistaking her silence for acceptance, her father's eyes grew hard as he shifted his gaze back towards Emmett. "Now, Dr. Maddix, I have not been formally introduced to you, but I am aware of your familial connections." He leaned forward in his seat but maintained his hold on her hands. "I have just become reacquainted with my daughter, and I do not wish her to choose a suitor at this time. The Season has just begun, and there are so many worthy men for her to meet."

Martha gasped. "Dr. Maddix is not my suitor. He is my friend."

Emmett's eyes sparked with fury as he glared at her father. "Sir, I became acquainted with Lady Martha when I..."

Lord Waterford waved his hand dismissively. "I know all of this. Lady Lansdowne sent me missives, updating me on my daughter's condition."

Emmett's back grew rigid as he observed, "Then you would know that your daughter and I struck up a friendship during that time."

"I am aware," he replied with a bob of his head. "However, I wish you to sever all ties now."

"You cannot be serious!" Martha exclaimed.

"Perfectly serious," her father stated sternly. "Dr. Maddix, you are no longer welcome in our home."

Martha jumped up, standing beside Emmett. "No, Father, I won't let you do this."

Barely sparing her a glance, he kept his gaze fixed on Emmett. "I am your father, and I know what is best for you."

Emmett calmly tugged down on his waistcoat as his eyes grew calculating. "I will honor your request. However, Lord Lansdowne has just requested Lady Martha to head the endowment for a charity hospital at the St. George's parish in Gravesend."

"What is this?" her father roared, redirecting his fury to her.

Seeing Emmett's eyes imploring her to play along, she nodded. "Yes, Father. Lord and Lady Lansdowne have asked me to head the charity hospital, and I have agreed."

Lord Waterford shook his head emphatically. "I forbid it."

Emmett lifted a brow in disbelief. "Just to clarify, you are forbidding your daughter to head a charity hospital, thus insulting Lord and Lady Lansdowne? Furthermore, need I remind you that Lady Lansdowne's father is the Duke of Remington?"

Frowning, her father replied, "She might catch an illness from those slothful, vile people."

"Were you not a vicar?" Emmett asked in disgust. "Do you have any compassion for people in lower stations than you?"

"Why would I?" he scoffed.

"Father…" Martha started.

"You were a man of God!" Emmett shouted over her.

Her father walked to the drink tray and took the lid off the decanter. "God is tired of hearing from the indolent men and women who choose to depend on others. They are undeserving of the benefits given by the parish and should be cut off."

"By 'benefits' do you mean food, clothing, and other basic necessities?" Emmett's tone was harsh.

Martha attempted to speak up again. "Do you want to…"

"If the poor worked harder, they would have more money to spend," her father declared, interrupting her.

Emmett stared at him, perplexed. "You have no concept of how the poor live, do you?"

Her father tossed back his drink. "I have no time for a radical social reformer. If we keep giving the poor handouts, then what are we teaching them?" He held his glass up. "I will tell you. We are encouraging them to be idle."

Martha looked down at Emmett's hands and saw his fists balled so tightly that his knuckles appeared almost white. Recognizing that she must do something before things became violent, she interjected, "Father, I disagree with your argument."

Lord Waterford's glance was condescending. "You are just a woman, dear, and cannot possibly understand the complexities of social issues."

Her hands balled into fists at her sides as she proclaimed, "I knew this was a mistake." She took a step closer to her father. "You almost had me fooled into believing that you had changed, but you are the same hard man that I grew up with."

Placing his glass down on the tray, her father opened his mouth, but she continued, "I don't need your money, nor do I need you in my life." She glanced at Emmett. "Dr. Maddix will escort me over to Lady Lansdowne's townhouse, where I will remain for the rest of the Season."

Her father took a step closer. "Wait! No... stop." His eyes grew solemn. "Please don't move out. I was just having a lively debate with Dr. Maddix."

"Were you?" she demanded.

Lord Waterford observed her carefully. "I apologize for my ranting, but I was beside myself when I thought you had run away again." He sighed. "My heart is still racing."

Martha eyed him suspiciously. What game was he playing? Why was he fighting so hard for her to remain with him when it was clear that he had not changed? Sneaking a peek at Emmett, she saw he was watching her closely.

"Father," she began, "I will remain under your roof, assuming Dr. Maddix is welcome in our home."

"But..."

She cut him off. "I'm not finished. I will also volunteer at the hospital."

His jaw grew hard as he stared at her. Finally, after a long moment, he conceded, "Fine, if that is what will make you happy."

"It will," she replied, lifting her chin defiantly.

Her father curled his lip in response as he regarded her. "If you will excuse me, I am going out for the rest of the day." He took a few steps, then spun back around. "You will be here when I get back, won't you?"

"Yes, I will," she agreed.

"Excellent," he mumbled, casting one final glare at Emmett before departing.

Emmett took a few steps closer to her. "Are you all right?"

Martha kept her eyes trained on the door, ensuring her father was gone. "I don't understand my father. His views and vices haven't changed, but he is passionate about me staying with him."

"Perhaps only his views about you have changed."

"Possibly," she muttered. Looking at Emmett with a bright smile, she added, "Apparently, I am volunteering at the charity hospital, which is ironic, since you just informed me that it was too dangerous for me to visit."

Emmett shrugged unapologetically. "I had to come up with a reason to see you tomorrow, and now I believe it is safer for you at the hospital than at your father's townhouse."

"I really would like to help those people," she admitted as her pleading eyes roamed his face. "What does it mean to 'head the endowment'?"

"You report to the gentleman who is running the charitable hospital."

"Who is…"

"Me." He grinned smugly. "Technically, it is an invented assignment, since Lord Beckett assigned me to run the hospital."

Martha found herself returning his smile. "Regardless, what will you expect me to do in the hospital now that I have committed to going?"

Emmett rubbed his chin thoughtfully. "You could take notes for me?"

She pressed her lips together. "I want to do more than just sit in a corner and take notes."

"Who said you had to sit in a corner?" he teased.

Playfully narrowing her eyes, she said, "As the head of the endowment, I will assign myself tasks once I arrive and see the needs of the patients." She crossed her arms and waited for Emmett to back down.

His lips twitched before he graced her with a warm, tender smile. "When you look at me like that, I find I would do anything to see you smile."

She gave Emmett a confused look. "How am I looking at you?"

"That is the problem," he explained, maintaining his gaze. Ever so slowly, he lowered his head till he whispered in her ear, "You have a hold over me, and you don't even realize it."

For a moment, she couldn't speak as his warm breath tingled on her skin, causing her to lose all rational thought. Before she could open her mouth to respond, he stepped back and bowed.

"Until tomorrow, Lady Martha." He walked swiftly out of the room, leaving her utterly baffled.

What did he mean that she had a hold on him? How was that possible? She wasn't flirting or encouraging him. Wait, did she want to encourage him? No, she thought. She needed a man in her life like she needed a thorn in her boot. Whatever she was doing, she must stop it before… well, she simply must stop.

AFTER A FEW HOURS OF SLEEP, EMMETT DESCENDED THE STAIRS of his uncle's townhouse and hopped into the waiting coach. However, before the footman closed the door, Mr. Martin stepped into the coach and sat on the opposite bench.

"Get out of the coach," the footman ordered as he reached in to grab Mr. Martin's sleeve.

"Leave him be," Emmett ordered, keeping his steely gaze firmly on Mr. Martin. "If I need assistance, I will bang on the wall."

"Yes, Dr. Maddix," the footman huffed as he closed the door.

Emmett lifted his brow as he waited for Mr. Martin to explain his behavior. As the coach lurched forward, they stared stubbornly at each other, each refusing to speak first.

Finally, after a long moment, Mr. Martin broke the silence. "I was told I need to apologize for my behavior."

"By whom?"

He frowned, shifting his gaze. "Sir Nathaniel Conant."

Stifling a laugh, Emmett confirmed, "Sir Conant, the chief magistrate of Bow Street?"

"I see that you have heard of him," Mr. Martin mumbled. "Apparently, he heard that I was tossed out of your coach, and he personally came to call."

"How was he informed so quickly?"

"You clearly underestimate the reach of the Bow Street Runners."

"Perhaps, but I am aware that the majority of the Bow Street Runners are a remarkable group of highly intelligent, motivated, and capable men." Emmett leaned forward in his seat. "Just last year, two Runners somehow matched a bullet retrieved from a murder victim with a bullet mold that they had subsequently discovered. Thus, identifying the murder suspect."

For a brief moment, Mr. Martin looked impressed before he wiped a hand over the side of his face. "Regardless, this case is extremely personal for me, and I may have taken out my frustrations on you."

"May have?" he repeated back sarcastically.

"All right, there is a highly probable chance." A slight smile came to Mr. Martin's lips before it disappeared.

"Why is a smuggling case in Gravesend so important to you?"

Mr. Martin shifted in his seat before answering, "There are many gangs in Gravesend that are smuggling contraband, but only one street gang plagues the town, terrorizing the weak and vulnerable. They are known as The Cursed Lot."

Emmett nodded. "Lord Beckett handed me a file, which contained a list of all the gangs in and around Gravesend. The Cursed Lot were at the top of the list." He took a moment to recall the specifics he'd read before adding, "In addition to smuggling, The Cursed Lot also operate a disreputable gaming hall out of The Cloven Hoof pub."

Mr. Martin leaned forward and adjusted his coat before sitting back. "My partner was undercover as a customs official. He boarded a ship looking for the smugglers. The following day, Jared left a note for me at The Frisky Hound Inn, informing me that he was onto something big."

"Which was?"

Mr. Martin shook his head. "I don't rightly know. His note ended with the statement that The Cursed Lot had most of the town on its payroll and not to trust anyone."

Emmett glanced out the window as he asked, "Do you have any idea what lead he was chasing down?"

"None," he replied despairingly. "The next morning, Jared was found dead, floating face-up in the Thames."

Silence descended over them before Mr. Martin asserted, "I

should have been there to help him, but I was watching the entrance of The Cloven Hoof." He slammed his leg with his clenched fist. "Contraband goes in, but it never comes out."

Curious, Emmett asked, "Why are Bow Street Runners concerned with smuggling in Gravesend in the first place? That seems too far away from Bow Street to involve you."

"There has been an increase in smuggling recently. The customs officials don't have enough men to handle it, so they hired us to identify the ships that are involved," he explained. "Our job is to report the merchant ships that are smuggling but not to engage them."

"Why not?"

Unclenching his fist, Mr. Martin took a deep breath. "It has been decided that the Navy will intercept those ships, impress the crew into service, and confiscate the smuggled contraband. Furthermore, those ships would revert to the Crown and expand their fleet."

Emmett nodded in approval. "That sounds like a reasonable plan."

"It should have been," Mr. Martin agreed, "but someone betrayed us."

"Who?"

He shook his head. "I know not."

"Who knew about the plan?"

"A select few Bow Street Runners, customs officials, revenue officers, officers in the Royal Navy, and the commanding officers at New Tavern Fort."

Emmett gave a low, disapproving whistle. "That is a lot of suspects." He took a moment to consider a different explanation. "Perhaps The Cursed Lot discovered Jared's involvement and killed him."

"No," Mr. Martin insisted. "Jared was a good Runner. He wouldn't have slipped up."

"People make mistakes."

The Runner leveled a hard gaze at him. "Not Jared."

Emmett turned his gaze back towards the passing countryside, knowing nothing he could say would change Mr. Martin's mind.

"Have you had the chance to become familiar with Gravesend?"

"Not yet," Emmett replied, returning his attention to the conversation. "I saw patients throughout the night, and I only just finished with my last patient at dawn."

"You must be exhausted," Mr. Martin voiced.

"Not particularly."

"You don't sleep?"

"Not really."

"Me neither."

For the first time, Emmett noticed the dark circles under the man's eyes. "Why don't you sleep?"

"I lost someone... someone I loved very deeply," he responded with a haunted look. "When I close my eyes, I see her, and the memories are too painful to bear." He lowered his gaze. "I sleep only when I have to."

"My condolences for your loss," the doctor expressed.

Mr. Martin's gaze shifted sadly to the side of the coach. "She didn't die; she just left me." After a moment, he asked, "And you? Did you lose someone dear as well?"

"I did," Emmett admitted. "Her name was Eleanora, and she was murdered by my commanding officer."

"This must be the 'cabin boy' that was impressed into service but turned out to be a girl," Mr. Martin observed. At Emmett's surprised look, he huffed in wry amusement. "Sir Conant informed me of my error."

Emmett shook his head, his somber eyes drifting off. "I was court-martialed under the vague charge of 'conduct unbecoming an officer and a gentleman'."

"That is rubbish," Mr. Martin declared. "Your actions were the definition of a true gentleman."

Giving him a grateful glance, he said, "It is in the past."

"Is it?"

"It is," Emmett stated, in a tone that effectively ended the inquest. "Tell me about Gravesend."

A SHORT WHILE LATER, EMMETT EXITED THE CARRIAGE IN FRONT of the Gravesend hospital with Mr. Martin.

Glancing around the churchyard, he recalled Mr. Martin's words about the history of the village. Besides being on the south bank of the Thames Estuary, it was an ancient town with a rich history, dating back hundreds of years.

Sister Mary stepped out of the main door to greet him. "Dr. Maddix, I didn't expect you for a few more hours."

"I found myself eager to see patients," he explained as they walked closer to the hospital.

Watching them approach, she shared, "The sisters have tended to the basic needs of our community, thanks to your supplies. However, I instructed the patients that wished to see you to do so after their supper."

"Thank you, Sister Mary," Emmett said.

She tilted her head in acknowledgement and disappeared back into the hospital.

Mr. Martin's voice drew back his attention. "This would be a good time for me to help you become familiar with Gravesend.

To your left, about a mile down the road is a pub called The Three Daws. It is a known hangout for smugglers and locals who want to avoid being impressed."

"How so?"

"Rumor has it that The Three Daws has seven staircases that lead to escape routes allowing them to avoid capture by the press gangs," Mr. Martin explained, "but I have not confirmed that to be true."

"Is Gravesend raided often?"

"I am surprised that the town has any men left," he scoffed. "The press gangs show up constantly, but they seem to target specific people."

"Like watermen?" he asked, attempting to understand what Mr. Martin was alluding to.

He nodded. "Yes, and sailors on merchant ships. However, recently they have begun impressing locals that have no seafaring experience."

"Perhaps these press gangs are impressing men into the British Army as well," Emmett suggested. "After all, I was under the impression that press gangs are notorious for rounding up unemployed and able-bodied men throughout England to act as infantry soldiers."

Mr. Martin shook his head. "That is not entirely accurate. The Royal Navy does prefer experienced seamen, but they will take common laborers to help man their ships if the need arises." He paused, then continued, "Something seems different about the press gangs in Gravesend, but I can't identify it."

With a little shake of his head, Mr. Martin started walking down the road with Emmett close behind. A moment later, they turned right. "About one mile ahead of us, and off the main road, is The Frisky Hound Inn. That is where I am renting a room. It boasts a bar, but it is mainly used for people to lay their heads at night."

"Would you prefer to walk or hop back in the coach?" Emmett asked.

"Normally I would walk, but I think the coach would be more conducive for my tour."

After they were situated in the coach, it jerked forward as Emmett teased, "I was informed you will act as my 'head nurse'."

Mr. Martin's face blanched. "I have no medical training."

"Not required," Emmett informed him. "Sister Mary has been a godsend. She has been formally trained as a midwife and diagnosed most of the patients correctly last night."

"I would prefer to monitor the comings and goings at The Cloven Hoof," Mr. Martin expressed. "I can't figure out how they are smuggling out the goods without us seeing them. I have searched for another entrance, but I haven't found one."

Glancing out at the passing countryside, Emmett saw several boarded-up cottages with three bay windows and thatched roofs sitting back from the road in picturesque green fields with brightly colored tulips, blowing in the wind. "These cottages could house several families each. Why are they abandoned?" he asked curiously.

"Those abandoned cottages represent the men that spoke out against the smugglers, particularly The Cursed Lot."

"Were they killed?"

"No," he responded, shaking his head. "The press gangs showed up one night and ambushed them." He pointed at one of the cottages with a burned thatched roof and one side of the building collapsed. "Sadly, some of the homes were burned to the ground during the scuffles."

"Where did all those displaced families go?" he asked, his heart swelling with compassion for the victims.

"It would be best if I show you," Mr. Martin responded vaguely.

Gazing at the horizon, Emmett saw a broad, stone rampart with a wide ditch in front of it. However, the structure had a most unusual construction. It was built in a zig-zag pattern. The manned watchtowers were pointed towards the bank of the Thames River, and men were patrolling along the parapet.

He pointed at the horizon. "What are those structures?"

Looking where he'd pointed, Mr. Martin replied, "That is the New Tavern Fort."

"Is there an Old Tavern Fort?" Emmett joked.

Mr. Martin grinned. "The artillery fort got its name from the previous occupant, the New Tavern Inn." As the coach continued down the dirt path, he pressed on with his tour. "Further on, past the fort, is the industrial side of Gravesend. Most notably, the sulphur mill and The Cloven Hoof pub."

"And The Cloven Hoof is the base for The Cursed Lot gang?"

"We believe so, but we have not corroborated that yet," Mr. Martin said. "I want to show you the workhouse."

Suddenly curious, Emmett asked, "How do you know so much about Gravesend?"

A detectable sadness swept over his face. "I grew up in Dover, but my father owned businesses in Gravesend when I was young."

"Do you still have family there?"

"I do."

"Are you close?"

"Not any longer."

"May I ask why?"

Mr. Martin tilted his head, frowning. "My father does not agree with my life choices."

"Ah, the prodigal son," Emmett teased.

He huffed under his breath. "Let's just say I followed my own path."

"Which is?"

"Dr. Maddix, I believe some anonymity should exist between us," Mr. Martin declared, forestalling any further questions.

"Understood." Emmett smirked. "Although I must admit, I felt like we were bonding as partners for a moment."

"We were most definitely not bonding," Mr. Martin stated firmly, although his lips twitched in amusement.

At that moment, a wagon full of soldiers charged down the road, and the coach moved to one side, waiting for them to pass. Looking beyond the fort, the slanting rays of bright sunlight broke through the darkening clouds, causing shimmery rays of light on the rippling water.

About two hundred yards past the fort, the scenery became dreary. Back-to-back, ramshackle, brick-terrace houses dominated both sides of the road, with tattered linens covering the window openings. Street urchins ran out into the road, skirting the coach as they played with each other.

Mr. Martin grinned. "Wait for it," he murmured with a devilish gleam in his eye.

"Wait for..." Emmett's words tapered as the wind shifted and a foul, offensive stench reached his nose. He reached into his waistcoat pocket and removed a handkerchief. "Cesspits," he muttered.

"At least it is not as bad as the rookeries in London."

"I will give you that."

Emmett closed the window but kept his eyes trained on the road. Further ahead sat large brick buildings, with nearly no room between them.

Following his gaze, Mr. Martin informed him, "Those are the factories." He then pointed to a blackened building with a dilapidated roof. "That one is the workhouse and home to the displaced families."

Emmett's eyes grew wide. "That building is not abandoned?" he asked in surprise.

"No, sadly."

"Beyond that building is the sulphur mill," Mr. Martin explained, pointing towards the shoreline. "The Cloven Hoof is about a mile down this road." Reaching into the pocket of his waistcoat, he pulled out a gold pocket watch and looked at the time. "It's time to take you back to the hospital."

"And you," Emmett reminded him.

Mr. Martin huffed his disapproval.

Leaning forward, Emmett could not help but admire the beautiful craftsmanship of Mr. Martin's pocket watch. "May I see your watch?" he asked when he started to return it to his waistcoat pocket.

Reluctantly, Mr. Martin handed it to him, and he carefully slid his fingers over the heavy, richly engraved gold. Emmett lifted his brow in question. "This is an exquisite pocket watch."

"It was my grandfather's," Mr. Martin explained. "When he died, it was passed down to me, despite my father's complaints."

Emmett eyed Mr. Martin with curiosity. Apparently, he had been raised as a gentleman. What led him to become a Runner?

As he opened his mouth to ask the question, Mr. Martin admonished, "I will not discuss any more personal details about myself, so kindly refrain from asking those questions."

Extending the pocket watch back to him, Emmett nodded. "Fair enough."

Placing the watch back in his waistcoat, he asked, "How long do I have to pretend to be a nurse tonight?"

"Why?"

"I was planning to stake out The Cloven Hoof."

Emmett bobbed his head in approval. "I will go with you."

"You?" Mr. Martin frowned. "You have a hospital to run."

"We could leave the hospital at midnight."

Mr. Martin shook his head. "That might be too early, but I can't say for sure, since the drop times are sporadic. The only recurring pattern is that the unloading is done at night."

The coach lurched to one side and turned sharply down a side road. Emmett placed his hand against the wall to steady himself. "All right, I will ask Sister Mary to take over my duties at two in the morning. That should give us enough time to arrive at The Cloven Hoof."

"There is a chance that nothing will be unloaded tonight."

"Regardless, it will be good to have two sets of eyes on the pub," Emmett stated.

Mr. Martin gave him a tight nod but did not speak again.

Emmett stifled a sigh. He didn't know what to think of this odd Bow Street Runner. Only time would tell.

DRYING HIS HANDS WITH A LARGE CLOTH, EMMETT'S EYES drifted over the main room in the hospital. Sister Mary had brought in half a dozen straw mattresses and laid them down against the walls. Only a few were occupied by patients at this late hour, and several nuns were attending to their needs.

Sister Mary approached him and smiled through tired eyes. "Mr. Martin has reminded me for the hundredth time that you need to depart within the hour."

"Yes, we have some business we must attend to." He hesitated, concerned. "You appear ragged, Sister. It might be best if I stay behind and let you rest."

"Nonsense," she admonished with the wave of her hand. "The sisters all rotate, and I am more than capable of taking the night shift, especially since it is for such a good cause." Lifting her brow, she asked knowingly, "Am I to assume that you are a Bow Street Runner, as well?"

"Why do you ask?"

She gave him a disapproving look. "It is painfully obvious that Mr. Martin has never been around sick people before, which made me wonder what his profession truly was." Stepping closer, she lowered her voice. "He is either an agent of the Crown or a Bow Street Runner."

Emmett laid the cloth down on the table, keeping his tone neutral. "And what led you to this conclusion?"

"Despite Mr. Martin's attempt to hide the pistol tucked into his trousers, the outline is still visible, as is the dagger hilt sticking out of his right boot."

"Mr. Martin is adamant he carries weapons for his protection," Emmett tried to explain.

Sister Mary huffed emphatically. "Dr. Maddix, I am not a simpleton. You can hide behind a veil of secrecy, but I would like to help you." She glanced over her shoulder at the other nuns in the room before she turned back, keeping her voice low. "For so long, Gravesend has been a den for smugglers, but The Cursed Lot are holding this town captive with their corruption and greed. It is widely known that they murder to achieve their evil purpose and do not hesitate to kill women and children."

Opening the main door, Mr. Martin walked into the room with a chamber pot in his hand, disgust on his face. Placing it down on the ground next to an occupied bed, he wiped his hands on his trousers.

Sister Mary watched him with disapproval. "He hasn't even learned the basics of hygiene." Raising her voice, she ordered from across the room, "Mr. Martin, you will wash your hands this minute."

He looked up in surprise but nodded as he walked over to the table. Without saying a word, he grabbed the soap and placed his hands into the basin of water.

"Cleanliness is next to godliness, Mr. Martin," Sister Mary informed him.

Emmett watched her with approval. "I am impressed with

how orderly this hospital is. The rooms have been scrubbed clean, the beds are free of bugs, the meager fare for the patients is quite tasty, and you have managed to staff the hospital with an impressive group of sisters."

She smiled at his praise. "It is far easier to accomplish one's goals when funds are forthcoming." She glanced up at the rafters before adding, "We have been praying for a hospital in Gravesend, and our prayers have finally been answered."

Laying the cloth on the table, Mr. Martin turned to address him, his voice full of eagerness. "Are you ready, Dr. Maddix?"

In a hushed voice, Sister Mary expressed, "You must be careful of The Cursed Lot. From what I have been told, they spend most of their time at The Cloven Hoof."

"That is our understanding as well," Emmett confirmed.

Glancing nervously around the room, she leaned closer to the men to ensure the conversation stayed private. "It is widely rumored that tunnels lay beneath Gravesend; tunnels that have been carved out of the chalk."

Mr. Martin turned to face him, his eyes lit up in excitement. "Of course! Those tunnels would be the perfect way for the smugglers to move their contraband undetected. I don't know why I didn't think of that."

"You must promise to be careful," Sister Mary admonished. "Our parish won't even whisper The Cursed Lot's name for fear of retribution."

"Do not fret. We promise to take precautions," Emmett assured her. As he started to brush by her, he stopped and shared, "Tomorrow, I will be bringing a young woman to help around the hospital."

"Your betrothed, perhaps?" Sister Mary questioned with a smile.

He shook his head in response. "She is just a very dear friend."

Mr. Martin gave him an annoyed look. "You are bringing a lady to the hospital? Are you mad?"

"Why do you assume that I am bringing a lady?"

"Who else do you associate with besides lords and ladies?" Mr. Martin asked, crossing his arms over his chest.

Ignoring Mr. Martin, he smiled at Sister Mary. "We will be back tomorrow."

A short drive later, the coach stopped about a mile from The Cloven Hoof. Stepping out, Emmett removed his coat, tossing it back into the coach, and followed Mr. Martin as he weaved between the buildings.

Arriving along the shoreline of the Thames estuary, Mr. Martin veered towards the low-lying land, which was filled with pools of different sizes and a broad drainage watercourse. The next few miles were slow and arduous.

Approaching the top of a slight knoll, Mr. Martin put up a hand to stop him and crouched down low. Whispering, he nodded in the direction of the water. "There is a ship ahead that is stuck in the mud."

"Should we help them?" Emmett asked in concern.

"No," Mr. Martin stated firmly. "Do you think a ship that could maneuver their way this far through treacherous channels and mud-banks would unintentionally get grounded in the mud and be forced to wait for a shifting tide?"

"I feel as if the answer is no," Emmett replied dryly.

A barked order drifted in the wind and over the long reeds in the lowland. They cautiously crept higher until they could look over the top of the knoll. The immobile merchant ship sat in the calm, dark waters of the estuary.

Then, as if by magic, small rowboats emerged from the tall reeds and approached the ship. Without hesitation, the crew started tossing barrels into the water. A few boats slid alongside the ship, and large chests were slowly lowered down, causing the rowboats to sit low in the water as they crept away. Over and over, they watched as the cargo was unloaded under the darkness of night, until the rowboats disappeared into the foggy reeds.

Tilting his head towards Mr. Martin, he asked, "Won't the customs officer become suspicious at the lack of cargo aboard that ship?"

He nodded. "He will take note, but the captain can maintain the off-loading was necessary to float the ship off the mud." Not sparing him a glance, his eyes remained fixed on the ship. "The customs officers and revenue men have little recourse if they can't locate the contraband."

"What is the difference between revenue men and customs officers?"

"Revenue men are responsible for collecting the taxes on goods imported, whereas customs officers are the ones who board the ship and take a log of the inventory, turning that log over to the revenue men. Both entities are supposed to work together to help stop the corruption involved with smuggling."

"Supposed to?"

Mr. Martin's sharp eyes scanned the horizon until he said in a hushed voice, "We have to go now."

Crouching low, Emmett followed closely as Mr. Martin expertly skirted the low-lying land. He kept quiet, even when he stepped into some mud and sank in to the top of his boot. As he yanked it out, Mr. Martin dropped low to the ground, hiding in the tall grass, urging him to do the same.

Lowering himself down next to his partner, Emmett watched as a line of rough-looking men, carrying parcels and barrels in their hands, marched silently towards town. The last few men helped carry chests, grumbling quietly about their lot.

Staying close, but far enough away to avoid detection, they followed the men until they walked into a side door of The Cloven Hoof. Loud, boisterous noise came from the pub's main entrance, and a rectangular light from an open door illuminated the dirt road.

Emmett noted the weatherboard siding and a tiled roof on the two-level structure. He wondered how easy it would be to climb to a second-floor window. Perhaps that would be the best way to enter undetected. When the last man entered the side door, a burly man exited the door, closed it firmly behind him, and positioned himself to stand guard.

Turning towards Mr. Martin, he asked, "Do you want me to take out the guard?"

"No, too risky," he replied. "I doubt we could get into the tunnels before we were discovered."

Emmett looked towards the main entrance and watched finely-dressed gentlemen and seamen walk side-by-side as they left the pub. "It appears that The Cloven Hoof caters to all levels of society."

Mr. Martin nodded. "The advantage of The Cloven Hoof is anonymity. Gentlemen play next to merchants, assuming they bring enough coins to the table, and the pub hosts more unique bets than London's gambling dens offer."

Emmett glanced over in confusion. "Like what?"

A deep frown creased Mr. Martin's face. "Last week, I went into the pub to play a game of cards and listen to the chatter in the room, hoping to get a lead. There were no leads, however, because everyone was still discussing how a gentleman had bet his own daughter a couple of months back during a high-stakes game of chance called queek. He lost."

"The scoundrel!" Emmett exclaimed. "That poor girl."

"I agree, which is why I informed the magistrate. But without knowing the identity of the man, there is little that can be done."

Watching as a gentleman hopped into a black coach, a sudden thought came to Emmett's mind. "I have an idea," he shared in an excited tone.

"Is it a good one?" Mr. Martin responded dryly.

He smirked. "It is quite clever."

"I highly doubt that, since the idea is coming from you, Dr.

Maddix," Mr. Martin said, his expression stoic. But a moment later, he could not hide the smile forming on his lips.

"We need to create a diversion; one that would let us slip past the guard near the side door," Emmett started to explain, "and I know just the agents to help us."

❧ 15 ❧

THE SUN WAS JUST RISING AS EMMETT'S COACH PULLED TO A stop in front of the Lansdowne's townhouse located in Portman Square. It was still hours before any respectable person would roam the street, but he wanted to speak to Lord Lansdowne before he went home to rest for a few hours.

This morning, he had promised to escort Lady Martha to Gravesend so she could volunteer at the hospital. She seemed eager to help, and it warmed his heart. To be honest, he had wanted to share that part of his life with her, but he knew it was not fair of him to expect her to appreciate what a sacrifice it would be.

Being a doctor consumed all aspects of his life. It was his calling and, at times, was the only reason he kept moving forward. Every person he helped, every child he healed, seemed to gradually mend his broken soul. He did not believe he was worthy of atonement, but he would spend his last breath trying to achieve that end.

The carriage door opened, and he took a step outside. Quickly striding up the steps, he knocked loudly and waited, knowing it might take some time for the butler to make an appearance because of the early hour.

To his surprise, the door flew open almost immediately, and Lord Lansdowne, with his daughter in his arms, greeted him with a smile. "Good morning, Emmett." At his surprised expression, Benedict admitted, "I saw your coach pull up."

"Ah," he replied as he entered, closing the door behind him. "I am sorry for calling so early, but I was hoping to steal a moment of your time."

Benedict tossed the baby in the air, laughing as she giggled. "You will find it is not so early when you have children." He drew his daughter close and kissed her on the cheek. "I have discovered the mornings are my favorite time to spend with Caroline."

"Is Lady Lansdowne still asleep?" he asked, glancing up at the stairs.

Benedict made an amused huff. "Eliza has been up for hours. She's outside training."

"Training?"

A smirk lit his friend's face. "You will see."

He followed Benedict across the expansive marble floors, bypassing busy servants going about their duties, until he stepped outside into a paradise. The gardens were pristine, with bright flowers filling the air with delightful scents.

Eliza's voice floated on the wind. "You need to be faster. If you continue to be so cautious, you will be discovered."

Turning towards the voice, he saw Eliza with her head out the second level window, instructing Miss Josette at the base of the brick townhouse. Josette was dressed in men's clothing, and her hair was pulled back and fastened with a ribbon.

"Try again," Eliza urged, "but this time, be faster."

Emmett watched in amazement as Miss Josette acknowledged Eliza's words with a nod, then proceeded to scurry up three levels and push open a window.

After she pulled herself into the room, she poked her head out the window and shouted down to Eliza, "How was that?"

"Better," Eliza praised. "I will meet you on the veranda for breakfast." Her gaze shifted down, landing on him. "Emmett, what a pleasant surprise. Stay right there."

Expecting her to disappear from his view, he was shocked when Eliza, also dressed in men's clothing, exited the window and scaled down the brick wall. His shock turned to admiration at the way she expertly descended with grace and poise. How was that possible?

Once Eliza jumped down the last few feet, she rushed over to him. "Please join us for breakfast." Stepping next to Benedict, she took Caroline into her arms, then led the way to the veranda where a sumptuous breakfast waited. Glancing back, she added, "Unless this is not a personal call."

Knowing he could trust Eliza, he said, "I need to consult with your husband."

A deep laugh came from behind him, followed by the words, "I hope you are not asking him for fashion advice."

Recognizing the voice, he turned and saw Adrien and Kate approaching.

"Why are *you* here so early?" Benedict asked Adrien.

Kate's eyes widened at the buffet table filled with food and waddled over to grab a plate. "I smelled bacon." Her simple explanation was all that she gave before she filled her plate with food.

Adrien watched his wife with pride as he escorted her to a table. "Our window was open, and Kate smelled food."

"Do you not employ your own cook?" Benedict huffed.

Adrien shrugged. "We do. I daresay he is better than yours," he challenged. "However, my wife was ready to break her fast now."

Shaking his head, Benedict leaned down and kissed his sister-in-law on the cheek. "Kate is always welcome in our home, but I can only handle you in limited doses," Benedict stated.

Reaching for a piece of fruit off Kate's plate, Adrien plopped it into his mouth, not even remotely deterred by Benedict's disparaging words. "As Caroline's godfather…"

"You are one of many," Benedict reminded him.

"As I was saying," Adrien drawled, reaching for a piece of bacon, "I feel it is my duty to spoil my niece as much as possible." Wiping off his hands, he reached into his coat and pulled out a doll, extending it towards Caroline.

Caroline grabbed it and pulled it close as Eliza sat her down on the ground. "Thank you, Adrien." Taking a close look at the doll, she asked, "Is that doll's head made out of wax?"

"It is," Adrien responded proudly. "As soon as Caroline was born, I sent a missive to the Dressel business in Sonneberg, Germany and ordered multiple dolls."

Eliza glanced curiously at him. "Multiple?"

Adrien gazed fondly at Caroline as she played with the doll. "Every girl deserves a doll, and I hope to have many girls."

Benedict's smile grew tender. "I feel the same way."

Emmett cleared his throat to break the spell that had descended over the group. "I wanted to bring you up to speed on my assignment in Gravesend."

Benedict's sharp eyes landed on him. "I am listening."

As he explained the events of the past two days, he ended with, "I was hoping to create a diversion using *Sunshine* and *Hawk*."

Adrien roared with laughter, and Benedict glared at him. "What did you just call me?"

Emmett shrugged unrepentantly. "Adrien offered to name his first-born son after me if I referred to you as *Sunshine*."

Benedict shook his head, his lips pursed together. "Did he now?" he grumbled under his breath, staring at Adrien, who was still laughing. "I really should have challenged you to a duel months ago."

Eliza laughed as she sat down next to Kate. "Behave, husband. You know you love Adrien."

Returning to the task at hand, Emmett said, "I was hoping for you both to be high-end gamblers and create a ruse to draw attention to yourself. If you can command the room's attention, we hope to sneak into the side door and look for underground tunnels."

Adrien leaned forward in his seat, all humor gone from his face. "Do you truly believe there is a tunnel that leads underground at The Cloven Hoof?"

"I do," Emmett responded. "It would explain how they are unloading the contraband."

After Eliza took a sip of tea, she asked, "Assuming there is a tunnel, do you have any idea where it would lead?"

"None," he admitted freely.

Adrien bobbed his head but then glanced down at Kate's protruding belly. "As much as I hate to say this, I feel I need to sit this assignment out, since my wife could give birth any day now."

Kate smiled gratefully at her husband. He reached over and clasped her hand, the love evident between them.

"What about Jonathon?" Eliza asked. "They just arrived yesterday, and it would give Hannah time away from him."

Emmett grew concerned as he inquired, "Why would Hannah want to spend time away from Jonathon?"

Kate laughed. "Jonathon is the most attentive husband." The way her words were carefully chosen made him feel there was more to the story.

"Is that an issue?" he pressed.

Eliza grinned. "My brother has been a bit overbearing in his care of Hannah since she announced her pregnancy."

"Wasn't that more than six months ago?" he asked.

"It was," Eliza confirmed, reaching for her fork. "Jonathon is quite attentive."

Not understanding the problem, he turned back to address Benedict. "According to Mr. Martin, the next shipment should be in tomorrow evening. Would you and Lord Jonathon be available?"

"We will," Benedict assured him.

Glancing back at the townhouse, Emmett frowned. "Why hasn't Miss Josette come down to break her fast?"

As she brought the teacup up to her lips, Eliza replied innocently, "Most likely, she is still trying to pick the lock of the room she entered."

Benedict chuckled under his breath. "I hope Josette knows what she is getting into, training with you."

A victorious voice came from behind. "I do, Lord Lansdowne. I have learned to always expect the unexpected from your wife, and she has yet to disappoint me." Josette smiled as she stepped onto the veranda.

Emmett's stomach growled, and he reached for a plate. "After a nap, I plan to escort Lady Martha," he paused, switching his gaze towards Josette, "and Miss Josette, to Gravesend to work at the charity hospital."

Eliza's hand stilled as she prepared to take a bite of food, and she lowered her fork. "Is that wise?"

"I don't see why not," he stated as he sat down next to Benedict, preparing to eat. "I hadn't planned on it, but Lord Waterford ordered me to end my friendship with Martha, which was odd, and it was the first plan that I could come up with."

Picking up Caroline and placing her on his lap, Benedict offered her some eggs before saying, "That was what Josette told us earlier. Apparently, he also has unpaid notes from The Cloven Hoof and a brothel in Gravesend."

Smiling, Emmett asked Josette, "How exactly did you discover those tidbits?"

"He may have left those bills laying on his desk," she replied, placing her hand to her chest, feigning surprise. "If the door to his study hadn't been locked, I wouldn't have felt the need to search it."

Giving her an exasperated look, he turned back to focus on Benedict. "Have you met Lord Waterford?"

"No, I have not," he confirmed.

"Good," Emmett nodded. "Let's just hope Lord Waterford doesn't decide to gamble in Gravesend when you create your diversion." Wiping his mouth, he pushed his plate back and stood. "I have been up all night, and I find my eyes need a short rest."

Eliza's eyes were filled with compassion as she watched him. "You need to sleep more, Emmett."

"No need," he replied, dismissing her concerns. "I am well enough."

Kate spoke up. "Are you?" Her eyes also reflected worry.

Pushing in his chair, he bowed. "No need to fret over me." Before he turned to leave, he lifted his brow at Josette. "I will see you in a few hours. Make sure you come prepared, because the road to Gravesend can be treacherous."

Without waiting for her reply, he moved towards the main door. He sighed as he remembered the pity reflected in his friends' eyes as they gazed at him. How could they understand what he had done?

They couldn't. Which is why they deserved their perfect lives, with their perfect love for each other. He would never have that. He wasn't worthy of another's love. Stepping into the carriage, he leaned his head back, and that was the last thing he remembered.

OPENING HER BEDCHAMBER DOOR, MARTHA STEPPED INTO THE hall wearing a simple, pale blue gown. She moved towards Josette's room, knocked, and announced, "Josette, it's me."

"Come in," came the faint reply.

Martha opened the door, and her steps faltered. Josette's room was in shambles. Gowns were sprawled out along the floor, white stays were draped over her settee, and boots were haphazardly lying around the room.

Arching an eyebrow, Martha looked at Josette sitting on the dressing table chair, appearing unconcerned by the state of her room. Instead, she was inspecting a row of knives, one by one. A small, satisfied smile came to her lips as she pressed a finger to the tip of one dagger. "This one will do nicely," she remarked.

Scooping up the rest of the daggers, Josette opened a drawer and carefully deposited them, hiding them away from view. Turning in her chair, she smiled, unassuming. "Are you ready?"

Even though she wanted to address the mess, Martha was more curious about the daggers. "Why do you have so many daggers?"

Josette gave her a surprised look. "I only have six."

Rolling her eyes at her companion's response, Martha decided to change topics. "May I ask what happened to your room?"

"I had to change after going riding."

"You went riding this morning?" she asked in surprise.

"I did," Josette replied nonchalantly. "How else was I going to get to Lady Lansdowne's townhouse and back before you broke your fast?"

She put a hand up to the side of her head. "Why did you have to see Eliza so early? We could have visited her after our errand to Gravesend."

Josette took out the pins in her hair as she explained, "Lady

Lansdowne requested that I report every morning about what has transpired with you. Plus, it gives me an opportunity to work on a few things."

Martha lifted a brow, knowing the 'few things' would be very atypical for a lady. "Such as?"

After pulling her hair into a chignon, Josette replaced the pins. "Today, I climbed up the back of the Lansdowne's townhouse."

"In a dress?" Martha asked in disbelief.

She shook her head. "No, Lady Lansdowne has no objection to me wearing men's clothing."

Noticing the pile of men's clothing for the first time in the corner of the room, Martha just smiled, remembering her own training. "That still does not explain why your clothing is all over the floor."

"Oh, I started searching for something." Josette shrugged. "I will pick up the clothes later."

"What were you searching for?"

"This," Josette revealed as she held up a dagger with an ivory hilt.

Walking over, Martha leaned down and picked up the stays, placing them on the bed. Noticing a line of dust on the table near the bed, she asked, "Why hasn't Anna been in to clean up after you?"

"I told her not to."

"Why?" Martha asked baffled.

"Because I am fairly certain that I cannot trust your father's household staff," Josette responded as she rose from the chair.

Martha was perplexed. "So, you plan to live in filth rather than let a young maid into your room?"

"I would hardly call this room filthy. I may have made a mess while searching for my dagger," Josette started, then paused as she picked up a white gown off the floor. "I know this dress alone costs more than most people make in a year. Perhaps I should take better care of it."

At the sight of Josette holding a gown in one hand and a dagger in the other, Martha couldn't seem to control the laughter that escaped her lips. "You are an untidy guest," she declared after her burst of emotions. "I did not expect that."

"I am no such thing," Josette denied. "I have been busy."

"Busy?" Martha asked slyly. "Do you find being a companion is too time-consuming for your schedule?"

Josette's face softened, and a smile appeared on her lips. "I would have you know that I discovered your father has a safe in his office, and I have been trying to open it."

"I would give the safe no heed. Most likely, it just holds the family jewels," she commented.

"Perhaps," Josette stated, pausing, "but I don't trust your father."

"Neither do I," was Martha's quick reply. "What do *you* think you will find in his safe?"

Josette scrunched her nose. "I don't know."

A knock on the door interrupted their conversation. Martha opened it to find the young maid, Anna, who curtsied as she informed her, "My lady, you asked me to notify you the moment Dr. Maddix's carriage arrived." The maid's eyes drifted over her shoulder, and she knew the moment they landed on Josette, because her eyes grew wide and fearful.

"Thank you, Anna," Martha acknowledged, blocking her maid's view. Before she walked out of Josette's bedchamber, she said over her shoulder, "You might want to put that dagger away."

Josette caught up to her as they glided down the stairs.

Turning her head, Martha asked her companion, "Why are you bringing a dagger?"

Josette glanced at her. "Why wouldn't I?"

Lifting her arm, Martha displayed her reticule. "Why not just put an overcoat pistol in your reticule?"

Her companion's expression turned mischievous. "I also have an overcoat pistol, but it is on my person. I prefer to have it close at hand."

As they exited the townhouse, Emmett was just stepping out of the coach, and his eyes lit up as he saw her at the top of the stairs. "Good morning, Lady Martha." He acknowledged Josette. "Good morning, Miss Josette."

Rushing up the stairs, Emmett presented an arm to each woman. "Allow me," he offered, escorting the ladies down the few steps.

Standing in front of the coach, Martha removed her hand from his arm as Josette moved to stand by her. "My father is at home, so I thought it would be best if I met you outside," she explained.

"You are as wise as you are beautiful," Emmett said softly.

Martha felt quite desirable as she smiled up at him. He was such a handsome man, and his eyes quite captivated her. They were filled with genuine engagement and warmth. When she was around him, she felt protected and cherished. What would it feel like to have his arms wrapped around me, she wondered. My goodness, she was acting just like a debutante.

"Don't you agree, Lady Martha?" Emmett asked with a boyish grin on his face.

Realizing she had been caught staring, she lowered her gaze and blushed. "I'm afraid I was wool-gathering."

Emmett stepped closer to her but still maintained proper distance. In a hushed tone, he commented, "You seem to be in good spirits this morning."

"I am." She put her hand up next to her mouth and informed him, "I just discovered that my companion keeps her bedchamber in shambles."

"I do not," Josette denied. "I just didn't have time to clean up after myself."

"Does your father not employ maids?" Emmett asked, glancing between them, humor in his eyes.

Martha grinned. "Josette doesn't trust maids."

"All maids, or is there one in particular you mistrust?" Emmett teased.

Josette rolled her eyes and stepped into the awaiting carriage, politely declining Emmett's outstretched hand as he reached to assist her. Once her companion was situated, Martha tilted her head towards Emmett and caught him watching her.

He quickly shifted his gaze and cleared his throat. "I should warn you that the drive to Gravesend will take between two and a half to three hours." He extended his hand to assist her into the carriage. "Are you ready, my lady?"

"I am," she replied, placing her hand into his without hesitation.

Before Martha stepped into the carriage, Josette shouted, "Wait!" She hopped out and waved her hand towards the alley.

Martha turned her head to see who Josette was greeting, but she saw no one. "Who are you waving at?" she questioned as Josette brushed past her on the pavement.

Stepping into the alleyway, Josette was lost from view. "Should we go after her?" Martha asked after a few moments.

"You stay here," Emmett directed as he started towards the alley.

Before he took two steps, Josette emerged with a man following her. He was dressed as a gentleman, although his brown hair was brushed forward, and a line of stubble was present on his strong jaw. A pistol was tucked into his trousers, but he did not appear overly-threatening.

Josette didn't say a word to the man as he trailed behind her, but she stopped in front of Martha. "I wanted your guard to catch a ride, since we were traveling all the way to Gravesend."

Tilting her head, she asked the man, "Do you even own a horse?"

"My guard?" Martha turned her surprised gaze towards Josette. "I thought *you* were assigned to protect me."

The man in question stepped forward. "I propose we have this conversation in the post-chaise."

Standing aside, the unknown man offered his hand to Josette, but she brushed it aside. "I do not require assistance."

Taking a step closer to Emmett, Martha was pleased when he offered his hand. She smiled as she accepted it and stepped into the carriage. Sitting next to her companion, she gave her a curious glance.

"Now will you explain what is going on?"

Josette gave the man a hard stare as the coach jerked forward. "This man has been following you since we first arrived, but I concluded he must be an agent."

Martha's eyes shot towards the man. "You have been following me? For what purpose?"

The man nodded. "I was assigned by Lord Beckett to guard you from afar."

"It appears that you are not very proficient at your job," Josette huffed.

"I am very proficient at my job," the man defended with amusement in his eyes. "Have you considered that I allowed you to spot me?"

Josette's mouth gaped open. "No, sir, you did not."

"Maybe I did," he replied nonchalantly as he wiped the sleeve of his coat, "maybe I didn't."

In response, Josette's eyes narrowed. "If that were the case, you would have given me some indication that you knew I had spotted you."

He lifted his brow. "You didn't think Lord Beckett would assign just one girl to guard Lady Martha?"

Josette's eyes grew wide, indignation on her face. "How dare you!" she exclaimed. "I am skilled with multiple weapons, and I am far more adept than you are in espionage."

"I highly doubt that," his tone was cocky as he replied.

"Just for the record, I am not a 'girl' anymore. I will be nineteen next month," Josette informed him.

"Thank you for clearing that up," the man stated quickly. "I was curious about your age." Turning his attention towards Martha, he introduced himself. "As I previously said, I was assigned by Lord Beckett to guard you from any impending threats. My name is Lord Morgan, but I prefer just to be called Morgan, especially when on assignment."

"Lord Morgan," Josette mocked under her breath.

"Just Morgan," he corrected her with a smile.

Martha tipped her head graciously. "Thank you, Morgan."

Morgan turned his gaze towards Emmett. "And it is an honor to meet you, Dr. Maddix."

Emmett chuckled. "I am not sure if 'honored' is the right word."

"No, sir," Morgan defended himself. "All the agents were informed of your valor when you helped defeat the French army on the shores of Rockcliffe. 'Honored' is exactly the right word."

"Many brave souls fought till their dying breath on the shore that day," Emmett asserted as he deflected the praise. "I thank you for guarding Lady Martha so diligently."

As Martha listened, she realized two things. First, that Emmett was more uncomfortable with praise than she'd first thought. Second, that she felt more comfortable in the presence of another man than she'd been in her entire life. She smiled a little, deciding that the presence of the modest doctor must be the reason.

Glancing at Josette, Morgan asked, "Were you aware that someone else began trailing Lady Martha last night?"

"No," Josette replied with a stunned face.

Morgan gave her a smug smile. "Interesting."

With an annoyed expression, Josette pressed, "Do you know why he was following Lady Martha?"

He lifted an eyebrow. "When should I have approached him? When he was lurking in the alleyway or when he watched you ride off in the wee hours of the morning?"

Rolling her eyes, Josette turned her head towards the window.

Morgan leaned forward in his seat. "May I ask where you went this morning?" he asked Josette.

"No, you may not, Lord Morgan," Josette replied dryly, barely sparing him a glance.

"Oh, just Morgan is fine," he reminded her with a smile.

Josette's lips tightened. "I do not wish to be so informal that I call you by your given name."

Morgan nodded as if mulling over her words. "I'm afraid we are going to have to agree to disagree on that, Josette."

Josette's mouth gaped open as she turned to glare at him. After a moment, she shook her head and turned back towards the opened window.

Martha held her gloved hand up to her mouth, hiding her smile. For whatever reason, Lord Morgan caused Josette to become quite contrary. Interesting.

❦ 16 ❧

On the ride to Gravesend, Emmett sat across from Martha. He noticed she sat close to the wall, distancing herself from Morgan. Her knees frequently brushed against his as the coach rocked back and forth. He relished the fact that he was touching her, but he pretended to give it no heed.

When they arrived, he exited the carriage, then turned back to assist the ladies as they stepped out. He stifled a smile as Martha placed her hand in his without a hint of hesitation. She was beginning to trust him, and that pleased him immensely.

Wanting to spend a little more time with her, Emmett led her down the path towards St. George's gardens between the church and the hospital. He heard, rather than saw, Josette and Morgan following behind them.

Tilting his head, he took the time to admire Martha's wide-set blue eyes with their long, black lashes, and her flawless skin, radiant with a morning glow. He cleared his throat as he tried to banish the inappropriate thoughts that flittered through his mind.

Breaking the silence, Martha glanced over her shoulder before saying in a hushed voice, "I thought we would have time during the ride to go over my duties, but Morgan was far more interested in discussing the battle in Rockcliffe with you."

"My apologies…"

"Nonsense," she replied, cutting him off with a grin. "I enjoyed learning more about the battle and your bravery."

He gave her a faint smile. "There were many brave…"

Martha stopped and turned to face him, all humor gone from her face. "You are always so quick to deflect praise for your role at Rockcliffe. Why?"

He clenched his jaw and glanced over her shoulder at Josette and Morgan, who had discretely kept their distance. "I only did what my conscience dictated."

Compassion crept into her eyes as she gazed at him. "When will you see yourself as I see you?"

"Which is?" he asked curiously.

"An honorable man." At his huff, she continued, "You may deny it, but I know it is true."

He tensed. "I'm afraid you are confused."

"I am not."

"You are," he said as he turned to resume his walk towards the hospital, but Martha did not follow his lead.

Her eyes reflected vulnerability as she stood her ground. "Fine. Forget Rockcliffe. Let's examine what you are doing now." She looked towards St. George's Church. "You spend every waking moment helping the poor, ensuring they have some medical care. And what do you get in return?"

Emmett sighed, choosing to remain silent, knowing Martha would answer her own question.

He didn't have to wait long. Martha took a step closer, her gaze locking with his.

"You are a champion for the weary and downtrodden, the poor and the meek, but you do not fight for yourself."

"Martha…" His voice trailed off because he couldn't find the words to express his emotions. Her words were passionate and seemed to speak directly to his soul.

"I will fight for you," she declared.

"Pardon?"

"After everything you have done for me, I owe it to you to help you."

"I don't need your help," he stated gently.

"No?" she inquired in a disbelieving tone. "Did you, by chance, stay up all night tending to the sick at the hospital?"

His eyes shifted towards the small building. "I did, but…"

"When was the last time you slept?"

"I slept in the carriage on the way back to town," he informed her. "And after I changed at my townhouse, I took a nap." He smiled, hoping that would appease her.

She arched an eyebrow. "How long was your nap?"

"A little over an hour."

"Only an hour?" she asked. "That is not sufficient."

He smirked. "It is for me."

"Interesting," she mumbled. "I want you to start sleeping at least four hours a night."

"Four hours?" he repeated as he processed what she was dictating.

"Yes, four hours." She nodded decisively. "And you must sleep in a bed during that time, not in the back of a carriage."

For the first time in years, Emmett felt his heart soften. He was touched by the compassion she bestowed on him. He wasn't angered by her words. Quite the opposite. He felt overcome by her sincerity.

"I am flattered that you are concerned about my well-being, but I assure you that it is not necessary."

Her chin tilted in determination. "And I assure *you* it is necessary."

"I am a grown man…" His words stilled when Martha abruptly turned and started walking towards the hospital. In two strides, he caught up to her and reached for her arm. "Wait, please."

He was not prepared for the pain etched on her face. Instead of dropping his hand as he intended, he wrapped his arms around her, gently, so he wouldn't scare her.

Tentatively, she brought her arms around him. "I am sorry, Emmett."

"You have nothing to apologize for. I am touched by your thoughtfulness." He rested his chin on the top of her head and savored that she was in his arms.

After a few moments, she lowered her arms, and he reluctantly released her. She took a step back, her eyes imploring. "No man can endure your grueling pace. You must take care of yourself, first and foremost."

A sad smile came to his lips. "You must understand that this is my penance."

"For what?" she asked. "You did nothing wrong."

He dropped his head in shame. "I should have done more to help Eleanora."

"You must stop blaming yourself for Eleanora's death. Your guilt is misplaced," she asserted in a soothing tone. "You are misinterpreting your sadness and empathy as a feeling of guilt."

A tear leaked out of one eye, and he brushed it aside. "I wanted to save her," he breathed, his voice hitching with emotion. "I tried, but I couldn't save her." More tears rolled down his face. "I failed her... I failed myself."

"No," Martha said firmly. "You did not fail her. You tried to save her, but your captain killed her, not you." Her hand came up and cupped his right cheek, urging him to look at her. "You have punished yourself long enough for a murder that is on someone else's hands."

"I should have done more," he insisted. "Had I known what Colonel Allister was capable of, I could have stepped in earlier."

Martha pursued her lips. "And I should have known my

fiancé was a blackguard." Her hand dropped from his cheek. "You have to start taking care of yourself, or you will have nothing to give your patients."

Deciding to forestall this uncomfortable conversation, he attempted a smile. "I will agree to your terms, but only if I get something in return."

"Which is?"

"That you take your own advice."

She offered him a perplexed look. "I already sleep more than four hours a night."

"No." He chuckled. "I am referring to how you are punishing yourself for something that was out of your control."

Martha visibly stiffened. "That is entirely different."

"Is it?"

"I have every right to be angry," she protested.

"You do."

Crossing her arms over her chest, Martha stared out over the gardens with a fixed stare. Finally, she brought her gaze back up to his. "You are right. Perhaps we both need to stop punishing ourselves for our past mistakes."

Sister Mary stuck her head out of the hospital building and gave him a questioning glance. Nodding his understanding, he offered his arm to Martha.

"Are you ready to learn the duties of a nurse?"

"I am," she answered, accepting his arm.

PLACING A HAND ON THE SMALL OF HER BACK, MARTHA TOOK A moment to stretch her weary body. For the better part of the day, she had helped Sister Mary and several other sisters from the convent with the patients' needs. A steady stream of men, women, and children walked through the doors of the hospital. Most suffered from simple afflictions; rashes, mild burns, infections, coughs, and colds.

Straw beds were placed along the walls to best utilize the small room, but only a few were in use. A young boy named Johnny occupied one of the beds. His face was pale, his eyes sunken, and his cough seemed to rattle his whole chest.

Leaning forward in the rickety wooden chair, Martha brushed a lock of brown hair off Johnny's sweaty brow. She watched the rise and fall of his chest, assuring herself that he was still alive. It had only been a few hours since the boy's mother had brought his nearly-lifeless body into the hospital, pleading for help.

Emmett had been tending to another patient in the back room, but he immediately appeared and ran over to collect Johnny, cradling him in his arms. After his examination, he had given him willow bark and had ordered a cold bath to lower his fever. Now that Johnny was finally asleep, she stood and covered him with a thin blanket.

Sister Mary gave her a warm look from the opposite side of the room before continuing with her current patient. The woman had complained of itchy skin, and Sister Mary had just washed the area with a solution made from camphor.

A young woman was next in line, and Josette led her over to a wooden chair. After a few moments, Josette nodded her head, rose, and went to the table where the powders and medications were. As she rifled through the jars and bottles, she sighed in exasperation.

Martha walked over and asked, "Is everything all right?"

Josette let out another sigh. "No," she whispered. "That lady is complaining about pain during her monthly courses, and I forget what we are supposed to give her."

Reaching down, Martha lifted a jar of the lucerne leaves, showed Josette the label, and reached for a cloth. As she deposited a handful of leaves into it, she instructed, "As a pain reliever, the leaves may be eaten as vegetables or steeped in boiling water to make a tea."

Josette looked amazed. "How do you remember that?"

Glancing over her shoulder at Sister Mary, she turned back towards Josette. "I suppose I took to it right away when Sister Mary explained all the basic medication and procedures we would be expected to know."

As Josette accepted the tied cloth, her eyes wandered towards Johnny's still body. "How is he?"

"About the same," she replied sadly. "He keeps drifting in and out of consciousness."

Josette nodded. "I will sit by him after I see to this patient."

Martha looked at the small line of people hovering in the doorway. "Unfortunately, we won't have time to sit by Johnny until that line is gone."

Putting on a brave face, Josette clutched the cloth to her chest. "I am exhausted," she admitted. "I have been on my feet all day."

For the first time, Martha realized that the sun was low in the sky. "I must admit that time has flown by for me. It seems like only a moment ago that we stopped to eat our sandwiches."

Sister Mary approached them with a smile on her face. "That is because you are a natural nurse, Lady Martha."

"Please call me Martha," she responded in a hushed voice.

Sister Mary smiled in approval. "How many patients need to see Dr. Maddix?"

"Three," she replied. "And the other line is out the door."

"All right." Sister Mary nodded. "Why don't you depart for London before it gets too late?"

Martha shook her head. "We still have a few hours before the sun sets, and I would like to help you thin out the patients."

"Let's begin then, shall we?" Sister Mary said as she approached another patient.

As Martha started to follow Sister Mary, a hand reached out and grabbed her arm. "I need water, miss." The male voice was raspy.

Her initial reaction was to yank back her arm and shout in protest. However, when she looked at the old man sitting on a wooden stool, her heart ached in compassion.

The man had thin, white hair, his clothes hung on his body, and the lines on his face were deep. His clothes were tattered, and his eyes made her pause. They were full of sadness and pain, much like her own. His touch didn't seem to burn anymore, but it gave her a sense of connection to him.

"Of course, sir, right away." She walked over to the bucket of water and placed it on a nearby table. Reaching in, she picked up the ladle and offered him a drink.

After he took a long sip, he said, "Thank you, kindly, lass."

"You are Scottish?" she asked curiously.

"Aye," he confirmed as he handed her back the ladle, turning his gaze towards the closed door. "Will Dr. Maddix be available soon?"

She smiled at him. "You are next in line."

"Are you always this cheerful?" he inquired with a weathered smile on his face.

His question took her aback. She was happy in the hospital. Never before had she found such joy in her tasks. Realizing she hadn't answered his question, she replied, "I enjoy helping people that are sick."

He dipped his head in acknowledgement. "You are a good lass. Thank you."

His kind words touched her again. In this setting, she was not afraid or fearful of men but had a desire to help them, to ease their pains. Choosing not to dwell on that for too long, she clasped her hands together.

"May I get you another drink before I go help another patient?"

"No," he said with a smile. "I will be here... waiting."

She chuckled. "Yes, you will," she paused, "but if you need anything..." She let her voice trail off intentionally.

He nodded. "Thank you."

Martha's next patient was a young woman who suffered from fainting spells, and she was given a large jar of vinegar. The next patient was a young boy that needed a compress soaked in tea, to help soothe a burn he had received while working at the workhouse.

Again and again, she helped patients with these simple procedures, and she loved it. Morgan walked into the room, holding a stack of wood. He placed it near the fireplace. As he rose, he said, "We will need to leave in the next few minutes if we want to arrive home before dark."

"I agree, especially since the last patient is in with Dr. Maddix, and the hospital will be closed for a few hours," Martha informed him. "Let me help Sister Mary by putting the powders and medication in the chest before we leave. The other sisters left for their evening prayers."

Morgan nodded. "Dr. Maddix informed me that he will be staying overnight in Gravesend."

"I assumed as much, since Johnny will be staying," she said as she turned her back to him and started organizing the medication.

"Yes, he needs to look into something..."

He was interrupted by a male voice she thought she would never hear again; a voice she had only heard in her nightmares.

"Martha."

Simeon.

Keeping her back rigid, Martha slowly reached into her reticule and pulled out her pistol. With the firm intention of shooting him, she turned around and aimed for Simeon's cold, blackened heart.

❧ 17 ❧

As Emmett placed his hand on the door handle, he gave Mrs. Willow a friendly smile. "Drink that calendula tea, and it will clear up your bladder infection," he reminded her.

Opening the door, he waited until Mrs. Willow walked out of the room, then followed behind. Unexpectedly, Mrs. Willow stopped short, and he bumped into the back of her.

"Excuse me…" His voice trailed off when he saw Martha pointing a pistol at Mr. Martin.

Placing a hand on Mrs. Willow's arm, he pulled her back into the examination room, giving her a warning glance and pointing toward the open window as an alternate exit. Entering the main room, he assessed the situation. Mr. Martin's gaze was firmly fixed on Martha. Martha, stone-faced, hadn't moved.

After he closed the exam room door, Emmett took a tentative step towards Martha. Keeping his voice steady, he asked, "Martha, why are you pointing a pistol at Mr. Martin?"

Her eyes didn't leave Mr. Martin as she explained, "He was my fiancé."

"I am still your fiancé," Simeon declared.

"No," she stated, her voice menacingly quiet. "I would die before I ever marry you."

Recalling what Martha had told him, Emmett asked, "Is this the same Simeon that…"

"The same," she replied, her voice devoid of all emotion, "and I am going to kill him."

"Not if I kill him first," Emmett growled, advancing towards Simeon. Morgan stopped him by pressing a hand against his chest.

"Go back to Martha," Morgan urged, his voice holding a warning. "She needs you."

An eerie silence descended over the room. Tilting his head to look at Martha, he saw her eyes were expressionless, the light gone. The woman he had come to know had been replaced with a woman who was hell-bent on revenge, regardless of the consequences.

Stepping back towards her, Emmett spoke her name calmly, "Martha." He took another step, but she didn't seem to care. She was focused only on Mr. Martin. "You don't want to kill Simeon," he insisted.

"Yes, I do," came her swift, cold reply.

Emmett stopped next to her, close enough to reach out, but he kept his hands by his sides. If needed, he could reach for the pistol, but he hoped it would not come to that.

"If you kill him, then you will be no better than he is."

"But I would be free of him," she asserted.

Knowing there was still good in Martha, he appealed to her sense of compassion. "It would ruin you. Killing another person would gnaw at your heart until nothing was left."

"Simeon doesn't deserve to live after what he did to me," she whimpered, her voice now filled with pain and torment.

Mr. Martin took a step closer, and Martha cocked the pistol. His eyes were wide in shock. "What I did?" he asked in anger. "You were the one who left me!"

Her mouth gaped. "I did leave you, but not by my choice."

Josette spoke up, "Is this the man who hurt you, Lady Martha?"

"Lady Martha now, is it?" Simeon repeated in disbelief, shaking his head. "No wonder you left me."

"I left you? You sold me!" Martha exclaimed.

"What?" Simeon yelled. "I did no…"

"I will kill him for you," Josette offered, a dagger suddenly appearing in her hand.

Emmett frowned. "Where did you get that dagger?"

"It doesn't matter," Josette replied, taking a step closer to Simeon.

Before she could take another step, Morgan wrapped his arm around her waist and forced her back against him. "Let's allow Lady Martha and Simeon to settle their own differences, shall we?"

Martha shifted her heated glare towards Morgan. "Differences? Simeon destroyed my life. He forced me into a life of slavery and…" Her voice trailed off as she took a deep breath, visibly trying to control her emotions. "He did it for profit."

Turning her fiery glare towards Simeon again, her loathing palpable, she demanded, "How much did you make? £20? £50?"

Mr. Martin's expression grew bleak for a moment. "What happened to you, Magpie?"

"No!" she shrieked. "You do not get to call me that."

Simeon's eyes filled with tears. "I don't know what you had to endure these past years, but I had nothing to do with it."

"You are a liar!" she yelled as the pistol shook in her hand. "I hate you!" Her words were filled with heartache.

"I had nothing to do…"

Martha took a step closer, her pistol leveled at Simeon's chest. "For the first week, I was in denial that you could have betrayed me, but that quickly turned into loathing." Her eyes narrowed. "I want to kill you. I want you to feel the same pain and betrayal that you bestowed on me. I want…" A loud sob interrupted her words.

"Oh, Magpie," Mr. Martin breathed as he put his hands out. When she didn't respond, he dropped them helplessly by his side. "After I left you in the room at the inn, I took my savings and bought a special license, just as we'd discussed." He sighed and ran a hand through his hair. "But when I came back, the innkeeper told me that you'd changed your mind, and he'd hired a hackney to take you home."

Shoving the pistol forward, Martha declared, "You are lying. I was told that you betrayed me."

"Who told you that?" Simeon asked in disbelief.

"Mr. Wade," Martha spat.

Everyone's eyes turned towards Martha as they realized what she had just admitted. Simeon slowly sank into a chair, his eyes never leaving her face. "You were one of the girls taken by Wade."

Martha scoffed. "You would know, you sold me."

"No," Simeon declared passionately. "I thought you changed your mind about eloping."

"Liar," Martha whimpered with tears in her eyes. "I would have never changed my mind; I loved you."

As his shoulders deflated, Simeon replied, "And I love you with all my heart." A tear rolled down his cheek, but he didn't bother to wipe it away. "After I discovered you were gone, I rushed back to your estate, but your father told me that you'd decided to live with your uncle."

"Even if he said that, why would you believe him?" Martha asked skeptically.

Simeon leaned forward in his seat. "I went to your uncle's estate to demand an answer from you, but I wasn't even allowed in the gates." His eyes were filled with anguish. "I spent all my money on the special license, so I went back to work for my father."

"Why would you do that?" Martha contended. "You hated being a merchant."

Simeon just blinked back his disbelief. "I would have done anything to get you back." He glanced at Morgan and Josette. "I worked constantly, establishing my own fortune. And I waited for an opportunity to present myself as a worthy suitor. However, you were never presented in court, nor did you have a Season, so I started asking questions."

The pistol faltered in Martha's hand, but she didn't lower it. "To who?"

"Mainly to your uncle," he replied. "But he was an earl, and I was just a young merchant asking too many questions about his niece." He paused before adding, "So I became a Bow Street Runner, which allowed me unparalleled access to both worlds."

"And what did you discover?" Emmett asked.

Simeon frowned. "At that time, I discovered that no one had seen you in over four years." The anguish in his eyes proved that he was every bit as tortured as she. "I have been searching for you ever since."

"I don't believe you," she proclaimed, although her voice was not as shaky as before. "How else would Mr. Wade have known that I was in that room?"

"I do not know," Simeon expressed, his voice hitching. "For the past few years, I have studied every woman's face, looked deep into their eyes, and wished they were you." His voice hitched again as he continued, "You may have stopped loving me, but every time I close my eyes, I see you, and my heart aches with the love that I feel for you."

Emmett took a step closer. "Martha." He waited till her eyes drifted towards him. "It is time to put your pistol down."

"I can't," she sobbed. "I have hated him for so long."

"I understand," he assured her. "You hated Simeon because he was the face of your trauma. But... I believe him." He turned his gaze towards Mr. Martin for a moment. "However, the question remains, do you?"

The indecision showed on Martha's face. "I don't know," she admitted weakly.

Taking a small step forward, Emmett put his hand gently on her sleeve. "No one will ever hurt you again, Martha. Morgan, Josette, and I will keep you safe at all costs."

With sad eyes, Martha nodded and handed him the pistol. After he deposited it into his coat, Martha surprised him by turning into his arms. Elated by the opportunity to comfort her, he brought his arms up to embrace her, being mindful to not pull her in too tightly.

Simeon started to stand, but Morgan was instantly by his side and placed a hand on his shoulder. "I don't think it is wise to approach Lady Martha at this time," Morgan admonished.

After a long moment, Martha leaned her head back and looked up at him, wiping the tears from her cheeks. "What do I do now?" she asked in a pained whisper.

He brought his hand up to wipe another tear from her cheek. "You can do anything you want, my dear," he responded, his words full of sincerity.

Martha's eyes nervously shifted towards Simeon. "I think I need to tell him what happened."

"Are you sure?" Emmett asked.

"Yes," she replied, shaking her head, "but only if you stay by me." Her eyes searched his, the vulnerability shining through. "I am not strong enough, and I find that I need to borrow your strength."

"You are wrong, Martha," he sighed, hoping his eyes conveyed his sincerity. "You are the strongest woman I know."

Offering him a grateful smile, she took a deep breath, then turned to face the group. "It is time for me to share what happened."

MARTHA FOUND HERSELF STARING INTO SIMEON'S BLUE EYES, unable to look away. His eyes held sadness and grief as emotions flittered across his face. This was her Simeon; the man she had given her heart to a long time ago. But he had abused it, turning it impenetrable.

The years had been kind to him. He appeared even more handsome than the last time she'd seen him. His brown hair was tousled, which highlighted his strong jaw. Even now, her traitorous heart lurched at the sight of him, but she pushed the emotion back down.

"Magp…" Simeon started, but stopped and corrected himself, "Lady Martha, what happened to you?" He tried to rise, but Morgan's large hand on his shoulder kept him seated.

When she didn't speak right away, Morgan asked, "Would you prefer that I stepped outside?" He glanced at Josette. "I could escort Miss Josette out as well."

Josette frowned at him. "Since I am Lady Martha's *protector*," she emphasized, "I need to stay and protect her."

Morgan gave her a half-smile. "I am confident that Dr. Maddix can protect Lady Martha from Mr. Martin."

"Perhaps," Josette replied as a mischievous smile came to her face, "but I will support Martha wholeheartedly if she decides to kill Mr. Martin."

Looking away from Simeon's intense gaze, Martha said, "You are all welcome to stay and hear my shame." She tilted her head towards Sister Mary. "You are welcome, as well."

Emmett's hand touched her elbow as he escorted her towards a chair, opposite Simeon and Morgan.

No one spoke as she lowered her gaze to the floor, attempting to gather her courage. So many thoughts filled her mind, some were full of venomous accusations, and others were heartfelt questions. Did Simeon betray her, or was she simply a victim of being in the wrong place at the wrong time?

"Martha," Emmett's voice was calming as he leaned over to speak to her, "you don't have to do this."

Raising her gaze towards his, Martha saw stern compassion in his eyes, holding her momentarily transfixed. Blinking back her trepidation, she replied, "Yes, I do."

Martha squared her shoulders, clasped her hands in her lap, and faced the man who, until just minutes ago, she had believed ruined her life. "After you left, I latched the door as you suggested," she paused for a long moment, "but three men barged into the room and quickly overpowered me. I was knocked unconscious. I woke up as I was tossed onto the main deck of a brig."

She shuddered at the memory of being thrown at Mr. Wade's boots and seeing the sneer on his face. His snide words, "Well, well, well... look at what I just bought," would forever haunt her dreams.

Glancing at Johnny on the mattress, she was relieved that he hadn't stirred. With another deep breath, she returned to her story.

"Mr. Wade enjoyed taunting me about how a loved one had betrayed me. He assured me that I would be well taken care of."

She tilted her head to look at Emmett before she continued, knowing he might hate her for what she was about to reveal.

"I was sent to a brothel in India and... um... was abused, even though I fought it. I was beaten as a punishment for my insolence," she revealed through gritted teeth.

Simeon broke free of Morgan's hold and started towards her. Pain filled his face, but Morgan pulled him back. He did not struggle, but as he returned to his seat, he declared, "I am so sorry. I had no idea."

Martha bit her lower lip before she added, "I was beaten so badly that I thought I would die, but I was not so lucky."

"Oh, Martha..." Simeon said sadly, his words tapered off, anguish in his voice.

She put up a hand. "I haven't even gotten to the worst part," she expressed. "Every time a man tried to abuse me, I fought back and refused to make it easy for them. I did not care if I lived or died, and I vowed never to stop fighting."

Wringing her hands in front of her, she swallowed slowly, hesitant to share the next part. "Eventually, the owner got tired of paying for medicine to keep me alive, so he allowed me to work as a maid in the brothel for years. I even managed to escape a few times, but I was always quickly captured. My light skin made it impossible to blend in."

Unable to stop fidgeting, Martha rose, moved to stand in front of the small crude window and stared out. Dusk had now descended over the town, casting shadows in the garden of St. George's. Turning back around, she placed her hands over her arms.

"I have scars from the beatings and torture that I was forced to endure for my rebellion, but I continued to refuse to allow those vile men to think I was willingly letting them touch me." Her voice grew hard. "No, I would not."

Simeon's eyes reflected compassion. "How did you escape?"

She looked at the floor. "When the owner decided to use me

again, I changed tactics. When those revolting men came to see me, I laid flat as a board, refusing to move, despite their best efforts, and they would become frustrated, leaving unsatisfied." She brought her eyes up to see Josette's eyes filled with tears. "Eventually, the owner got tired of my emotionless reactions to the customers, and he decided to sell me at the market."

A tear rolled down Josette's cheek. "How are you still alive?"

Martha nervously shifted her eyes towards Emmett expecting to see judgement or repulsion, but instead, she saw love and acceptance. It took her breath away. "Lady Lansdowne bought me," she said with finality. "She is the only reason why I am alive."

Sister Mary walked over and took her hands. "You poor thing. What you were forced to endure was horrific."

Tears welled in Martha's eyes. "It was awful," she admitted. "I prayed for death every day for five long years."

Pulling her into an embrace, Sister Mary spoke softly into her hair, "You are a strong, fierce woman that fought to survive. Do not discount that."

"Thank you," she responded as she leaned back.

Simeon's voice filled the room as he asked, "If you were held for five years, where have you been these past two years?"

Martha turned towards him as she answered, "I have been Lady Lansdowne's lady's maid."

"Lady's maid?" Josette repeated in surprise. "Lady Lansdowne told me that you were her companion."

"Of course she did," Martha replied with a half-smile. "It took me months to start trusting Eliza. Finally, I trusted her enough to reveal what happened to me." She walked over and sat down, all eyes still watching her. "She tried to convince me to become her companion then, but I assured her that I was perfectly content living upstairs, quietly and alone."

Morgan's eyes reflected sadness. "I have no words for their ill-treatment of you. I am sorry."

Martha nodded her appreciation. "Thank you for that, Morgan. I do not want your pity, though."

Simeon's words were weak at first, but his voice became stronger as he announced, "I failed you, Magpie. I promised that I would protect you, but you were snatched right from under my nose. We can depart tonight for Gretna Greens and be married."

"I beg your pardon?" Martha huffed in disbelief. "What point in my story caused you to believe that I still wanted to marry you?"

Standing up, Simeon brushed Morgan's hand from his shoulder and took a few steps towards Martha before he was stopped again by Morgan's firm hold on his arm. "I have never stopped loving you, and I will protect you," he proclaimed.

Without warning, Emmett stepped in front of her and declared, "If anyone is going to marry Martha, it will be me."

Simeon took a step closer to Emmett, challenging him. "I am still her fiancé."

"No, you are not," Emmett stated. "I can give Martha a far better life than you ever could."

"I am wealthy in my own right, and I can provide her with a lavish lifestyle if she desires," Simeon countered.

Fisting her hands at her sides, she exclaimed, "What is wrong with both of you? I don't want to marry either one of you." As Emmett stepped to the side, both men lowered their gazes. "I have no intention of ever marrying. I refuse to let any man have control over my life again."

Martha could hear Josette say in a hushed voice to Morgan, "Why did you not offer for her?"

"It was clear she was not looking for a husband, or I would have," Morgan responded with a teasing tone.

Martha stifled a laugh at Morgan's response. Returning her gaze to the two men in front of her, she acknowledged in a soft voice, "Thank you both for your kind offers, but my heart has been closed since the day I boarded that brig." Her voice trailed off as she struggled to suppress her emotions. "My scars are daily reminders that my past is real."

With a determined gaze, Simeon replied, "You must not give up on me, Magpie."

Martha gave him a sad look. "Even if I still wanted to marry you, which I don't, you don't deserve a woman who has been ruined."

"You are not ruined to me," Simeon asserted. "You are more beautiful than when I last saw you."

"You are kind," Martha sighed. "But I know what I am, and it is time for you to accept that."

Simeon put his hand out to touch her, and she instinctively stepped back. He stopped, his eyes full of pain.

"I do not accept that, Magpie."

"Please do not call me that," Martha pleaded. "It reminds me of a future that I no longer have."

Emmett stepped closer and placed a hand on the small of her back, providing her with much reassurance and comfort. "It is too late for you to travel back to London, and I don't believe The Frisky Hound Inn would be a good option."

"Definitely not," Simeon agreed.

Sister Mary spoke up, "You are welcome to stay with us tonight at the convent. We only can offer you and Miss Josette a lumpy straw bed to share, but Sister Gertrude makes a delicious porridge for breakfast."

"I would hate to impose…" Martha started.

Sister Mary cut her off. "Nonsense, you both would make wonderful guests."

Leaning closer, Emmett informed her, "I will send footmen to alert your father that you are staying. I am sure he would rather have you stay in a convent than risk riding at night."

She tilted her head towards him, grateful that he was standing by her, supporting her. "I suppose you are right."

He smiled. "Did you just admit that I was right about something?"

She playfully rolled her eyes. "On a rare occasion, I find that you do make a suitable argument."

"I see," he replied, rubbing his hands together. "I can't wait to see what else you think I am right about."

"Do not let this go to your head, Dr. Maddix," she bantered back.

Simeon cleared his throat, loudly at that. "Would you allow me to escort you to the convent?" he asked her.

She started to open her mouth to decline when Emmett answered, "No need. I will escort her."

Martha could hear Sister Mary mumble under her breath, "Oh, dear."

Giving them both a gracious smile, she asserted, "It is not necessary for either of you to walk me to the convent. I feel confident that Josette and I can walk up a paved path, which is only a hundred yards from this building, unescorted."

Morgan moved to open the door and stood aside. "I will be standing watch all night, Lady Martha." The way he spoke made it clear that he would brook no argument.

Beaming at Morgan, she turned to the other two men. "There you go," she announced. "We will see you both in the morning."

Looping her arm through Josette's, they walked the short distance to the convent, giving Martha time to think about what she had just shared with the group. Previously, only Eliza had known her story, but it felt safe to share it with the others tonight, despite Simeon's presence.

Emmett had been right. Sharing her story seemed to have lessened her burden, although she still didn't know what to think about Simeon. If he hadn't been involved in her abduction, that would change everything. But if he was lying now, then she had every right to keep hating him. It was all so confusing!

EMMETT LEANED HIS HEAD BACK AGAINST THE PLUSH BENCH AND closed his eyes. The sun was barely peeking over the horizon as he made the trip back to London to get a fresh change of clothes and tell Eliza about the arrival of Martha's former fiancé.

He had sat by Johnny's side most of the night. When his fever broke early this morning, Sister Gertrude had relieved him, bringing a bowl of broth to feed Johnny. Reflecting on the boy's survival, he knew this was why he had become a physician. He wanted to help people, especially the ones that did not have access to medical care. Usually, the poor only had access to apothecaries who would offer solicited advice, but they would never have the funds to see a doctor. He wanted to change that.

Emmett sighed as he thought about the disaster of last night. After Martha departed for the convent, Simeon glared at him before he stormed out of the door.

Why did I offer for Martha, he wondered, closing his eyes in mortification. When Simeon had proposed marriage, Emmett had reacted and blurted out his own proposal. And it was a bad one, at that. The thought of Martha marrying Simeon had unnerved him.

Long ago, he had determined that he would never marry. His life was not conducive to having a wife or family. He was a physician who lobbied for the poor. He spent his evening hours in the rookeries, not at balls or social gatherings.

Emmett shook his head, realizing perhaps he had been chasing after the wrong things. The image of Lady Martha smiling at him came to his mind, and he found himself focusing on her beautiful lips. It had taken so long for him to coax a smile out of her, but when he'd heard her laugh, his life had changed. His entire focus had changed.

Before he could dwell on that any longer, the coach lurched to a stop, causing him to lunge forward. The door was jerked open, and a pistol was pointed at him. He was being robbed!

"Get out of the carriage," the highwayman ordered, tilting the pistol towards him.

Placing his hands in front of him, he exited the carriage and saw two other men on horses. They wore black cockades on their hats which were trimmed with bright, bold feathers. Their pistols were aimed at his footmen.

The standing highwayman stood in front of him and jammed the front of the pistol against his chest. His hat sat low on his head, shading his eyes, but it did not hide the silver hair poking out. This was not a young robber, but a mature criminal.

"Stand and deliver," the man said, slowly and deliberately.

Emmett met his gaze, not intimidated by his heated glare. "I will give you what you ask, but do not dare think about hurting my friends."

"Your friends?" the man repeated.

"Yes," he replied, turning his head towards the two footmen and driver. "They are my friends and are under my protection."

The highwayman smiled. "You are not in a position to make requests."

"Are you sure about that?" Emmett asked, knowing his own pistol was tucked into the waistband of his trousers, hidden by his waistcoat.

The highwayman stepped back and yelled, "I am going to look in the coach. Keep a pistol on him."

Emmett turned his head and saw his footmen's eyes were wide with fear. He wanted to reassure them but chose to remain silent.

Stepping out of the coach, the highwayman had his leather medical bag in his hand. He held it up and demanded, "Are you a doctor?"

"I am," Emmett confirmed.

Tossing the leather bag up to one of the other men, the highwayman grabbed his forearm and ordered, "You are coming with me."

Digging his heels in the ground, Emmett countered with, "Not until you tell me where I am going."

The highwayman dropped his arm and moved to place the pistol up to his head when Emmett reacted. With a rapid motion, he grabbed the man's wrist, twisted it, and stepped to the side. With his other hand, he yanked the pistol from the man's hand, repositioned it, and pointed it back at the robber's chest.

Narrowing his eyes, he grunted, "As I said previously, 'Not until you tell me where I am going'."

Instead of the anger he expected to see in the highwayman's eyes, he saw respect. Emmett heard the other pistols cocking, but he gave them no heed.

"We need a doctor," the highwayman admitted, somewhat urgently.

"Why?"

Glancing over at the footmen, he murmured, "I would prefer to tell you when we are on the road."

There was a hint of desperation in the highwayman's eyes, which caused Emmett's resolve to soften. It was clear that this man really did need a doctor.

"Fair enough," Emmett replied. Turning toward his footmen, he directed, "Stay here for a few hours. If I am not back by noon, then go inform Lord Lansdowne of my predicament."

His lead footman hesitated as he asked, "Would you not prefer us to contact the constable?"

"No," Emmett stated. "Do as you are instructed." He rotated the pistol in his hand and extended the handle towards the highwayman. "I do not require your pistol any longer."

The man accepted it, placing it into the waistband of his trousers. "Follow me," he ordered as he walked towards a chestnut mare. "We can share a horse, since we are only going a short distance."

The man mounted and offered his hand to assist Emmett. When he was on the back of the horse, the man said over his shoulder, "We will not blindfold you, but if you betray us, we will kill you."

Emmett chuckled. "It would be more effective if you threaten my friends and family's lives as well." He paused before adding, "My uncle does have a dog. You could extend the threat to include the dog's life, I suppose."

The highwayman gawked at him. "You seem immune to threats."

"I am," he admitted as the image of Mr. Larson floated to his mind. "I find I am threatened on a regular basis."

"Do your patients threaten you that often?"

"No," Emmett replied as the horse trotted up a small hill bordering the road. "My friends do."

The highwayman chuckled. "Those don't sound like very good friends."

Gripping the edges of the saddle as the horse increased speed, he responded vaguely, "On the contrary, I assure you. They are the best."

"Fair enough," the highwayman acknowledged as he ducked low in the saddle. "Keep your head down and hold on tight."

After a short ride up a steep hill shrouded by large trees, they wove in and out of the dark green foliage. Pulling to a stop, the man dismounted and shouted towards a canvas of trees, "Prinny is a fine dandy."

Tossing his leg over, Emmett slid off the horse as he saw two armed men walking out of the trees. They watched him warily as one came over to collect the saddled horse. Neither pulled their weapon, but it was clear they were puzzled by his presence.

A man approached him and extended his medical bag towards him.

"You are needed in there," he said, pointing at a small cottage buried deep within the trees. The tree branches rested on top of a thatched roof, and a small billow of smoke came from the fireplace.

Emmett reached the door and ducked into the cottage. A young man lay on the straw mattress, his painful moans echoing throughout the small room. Another man was sitting next to him, attempting to place wet cloths on his face, but the patient continually thrashed about, knocking them away. A third man sat next to the fireplace stirring a pot, his back turned towards the young man.

Without hesitation, Emmett strode over to the young man and crouched down to examine the injury. He had a familiar red, oozing wound on his right upper arm. "When was he shot?"

The man lowered the wet cloth as he stood. "Two days ago."

Taking another long look at the wound, Emmett wiped his hand over his chin, hesitantly. This did not look good. "And did no one think to retrieve the bullet?" Emmett asked as he opened his bag and reached for a piece of willow bark. When no one answered, he ordered over his shoulder, "I need some fresh water boiled and clean linens."

When again no one moved, Emmett shouted, "Now!"

As the two men began doing his bidding, the silver-haired man who had brought him to this place walked into the cottage and grabbed a stool, placing it next to him. "How does it look?" he asked warily.

Emmett shook his head. "To be frank, it does not look good. He has a fever, infection has already set in, and the bullet is lodged deep into his arm." He turned his gaze towards the young man. "Is he a fighter?"

The highwayman's eyes grew pensive. "He should be. He is my son."

Emmett knew there was an obvious solution, as much as he

hated to admit it. "It might be best to remove his arm to prevent the infection from spreading."

"No!" the highwayman cried out. "My son wouldn't want that."

Giving him a sad look, he informed him, "In that case, I will do everything I can to save your son's life, but you need to prepare yourself for his death."

"I could threaten to kill you if he doesn't live," the man said. His tone was gruff, but it held no real malice.

"You could," Emmett admitted, "but if I thought you intended to kill me, I would never have come along."

"I didn't give you much of a choice."

Reaching for a piece of cloth in his bag, Emmett set a tourniquet above the wound. "Believe me, I came willingly," he stated as he leaned back.

The highwayman gave him an odd look. "You are quite confident in your abilities, Doctor…"

"Dr. Maddix," Emmett offered.

"Call me Gaspard."

"Is that your real name?"

"No," he confirmed, then he glanced down at his son. "What can I do to help?"

Giving him a hard look, Emmett explained, "I am going to put this willow bark into his mouth. It will dull the pain and give him something to bite down on. I need you to hold him firmly." He touched the exceedingly warm wound with his finger, and the boy let out a pain-induced moan. "I need to remove the bullet, and it will be excruciatingly painful." He sighed. "Do you by chance have any whiskey?"

"We do," Gaspard confirmed as he walked over to a cabinet. "We took it out of a fancy bloke's carriage a few weeks back."

Accepting the whiskey, Emmett poured a generous amount over the wound, causing the boy to scream in pain. Before he placed the whiskey bottle down on the ground next to him, he poured some over his hands.

Once the hot water was brought over, and somewhat clean linens were procured, Emmett took his forceps and began digging for the bullet in the young man's arm. He stiffened as his pitiful screams echoed through the room. Within moments, the young man started to thrash about, but his father pinned him in place.

As Emmett continued to use his forceps to search for the bullet, the young man's agonized groans seemed to come from the very depth of his body. Still, he could not quit and spare him this pain. If he stopped, the young man would surely die. This was his best chance for survival.

Finally, he felt the bullet, and clamped his forceps around it, pulling it out. Dropping the blood-coated bullet to the ground, he barely acknowledged the noise as it hit the wood. He was more concerned about another obstacle.

A large abscess sat next to the wound, and it needed to be drained. He made a small cut with his scalpel. Yellow pus started oozing out of the wound, a horrible odor emanating as he rubbed around the wound to ensure all the pus had been removed.

Grabbing a cloth, he placed it over the incision and allowed it to saturate with blood and discarded pus. The next step was to take his scalpel and remove all the damaged tissue around the wound. Once he finished, he dabbed the affected area with a cloth to remove the excess blood.

Tossing aside the linen, he reached for a needle, which was already threaded with catgut. He preferred the fine thread woven from sheep intestines rather than the silk used by many of his compatriots at the hospital.

After he closed the wounds, he dumped some herbs into the hot water and created a poultice for the boy's arm, covering it with bandages. Then, he removed the tourniquet. "I need more water," he ordered, pushing the pot back towards Gaspard. "We need to give him some tea, mixed with laudanum to help him sleep."

After the medicine was administered, Emmett acknowledged that he'd done all that he could to save the boy's arm. "If this doesn't work, we will need to amputate his arm for his best chance at survival."

Looking in shock, Gaspard just stared at his son. "Do we need to decide now?"

"No," Emmett admitted. "First, we will see how his body responds."

"Timothy," he stated gruffly. "My son's name is Timothy."

Giving him a tentative smile, Emmett said, "Let's hope Timothy is willing to fight to stay alive."

❧ 19 ❧

Hours later, sitting alone on the filthy, wooden floor, Emmett leaned his back against the wall and listened to Timothy's heavy breathing. He heard only occasional words from the men outside. Apparently, no one was in a talkative mood right now.

The door opened, and Gaspard walked into the room with a dead rabbit in his hand. "You hungry?"

"Famished," he replied honestly. "I must admit that I have never had rabbit to break my fast, though."

Gaspard smirked. "It is an acquired taste."

"Much like hardtack."

Gaspard glanced at him curiously. "Were you in the Royal Navy?"

Stretching his neck, Emmett yawned before he answered, "I was."

"So was I," murmured the highwayman.

Reaching over, Emmett placed his hand on Timothy's forehead, pleased that he was not hot to the touch anymore. "His fever finally broke," he reported. "That is a good sign. Timothy should be able to keep his arm."

"That is wonderful news," Gaspard responded as he tossed the rabbit carcass onto a small table and pulled out his knife. Without hesitation, he chopped off the head and the lower half of each leg before he peeled back the skin from the neck.

While Gaspard continued to prepare the rabbit for cooking, Emmett asked, "When were you in the Royal Navy?"

"About four years ago," the man answered, focusing on the task at hand.

Emmett sat straighter against the wall. "Why did you become a highwayman?"

Gaspard removed the guts and placed them aside before he acknowledged his question. He pointed his blood-coated knife at him. "I think of myself as more of a Robin Hood to the people of Gravesend."

Emmett was amused. "Do you expect me to believe that you rob from the rich and give to the poor?"

Gaspard shrugged. "I don't expect you to believe it, but it is true."

Emmett's eyes drifted towards his patient as he exhaled loudly. "Isn't Timothy a little young to be a highwayman?"

"He is sixteen," Gaspard remarked under his breath. "But to answer your question, Timothy is not a highwayman."

"Then how did he get injured?"

Flattening the rabbit out on the table, Gaspard roughly chopped it into large pieces. "He was running from a press gang."

"Press gangs don't usually shoot people," Emmett commented. "They want to impress men into service, not kill them."

Gaspard shook his head. "Not these press gangs. Anyone opposing The Cursed Lot is either impressed into service or killed. They have overtaken the town, and no one can stop them."

LAURA BEERS

Emmett brought his knee up and rested his elbow on it. "Have you sought out the constable?"

"The constable is in The Cursed Lot's pocketbook," he said. "As are the magistrate, customs officials, and revenue men."

"Surely, not all those people are conspiring with them?"

"Perhaps not all of them, but everyone in Gravesend is petrified of The Cursed Lot gang," Gaspard said as he scooped up the meat and dropped it into an iron pot hanging above the hearth floor. "All my men barely escaped from Gravesend with their lives."

Trying to understand the extent of The Cursed Lot's reach, the doctor asked, "I was led to believe that The Cursed Lot only dealt with their smuggling operation and gambling den."

Gaspard scoffed. "Who do you think rows out to the ships to unload their cargo?" He lifted his brow. "Who do you think carries all those parcels into The Cloven Hoof and down those long tunnels?"

"Have you been inside of the tunnels?" Emmett asked, dropping his arm.

Shaking his head, Gaspard admitted, "Not me, but my lad has." He took a moment to stir the contents of the pot. "He said the tunnels are miles long. But he had to run when he was spotted by one of the gang."

Emmett ran his hand through his dirty hair, knowing he needed a long soak. "Why not go to the commander at the New Tavern Fort and seek his help?"

Gaspard laughed dryly. "That is rich." When his laughter subsided, he explained, "Colonel Allister is running the whole operation."

"Did you just say Allister?" he asked in dread. Surely, it could not be the same Allister, his former captain.

"I did."

Emmett closed his eyes and leaned his head back against the

wall. "I knew of a Captain Allister. He was my commanding officer when I was in the Navy."

Gaspard grabbed the discarded pieces of the rabbit and tossed them into a small bucket. "Rumor has it that Colonel Allister was relieved from duty as captain of his own ship after he was court-martialed for killing a girl under mysterious circumstances." He scoffed. "And some dim-wit offered him the position as colonel of the New Tavern Fort."

"There were no mysterious circumstances," Emmett grunted. "It was murder. I was serving under Captain Allister when he killed that poor girl for rejecting his advances."

"That doesn't surprise me," Gaspard said, eyeing him curiously. "That man has blood on his hands."

Opening his bag, Emmett removed a small pouch of herbs and willow bark. "I need to go," he declared as he stood. "I need to act on this information."

Gaspard placed the bucket on the floor near the hearth. "You are not just a doctor, are you?"

Emmett shook his head, knowing there was no reason to hide it. "I have been tasked to help stop the smuggling in and around Gravesend."

"You will never be able to stop the smuggling," Gaspard said definitively with a shake of his head.

Reaching for his bag, Emmett placed it under his arm. "Then we will stop The Cursed Lot."

"That is impossible."

"You are wrong," Emmett replied. "Every criminal slips up. They become too comfortable and believe that they are smarter than everyone else around them."

Wiping his hands on his trousers, Gaspard looked at him with concern. "Not these men. Colonel Allister is ruthless and will chop down anyone in his path."

Walking to the table, Emmett placed the pouch onto a non-bloodied section of the table. "Boil this and place it in his broth.

Start off slow and don't give him too much at once, or it will make him sick."

"You can't go now," Gaspard stated. "I can't just let you walk out that door. You will have to wait till dark. Then I will take you to the village."

"By now, my footmen have informed Lord Lansdowne of my abduction, and I have no doubt he will be here shortly to collect me," Emmett informed him.

Gaspard emitted a single bark of laughter. "As if an entitled lord could track down your location…" His voice trailed off as loud banging at the door echoed throughout the small room.

"Dr. Maddix, are you in there?" Benedict called from outside the door.

Smirking, Emmett enjoyed seeing Gaspard's shocked expression.

"I am!" he answered loudly.

Jonathon's voice asked, "Are these men friends or foes?" There was a pause before they heard a loud thud on the front porch. "An answer would be appreciated."

Emmett walked over and opened the door. He smiled at Jonathon and Benedict, who held pistols in their hands and had daggers tucked into their trousers.

"These are friends," he paused and glanced over his shoulder at Gaspard, "for now."

Gaspard joined him at the door. "Thank you for what you did for my Timothy. I owe you my life."

"No, you owe me nothing," Emmett assured him. "Thank you for the information about Colonel Allister."

He started to step out of the door but stopped as he noticed two unconscious men sprawled out on the porch. Before he stepped over them, he turned back towards Gaspard.

"In two days, bring Timothy to the hospital near St. George's Church so I may change the bandaging. If he is unable to travel, please send for me, and I will come post-haste."

Turning back towards Benedict and Jonathon, he smiled broadly. "I expected you hours ago."

Jonathon gave Benedict an exasperated look. "I wanted to depart as soon as your footmen arrived at Benedict's townhouse, but *someone* wanted to give you time to escape on your own."

Benedict grinned knowingly at him. "As soon as the footmen informed us that you were captured because you were a doctor, I knew I didn't have to finish my tea and biscuits too quickly."

Emmett chuckled. "Thank you for prioritizing me under your tea and biscuits."

"What?" Benedict declared. "Have you had my cook's biscuits?"

Shaking his head in amusement, Emmett followed the two men over to their horses. Before they mounted, he revealed, "Colonel Allister is the commanding officer at the New Tavern Fort and is the rumored leader of The Cursed Lot gang."

Jonathon eyed him warily. "Is this the same Allister that was your commanding officer in the Navy?"

Emmett nodded.

"Do you have proof of this?" Benedict asked.

"No," he admitted reluctantly. "The highwayman just informed me."

Jonathon's face was set, his lips a thin, grim line. "We need to speak with my uncle."

"Why didn't you just shoot the blackguard?" Eliza demanded, her eyes blazing with fury.

Emmett chuckled at Eliza's misplaced anger. "Did you miss

the part where I told you that Simeon claims he knew nothing of her abduction?"

Eliza waved a hand in front of her dismissively. "Am I expected to believe that it was just a grand coincidence that Wade knew which room Martha was staying in at the inn?"

Reaching for his cup of tea from the table, he took a sip before attempting to explain the events of Lady Martha's abduction for the third time. "Why would Simeon spend all of his money for a special license if he planned to betray her?"

Tapping her foot rapidly, Eliza pursed her lips. "Simeon is a scoundrel. He was the only one that could have betrayed her."

Placing the cup back on the table, Emmett leaned back in his seat before saying, "Be that as it may, I do not believe Simeon is capable of such underhandedness."

"Now you are spouting nonsense," Eliza declared harshly. "If not him, then who?"

"Dearest," Benedict started as he placed his hand on her arm, "women go missing all the time from the docks."

"But she wasn't at the docks," Eliza reminded him. "She was miles away at a respectable inn."

Jonathon spoke up, giving Eliza an apologetic look. "The innkeeper was not a reputable man. After you first shared a small tidbit of Martha's story with me, I went to investigate the inn. At the time, I thought we could use the inn to lure in Wade and set a trap for him."

"And what did you discover?" Eliza asked with an uplifted brow.

Jonathon crossed his arms over his chest as he leaned back onto the window sill. "Apparently, the innkeeper was known for selling women to Wade for a tidy sum, but he was murdered around the same time that Martha went missing."

"Did they catch the killer?" Benedict asked.

Jonathon shook his head. "No. His body was found in an

alleyway, his throat slashed. It caused such a scandal that the innkeeper's wife had no choice but to close the inn."

Eliza gave them an exasperated look. "Again, Simeon took Martha to a disreputable inn. He had to be in collusion with the innkeeper, then killed him to keep his secret."

"Or," Benedict began with a smile, "Martha was just a victim of circumstance, and the murder of the deplorable innkeeper was not related."

"Simeon appeared genuinely relieved to see Martha. He even offered for her," Emmett reminded her.

Eliza huffed loudly. "Martha is now a titled lady with a dowry. Additionally, she is a kind-hearted, loving woman. Any man would be lucky to have her as a wife."

Emmett sighed. "I don't dispute that..."

Interrupting him, Eliza pressed, "You cannot truly believe that Simeon is just a star-crossed lover?"

Emmett attempted to speak again. "It is not that simple..."

Eliza cut him off. "But it is. Next time you see Simeon... kill him."

"Eliza," Benedict warned.

She rolled her eyes. "Fine, next time you see Simeon, will you *please* kill him?"

Jonathon walked over and sat on a chair near Eliza. "Until we find proof of Simeon's treachery, no one is going to kill him. I, for one, believe that Martha's father had something to do with her abduction."

Although obviously displeased by Jonathon's comment, Eliza's eyes grew reflective. "No father could be so cruel to their own daughter."

Jonathon shrugged. "If so, our mother looks like a saint compared to Lord Waterford."

Eliza sighed, then turned back towards Emmett. "How is Martha holding up?"

Emmett placed his elbow on the chair's armrest, and his

fingers cupped his chin. An image of Martha holding a pistol at Simeon, defending herself, came to his mind. She was brave and... magnificent.

Turning his attention back to Eliza, he answered, "She appears to be holding her own."

A sad expression flittered across Eliza's face. "Martha may put on a brave face, but she has suffered greatly at the hands of others. I am surprised she didn't shoot Simeon."

Benedict smirked. "Martha tends to think before she acts, my love."

Eliza playfully narrowed her eyes at her husband. "Traitor," she mumbled under her breath.

Reaching over, Benedict kissed her on the cheek before asking Jonathon, "When is Lord Beckett scheduled to arrive?"

Jonathon pulled out his pocket watch. "Any moment now."

"Good," Emmett said. "I do have a hospital to run and smugglers to apprehend."

"Don't forget Martha's ball tomorrow evening," Eliza reminded the group.

Jonathon grinned. "How could I forget? Hannah is thrilled to be going, despite being heavy with child."

"You didn't convince her to stay back with Kate for the evening?" Benedict asked.

He shook his head. "As soon as Hannah heard Rachel and Luke were coming, I couldn't talk her out of it."

"Trust me, life is easier when your wife is happy," Lord Beckett advised from the doorway with a bulging file in his hand.

"Uncle," Jonathon greeted. "Thank you for coming on such short notice."

Lord Beckett sat down on a chair next to Benedict. "I apologize for not being at my office when you came to call, but I was at the palace." He laid the file down on the table and added, "My agents have discovered the most unusual inconsistencies regarding Lord Waterford."

"Such as?" Eliza asked.

Reaching for a piece of paper, Lord Beckett held it up. "His brother and nephew both died in a carriage accident."

"That is not highly unusual," Jonathon remarked. "Carriage accidents are quite common."

"True," Lord Beckett admitted. "However, if you take into account that Lord Waterford moved in with his brother and nephew two weeks prior to their death…"

"Why would Lord Waterford move in with his brother?" Emmett asked curiously. "I thought he was a vicar."

Lord Beckett grabbed another piece of paper and reviewed it. "He was fired from his post at St. Edmund's church."

"He was fired?" Jonathon inquired with a frown. "How does a vicar get fired?"

"You would be surprised," Lord Beckett mumbled under his breath. "An agent interviewed the bishop of St. Edmund's, but he was surprisingly tight-lipped about Lord Waterford." He extended the paper towards Jonathon. "The agent then took it upon himself to interview some members of the parish, and they claimed Lord Waterford was a delightful man."

"Delightful would not be a word that I would use to describe him," Emmett offered.

"Nor I," Lord Beckett agreed. "Luckily, the agent pressed more people for information, and he discovered that the people in the village feared Lord Waterford. He was belligerent, cruel, and forced his intentions on several women."

Going back to the previous conversation, Emmett asked, "What did Lady Waterford die of?"

"Good. I wanted to broach that subject." Lord Beckett frowned, reaching for another paper. "Her death certificate listed consumption, but my agents discovered she had not been under a doctor's care." His eyes scanned the document. "In and of itself, that was not suspicious, but she supposedly fell into a coma only days after Lord Waterford and his son died in a carriage accident."

"That is not at all suspicious," Eliza remarked sarcastically as she rose. "I will bring Martha back to our townhouse as soon as possible."

"No," Lord Beckett ordered. "We have no proof tying Lord Waterford to these murders, and Lady Martha is in an ideal situation to spy on her father."

"But, sir, Martha is not an agent," Benedict reminded him.

"I agree," Lord Beckett said, "but she is protected by Miss Josette and Lord Morgan."

"Speaking of Josette," Eliza began, "she informed me that Martha's father has unpaid notes from a pub called The Cloven Hoof."

Lord Beckett bobbed his head up and down. "That does not surprise me. There are a few outstanding debts that Lord Waterford has accrued at gaming halls around London. He appears to be an incompetent gambler." He reached for another piece of paper from the file. "Before his brother's death, Lord Waterford had a few creditors calling for his arrest and demanding that he be tossed into Marshalsea."

Jonathon swiped his hand across his mouth. "That sounds a lot like motive. Lord Waterford didn't want to spend his days in a debtors' prison, so he killed his brother to inherit the earldom."

"Regardless, let's hope that Lord Waterford won't be at The Cloven Hoof tonight, or else he might ruin our plan," Emmett shared.

Lord Beckett glanced curiously between the group. "What plan?"

"Did you have a chance to read the missive that I left at your office?" Jonathon asked his uncle.

"I did," he confirmed. "I just ordered an investigation into Colonel Allister's conduct."

"Good," Emmett muttered. "That man is the devil himself."

"Now back to 'the plan'," Lord Beckett redirected with a lifted brow.

"Jonathon and I are going to The Cloven Hoof and participate in some high-stakes gambling," Benedict said, wiggling his brow. "However, it may end in a brawl."

"May?" Eliza asked with a knowing look.

With a widening smile, Benedict admitted, "It will definitely end in a brawl."

"At which time, Mr. Martin and I will attempt to locate the tunnels that run beneath the pub," Emmett said.

"How do you know there are tunnels beneath the pub?" Lord Beckett asked.

"Not only did Sister Mary of St. George's Church inform us that underground chalk tunnels run the length of the town, but I recently confirmed that a tunnel runs directly below The Cloven Hoof," Emmett shared. "It would explain how the smugglers freely move their contraband around."

"Good plan," Lord Beckett agreed, then added with a smirk, "assuming you don't get yourselves killed."

Jonathon huffed. "Thank you for the vote of confidence, dear uncle."

As Lord Beckett rose, he asked, "How did you discover that Allister was the colonel stationed at the New Tavern Fort? The note did not address that."

Emmett rose and answered, "A highwayman told me."

Lord Beckett reached down and picked up the file. "Good work, Dr. Maddix." Tipping his head towards the group, he left without another word.

"Shouldn't we be on our way to Gravesend?" Benedict asked, rubbing his hands together in anticipation. "I always look forward to a good fight, especially when I get to hit Jonathon."

Eliza walked over and kissed Benedict on the lips. "Have fun, my brave husband."

In response, Benedict wrapped his arms around Eliza's waist, ignoring everyone else in the room. "I suppose I have some time before we must leave."

Jonathon shook his head, but a smile played on his lips. "If you will excuse me, I will go check on my wife before we depart."

Emmett trailed behind Jonathon and closed the door behind him, granting Benedict and Eliza some privacy. It was refreshing to see couples in love.

❧ 20 ❧

MARTHA HANDED A SECOND BOWL OF BROTH TO JOHNNY'S outstretched hands. "You seem to have your appetite back," she teased. "If you keep this broth down, we will feed you something more substantial later."

Johnny gave her a toothless grin. "Thank you, Sister Martha."

She laughed at his innocent mistake. "My name is just Martha."

Bringing the broth to his mouth, Johnny gulped it down quickly. As he lowered the bowl, he said, "This soup is delicious."

Martha sat on the chair next to Johnny's straw pallet. "What you are eating is actually called broth."

Johnny tilted his head and wiped his mouth on his dirty, tattered shirt. "Doesn't matter what it's called. It's better than what I get at the workhouse," he informed her.

"What do you usually eat there?"

"Soup with moldy vegetables and dusty bread." Johnny shuddered. "But at least it tastes better than it smells."

"How awful," she murmured under her breath.

"Martha," Josette said from behind her, "Sister Mary is requesting your help with a patient in the back room."

Nodding her understanding, she rose and attempted to smooth out her wrinkled gown. Turning, she saw Josette had a book in her hand. "Are you going to read to Johnny?"

"Worse," Josette declared as she gave him a frightful expression. "I am going to give him reading lessons."

Johnny's eyes grew wide with excitement as he placed the bowl on the ground. "If you teach me how to read, then I can read to my momma." He scooted over in his straw pallet and patted the seat next to him. "Come sit by me."

With a smile, Josette sat next to Johnny and opened her book. "First, let's see if you can recognize any letters..." Her lesson continued as Martha started towards the back room where Sister Mary was treating patients.

The previous evening, they'd eaten a light supper at the convent, then went to bed. Even though the sisters had extra nightshirts for them to sleep in, her gown had still managed to get horribly wrinkled.

Martha had spent most of the night thinking about Simeon and the fact that he had not betrayed her. At least, she was fairly confident he hadn't. Still, she had some reservations. For so long, she had held anger and revenge in her heart for Simeon, and she wasn't ready to let it go. If he wasn't to blame, then who was?

Was she to blame for leaving the safety of her family and her town? If she hadn't followed her heart, then she wouldn't have eloped with Simeon. Well, she certainly wouldn't make that mistake again. Her heart was not to be trusted when making important decisions.

Knocking softly, Martha waited until she heard Sister Mary inviting her in before she pushed open the door. As she started to close the door, she saw Sister Mary with an arm around the shoulders of a young woman who had tears flowing down her cheeks.

"It's heart-breaking to lose a babe. Allow the tears to flow, my child. There is no shame in crying over such a loss."

The young woman nodded but did not appear convinced. Feeling the need to provide comfort, Martha stepped closer, keeping her voice encouraging. "You may feel that hope is lost, and you don't have the strength to take another step." She paused as the young woman looked over at her. "But don't let that fear rule your life. Hope can always be found again."

"This is my second time losing a babe," the young woman cried. "What if I am not meant to have children?"

Taking in the disheveled appearance of the young woman, it was clear that she was overwhelmed with emotion. With compassion in her heart, Martha took a step closer to the struggling young woman.

"How long have you been married?"

"Eleven months," came her weak reply.

Lifting a knowing brow, Martha asked, "And during that time, has everything come easily to you?"

"No, ma'am," the young woman mumbled.

She lowered her brow. "Anything worth having in this life is worth the heartache that comes along with it."

The young woman stayed quiet, and her eyes were full of sadness.

"Do you have enough to eat?" Martha asked as her eyes took in the small thin figure in a shapeless brown frock.

"No, ma'am."

"I see," Martha remarked as she reached into her reticule and grabbed two shillings. Extending the coins, she stated, "You need to eat more, especially when you are carrying a babe."

The young woman shook her head. "I don't accept charity."

"Good," Martha said, withdrawing her hand. "I was looking to hire a hard worker to clean this building every day." She looked up at the rafters. "If you believe you can keep this place clean, then the pay is five shillings a week."

With wide eyes, the young woman repeated, "Five shillings a week?"

Martha nodded. "But you will be expected to arrive early and report to Sister Mary."

"When can I start?" the young woman asked eagerly.

"I have a few more questions." Keeping her face expressionless, Martha inquired, "Is your husband employed?"

"At the workhouse."

Martha pressed her lips together. "Do you suppose he would be willing to work odd jobs for the sisters? I noticed that their convent needs repair."

"Yes, ma'am."

Martha gave her a friendly smile. "What is your name?"

"Cynthia, ma'am."

Martha chuckled. "Please stop calling me ma'am. My name is Martha."

Cynthia curtsied. "Yes, Martha."

"If Sister Mary agrees, I believe we have found our housekeeper and groundskeeper. Each of you will earn wages of five shillings a week," Martha shared with a bright smile.

Cynthia's mouth gaped open. "Ten shillings?"

Martha extended her hand with the coins. "Take these coins and go celebrate. I expect you both to report here first thing tomorrow morning."

Cynthia accepted the coins and threw her arms around her. "Thank you, Martha. Thank you!"

As Cynthia raced out the door, Martha looked over and saw approval in Sister Mary's eyes. "Ten shillings? That was quite generous."

"When I worked as a lady's maid, Lady Lansdowne set my wage as one guinea per week."

"A week?" Sister Mary blurted out. "That is an exorbitant wage, indeed."

Martha shrugged. "I never collected the money. I was just grateful to be alive."

Sister Mary eyed her for a moment before saying, "Thank you for helping Cynthia. You have just given her a boost of hope."

"Everyone needs hope in their lives," she murmured.

"Do you?"

Martha gave her a perplexing look. "Do I what?"

"Have hope in your life?"

Martha frowned. "I have seen the evils of this world and somehow was lucky enough to survive. I suppose I don't hope for anything anymore."

Sister Mary walked over to the table and picked up a small box of supplies. "That is a sad way to live."

Accepting the box from Sister Mary, Martha took a step back. "I disagree. It is a realistic way to live."

Reaching down to the table, Sister Mary took a cloth and wiped the table clean. "And what about matters of the heart?"

Martha huffed. "I am not interested in marriage or love."

"Interesting," Sister Mary mumbled under her breath. "I surmise that Mr. Martin might fight to win your heart again."

"I highly doubt that," Martha asserted. "I believe I made my point perfectly clear last night."

Sister Mary humphed, then nodded in the direction of the door. "I don't think he listened."

Turning her head, Martha saw Simeon holding a bouquet of flowers. A bright smile lit up his face when he saw her.

Martha just sighed.

UPON SEEING THE SMALL BOX IN HER HANDS, SIMEON MOVED THE bouquet of flowers to rest in the crook of his elbow, then placed his hands out. "Please let me carry that for you."

"No need," Martha replied. "If you are looking for Dr. Maddix, we expect him shortly." She walked past him and into the main hall, setting the box on the table with the other crates of supplies.

"I... um..." Simeon sputtered, looking entirely unsure of himself.

Sister Mary approached him and pointed at the flowers. "Those are beautiful, Mr. Martin. Are they for anyone in particular?"

He nodded, keeping his gaze on her. "Yes, they are for Lady Martha." He extended the flowers towards her, but she did not move to collect them.

"No, thank you." She turned with the intention of helping another patient in line.

"Magpie... wait," Simeon pleaded as he took a few strides to catch up to her.

Spinning around, Martha admonished in a hushed voice, "Do not call me that."

Simeon took a step closer. "Would you prefer Lady Martha?"

She glared up at him. "I would prefer if you would call me Martha."

"But I have called you Magpie since you were little," he reminded her with a boyish grin.

"I am not a little girl anymore."

Simeon slowly perused her face with admiration. "I can see that," he said softly. "Would you like to go for a walk? Perhaps we could walk by the shoreline."

Martha matched his gaze, daring him to continue staring at her. "I am much too busy to leave the hospital."

Simeon's eyes scanned the room. "I count three sisters from the convent and Miss Josette. I am sure they wouldn't miss you for an hour."

Squaring her shoulders, she challenged, "This is not a passing whim, Simeon. I enjoy helping these patients."

"And these patients will be here after our walk," he pressed.

Martha's eyes narrowed. "How dare you presume…"

Her words faded as Sister Mary placed a hand on her shoulder and leaned in. "Would you mind having this conversation outside?"

Glancing over at Josette, she saw her studying with Johnny. Pointing in their direction, Martha said, "I don't want to interrupt Johnny's lesson by asking Miss Josette to chaperone." She gave Simeon what she hoped was an apologetic smile. "Perhaps you could come back at a more convenient time."

Unexpectedly, Morgan spoke up from behind them. "I am more than capable of chaperoning outside in the garden."

"No, thank you," Martha huffed in irritation.

"Please," Simeon pleaded. "Just give me a few moments of your time." He extended the flowers towards her.

She sighed as she stared deep into his eyes. They were so familiar to her, and she could see the vulnerability in them. Finally accepting the flowers, she took a moment to breathe in their delightful smell before handing them off to Sister Mary.

"As you wish," she conceded, "but only for a few moments."

Simeon offered his arm, but she pretended not to see it as she walked out the door. Once outside, she veered towards the gardens and stopped when she reached the center. Turning around, she saw Simeon watching her carefully. He was dressed in a dark blue tailcoat, a paisley waistcoat, and tan trousers. His brown hair was now impeccably groomed, and she was reminded of how she used to love to run her fingers through his hair.

Simeon was a handsome man; a man that she'd loved wholeheartedly during her childhood. In her youthful naïveté, she always thought they would be married, have lots of children, and spend their days in bliss. However, that was not meant to be. Simeon may not have betrayed her, but her soul was darkened regardless. She was not the same girl that fell in love with him so long ago.

Simeon put his hands in front of him. "Magpie…" His voice trailed off.

Martha clasped her hands in front of her. "Say what you need to say, Simeon."

Instead of saying anything, he sat on a nearby wooden bench. He looked towards the horizon. His words started off soft at first. "I can't believe you are finally here. I have been searching for you for so long."

"You have?" Martha asked, moving slowly towards the bench.

Maintaining his gaze on the horizon, he looked crestfallen. "I truly had no idea you were sold to Wade, or I would have gone to hell and back to retrieve you." Tears filled his eyes, but he blinked them away. "I have missed you, Magpie. I have missed you more than I can possibly express."

Any residual anger melted away at the sight of his tears, and Martha sat on the bench next to him. "For so long, I thought you betrayed me. I spent years thinking of how much I loathed you."

He furrowed his brows together as he turned towards her. "How could you think that of me?" he asked. "We were supposed to be wed."

Tucking a few pieces of her blonde hair behind her ears, Martha gave him a sad smile. "Those were simpler times."

Simeon angled his body towards her. "We can go back to that. We can be wed and…"

Martha stood abruptly and walked a few paces away. "No, we can never go back to what we were."

"Yes, we can," Simeon insisted as he remained seated. "I have merchant ships of my own and have amassed a sizeable fortune." He ran his hand through his hair. "We could set sail and never look back."

"Why?" she asked forcefully. "Why would you want me? I am ruined."

He smiled tenderly at her. "I have wanted you from the moment we used to climb trees near the village." He slowly rose as he pulled out a small piece of paper from his waistcoat. "Do you remember this?"

Simeon extended the paper towards her, and she accepted it. Carefully unfolding it, she realized it was the sketch of her that he'd created one lazy afternoon. "Do you remember that day?" he prodded.

She nodded as she ran her fingers over the sketch. "That was the day you proposed."

He took a step closer. "And we agreed to keep it secret, until we learned of your betrothal to Baron Whitehall."

Martha folded the paper and handed it back. "Father was furious when I told him that we wished to be married."

Simeon carefully placed it back into his waistcoat, his gaze never wavering from her. "And we decided to elope instead."

"That was our mistake," Martha remarked as she started to turn.

Simeon put his hand out and reached for her, but she stepped back out of his reach. He dropped his hand. "I apologize, I didn't think."

Martha closed her eyes. He had meant no harm, but she had just reacted, as she always did. Putting up her hands, she said, "This is why it could never work."

"I disagree."

"I don't like to be touched," she asserted.

Simeon huffed as he turned his head away, but she heard him mutter under his breath, "You let Dr. Maddix hold you."

"That is entirely different," she declared.

"Is it?"

"Yes," Martha insisted. "We are just friends."

"Are you?"

Martha frowned. "You know nothing of our friendship."

His eyes were sad, but his tone was stern. "I have eyes, Magpie."

"I am not sure what you are referring to."

Simeon sighed; a deep, heartfelt sigh. "I am not giving up on you."

"Please..."

He spoke over her soft plea. "I understand you have endured much, but I want you in my life." He took a small step forward, still maintaining distance. "I love you."

Before Martha could respond, Emmett's voice filled the gardens. "Pardon me for interrupting, but may I have a moment of Lady Martha's time?" When she glanced his way, he tipped his head. "It is about a patient."

"Of course," she replied with a grateful smile. "I will be right in."

Turning back towards Simeon, she opened her mouth, but he interrupted, "Don't say anything. It won't change how I feel about you."

Martha watched as he walked away, wishing things were different.

STORMING INTO THE HOSPITAL, EMMETT IGNORED THE SISTERS and patients as he strode back into the examination room. In a huff, he closed the door and tossed his hat across the room.

He had been excited at the prospect of seeing Martha today, but that joy vanished when he saw her with Simeon in the gardens. Feeling an unfamiliar surge of jealousy, he'd moved to interrupt them when he heard Simeon give her a declaration of love. That had stopped him in his tracks.

Lowering himself onto the straw bed, he dropped his head into his hands. He hadn't planned on Simeon attempting to woo Martha so quickly. What if she decided to marry Simeon and left him? Martha isn't mine, he reminded himself.

He lifted his head when he heard a quiet knock on the door. "Enter."

Martha opened the door, stuck her head in, and smiled sweetly. "You wanted to see me, Dr. Maddix?"

"Yes, please come in," he replied as he stood.

Walking further into the room, Martha stopped and looked at him expectedly. Instead of immediately responding, he took a moment to admire her. Her dress was wrinkled, her blonde hair was pulled back into a low chignon, and wisps of her hair were already escaping down her back. But she had never looked more beautiful to him.

Furrowing her brows, her eyes scanned his face. She took a small step closer to him and asked, "Are you all right, Emmett? You seem distracted."

Blinking back his stare, he shifted his stance. "I apologize. I've had a rough day."

"I am sorry to hear that," Martha replied. "May I help you somehow?"

His heart softened at her kind words. "No, thank you." He wanted to tell her that just seeing her had already buoyed his spirits. Instead, he shared, "This morning I met with an unusual patient, and he should arrive in two days for follow-up treatment."

"Oh?" Martha asked. "You saw a patient this morning?"

An impish smile came to his lips. "Yes, when I was robbed by highwaymen."

She gasped, her hand covering her mouth. "Oh, Emmett. Did they shoot someone?"

He shook his head. "No, I was taken back to the robber's hideout, and I ministered to the leader's son."

"What was wrong with him?"

Emmett pointed to the straw pallet indicating Martha should sit. As she lowered herself onto the bed, he explained, "He was shot trying to run from a press gang."

Placing her hands into her lap, she leaned forward and asked, "Doesn't that make him a criminal?"

He sat down next to her. "I do not believe that this group of highwaymen are the criminals we perceive them to be."

"But they are highwaymen?"

Placing his hand back behind him, he leaned back. "True, but perception can be relative."

Shifting her body, Martha pressed, "But they attempted to rob you."

Emmett smirked. "I let them believe they were robbing me."

She rolled her eyes. "I fear you are quite conceited about your fighting abilities."

"You wound me, my fair maiden," he mocked, feigning disappointment.

"I doubt that," she bantered back. "Your ego is too large, doctor."

He chuckled. "Regardless, a young man named Timothy might appear at the door, and I would like you to keep his identity a secret."

"You are entrusting me with this secret. I am honored," Martha said with a bright smile.

As she moved her head, a piece of her blonde hair fell from behind her ear and hung near her face. Without thinking, he reached over and tucked it behind her ear, his fingers lingering on her skin. He heard her soft intake of breath and immediately dropped his hand.

When he opened his mouth to apologize, he noticed that Martha was watching him, not with fear in her eyes but with something else. It was that something else that caused him to stare deep into her pale blue eyes. Unconsciously, he leaned his head forward until he was close enough to see the tiniest green flecks in her eyes.

When he realized what he was doing, Emmett was afraid to move for fear of breaking this spell that had come over them. He felt his heart pounding in his chest and feared that she could hear it.

Finally, he broke their gaze as his eyes roamed over her enchanting face, then focused on her lips. Looking up, he saw Martha looking at his lips. She blushed slightly. Then, she looked up at him, a radiance transforming her expression, causing his heart to overrule his good judgement.

Mindful of Martha's feelings, he watched for any signs of distress, but all he saw was longing in her eyes. At least, he hoped it was longing and not just his wishful thinking. Hesitantly, he dipped his head closer and was encouraged by the ever-so-slight parting of her lips.

As his mouth neared hers, he felt Martha's warm breath, and it was intoxicating. Then, just before his lips brushed against hers, the loud clearing of a throat echoed in the small room.

Rearing back, Martha's eyes grew wide as she jumped up. Without sparing him a glance, she ducked her head and ran out of the room, brushing past Sister Mary and Miss Josette. Intending to race after Martha, Emmett stood but was stopped by heated glares from Sister Mary and Miss Josette.

"Dr. Maddix," Sister Mary chastised sternly, "did you forget that you left the door open?"

Emmett sighed in frustration as he looked at the ceiling. "I hadn't planned that."

"Obviously not," Sister Mary replied with pursed lips.

Miss Josette brushed past Sister Mary and stood in front of him. Her eyes were narrow, accusatory, and sparking with fury.

"What were you thinking?" she challenged in a hushed but intense voice.

Looking over Sister Mary's shoulder, he asserted, "I need to see if Lady Martha is all right."

Miss Josette frowned. "No, you need to stay here. I will go check on her." With a flip of her head, she left the room.

Disapproval laced Sister Mary's features as she watched him. "Mr. Martin informed me that you need to depart in a few hours, so I will send in the most urgent cases."

"Thank you."

She nodded and turned to go.

"Sister Mary," he called, "wait."

She turned back to face the doctor with an uplifted brow.

"Will you please ensure that Lady Martha is all right? I

hadn't thought that through, and she may be upset by my brazenness."

Her eyes warmed. "As you wish," she responded as she continued to regard him for a long moment. "If it helps, Lady Martha would have let you kiss her."

A relieved smile came to his face. "That does help, Sister Mary."

The warmth faded from her eyes, and her next words were anything but kind. "But do not let it happen again, Dr. Maddix. This is a charity hospital, not a marriage mart." With a final stern look, she departed from the room.

THE SUN WAS SETTING AS EMMETT AND SIMEON STOOD IN FRONT of St. George's Church, watching as the coach pulled away, taking Martha, Josette, and Morgan back to London.

When the coach was out of sight, Simeon's voice broke the silence. "How was the hospital?"

"Busy," he answered. "I noticed you didn't work there today."

Simeon cleared his throat. "I thought it might be awkward for Martha if I was there all day, especially since I am not really a nurse."

"Good point." Several uncomfortable moments of silence passed between them before Emmett asked, "Were you able to acquire the horses?"

"I did."

"And they would be where?" His eyes scanned the area.

Mr. Martin jerked his head towards St. George's Church. "In the back. I thought it would be suspicious if two horses were in front of the hospital waiting for us."

"Good thinking," he replied, attempting to ignore the awkwardness between them.

Turning to face him, Simeon gave him a hard, pointed look. "What are your intentions towards my fiancée?"

"Your fiancée?" Emmett repeated, his sarcasm thinly veiled. "I daresay that Martha does not know she is betrothed."

Crossing his arms over his chest, Simeon stated, "Martha will come around, and we will be wed. It will just take time." Irritation flashed in his eyes. "And you trying to come between us will only complicate matters."

Emmett crossed his own arms over his chest, matching Simeon's stance. "I disagree. I believe Martha has made it quite clear that she has no intention of marrying you."

"Be that as it may, I request that you step down and allow Martha and I to settle our own disagreements."

"I will not."

"No?" Simeon huffed. "Surely as a gentleman…"

"I am a gentleman, but I am loyal to my friend, Martha, not you."

"You have more than friendship in mind with Martha. Don't try to deny it," Simeon challenged.

"That is true," Emmett admitted, "but Martha is still healing, and I am giving her time to find her own path, whereas you are trying to pressure her into something she may never be ready for."

Obviously aggravated, Simeon pressed his lips together tightly. "I always knew I was going to marry her. I love her."

Emmett sighed and lowered his arms. "I won't agree to stop pursuing Martha's heart, but if she makes her intentions known towards you," he paused, reluctantly, "I will bow out and accept her decision."

"Thank you," Simeon stated with a smug smile.

Watching the horizon, Emmett saw familiar riders approach

as he said, "I care only about making Martha happy. It has nothing to do with you."

"Understood," Simeon replied quickly. "I feel the same way."

As the riders grew closer, Emmett raised his hand to welcome Benedict and Jonathon. They were dressed in riding coats, looking the part of wealthy lords, which was an intricate part of their plan.

When they reined in their horses, he provided the introductions. "Mr. Martin, may I introduce Lord Lansdowne and Lord Jonathon?"

Jonathon glowered down at Mr. Martin. "Is this Simeon, Martha's supposed fiancé?"

"I am." Simeon bowed, unconcerned, not anticipating the danger. "It is a pleasure to meet you, Lord Jonathon."

Without another word, Jonathon dismounted and came around his horse. Drawing back his fist, he punched Simeon in the face, causing him to tumble back into the dirt.

Simeon covered his left eye. "What was that for?" he growled.

Jonathon stood over him with a murderous expression on his face. "That is for failing Martha." His words were slow, deliberate, and downright terrifying.

"I did no such thing!" Simeon protested. "She was abducted at the inn. I had no knowledge of where she had gone. I thought she had decided not to go through with the elopement."

Shaking his head, Jonathon declared, "When my Hannah was taken from me, I went through hell till I got her back in my arms. I couldn't think straight, I couldn't function, and I nearly died trying to find her."

"It is true," Benedict acknowledged. "Jonathon was more unbearable than usual during that time."

Ignoring his friend, Jonathon continued his hardened stare at Simeon. "You should have done the same for Martha."

Jumping up, Simeon lowered his hand as he shouted, "Do you think I ever stopped looking for her? There is not a day that goes by that I don't relive the moment I left the inn, leaving her alone and vulnerable. It plays in my mind repeatedly..." His voice hitched as his words trailed off.

Some of the anger faded from Jonathon's expression, but his jaw was still clenched. "This is your one warning, Mr. Martin. If I believe for even a moment you may hurt Martha again, then I will kill you."

Benedict adjusted the reins in his hands. "And I would cover for Jonathon."

"And I would help hide the body," Emmett offered, joining in on the conversation.

Jonathon smirked at his friends. "I have no doubt I can make his body disappear."

Simeon did not appear as amused as he gingerly touched his swelling eye. "May I ask what your personal connection with Lady Martha is?"

Benedict's eyes narrowed dangerously, and his words held a warning. "Martha is my wife's dear friend and my child's godmother."

Jonathon's face was filled with barely controlled fury as he addressed Simeon. "And I was in India when my sister bought her freedom. Lady Martha has become a dear family friend, so I hope you are not implying we have ulterior motives for protecting her."

"I am not. I am not a complete fool," Simeon replied. "I am pleased that my fiancée has such close friends."

"Fiancée?" Benedict lifted his brow and shifted his gaze towards Emmett. "How do you feel about that, Dr. Maddix?"

Emmett shrugged. "He is welcome to attempt to pursue Martha, but I have no intention of stepping back without a fight."

"My money is on Emmett," Jonathon proclaimed.

Without hesitation, Benedict stated, "I concur."

Simeon stood, dusting off the back of his trousers. "Martha and I fell in love in our youth, and I plan to woo her until she agrees to marry me." With a flick of his wrist, he argued dismissively, "Besides, Dr. Maddix and Martha barely know each other."

Placing his foot into a stirrup, Jonathon reached up and grabbed the pommel of his saddle. "Yes, but Dr. Maddix saved Martha's life and nursed her back to health."

Sitting tall in his saddle, Benedict added, "Plus, I have seen the nauseating looks they share when they think no one is looking."

"Really?" Emmett asked. "Do you think Martha has feelings for me?"

"There is no doubt," Jonathon answered for his friend. "And," he paused, smirking at Simeon, "Emmett has never lost Martha."

Benedict chuckled. "The same could not be said of Mr. Martin."

"Exactly," Jonathon agreed with a smile.

With fire in his eyes, Simeon took a bold step towards Jonathon's horse, but Emmett put his hand out to stop him. "Trust me, you do not want to fight these two men."

"I can take down two entitled lords," Simeon growled.

Keeping his hand on his chest, Emmett turned to give Simeon his full attention. He lowered his voice. "Do you have any idea who these two men are?"

"Yes, one is a marquess, and the other buffoon is the son of the Duke of Remington," Simeon answered, looking towards them, anger still sparking in his eyes.

Jonathon leaned low on the pommel of his saddle. "Did you just call me a buffoon?"

With a low whistle of disapproval, Benedict started backing up his horse. "That was not a wise move, Mr. Martin."

"Apologize," Emmett asserted under his breath. "Do it now, before he kills you."

"I am not going to apologize to…" Simeon started.

"Do it!" Emmett demanded. "You insulted an agent whose caliber is equal to *Shadow* and *Hawk*. He has fought side by side with them countless times."

The anger faded from Simeon's eyes and was replaced with newfound respect. "I apologize for my harsh words, my lord."

"Thank you for that." Jonathon graciously tipped his head. "Now, if you don't mind, Benedict and I are anxious to start a fight at The Cloven Hoof."

With his free hand, Benedict rubbed his horse's neck. "I have been looking for a good reason to hit Jonathon."

Emmett smiled. "Just keep them distracted long enough for us to explore the tunnels."

Jonathon looked down at Emmett's clothing. "Why aren't you wearing the clothes you requested from my valet?"

"I haven't removed them from the sack yet," Emmett confessed, then deliberately made a gagging noise. "I haven't dared."

Simeon glanced curiously at him. "What clothes?"

A slow smile formed on Emmett's lips as he explained, "Jonathon's valet was gracious enough to give us clothing that will help us blend in as poor blokes from the workhouse."

Benedict saluted him. "We will wait for you at the rendezvous point."

Before kicking his horse into a run, Jonathon urged, "Be careful, and try not to get yourselves killed."

❧ 2 2 ❧

"TELL ME AGAIN WHY THESE CLOTHES SMELL LIKE THEY HAVE been washed in excrement?" Simeon grumbled under his breath as they waited behind the knoll near the side door of The Cloven Hoof.

Emmett gave him a side-long glance. "Has anyone ever told you that you complain too much?"

"Never," he replied. "However, I smell like I took a dip in the River Thames on the east side."

"Haven't you ever gone undercover?" Emmett asked as he kept his eye on the lower level windows. They were waiting for Jonathon and Benedict to start the fight to draw the attention of the guard at the side door.

"Many times," Simeon confirmed, "but I have yet to smell like a chamber pot."

The wind shifted, causing the reeds to sway over their still forms. "Perhaps you should consider serving aboard a Royal Navy ship. Between the stench of unwashed bodies, the musty odor of old, wet wood, and the aroma of the rats scurrying around the ship, it's a real picnic for the nose," he stated sarcastically.

"I do own three merchant ships, but I have only gone aboard to inspect them and their cargo," Simeon admitted as he stretched his neck. "It has been hours since your friends went into The Cloven Hoof. When are they going to pick a fight?"

Emmett's eyes scanned the structure. "They are seasoned agents and will make their move when the time is right."

Loud, unruly shouting came from the pub just before a man flew through the window, the sound of breaking glass echoing throughout the night. The man jumped up, dusted off his clothes, and turned in their direction. With a broad smile, Benedict nodded at them before running back through the open door.

"Is he mad?" Simeon asked with a concerned brow.

"Most likely," Emmett joked, "but he is one of the best agents that England has."

Through the window, they saw the brawl. Men were over-turning tables, tossing drinks to the ground, and everyone appeared to be engaging in fisticuffs. It was a full-on ruckus with Jonathon and Benedict in the middle of it.

The guard at the side door ran to help stop the brawl, but when he entered the pub, he slipped on the ale-coated floor, landing soundly on his back.

"Let's go," Emmett ordered as they kept low to the ground and ran for the side door.

Placing his hand on the handle, he was relieved that the door was unlocked. Opening it wide enough to let Simeon pass through, he followed and closed the door behind him.

Expecting to be plunged into darkness, Emmett was pleased to see sconces on the wall, holding lighted torches which illuminated a set of narrow stairs leading down towards another door. Jogging down the steps, Simeon arrived first and reached for the door's handle. When the door wouldn't open, Simeon lowered his shoulder and forcefully plowed his left shoulder into it. The sound of splintering wood could be heard echoing against the walls, and the door flew back, revealing a long tunnel.

Torch-light danced merrily off the white chalk walls. The tunnel was wide enough for them to walk side by side, and the ceiling was tall enough for them to walk without ducking. Pressing his hand against the cool, uneven chalk, Emmett could feel the grooves where the workers had cut into the walls to create this passageway.

Knowing their time was short, they rushed down the long tunnel urgently, but no outlet was in sight. After several twists and turns, it split into two paths. Standing at the fork, Emmett turned to Simeon.

"Meet back at the rendezvous point." He hesitated for a moment before adding, "Be careful."

Simeon acknowledged his comment with a nod before he disappeared down the right tunnel. Emmett continued to rush through the left fork until he came to four wooden stairs which led to a crudely hung door.

Placing a hand over the pistol tucked into his waistband but hidden by the wrinkled, smelly, tan shirt, he took his free hand and opened the door. He expected to be assaulted, or at least hear shouts and have pistols pointed at him. Instead, he was met with silence.

Walking further into the room, he saw that it was filled with barrels and a few chests stacked against the wall. A door on the other side had light filtering through the cracks. He inspected the nearest barrel, finding that the cover would not budge.

Seeing a crowbar on the ground, he opened the lid, revealing salt. Replacing it carefully, he opened one of the chests. It was filled with tea leaves. He tried another barrel, which smelled suspiciously like brandy, but he couldn't manage to pry off the lid.

Stepping back, Emmett placed the crowbar on top of the barrel. He needed to discover the location of this storage room. Moving towards the door, he reached to open it when it was flung open. The familiar red coat of an Army uniform was the first thing he saw before he heard, "Why are you still in the supply chamber and not unloading the vessel?"

Emmett dropped his gaze and hoped he appeared contrite. "Sorry, sir. I… um… wasn't as fast as the others and was locked in."

The officer let out a frustrated sigh. "I assume you are from the workhouse."

"Yes, Captain," he responded, intentionally using the wrong rank.

"You're new, aren't you?" the officer queried.

"Yes, Captain," Emmett responded again.

"Follow me," the soldier ordered. He turned around and walked out towards a cobblestone courtyard.

Emmett jogged up the few steps to keep up with the infantry soldier as he surreptitiously scanned the surrounding buildings, immediately recognizing these structures were part of the New Tavern Fort. The hour was late, so the courtyard was virtually empty. Guards walked the perimeter wall, which faced the River Thames.

When Emmett caught up to the soldier, the man shared, "You will need to work faster or there will be consequences." Suddenly, the soldier stopped and swiveled around. "I will caution you to avoid looking around. If you are found anywhere that you do not have a right to be, you will meet a similar fate." He tipped his head towards a darkened corner where three wooden gibbets displayed dead bodies. "This is your only warning."

Unable to keep his outrage hidden, Emmett demanded, "Why are those bodies hanging there?"

The soldier shrugged. "Colonel's orders. We rounded them up to impress them, but they refused to cooperate."

"Since when did the British Army start using gibbets in forts?"

"It is effective," the soldier replied, completely unaffected by his tone. "They will stay there until they start to stink as a warning to the worthless men and women of Gravesend."

The soldier turned and walked towards a large iron gate, swinging it out towards a cobblestone pathway. Nodding at the guards posted there, the soldier walked down towards a seawall where a ship was moored. Lines of men, women, and children were carrying parcels, barrels, and crates from the seawall up a small hill towards the sulphur mill. Standing back, the man pointed expectantly at the line.

"Now, do as you are told," he ordered, "and try to keep up next time."

"Yes, Captain," Emmett answered humbly.

Moving past the soldier, he kept his head down and walked down towards the vessel where items had already been unloaded. Grabbing a barrel, he tossed it over his shoulder and started up the hill, noting how low the countenance was of each person he passed.

As he neared the top, he noted the red-coated officers guarding the mill. When he reached them, he carefully lowered his load alongside the other contraband.

Over and over, he made the trip until he felt like his arms and legs would give out. Finally, a whistle was blown, and the crowd started marching back towards the village.

A guard stepped in front of him with a musket in his hands. "You stink," he gagged. "See that you bathe before tomorrow."

"Yes, sir," he replied submissively.

Staying with the crowd, Emmett trudged along with the expressionless group of people until he saw a little boy in front of him. The boy's shoulders slumped with exhaustion. Moving to walk alongside him, Emmett recognized him from the hospital.

Leaning down, he whispered, "Johnny."

The boy lifted his head, and his eyes grew wide. "Dr…"

"Shh," he instructed as his finger pressed against his lips. "What is going on here?"

The boy nodded and replied in a hushed voice, "Anyone that lives in the workhouse has to unload the ships when they come."

Afraid he knew the answer, Emmett still asked, "And if you don't?"

Johnny's eyes darted towards a red-coated soldier. "That's how my father died. He tried to ride out to get help."

"Where is your mother?"

The boy rose on his tiptoes, his eyes looking around. "She's up there somewhere. We always meet back at the workhouse."

Emmett kept his gaze forward and his eyes alert. "Do you have any other family?"

"No," Johnny replied, his expression downcast.

As they neared the doors of the deteriorating workhouse, Emmett's words were quiet but firm. "I want you to take your mother and flee to the convent. Leave everything behind so no one will ask any questions. At the convent, ask for Sister Mary and explain that I will pay a donation for your keep." They stepped inside the rotting home, and the doctor was horrified by the blackened walls and droopy ceilings. "You both can come work for me."

Johnny eyed him with apprehension. "What kind of work are you looking for us to do?"

Standing still as people brushed by him, Emmett answered, "I live in a townhouse in London. We always need capable, hard-working men and women."

"I'll tell her," Johnny said, sounding unconvinced.

Emmett crouched down to the boy's eye-level and placed his hands on his lean shoulders. "Johnny, let me help you and your mother. You should be resting, not working. You just left the hospital this morning."

"I had to," he defended himself. "If I don't work, then I don't eat."

"I understand, but you are in constant danger here. I can help you."

Johnny gave him a nervous look. "What if you forget about us at the convent?"

"Never," Emmett assured him with a smile. "Now," he paused, glancing around the room, "is there a back entrance?"

"If you go past the kitchen, there is a hole in the wall that's big enough to fit through," Johnny informed him, pointing towards the opposite end of the house.

Emmett lifted his brow in disbelief. "Even for me?"

"Yes."

Standing, he gave the boy an affectionate pat on the head. "With your dad gone, you are the man of the family. You need to get your mother to safety."

Hearing that, Johnny straightened his back and squared his shoulders. "We'll be waiting tomorrow."

"Good," he answered. "If not, I will come looking for you."

With a final dip of his head, Emmett swiftly walked towards the back and found the large hole Johnny had described. As he raced away from the workhouse, he hoped that Simeon fared as well as he had.

"THE HOUSE WAS COMPLETELY ABANDONED?" EMMETT ASKED AS he pulled a stitch through the wound on Simeon's buttock.

Looking over his shoulder, Simeon grimaced as Emmett pushed the needle through his skin again. "Yes."

Trying hard not to laugh, the doctor asked, "Can you explain to me how a sheep managed to bite you in the buttock?"

Turning back to look straight ahead as he lay flat on the straw mattress in his rented room, Mr. Martin shared, "The tunnel led me to a cottage near a jetty in the Thames estuary."

Emmett tied off the last stitch, cut the thread, and teased, "So, did the sheep jump out and attack you in the house?" He placed a bandage over the wound. "I am finished here."

As he turned to give Simeon privacy, his partner revealed, "The house was completely dark, and I stepped outside. That is when I encountered the guard." He grunted in pain. "I ran and hopped a fence while the guard was chasing me. Unfortunately, I ran into a field of sleeping sheep, startling them."

Wiping down his needle, Emmett put his tools back into his bag. Benedict and Jonathon opened the door and peered into the room. "Are you finally done?" Jonathon asked in frustration. "We have been waiting in the hall for twenty minutes."

"And that doesn't count the hours we waited before that," Benedict complained.

Closing the bag, Emmett set it aside. "My apologies, my lords, but I prefer to give my patients privacy when required to stitch up a sheep bite on their buttocks."

"How many other patients have you tended that have received such bites?" Jonathon asked as he entered. Benedict followed and closed the door behind him.

"None," Emmett said with a smirk. "Sheep are notoriously docile animals."

Tucking in his shirt into his trousers, Simeon grumbled, "Hilarious. I was bitten by a sheep. Can we discuss something more important, like what we learned tonight?"

"Yes," Emmett agreed as he sat on a chair in the corner.

He waited until Benedict and Jonathon sat down before he filled them in on his adventure into New Tavern Fort. He ended by explaining what he learned from Johnny.

Leaning his back against the wall, Jonathon shook his head in disbelief. "I can't believe these chalk tunnels run from The Cloven Hoof to the New Tavern Fort and an abandoned cottage near a jetty."

"Why would a tunnel lead to a sheep farm in the middle of

nowhere?" Emmett speculated.

"Perhaps so the sheep will wipe away all traces of footprints left by the smugglers." Jonathon's eyes sparkled with humor as he asked Simeon, "Despite angry sheep trying to attack you, do you think you can retrace your steps to the cottage?"

"Definitely," Simeon assured him. "Although, it would be much easier during the day."

"We need to discover who owns that property," Emmett said. "Would your uncle be able to discover that information?"

"I have no doubt," Jonathon confirmed.

Emmett glanced at Benedict with concern. "Are you all right?"

"I am incensed that the soldiers at the New Tavern Fort are involved in such corruption. Smuggling and murdering of innocent people? It's an outrage!" Benedict declared, the fury in his voice barely controlled. "It validates the highwayman's accusation."

"I propose we go directly to Lord Beckett and have him inform the commander-in-chief of Colonel Allister's deception," Emmett recommended. "I'm sure he would send soldiers to the fort and strip Allister of his command as colonel."

Jonathon shook his head. "Before we bother Prince Fredrick, we need to approach the general over New Tavern Fort. The general would be Colonel Allister's commanding officer."

"And what if the general is aware of the smuggling?" Emmett asked.

Benedict pursed his lips. "If the corruption extends to the general, then we will inform Prince Fredrick. His retribution will be swift and just."

"Even if Colonel Allister is removed from his post and the soldiers are replaced, that still won't change the fact that The Cursed Lot are running a sophisticated smuggling ring," Simeon pointed out.

"True. However, Allister is the supposed leader of The

Cursed Lot," Jonathon countered. "Taking out Allister and the support of the British Army would be a huge blow to The Cursed Lot's operation."

Benedict sighed. "If you cut off the head of the monster, many more will emerge."

"Good point," Emmett agreed. "Unless we arrest all the key members of the gang, it would only be a matter of time until a new leader would emerge."

"It finally makes sense. The Cursed Lot have obtained so much power in the village because the British Army is involved with their treachery." Simeon ran a hand through his hair. "We need to end their rule over the people of Gravesend."

Agreeing with Simeon, Emmett nodded his support. "And we need irrefutable proof of Allister's involvement with the smuggling ring."

Benedict frowned. "I hate to say it, but by the time we go into London and get proper reinforcements, the contraband will already be en route to another location."

Simeon dropped into a chair and grunted in pain as he landed on his wound. "What do you propose?"

Benedict rubbed a hand over his chin. "We need to discover how deep the corruption goes. First, we need to find out who is running the workhouse, since someone had to give permission for the British Army to use them for unloading the smuggled goods."

"Agreed," Emmett responded. "Furthermore, we need to find out who is serving on the parish's vestry. After all, that committee is responsible for the workhouse and conditions of the poor."

"The vestry is also informed when the customs officers will board the ship," Simeon shared. "If the smuggling occurs the night before, there is a chance that the officers are not culpable in these crimes."

"That is a big 'if'," Emmett contended. "How could they not

know of the smuggling?"

Jonathon stood and stretched from side-to-side. "First thing tomorrow, I will inform my uncle of Allister's deceit, and I have no doubt that he will seek out the general in charge of the fort."

"Remember, without proof, it will be his word against ours," Simeon said.

Benedict rose. "If you will excuse me, I will go to my rented room for a few hours of sleep before we return to London."

Emmett lifted a brow in disbelief. "You rented a room at The Frisky Hound?"

"It is much too dangerous to travel to London at night," Jonathon answered. "We will leave at first light." He smirked. "After all, we want to be well rested for Martha's ball."

"Martha is having a ball?" Simeon asked with interest.

Benedict grinned. "She is."

"You are not invited," Emmett mumbled under his breath.

Simeon's eyes narrowed. "As her fiancé…"

"Will you stop saying that?" Emmett exclaimed, glaring at him. "You are not her fiancé anymore."

"We will see," Simeon replied simply.

Shaking his head in annoyance, Emmett turned his attention back to Benedict and Jonathon. "Would you like to ride in my coach back to town?"

"No, I have my horse," Jonathon said. "Besides, won't you have Johnny and his mother on your return trip?"

"I will," he confirmed, "but my coach is spacious."

Benedict chuckled. "I could ride with Jonathon, or I could spend time in an enclosed space with a doctor, an unfamiliar woman, and a little boy. I wonder, which will be more comfortable?"

"Point taken," Emmett responded with a smile. "If you change your mind, I will be sleeping at the hospital."

"We won't change our minds," Jonathon said with a tip of his head as he opened the door. "See you at the ball."

❦ 23 ❦

STARING BACK AT HER REFLECTION IN THE MIRROR, MARTHA couldn't believe what she was seeing. She looked and felt every bit the part of the English gentlewoman she was supposed to be. Her hair was piled high on her head, blonde curls cascading down her back, with pearls woven through it.

Standing, she smoothed down the white ball gown that Eliza had commissioned for her. She was certain it must have cost a small fortune. The gown had a square neckline and flecks of green emeralds sewn into the bodice, creating a dazzling display of sparkling color when the gems caught the light.

For the first time, Martha felt as though she belonged in this world and was not the interloper she had always believe. A world that she had been born into, but had no right to be in. Perhaps this life would not be as terrible as she had imagined. She had beautiful gowns, lived in a luxurious townhouse, and was able to spend her time helping patients at the hospital. That act of service gave her life purpose.

Emmett had shared that the charity hospital was a front so they could find information on the smuggling operations in Gravesend. Despite what he said, Martha knew that he enjoyed working as a physician and running his own hospital. Truth be told, she loved working beside him and seeing the light in his eyes as he helped his patients.

At the end of the Season, she would take her dowry and use it to fund the charity hospital. She would buy a small cottage and spend her time nursing the patients of Gravesend. Smiling, she was excited at last to see what the future held for her. She would spend her life serving others, which was something that made her happy; truly happy.

As she reached for her matching kid gloves, Martha was startled when the door was thrown open and slammed shut as Josette stormed into the room. "I opened your father's safe."

Pulling a glove onto her left hand, Martha asked, "And what did you discover?"

Josette's hands grew animated as she rushed to explain, "Your father spends money at an alarming rate and has no money left in his coffers."

Martha nodded. "That is not a surprise. My father is known for his extravagant ways."

"Your father owns multiple properties in Gravesend, including a sheep farm, of all things."

"A sheep farm?" Martha repeated as she started pulling on her other glove. "Did he inherit those properties from my uncle's estate?"

"No, they were purchased recently." Josette dropped down on the bed, her face grim. "How much do you know about your mother's death?"

With a perplexed look, Martha replied, "I was told she fell into a coma and her heart quit working."

"Your mother died just days after she inherited an estate in Liverpool," Josette shared.

"Yes, my great aunt's property," Martha mused. "Mother always spoke with fondness about spending summers in her youth in Liverpool."

Josette gave her a pained expression. "Your father sold the property."

"Why would he do that?" she asked in shock. "It has been in our family for centuries."

"Legally, that property belonged to your father, since they were married, but if your mother passed before she inherited, then it would have gone to you." Josette gave her a look of pity as she smoothed out her pale pink ball gown.

Martha cringed as she realized that her mother had died only days after she outlived her usefulness. But would her father be so cruel as to resort to murder?

"There is more," Josette continued.

Lowering herself onto the dressing table chair, Martha sensed she was not going to like what Josette was about to reveal. "I am ready."

"With that newfound money, your father bought those properties in Kent, despite owing multiple creditors large sums of money," Josette said. "Within a month of the purchases, his ledgers showed large deposits, but none of his properties are showing income."

Furrowing her brow, Martha asked, "So, how is my father earning these large sums of money?"

Josette shook her head. "I don't know, but it sounds like your father may be involved in illegal activities."

"That doesn't make any sense. He is an earl," Martha countered. "What kind of activities could he be involved in?"

As Josette opened her mouth to respond, a knock on the door interrupted their conversation. "Enter," Martha commanded.

A finely-dressed Lord Waterford pushed open the door, and his eyes sought her out. "Are you ready for your ball?"

Rising gracefully, Martha answered, "I am."

Lord Waterford turned his gaze towards Josette, his eyes holding irritation. "Your services are not required tonight, Miss Josette. I will accompany my daughter."

"But Father…" Martha's voice faded as Josette shot her a pointed look.

She watched in surprise as Josette rose from the bed and curtsied. "As you wish, my lord."

"Father, will you give me a moment before we depart?" She stretched her lips into what she hoped resembled a smile and not a grimace.

Her father tipped his head towards her. "Of course. I will wait for you in the entry hall."

Martha waited for the click of the door to confirm it was shut before turning to Josette. "I don't know which was odder, my father dismissing you for this evening, or you going along with it."

Josette stepped closer with her hand up. "Hear me out. I don't know what your father is up to, but I will still be at the ball."

Martha glanced at the door with a frown. "Why would my father not want my companion to accompany me to a ball? It doesn't make sense."

Josette smiled at her. "Do not fret. You will have an enjoyable time at the Duke of Remington's townhouse."

"The ball is at the duke's townhouse?"

"It is," Josette confirmed as she walked towards the door. "I will see you at the ball, Lady Martha."

A short time later, Martha sat across from her father in the closed carriage and fixed her gaze out the window, watching the street lamps as they passed by. Her face was expressionless. After what she'd just heard, she had no intention of engaging in a polite conversation with her father.

Lord Waterford broke the silence. "You look beautiful, dear."

"Thank you," she replied, barely sparing him a glance.

He cleared his throat. "I heard you were forced to spend the evening in a convent."

"It is true," she admitted as she faced him. "By the time we finished with the line of patients, the sun was starting to dip in the sky, so it was not safe to travel back to London."

Her father's lips tipped down in disapproval. "I have decided your time would be better suited staying in London with me, rather than traveling to help in a disease-ridden hospital."

"I have no intention of stopping," Martha replied through gritted teeth.

He gave her a stern look. "You promised to give me one Season, but you are failing to uphold your end of the bargain."

"I certainly am not," she defended.

Adjusting his black superfine coat, Lord Waterford pressed, "What if gentlemen come to call, and you are not at home to receive them?"

"Our deal was that I would come to London for one Season. Nothing was said about receiving gentleman callers," she countered.

"How will you entertain offers of marriage if…"

She cut him off. "You know I have no intention of getting married."

Lord Waterford stared at her for a long moment before saying, "Regardless, if you want your dowry at the end of the Season, then you must be present at the balls and soirées."

Turning her head back to the window, she didn't feel the need to respond to her father but instead watched the carriages as they lined the street leading to the Duke of Remington's townhouse.

"I have decided it is in your best interest to fire Miss Josette," her father announced unexpectedly. "The household staff informs me that she has been stealing from me."

Martha laughed. "Josette is not stealing from you."

Her father's eyes grew guarded as he attempted to press his point. "Were you aware that your companion sneaks out in the early morning hours and goes for a ride?"

"Are you spying on her?" Martha asked, already knowing the

answer. Her father must have hired the man Lord Morgan caught spying on them.

"Of course not," he said smoothly with no indication he was lying.

"I am keeping Miss Josette as my companion," she stated firmly.

The carriage slowed to a stop. Sitting in the darkness of the long drive, surrounded by trees and shrubs, they waited in line to be delivered to the entrance. Martha decided to shift the conversation to another topic.

"Remind me again how Mother died."

"She died from consumption," he said with a sad smile. "The last words that she uttered were about your welfare."

More lies. Martha pursed her lips. "I thought you said that Mother died from laudanum addiction."

Blinking rapidly, her father answered, "Actually, it was a combination of both."

"I see," she said deliberately, knowing that her father was lying to her again. She decided to ask another question. "Have you ever been to Gravesend?"

Her father shook his head. "I have not." He gave her a curious look. "Why do you ask?"

"No reason," she answered. "I've enjoyed my time in Gravesend at the charity hospital and wondered if you'd been there."

Lord Waterford leaned forward and patted her leg. "Your mother would have been proud of the lady that you have become."

She gave him what she hoped was a gracious smile. It was difficult, because Martha now knew that her father was responsible for her mother's death. But why? How did he benefit from murdering her?

She was no simpleton. Her father was using her, just as he had in the past, and she knew he had no intention of honoring their agreement. Again, she had no idea why. Either way, she would not spend another day with him. Tomorrow, she would visit Eliza and never see her father again.

The coach stopped again, and a footman opened the carriage door. Placing her hand into his outstretched hand, Martha exited the carriage and walked up the steps towards the stately home of the Duke of Remington.

WITH HER HAND ON HER FATHER'S ARM, MARTHA HELD HER head high as she walked into the ballroom. As their names were announced, she could see Eliza walking straight towards her, with Benedict following close behind. She started to remove her hand from her father's arm, but his free hand came up and held it tightly in place. Tilting her head, she gave him a questioning look, but he kept his gaze straight ahead.

Fortunately, Eliza approached them and pulled her into a tight embrace. Taking advantage of her nearness, Martha whispered, "I believe my father murdered my mother."

"Just keep smiling," Eliza murmured through clenched teeth. She released her and took a step back. "You look beautiful, Martha. That dress is exquisite."

"Thank you for commissioning it for me," she responded graciously.

"It is good to see you again, Lady Martha," Benedict addressed with a slight bow.

Martha curtsied. "Thank you, Lord Lansdowne."

Eliza smiled up at her father as she looped her arm through Martha's. "Lord Waterford, may I borrow your daughter for a moment?"

Martha was sure he would say no, but his face grew expressionless.

"You may, but bring her back before the first dance," he instructed.

"I will. Also, you may enjoy the card games that are being played upstairs," Eliza suggested as she began leading her towards the opposite side of the room.

However, instead of stopping, she continued walking, keeping a smile on her face as she greeted her guests. When they arrived at a side hall, Eliza pulled her into a small, fashionably-furnished room. Turning to face her, she placed a finger up to her lips.

Within a few moments, Benedict entered with Jonathon close behind. After the door was closed, they turned their keen gazes towards Eliza.

Without preamble, she shared, "Martha believes her father murdered her mother."

Jonathon's eyes burned with intensity. "Do you have proof of this?"

Martha shook her head. "No, but I caught him in a lie about how my mother died."

"Lord Beckett also found the circumstances around your mother's death suspicious and has launched an investigation into her death, as well as your uncle's and cousin's," Benedict informed her.

Frowning, Martha crossed her arms over her chest. "Why was I not informed of this?"

Jonathon sat in an upholstered armchair. "We have reason to believe that…" His voice trailed off as Lord Morgan opened the door and slipped in.

Morgan gave him a curt nod. "Sorry I'm late. I was dealing with scheming mothers," he remarked before his eyes turned to her. "Lady Martha, are you all right?"

"I am," she replied with a reassuring smile. "However, I just

LAURA BEERS

learned that everyone in this room except me knew my father was a murderer."

Morgan gave her a sheepish smile. "I was informed of that, as well."

"Again," she said, raising an eyebrow, "why was I not informed?"

"To protect you," Eliza assured her.

Before she could reply to that ridiculous statement, Jonathon spoke up, "As I was saying, we have reason to believe that your father murdered his brother and nephew to gain access to the earldom. He was heavily in debt to several gambling halls and needed the income."

Benedict joined his wife and added, "Currently, we are under the assumption that your father killed your mother to silence what she knew, because it doesn't appear that he financially benefited from her death."

Martha huffed her disbelief. "Make no mistake. My father benefited from my mother's death. She died just two days after inheriting my great aunt's property. Josette discovered that my father bought property in Gravesend with that newfound money, including a sheep farm."

"Did you say a sheep farm?" Benedict repeated, surprised.

"I did," she affirmed, giving him an odd look.

"What are the chances that it is the same property that Mr. Martin discovered?" Benedict asked.

"It feels like too much of a coincidence to ignore." Eliza cast her a worried glance. "After the ball, you will go home with your father, and I will come and retrieve you."

Martha raised an eyebrow. "Does 'retrieve me' mean I have to crawl out my window and scale down the wall?"

Eliza smiled. "This is precisely why I taught you how to scale a building."

There was a soft knock on the door before it was pushed open. Josette slipped through the door and closed it behind her.

"Sorry I'm late," she apologized. "I had to avoid being seen by Lord Waterford."

Martha watched as Morgan's eyes perused the length of Josette's pale pink ballgown, admiration clear on his face. Expecting a compliment, she was surprised to hear him clear his throat and say, "Don't fret. I ensured that Lady Martha stayed protected while you were shirking your responsibilities."

Josette gave him an exasperated sigh. "Lord Waterford is trying to keep me away from Martha, and I haven't figured out his intentions yet."

"Do you think he has caught you snooping?" Eliza asked.

"No, I have been careful," Josette assured her, "but he tried to do the same thing with Dr. Maddix."

"He did tell me that the staff informed him you'd been stealing from him," Martha interjected. "He wants me to fire you."

Josette frowned. "I didn't steal anything."

"I know," Martha reassured her.

Eliza's eyes turned calculating. "Martha, it is not safe for you to remain in Lord Waterford's townhouse anymore."

Martha nodded. "I agree, especially since my father has hired someone to spy on us." She frowned. "Why do you suppose he invited me in the first place?"

"Perhaps he truly missed you?" Benedict asked.

"That is definitely not the reason," she stated, shaking her head. "My father has never been described as sentimental."

"Either way," Eliza said, "until we discover his true intent, we will keep you safe."

Jonathon rose from his seat and addressed her. "Now, you will need to go and enjoy the ball being held in your honor."

Placing the palm of her hand on her stomach, Martha let out a shallow breath. "There are entirely too many people in your father's ballroom. I was expecting more of an intimate affair."

Benedict chuckled. "Eliza's mother never does anything halfway."

She was curious about that. "Why did the Duchess of Remington host the ball?" Martha asked.

Eliza smiled broadly, and Martha was briefly distracted by her exuberance. "The prince regent is my father's second cousin and agreed to stop by for the ball, assuming it was close to the palace."

Jonathon chuckled. "You forgot to mention that our step-mother was also a childhood chum of Prinny's. He could hardly say no to her request."

Another knock at the door interrupted them. Josette opened it, and Martha was relieved to see Emmett standing in the door-way. In that moment, she realized how happy she was to see him. He was in full dress, his brown hair well-groomed, but it was the way his eyes lit up when he saw her that made her heart fill with joy.

Ignoring everyone else in the room, Emmett walked up to her, reaching for her gloved hand. He brought it slowly up to his lips as he offered her a dashing smile, one that made her knees grow weak.

"When I saw Eliza dragging you in here, I was worried about you. I feared that the crush in the room was too much for you to bear."

"I did not drag her in here," Eliza mumbled under her breath.

Emmett's lips twitched at Eliza's words, but he kept his gaze fixed on her. "The dancing is about to start, and I was hoping you would allow me to be your first partner."

"I would like that very much," Martha replied, finding it nearly impossible to look away from his tender gaze. Why did he look at her with such care, making her feel infinitely adored?

Accepting his outstretched hand, she placed her arm in the crook of his elbow and allowed him to escort her out to the ball. Tilting his head, Emmett informed her, "I have taken it upon myself to secure you dance partners that will treat you with the respect you deserve."

"I don't wish to dance with anyone else," she stated honestly.

Emmett chuckled. "If that is the case, then we can announce our engagement tonight."

Her steps faltered, fearing she'd misheard him.

He turned to face her with a devilish twinkle in his eyes. "You are fun to tease, Lady Martha." Turning his gaze back towards the dance floor, he added, "Unfortunately, it is only appropriate for me to dance once with you tonight, and I have no doubt that you will have a line of suitors hoping to dance with you."

Martha tightened her hold on his arm. "This is a charade that I don't wish to continue."

Placing his free hand over hers, Emmett replied, "You can do anything you set your mind to. What seems like a mountain of an obstacle today will barely be of consequence tomorrow."

"I fear that I may disappoint you," she murmured as she looked up at him.

Emmett stopped and turned to face her, his eyes holding an intensity that she did not understand. "Oh, Martha," he breathed out, "nothing you ever do could disappoint me."

A deep clearing of a throat interrupted them. Looking over, Martha saw Jonathon and Hannah standing there with bright smiles on their faces.

Martha looked down at Hannah's large belly before she curtsied. "You are glowing, my lady."

"Thank you, *my lady*," Hannah drawled. "Why don't we drop our titles from here on out?" Her eyes took in Martha's dress and widened in surprise. "Your dress is exquisite."

Martha beamed at her friend. "Eliza commissioned it for me."

Before Hannah could respond, Martha saw Rachel, the Marchioness of Downshire, walking straight towards her. As she

LAURA BEERS

prepared to curtsy, Rachel pulled her into a tight embrace. "I am so happy for you, Lady Martha," she proclaimed.

Lord Downshire, a tall, handsome gentleman, stood back with his ward, Miss Emma Pearson, a beautiful young lady with deep brunette hair. He tipped his head graciously when her eyes landed on him.

"Lady Martha, it is a pleasure to see you again," he stated in a beautiful baritone voice.

Martha curtsied. "Thank you, Lord Downshire."

He gestured to his ward. "I presume you remember my ward, Miss Emma, from my niece's christening."

"I do," Martha replied. Addressing Emma, she asked, "How are you enjoying the ball?"

"My master won't let me dance," she answered, with a mischievous look in her eye.

Lord Downshire let out an aggravated sigh. "Please stop referring to me as 'master'. I am your guardian."

Emma clasped her hands demurely in front of her. "Same thing," she replied. "My *guardian* won't let me dance with anyone."

"That is not true," he replied. "You are free to dance with gentlemen that I believe are worthy of your notice."

"You glower at the gentlemen that are brave enough to ask me to dance," Emma pointed out.

"That is because you are only seventeen and too young to entertain a suitor," he declared flatly.

"I will be eighteen next month," Emma said, smiling, as her eyes roamed over the crush. "And my apologies, I forgot that a dance is synonymous with a marriage proposal."

"Emma..." Lord Downshire started before he turned his frustrated gaze back to his wife. "Rachel, can you please explain to Emma, *again*, why we feel that seventeen is too young to entertain an offer of marriage?"

Rachel laughed and brought her hand up to her mouth. "We

256

have enjoyed having Emma in our household. Her humor is so much like her brother's."

"It is good to see you, cousin," Emmett said as he embraced Rachel. "I was worried you wouldn't make the trip because of your condition."

"My condition?" Rachel repeated back. "Women have been having babies since the dawn of time. Besides, I am only three months along."

Without warning, the room grew silent as the prince regent was announced, along with his entourage. Wearing full dress, Prinny regally entered the room as everyone bowed respectfully.

The Duke of Remington approached the prince regent in the center of the room, and they began conversing. After a few moments, the duke nodded and turned to address the group.

"His royal highness wishes to honor Lady Martha by partnering the first dance of the evening with her." He paused dramatically before adding, "He has chosen the waltz."

Martha sucked in a breath but felt immediate relief when Emmett's hand sought out her own. He leaned in and said, "This is your moment; seize it."

Releasing his hand, Martha stepped out from the crowd and approached Prince George hesitantly. Once she was close, she dropped into a low curtsy and waited for him to approach. He approached, and she continued to keep her gaze lowered.

"Lady Martha, will you honor me with this dance?"

Nodding, she slowly rose. As she lifted her gaze towards his, to her surprise, she saw Prinny's eyes were filled with kindness. He stepped closer and ever so gently placed his hand on her waist and lifted her left hand. As the music filled the ballroom, he started dancing with her.

After a moment, she willed herself to relax, even though she was in the arms of a prince... a man... a man that wasn't Emmett.

Prinny smiled down at her. "You dance splendidly, Lady Martha."

"Thank you, your highness," she murmured.

His gaze left hers as his eyes roamed the ballroom. "I am glad that we have this moment alone, because I would like to commend you for your bravery."

"My bravery?" she asked, very much confused.

He brought his gaze back to scan her face, his eyes now reflecting compassion. "Lady Lansdowne spoke to me at length about your past. She has pushed for reform on punishments for people who are caught trafficking women."

"I had no idea."

"You managed to stay alive, against all the odds, in spite of the vile practices imposed on you. That proves to me that you are a fighter," he said.

She ducked her head, knowing she was unworthy of his praise. "I did nothing spectacular, your highness."

"You are wrong," he contended. "From what I understand, you are now helping others in a charity hospital. Your efforts should be applauded... and rewarded."

Not understanding what he meant, she remained silent.

A determined look came to his face as Prinny informed her, "I will ask my prime minister, Lord Liverpool, to bring forth a bill in Parliament that condemns trafficking of women and sets longer prison sentences against criminals who abduct our women to sell to brothels." He offered her a gentle smile. "I had not considered the plight of these women until I heard your story."

"Thank you," she managed to whisper, as she tried to reign in her emotions.

Prinny nodded. "By sharing your story, you have proven to those men that you are stronger than they are. You outwitted them."

The music came to an end, and Prinny released her, stepping back. She dropped into a curtsy and was rendered speechless when he tipped his head towards her. "It was an honor to meet you, Lady Martha."

Watching the prince regent as he left the ballroom, Martha could not believe what had just transpired. Not only had she just danced with a prince, but he had applauded her survival and was doing something to prevent other women from having to endure what she had.

Turning back to where she had left Emmett, she saw he was smiling proudly at her. Returning to him, she realized that he had been right all along… she was more than just a survivor; she was a fighter. She may not have been born strong, but she was made strong through her trials and experiences. And that is something she was proud of.

❧ 24 ❧

BEFORE SUNUP THE NEXT MORNING, MARTHA HEARD HER bedchamber window open as she packed a satchel full of clothing. The small fire still burning in the hearth and the moonlight streaming through the window helped her move about her room.

Turning towards the sound, she saw Eliza climbing through, dressed in men's clothing. Expecting to see Benedict come through as well, she was surprised when he did not appear. "Where's Benedict?" she asked quietly.

"On the ground," Eliza answered. "Are you ready?"

"I am." She was also dressed in men's clothing to make it easier to climb down the wall.

As she took a step closer to the window, they heard a loud knock on her door. With wide eyes, she turned to Eliza but discovered she was already hiding behind the floor-length drapes. Tossing her satchel under the bed, she jumped onto it and pulled the blanket up to her chest.

"Come in," she answered, trying to sound sleepy.

The door opened, and her father stood in the doorway with the light of the hall illuminating his body. "Did I wake you?" he asked in concern.

Martha kept her head on her pillow. "No. I am having a difficult time falling asleep."

"I am not surprised," her father acknowledged with pride. "I have no doubt that the ton will be talking about tonight for some time."

"I suppose so," she responded simply, hoping her father would leave her room.

Instead, he entered and sat down on the edge of the bed. "You did well, my daughter. I am proud of you."

"Thank you," she replied. "Now, if you don't mind, I am tired from tonight's festivities."

Lord Waterford smiled tenderly at her. "I understand perfectly." He stood up, bent down, and kissed her cheek. She could smell strong spirits on his breath. "Tomorrow, there is someone I wish you to meet. I believe you two would suit."

"Of course," she agreed, knowing she had no intention of meeting this suitor. "Good night."

Glancing down at her shirt, his brows furrowed slightly. "Are you wearing a man's shirt?"

"I am," she responded quickly. "I find I prefer a shirt over a nightgown."

He frowned. "That is an unusual habit. One that I wish you would break."

"Yes, Father."

He gave her a long, puzzled stare before he turned to leave, but his foot brushed against something under the bed. "What is this?" he asked as he leaned over and pulled out her satchel.

She sat up and attempted to grab it, but Lord Waterford held it out of her reach. "I think we should open up this bag, don't you?" He placed his hand in and pulled out a handful of her gowns. "Why do you have gowns in a bag?"

Martha recognized the moment that her father figured it out when he glanced towards the opened window then back down to the satchel. Without a word, he grabbed her blanket and yanked it back, revealing her trousers and boots. Tossing the bag across the room, he shouted, "You were going to run away again! Weren't you?"

"I am," she answered, feeling no need to deny it.

"No, you are not! I forbid it!" he exclaimed, pointing his finger towards the ground.

"You cannot forbid anything," she asserted as she rose from her bed. "I am of legal age to make my own choices."

His eyes narrowed at her words. "If you leave, you will be walking away from your dowry."

"I understand."

Her father had left the door open, and his shouting had attracted some of the household staff. They began to gather outside her door.

Lord Waterford took two powerful strides and stood above her. "You are not going anywhere."

Dropping her gaze, she turned to provide herself greater distance.

His hand snaked out and grabbed her upper arm, squeezing tightly.

"Let me go," she demanded.

"No," he grunted as he leaned closer to her. "I wanted to do this the easy way, but it appears that you are not going to be reasonable."

"I beg your pardon?"

Letting her arm go, her father took a step back but still stayed close. "I was going to make the announcement at the end of the Season, but you have left me with no choice."

"What announcement?"

Her father adjusted his waistcoat. "You are betrothed to Colonel Allister."

"No," she argued. "I will never marry him."

"You don't even know the man," he huffed.

Martha shook her head. "I have heard rumors about him, and he is not a good man."

He sneered at her. "I have heard rumors about you as well."

With horrified eyes, she declared, "I am leaving." As she leaned over to pick up her satchel, her father slapped her hard on the cheek, knocking her to the floor.

"You are not going anywhere!" her father exclaimed, his words filled with anger. "You will do as you are told this time."

Looking up in shock, Martha felt the familiar terror she'd had when he'd beaten her as a young child. Only this time it was different... she was different.

Holding her stinging cheek, she challenged, "I am not the scared little girl that you remember."

She started to rise, but her father crouched down and grabbed a handful of her white shirt. "Everything that I have done is because you did not marry Baron Whitehall." He shoved her back down to the ground. "You ruined everything."

Meeting his hardened gaze, she stated, "If you recall, I did not want to marry him. Baron Whitehall was older than you were."

Her father shook his head slowly as he straightened from his position. "I don't care about what you wanted. You are my daughter and are mine to do with as I please."

"No," Martha contended as she rose slowly. "I may be your daughter, but you have no hold over me."

A small, cruel smile came to his lips. "Are you sure about that?"

Hesitantly, she asked, "What did you do, Father?"

"Nothing that wasn't within my rights." He adjusted his waistcoat as he shared, "I informed the constable that Miss Josette stole from me, and she has just been carted away to Newgate."

"What did you say she stole?"

"A family heirloom."

Martha glared at him. "Why would you do that?"

With a glance over his shoulder, Lord Waterford smirked at the footmen. "You left me no choice," he stated, bringing his gaze back to her. "Miss Josette never left your side."

"That is her job. She is my companion," she asserted.

Her father ordered over his shoulder, "Close the door, but stay close." He gestured that she should sit in one of her upholstered armchairs. When she didn't move, he frowned, then sat in a chair near her. "When Lady Lansdowne sent a missive informing me that you were still alive, I had mixed feelings, but I knew you might come in handy one day."

Martha rolled her eyes. "I am glad I could oblige you."

Disregarding her sarcasm, he pressed on, "But I knew I needed to take you away from Lord Lansdowne's protection and be sure you would rely solely on me." He pressed his lips together. "I had not anticipated your close association with Miss Josette or with Dr. Maddix."

"They are my friends," she stated, not bothering to keep the annoyance out of her voice, "something that you must not be familiar with."

Fury flashed in her father's eyes, but he remained seated. "I am not a fool, daughter. Anyone with eyes could have seen the affection you and Dr. Maddix held for each other at the ball." He flicked his wrist at her. "I even saw you holding hands with him."

Feeling the need to defend herself, she responded, "He was encouraging me."

"Encouraging you to the bedchamber," her father mumbled under his breath.

"Father!" she exclaimed in outrage. "You have spoken out of turn."

Lord Waterford's eyes held no apology as he stood. "Tonight, at the ball, I knew I needed to speed up my plan."

"Your plan?" she asked.

He took a powerful step towards her. "For you to marry Colonel Allister."

"I will not," she declared.

"You have no choice." A cruel sneer came to his face. "I lost you in a gambling bet at The Cloven Hoof."

"You lost me?" she repeated in outrage. "You don't own me."

Her father took another step until he towered over her. "You are right. You belong to Colonel Allister now."

Shifting her gaze towards the curtain, she was pleased to see that Eliza's form wasn't visible. Martha had no doubt that her friend could take care of herself, but murdering an earl in front of witnesses would not be the best move.

Meeting her father's ire, Martha took a few steps back towards the table where her reticule lay. In it was a pistol that she could use to help her escape out the window, and if she started scaling the wall, she had no doubt that Benedict would keep her safe as soon as she made it to the ground.

Her father chuckled dryly. "You are becoming too predictable." He walked swiftly to the table, opened the reticule, and pulled out the overcoat pistol. "The maids informed me that you carried a pistol."

Placing it into the pocket of his black dress coat, her father dropped her reticule back onto the table. "If you don't behave, I will ensure that Miss Josette and Dr. Maddix meet an untimely death."

Knowing that her father vastly underestimated her friends was a relief. She had no doubt that they could take care of themselves. However, she needed a distraction so she and Eliza could escape out the window.

"I will do as you wish... assuming you do not hurt my friends."

Her father shook his head. "I had hoped to spare you this pain, but you have left me no choice."

"What are you referring to?" she asked, backing up towards the window. "What pain?"

"You are too clever for your own good," he said, his words holding no praise, only contempt. "You asked too many questions in the carriage, leading me to believe that you would not sit idly by and do my bidding."

Her heel hit the wall, and she swiftly turned towards the window. Grabbing the sill, she started to step up onto the frame, but her father caught her waist and pulled her back.

"Men!" he shouted over his shoulder. "Lady Martha is ready to depart." As she struggled in his arms, the footmen ran into the room. "We feel it is in your best interest to have a holiday before your wedding," he said next to her ear.

"No!" she exclaimed as she thrashed about. "I will not marry him."

A footman came closer to her with a large sack in his hand. She opened her mouth to scream, but before she heard her voice, everything went black.

STORMING INTO ELIZA'S DRAWING ROOM, EMMETT'S HAND WAS clenched around the missive that had just been delivered to his townhouse. As soon as he saw Eliza, he shouted, "What in blazes do you mean Martha has been abducted?"

Eliza, still dressed in men's clothing, gave him a sad smile. "Per our plan, I went to retrieve her, but her father prevented her escape."

His eyes were frantic as he glanced around the room, seeing Benedict, Adrien, and Jonathon were all assembled. "We will just go demand that Lord Waterford release his daughter," he declared.

"It's not that easy," Benedict informed him as he stood and walked over to the drink tray.

Crumbling the missive in his hand, Emmett shouted, "It *is* that easy. I will do whatever is necessary to ensure Martha is released unharmed."

"I applaud your efforts, but that won't work," Jonathon said, pausing, "at least right now."

Eliza rose slowly and stepped closer to him. "Lord Waterford intends Martha to wed Colonel Allister."

"What?" he roared. "No! He will have to kill me first." Spinning around, he moved towards the door intending to call on Lord Waterford.

"Stop," Adrien ordered from across the room. "Do not walk out of this room. You are acting mulish, and that could get you killed."

Turning to face Adrien, his eyes narrowed. "You do not get to dictate my actions."

"No," Lord Beckett stated from behind him, "but I do."

"With all due respect, sir…" he began.

Lord Beckett spoke over him, "Sit down, Dr. Maddix. There is much we have to discuss before you go half-cocked all over England."

Benedict walked over and handed him a drink. Accepting the snifter, Emmett begrudgingly sat on a camelback settee.

"I have just confirmed that Lord Waterford obtained a special license from the Archbishop of Canterbury for Lady Martha and Colonel Allister to wed," Lord Beckett confirmed as he placed a large file onto the table.

"What?" Emmett shouted as he jumped up from his seat, spilling his drink onto his hand.

Ignoring his outrage, Lord Beckett shared, "I have also

spoken to the magistrate about getting Miss Josette released from Newgate."

"Why is Miss Josette in Newgate?" Emmett asked Eliza.

Leaning forward in her seat, Eliza said, "When I went to retrieve Martha…"

As she continued the story behind Martha's abduction, Emmett found the anger raging inside of him. When she finished, silence descended over the room, and all eyes were on him. Ignoring their gazes, he placed his drink onto the table, rose, and walked to the window.

Clenching his jaw, Emmett placed his hands on the window sill and leaned in. He'd failed Martha. He promised he would protect her, but he'd failed; just as he'd failed Eleanora.

He slammed his hand down onto the sill, ignoring the pain radiating up his arm. It was happening all over again, he admitted to himself as guilt plagued his thoughts.

Caught up in his own unbridled grief, he barely registered his own name being called. "Emmett." Not in the mood to talk, he closed his eyes and lowered his forehead to the window pane. "Emmett," his cousin repeated next to him.

"Rachel?" He tilted his head towards her. "When did you arrive?"

Lady Downshire gave him a compassionate look. "Eliza sent over a missive informing us about Martha's abduction." She took a step closer and lowered her voice. "It appears I was correct to assume that you would blame yourself."

"She told me last night that she thought her father had a role in her mother's death and I…" His voice hitched as he blinked back his tears. "And I was too busy enjoying the nearness of her when we were dancing to assess the threat."

"It's not your fault," she asserted.

He shook his head, feeling sick in his stomach. "It is," he declared. "I gave her my word that I would protect her, and I failed." He clenched his jaw tight. "I failed her just as I failed

Eleanora." His voice was weak, but his words were no less painful.

Her hand rested on his sleeve as she whispered, "You did not fail Eleanora, and you did not fail Martha."

Not believing her, Emmett kept his eyes straight ahead, but her next words surprised him. "Despite what you believe, you did not fail Eleanora. Colonel Allister did." Rachel's words grew more intense. "And as for Martha..." Her words trailed off, causing him to look up at her. He was surprised to see a smile on her face. "You have powerful friends now."

Shifting her gaze towards the group, her smile grew. "You have *Shadow, Hawk, Sunshine...*"

"My code-name is not *Sunshine*," Benedict growled.

"...Jonathon and Lord Beckett," Rachel listed. "We are all on a team."

"What about me?" Luke huffed from his position by Jonathon.

With a mischievous smile, she added, "And you have a tall, handsome, brooding marquess."

Emmett shook his head, still not fully believing her, but he turned around when he heard Eliza say, "You are not the only one that blames themselves for Martha's abduction." When his eyes caught her fiery gaze, she said deliberately, "Lord Waterford has no idea who he is messing with, and that will be the cause of his downfall."

Emmett's heart was lifted by her words. Eliza was right. He was not alone, and everyone in this room would risk everything to save Martha. It was different this time. Together, they would free Martha from her father's clutches.

With a decisive nod, he responded, "Let's bring Martha home."

Eliza gave him an understanding look. "And we will, because Martha is family."

"That she is," he agreed.

Lord Beckett opened the file as he asked, "When was Martha taken from her home?"

"The carriage drove out of town around six in the morning," Eliza confirmed.

"She has been gone for over three hours?" Emmett cried out in frustration as he glared at Eliza. "Why didn't you just attack her father and set her free when you were in her bedchamber?"

Not appearing the least bit offended, she explained, "When I was in Martha's room, I could have killed Lord Waterford with my dagger. However, footmen were loitering in the hallway, and I didn't bring my longbow."

Tossing up his hands, he pressed, "Then why not attack the carriage when it left Lord Waterford's townhouse?"

Benedict lifted his brow. "Have you ever attacked a moving carriage?"

Emmett shook his head. "No, I have not."

"While Benedict followed the carriage, I raced over to our townhouse, and asked Mr. Larson to trail after the carriage," Eliza shared. "Furthermore, Lord Morgan was already following the carriage as they left London."

Lord Beckett nodded in approval. "Excellent. Both are adept at espionage, and I am confident in their abilities to trail behind a carriage undetected."

"As am I," Jonathon stated. "In the meantime, we need to discuss the connection between Colonel Allister and Lord Waterford."

"That is where it gets interesting," Lord Beckett shared, opening the file onto the table. "The only time it appears that their paths cross is when they both serve on the vestry in Gravesend."

Adrien leaned forward in his seat. "How is that possible? A vestry is composed of land-owning members of the parish."

Reaching for a piece of paper, Lord Beckett explained, "Eight months ago, Colonel Allister bought The Cloven Hoof from Mr. Allen Davies, but only after Davies had been picked up by a press gang and impressed into the British Army."

"We need to talk to Mr. Davies," Jonathon said.

Lord Beckett frowned. "Unfortunately, that is impossible. After serving for one month under the command of Colonel Allister at the New Tavern Fort, he was killed during a routine training exercise."

"And did no one find that suspicious?" Benedict scoffed.

"Apparently not," Lord Beckett answered. "Multiple sources indicated that Mr. Davies was the leader of The Cursed Lot gang up to that point, but he routinely escaped capture."

Emmett walked over and sat in an upholstered armchair. "When was Colonel Allister appointed as a colonel in the British Army?"

"Ten months ago," Lord Beckett confirmed after looking at a sheet of paper. "The Royal Navy terminated his commission for his role in the death of Eleanora, but he was friends with Charles Lennox, the Duke of Richmond, who campaigned for him to become the governor over Gravesend and Tilbury Fort. Fortunately, despite his connections, the British Army rejected him as a potential governor but allowed him to purchase a commission as a colonel, placing him under the command of Sir John Floyd, who is the current governor of Gravesend and Tilbury Fort."

Eliza spoke up, "If Colonel Allister owns The Cloven Hoof, which is a known gambling den, then why was he allowed onto the vestry?"

"Good question," Lord Beckett said. "However, I can't answer that." Slipping out another piece of paper, he shared, "Furthermore, if it weren't for Miss Josette's ability to open a safe, my agents would have never discovered the properties that Lord Waterford owns in Gravesend."

"Isn't it public record who owns the property?" Emmett asked.

Extending the paper to Benedict, Lord Beckett explained, "It is, but Lord Waterford didn't put the titles under his name."

"Who owns the properties then?" Adrien asked.

Benedict lifted an eyebrow after reading the page. "Miss Martha Haskett."

Eliza leaned closer to her husband as she read the paper he was holding. "Martha legally owns all these properties, but her father, Lord Waterford, must act as her representative at the vestry."

"Why would Lord Waterford put properties in his daughter's name?" Jonathon pressed.

"I can't say for certain, but it is clear that something is afoot," Lord Beckett stated.

Now standing next to her husband, Rachel asked, "Where do we go from here?"

"Oh, no," Luke declared, putting his arm around her shoulders. "You are pregnant and cannot go storming into Gravesend to save Martha."

A look of defiance came to Rachel's eyes as she said, "Need I remind you…"

Her words faded when Mr. Larson stormed into the room. "Martha is being held at a sheep farm in Gravesend."

Emmett jumped up from his seat. "Let's go save her."

Benedict rose quickly and put his hand up to stop him. "No, we need to develop a plan first."

The image of Martha sitting on the ground, afraid and alone, came to Emmett's mind, causing a lump to form in his throat. Pushing down his emotions, his next words were unyielding. "I am going to save my Martha… now."

"*Your* Martha?" Jonathon asked.

Ignoring Jonathon, Emmett started towards the door.

Mr. Larson stepped into his path, stopping him. "You won't be in a position to help Martha if you are dead."

Taking a step closer towards Mr. Larson, Emmett met his firm gaze with the same intensity. "You don't scare me, Mr.

Larson." Proving he was slightly mad, he took a step even closer. "And if I have to go through you to save Martha, then so be it."

Blinking slowly, Mr. Larson gave him a long, hard look before stepping aside. "Good luck," he drawled.

"Thank you." He was nearly out the door when he was stilled by Mr. Larson's voice.

"Just so you know, Lord Morgan remained at the cottage to watch over Martha. A cutter was having its cargo removed, and they were storing the contraband inside the cottage." He paused, dramatically. "If you go now, I would guess you'll have to battle fifty men... alone."

Emmett stared at the door, knowing he could not save Martha alone. "You are right," he admitted reluctantly. "I need help."

Eliza spoke up from behind him, "You were going to get it whether you wanted it or not."

"If you had walked out that door, Jonathon and I were prepared to restrain you," Benedict said with confidence.

"I could have fought both of you," he replied, turning back around to face the group.

Jonathon humphed. "I doubt that. I have fighting moves that you have never seen before."

Adrien lifted his brow. "Fighting moves?"

Pulling down on his coat, Jonathon smirked. "My fighting is legendary."

"Now I know you are goading me," Adrien said. "I could thump you any day of the week."

Lord Beckett rose and frowned. "Gentlemen, if you will sit down, we can discuss a plan to retrieve Lady Martha."

Mr. Larson gestured that Emmett should go first. As he passed, Mr. Larson assured him, "No one in this room will stop until we get Lady Martha home safely."

The way Mr. Larson spoke those words, it was clear that he meant them. Regardless, he was not going to rest until he had Martha back in his arms.

25

MARTHA'S HEAD JERKED FORWARD, AND HER EYES SNAPPED open. As she tried to bring her hand up to her throbbing forehead, she realized her hands were bound in front of her.

Laying her head against the wall behind her, she took in her surroundings. It was a small bedchamber with a four-poster bed against the opposite wall. She sat near a darkened fireplace, and a writing desk rested near the window. Fortunately, the tattered drapes were opened, allowing light to filter through the broken panes of glass.

Taking a deep breath, Martha knew she needed to keep all her wits about her in order to aid in her own rescue. She had no doubt that Eliza and Emmett would come for her, and she would be ready for them.

Relaxing her hands, she began to wriggle and twist them until the ropes dropped in front of her. Martha rubbed her reddened left wrist. Not stopping to rejoice in her accomplishment, she jumped up and ran towards the window.

To her left, she saw a large, gated pasture filled with sheep. Turning her head, she saw a jetty and marshlands. This must be the sheep farm her father owned in Gravesend. At least, she assumed it was.

A bright, flashing light in the distance caught her attention. Doubting her eyes, she took a second look. To her surprise, she saw Lord Morgan laying in the long reeds looking through a telescope, the light reflecting off the glass. Giving him a quick nod, she saw him lower his telescope and disappear back into the reeds.

She pushed on the window, but it didn't budge. Running her hand along the frame, she discovered that it was nailed shut. Reaching down, she ripped a piece from her white shirt and wrapped it around her fingers. She attempted to pry the nails up with her fingers, but she was not successful. After many failed attempts, she stepped back and looked at the only other escape route; the door.

With determination on her brow, she walked over to the door and put her hand on the handle. She pushed it down, but the door did not budge. It was locked. Not ready to give up, Martha walked around the room and looked for anything that could help her.

Stopping at the desk, she opened each drawer and searched them meticulously. Finding nothing that would help her, she felt ready to give up until she opened the last drawer. Inside was a long, bronze letter opener. It was dull, but it was something.

Tucking the letter opener into the folds of her trousers, she was startled when the door was thrown open and slammed against the wall. Her father loomed in the doorway holding her satchel, and he did not appear pleased by her actions. Taking a step further into the room, he closed the door behind him and glared at her with venom.

Squaring her shoulders, Martha boldly stared at her father. She would not make this easy for him, regardless of the consequences.

"Why am I not surprised that you managed to escape your restraints?" Lord Waterford asked gruffly.

She shrugged, choosing to remain silent.

Tossing the satchel at her, he ordered, "I want you to change into a dress before you meet your betrothed."

"I am not marrying Colonel Allister."

Her father scoffed. "Yes, you are."

Martha placed the satchel on the desk and took a step back. "I refused to marry Baron Whitehall, and I refuse to marry Colonel Allister."

Closing the distance between them in two strides, her father grabbed her blonde hair, yanking her closer, his foul breath warm on her cheek. "I tire of your insolence, girl. Because of your actions, I was forced to resort to this."

"What actions?"

Shoving her back, he released her hair. "If you had married Baron Whitehall, he was prepared to pay me a generous sum of money. Since you ran away from your responsibilities, you left me no choice."

Rubbing the back of her head, Martha watched her father with trepidation. "What did you do?"

"I was raised in privilege as an earl's son, but my father forced me to become a vicar. What was worse, he expected me to live on the paltry income the parish allotted me." His eyes hardened and turned cold. "How was it fair that my elder brother lived in extreme wealth as the heir, while I was forced to live in poverty?"

Martha remained silent. There were no words to be said. She felt no pity for her father.

"Did you know your uncle refused to pay my gambling debts?" Lord Waterford ranted in disgust. "The high and mighty lord thought I should be responsible for my own debts."

Walking over to the desk, her father trailed his finger along the top as he watched her with disgust in his features. "If you had married the baron, everything would have been perfect."

"But I wouldn't have been happy," she replied, hoping to appeal to his compassion.

Lord Waterford gave her a look of utter disbelief. "That is not my concern."

"What happened after I eloped with Simeon?"

He shook his head. "Baron Whitehall was furious and sued me over breach of contract. Between the money I owed him and my other debts, I was over £25,000 in debt. I pleaded for my brother to help me."

"Did he?"

"No, he refused to pay, despite my many requests over the years for help." He frowned. "My own brother even told me to prepare to go to debtor's prison or be shipped to the colonies."

"What about Mother's inheritance from her father? I understand he left her a small fortune when he died."

"Spent."

Her mouth gaped open. "All of it?"

He cast her a disappointed look. "How else was I to maintain the lifestyle that I was accustomed to?"

Leaning on the window sill, she couldn't comprehend what he was telling her. "You were a vicar."

"Not by choice," he scoffed. "About eight months ago, I was unable to pay my household staff, and my creditors were demanding that I should be arrested for my outstanding debts." He met her gaze. "I asked my brother for help one last time."

Her eyes tracked his every move as she asked, "What did he say?"

"He allowed me and your mother to move in with him, but he told me that I made my own bed and that I should lie in it," he grunted as an evil glint came to his eyes. "Two weeks later, they were killed in a horrific carriage accident."

Her hand went up to cover her mouth. "You killed Uncle Theodore and my cousin Daniel?"

"No, I did not." He smirked. "I hired someone to stage a carriage accident."

"How could you?" she breathed.

"How could I?" he argued. "This is all your fault."

She shook her head. "No, Father. You killed your own brother and nephew."

"I had no choice," her father replied with no hint of remorse.

"Did you kill Mother?" she asked boldly.

He sighed. "I didn't want to kill your mother, but it was inevitable."

Her hands covered her mouth in disbelief, and she stepped back. "You did have a choice, and you killed her."

His glare intensified, but she refused to cower. "Your mother was too smart for her own good. She discovered my role in my brother's death. For two months, I kept her drugged with laudanum, but eventually, she died."

"Only after you obtained her aunt's property," she remarked in disgust.

Her father looked at her in surprise. "How did you discover that?"

Ignoring his question, she asked, "Was it worth it?"

"Yes," he growled back, "but it wasn't enough." Running a hand through his hair, the frown lines around his mouth deepened. "I had a bad run at cards and wasn't welcome back in the gaming halls in London. So, I sought out a pub in Gravesend that was known for high-stakes gambling."

"The Cloven Hoof?" she said, already knowing the answer.

Giving her another inquisitive glance, he answered, "Yes, but eventually I owed too much, and the owner tossed me out." He gave her a cold look. "That was until Colonel Allister took over the establishment and let me use you as collateral. After I lost you, we came to a new agreement."

"I don't understand. Why do you need me to marry Colonel Allister?" she pressed. "I have no money, and I am of little value to you."

A sly smile came to his lips. "You do have money."

"I beg your pardon?"

Her father took a step closer and loomed over her. "Your Uncle Theodore started asking about your welfare after you disappeared. Your mother and I informed him that you were sent to a boarding school in Bath. When he pressed again, we informed him that you'd started working as a governess for a family in Yorkshire."

His eyes scanned her face. "That seemed to satisfy my brother until last year. He demanded to see you and even threatened to go to the magistrate if you didn't come to visit him." He sneered. "I informed Theodore that you would be coming home for the Season, knowing he would be dead by that time."

Martha just stared at her father, not able to comprehend how evil he had become.

"Your uncle left £25,000 in an account to be used as your dowry. However, there was a stipulation that the money could only be withdrawn by you on your twenty-fifth birthday, assuming you chose not to marry."

Her mind reeled with the knowledge that she was entitled to so much money. "Why wasn't I notified about the funds?"

"My brother altered his will last year after a pesky Bow Street Runner kept asking questions about your disappearance," Lord Waterford explained as he dropped his hand and stepped back.

"Again, why wasn't I notified?" she asked. "You knew I was living with Lady Lansdowne."

Swiping a hand in front of him, he declared, "That money deserved to be mine." A small smile formed on his lips. "Lucky for me, I discovered Colonel Allister and I share similar interests."

"Similar interests?" she challenged with an uplifted brow. "You mean murder."

Unexpectedly, her father punched her left eye, knocking her to the floor. "You are nothing, you worthless chit." He crouched down next to her. "You will do as you are told, or you will die in this room."

Bringing her hand up to her throbbing eye, she asserted, "I will never consent to marry Colonel Allister."

"We shall see," he replied. He glanced down at her with disgust. "You look a fright. When I come back into this room, you'd better have yourself cleaned up."

EMMETT WATCHED SIMEON PACE BACK AND FORTH IN THE MAIN room of the charity hospital. Sighing, he turned to Benedict and asked, "Did we have to tell Mr. Martin?"

"We did," Benedict confirmed as his eyes tracked Simeon who was muttering to himself.

Jonathon spoke up from behind him. "Now you can understand how infuriating you were earlier."

"I apologize for that," Emmett replied. "Should I stop him?"

"Not yet," Adrien stated. "I made a bet with Jonathon that Simeon wouldn't acknowledge us for another ten minutes."

Benedict nodded. "That is a sound bet."

Simeon turned and faced them, annoyance was on his features. "I hear you, you know."

"I am no doctor, but I assumed you could hear us over your random mutterings," Adrien joked.

Simeon ran a hand through his hair. "I just can't believe that

Martha was abducted by her father to force her to marry Colonel Allister."

Benedict's authoritative voice took over the conversation. "We have given you enough time to process this information. Are you ready to go forward with the plan?"

Simeon's eyes grew wide. "It's a horrible plan."

Jonathon leaned up against the wall, completely undeterred by Simeon's negativity. "I admit, it's not one of our strongest plans, but it will get the job done."

"You want Dr. Maddix and me to stroll up to the Tilbury Fort and ask for a meeting with Sir John Floyd, the governor of Gravesend and Tilbury Fort," Simeon said in a mocking tone. "How do we know he is not conspiring with Colonel Allister?"

"We don't, but you are not going in alone," Benedict reminded him. "Adrien is going with you."

Simeon looked exasperated. "He is an earl and is incapable of handling the demands of espionage."

Jonathon laughed "I completely agree with you, Mr. Martin."

Lowering his voice, Emmett whispered to Benedict, "Are you sure we can't just have Mr. Martin sit this one out?"

Benedict shook his head. "No, Lord Beckett reminded us that this is a joint operation, and we need the Bow Street Runners' support on this."

"But he is so… frustrating," Emmett admonished.

"Bow Street Runners usually are," Benedict confirmed. Raising his voice, he added, "Lord Beckett has confirmed that General Floyd has been touring the forts in Scotland for the past four months and has just returned to his post at Tilbury Fort."

Jonathon leaned his shoulder against the wall. "We don't have time to wait for him to tour New Tavern Fort, nor do we have time to wait for him to go home to his estate in Gravesend. We need to approach him now and ask him to arrest Allister."

"As agents of the Crown, why don't you take Allister into custody?" Simeon questioned.

Sitting in a nearby chair, Adrien explained, "There is no protocol for agents to arrest military officers. Besides, right now we only have hearsay about Colonel Allister's role in the smuggling operation."

"And it is not illegal to own a pub," Jonathon reminded Simeon, "or to be on the vestry."

"What about all the people that Colonel Allister has killed?" Simeon pressed.

Emmett frowned. "According to the British Army, they were deserters, and that is punishable by death."

Simeon started pacing back and forth again, and Adrien's eyes tracked him before saying, "You have to trust us on this."

"Why can't we just storm the cottage and free Martha?" Simeon asked as he stopped pacing.

"Mr. Larson informed us that the cottage is well guarded, and Martha won't be safe until Colonel Allister and her father are taken into custody," Benedict reminded him.

Emmett was tired of the delay and pressed his fingers to the bridge of his nose. He thought about poor Eliza who had been in the coach waiting while they met with Simeon privately. They did not want to disclose her identity. At least Miss Josette was keeping Eliza company.

Frustrated, he raised his head and demanded, "Mr. Martin, if you are unable to complete this assignment, please let us know now so we may get on with it. A waterman is waiting to take us across the Thames."

"I am ready," Simeon said in a determined tone.

A short while later, Adrien, Simeon, and Emmett rode up a long-paved path that ended at the main entrance of Tilbury Fort. Three soldiers stood guard near the large, copper gate and watched them approach. Once they were within twenty yards, the soldiers aimed their muskets at them. The tall, lanky soldier ordered, "State your business at Tilbury Fort."

Emmett reined in his horse. "We are here to request an audience with General Floyd."

All the soldiers smirked at his words. "The general does not have time to meet with the likes of you," the shorter soldier responded.

"Will you at least ask General Floyd if he will meet with a Bow Street Runner?" Simeon asked.

"Turn around, or we will shoot you," the tall, lanky soldier demanded. "Our general is a busy man and no Bow Street Runner will deprive him of his time."

"What is the plan?" Simeon mumbled under his breath as his horse pawed at the ground.

Dismounting, Adrien took a few commanding steps forward. "Inform General Floyd that *Hawk* is here to see him."

The last guard spoke up, laughing. "You expect us to believe that you are *Hawk*?"

Adrien took another step closer, ignoring the cocking of their muskets. "You have ten minutes to alert General Floyd of my arrival, or *Shadow* and I will take this fort by force." His words were spoken so matter-of-factly that there was little doubt of the validity of his words.

Their eyes grew wide as they scanned over the marshes that surrounded the fort. The shorter soldier started to say, "Why would *Shadow*..." but his words were stilled when an arrow landed next to his boot.

Immediately, the soldier lowered his musket, and gave Adrien a salute. "Wait right here, sir." He pushed open a side door, and it slammed shut behind him. The other two soldiers had lowered their weapons as well and stood staring at Adrien with admiration.

Shaking his head, Simeon murmured, "You are *Hawk*." His

eyes tracked over the marshes. "And apparently are good friends with *Shadow*."

Adrien nodded without removing his piercing gaze from the soldiers. "I am."

"Right," Simeon stated dryly.

The soldier returned and indicated they should follow them into the fort. Leaving their horses at the stable, it was a long walk to the general's office, located in the back of a brick building along the fortification's wall. The soldier knocked on the door and pushed it open.

A tall man, dressed in full military uniform, lowered his quill and leaned back in his chair. He had a slender face, sharp nose, long sideburns, and his dark hair had started to recede.

"Which one of you claims to be *Hawk*?"

Adrien stepped forward, his commanding presence dominating the small office. "I am," he answered. "And I assume that you are General John William Floyd, the Governor of Gravesend and Tilbury."

"I am. However, I am reluctant to believe your claim to be the legendary spy."

Reaching into his waistcoat pocket, Adrien pulled out a small slip of paper and extended it towards General Floyd. "This is a letter from the prince regent himself confirming my identity."

General Floyd accepted the paper and read it then turned it over. He frowned as he extended the note back to Adrien. "All this note says is 'This man is who he claims to be' and has the prince regent's signature and seal."

While depositing the note back into his waistcoat, Adrien acknowledged, "Prinny is a man of few words."

General Floyd huffed as his lips twitched. "Yes, he is." His eyes gravitated towards Emmett and Simeon. "And are you agents as well?"

Emmett nodded and bowed respectfully. "I am Dr. Maddix."

"I have heard of you, Dr. Maddix," General Floyd stated as

he shuffled some papers in front of him. "I have read about your work as a doctor in the rookeries, and I am quite impressed. Now I understand that you are running a charity hospital near St. George's Church."

"That is mostly true," Emmett replied.

General Floyd took a paper and folded it. "You are a man of action, and I respect that." As he extended the paper towards the soldier in the room, he ordered, "Ensure this is mailed and leave us."

As the soldier saluted and walked out of the room, he closed the door behind him.

Simeon bowed as he introduced himself. "I am Mr. Simeon Martin. I am a Bow Street Runner."

"And why is a Bow Street Runner in my office?" the general huffed, unimpressed.

Giving an uneasy look to Emmett, Simeon said, "The Bow Street Runners were hired to help combat the smuggling in Gravesend…"

Interrupting him, General Floyd turned his gaze towards Adrien. "Perhaps *Hawk* can explain why a lowly Bow Street Runner is in my office."

"He is with me," Adrien asserted, taking a seat. "We are here because we have a problem with Colonel Allister."

"And that problem would be?" General Floyd asked with a guarded expression.

Emmett claimed the other open seat before he explained, "Colonel Allister is using his position as colonel of New Tavern Fort to smuggle contraband ashore and oppress the citizens of Gravesend. We have reason to believe he is the leader of The Cursed Lot gang."

The general's face broke out into a broad smile. "That's a great joke. I haven't had a good laugh in a while." When they didn't return his smile, it disappeared. "You can't be serious? Those charges are ludicrous."

"I'm afraid we are deadly serious, General," Adrien replied. "We have since learned that Allister owns The Cloven Hoof pub, which is a known gambling den."

Placing his arms onto his desk, General Floyd leaned forward. "That is distasteful, but it's not a crime to own a gambling den."

"A tunnel leads from The Cloven Hoof to the New Tavern Fort," Emmett shared. "And I was present when your soldiers forced members of the workhouse to unload cargo and store it in the sulphur mill."

A wave of General Floyd's wrist dismissed his comments. "The British Army contracts with the workhouse to help with mundane tasks around the fort. Most likely, you were confused with the task at hand."

"There was no confusion," Emmett replied, his gaze firmly latched onto General Floyd's. "It was a merchant ship, and they were lightening their load. I even saw contraband stacked in the fort's storage room."

General Floyd stiffened before a deep frown formed on his lips. "I have over two hundred soldiers stationed at the New Tavern Fort. If what you are saying is true, I have a bigger problem than just Colonel Allister." His eyes darted to the window before he asked, "What proof do you have that Allister is the leader of this Cursed Lot gang?"

"We are still gathering proof confirming Colonel Allister's role in The Cursed Lot gang," Simeon ventured, hesitantly.

General Floyd shot him a frustrated look. "You want me to arrest my colonel for crimes that you have no proof he committed?"

"Regardless of his status in The Cursed Lot gang, he commands the New Tavern Fort and is responsible for any smuggling that occurs under his command," Adrien asserted. "If a tunnel exists between The Cloven Hoof and ends inside the fort, that should certainly be enough evidence to arrest Colonel Allister while you investigate his crimes."

"Fair enough," General Floyd agreed, pushing back his chair. "I had planned to tour the New Tavern Fort today, anyway." As he rose, his gaze turned firm. "But if we do not find any proof of Colonel Allister's treachery, you will drop this matter for good. Understood?"

"Agreed," they said in unison as they stood.

As Emmett trailed behind, he knew that it was time to face his former commanding officer again. Only this time, he would come out the victor.

26

WALKING INTO THE COURTYARD OF THE NEW TAVERN FORT, Emmett's eyes darted towards the corner and found the gibbets and bodies had been removed. Red-coated soldiers were in line formation and going through drills, but they stopped to acknowledge their general as he walked by.

"Didn't you say there were bodies in a corner somewhere?" Adrien asked.

He pointed towards the right corner. "A few nights ago, three gibbets were displaying dead bodies."

"Where do you think they were put?" Adrien inquired.

Emmett shrugged. "I have no idea, but I assure you they were there."

Grinning, Adrien replied, "You don't need to convince me." He tilted his head towards General Floyd. "You just have to convince him."

As they followed the general into the officer's barracks, Emmett kept his eyes out for any signs of the soldiers that were present when he helped unload the ship's cargo. The general ducked into a room and stood to the side, waiting for them to enter.

Stepping into the room, he saw Colonel Allister standing behind his desk. His eyes sharpened when Emmett walked in. He sneered as he acknowledged him.

"Well, well, well, look who it is," he scoffed, "a man that is not fit to wear the Royal Navy uniform."

The general glanced curiously at him. "What is Colonel Allister referring to?"

Colonel Allister's sneer grew bigger. "General, were you not aware that Dr. Maddix was under my command when he refused to act on a direct order, shot me in the leg, and was court-martialed?"

General Floyd's eyes held censure, but Emmett decided to clarify a few things. Rather than cower in front of Allister, he drew himself up, determined to stand his ground.

"Everything the colonel has said is true, but he left out his part in the story. I refused his order and shot him in the leg because he murdered a girl when she refused his advances."

Colonel Allister's eyes grew hard. "That girl was mad."

"No," Emmett exclaimed, "that girl was named Eleanora, and she was an innocent." He took a strong step forward. "You killed her and had her body tossed overboard."

As Colonel Allister came around his desk, Adrien stepped up and stood next to him, his hand on the pistol in his waistband. "I warn you to not aggravate my friend, Colonel Allister," Adrien warned.

Colonel Allister chuckled dryly. "As if you could stop me."

General Floyd cleared his throat and took control of the conversation. "Allister, I have come personally, because these men have brought forth some mighty strong accusations against you."

"These men being…" Colonel Allister asked with a lifted brow.

"I work for the home office," Adrien stated.

Colonel Allister frowned. "I didn't catch your name."

Adrien's face grew expressionless. "I didn't give you one."

Simeon stepped up and introduced himself. "I am Mr. Simeon Martin, and I am a Bow Street Runner."

"Interesting," Colonel Allister grunted as he sat back down in his chair. "Another Bow Street Runner was poking around Gravesend just a few weeks ago." With the casual arrogance of one used to having power, he shifted his gaze towards the general. "I informed him that he should be careful. Apparently, he did not listen to me."

It was Simeon's turn to grow angry. "Did Mr. Jared Rogers come to you for help?"

Colonel Allister nodded. "He did." There was no discernable movement of his features, but his eyes grew cold, cruel. "Mr. Rogers was a little too eager, in my opinion, and it must have cost him his life."

Simeon tensed, his eyes sparking with fury. "Did you have something to do with his death?"

"Heavens, no!" Colonel Allister vehemently denied, but Emmett did not miss the faint smile that twitched on the corners of his lips.

General Floyd sat on a chair, appearing oblivious to the tension in the room. "Let's get back to these accusations," he said, shifting in his seat. "These men claim you are the leader of The Cursed Lot gang, and you have been using the British Army's resources to assist in smuggling contraband."

Colonel Allister wiped a hand over his face, appearing stunned. "I don't even know where to start, General." He turned his gaze towards Emmett. "I thought we let bygones be bygones after your court-martial. I had no idea you would stoop so low as to fling false accusations my way."

Emmett watched him with a wry smile. "You are not as clever as you think you are."

Leaning back in his seat, Colonel Allister clasped his hands in front of him. "Pray tell, if I am guilty of what you say I am, then please show me your proof."

"You have enslaved everyone who works at the workhouse. They are forced to help unload contraband from the ships before the customs official boards," Simeon accused.

Reaching under a stack of papers, Colonel Allister grabbed a file and placed it in front of him. Opening it, he pulled out a paper and extended it towards the general.

"Per your orders, we have contracted with the parish workhouse to supply jobs." When the general accepted the paper, he continued, "One of their duties is to unload supplies from ships and store them in specific storage rooms."

The general handed the paper to Simeon. "This report appears to be in order. The British Army likes to support the workhouse by offering them odd jobs."

Adrien leaned his right shoulder against the wall. "Who owns the workhouse building?"

Colonel Allister blinked slowly, not answering right away. "I cannot presume to know."

"Have you toured the workhouse recently?" Emmett asked.

Shaking his head, Colonel Allister replied, "No, I am much too busy."

"I have," Emmett stated. "The building is on the verge of collapse."

Accepting the paper back from Simeon, Colonel Allister placed it back into the file before saying, "I will ask Lieutenant Johnson to tour the building at his first availability."

"Who does the British Army pay for the odd jobs that the members of the workhouse perform?" Adrien pressed.

Colonel Allister gave a slow shake of his head. "I assume the wages are given to the parish vestry so they may continue their support of the workhouse."

"Most likely," Adrien agreed deliberately, "but wouldn't you know since you are on the vestry?"

"Why do you assume I am on the vestry?" Colonel Allister asked cautiously.

"The home office supplied me with that information," Adrien admitted with a one-shoulder shrug. "Another interesting fact I learned was that you own The Cloven Hoof."

Colonel Allister's eyes shifted nervously to General Floyd. "I did buy that property, but…"

"Don't you mean you took it?" Emmett asked.

"I purchased that property fair and square!" Colonel Allister shouted, slamming his fisted hand on the desk.

"Interesting," Simeon remarked, "the previous owner was rounded up by a press gang and died less than a month later during a routine training exercise."

Colonel Allister frowned. "A horrible shame, but that had nothing to do with me."

"And the press gang?" Emmett pressed.

With a blank stare, Colonel Allister contended, "I have no control over who the press gang picks up."

"You are a liar!" Simeon exclaimed. "You send out your press gangs to force the citizens of Gravesend to bend to your will and ensure their loyalty. These so-called 'press gangs' burn people's homes and businesses."

"That is ludicrous," Colonel Allister barked back. "In case you have forgotten, we are still at war, and press gangs are crucial to the success of our military."

General Floyd propped his right elbow onto the arm of his chair and rubbed his forehead. "Have you been storing supplies at the sulphur mill?" he asked in mild frustration.

Colonel Allister shook his head. "No, General. The mill has been abandoned for years." He shifted his gaze back towards the window. "If you require more proof, I would be happy to give you a tour of the sulphur mill right now."

"Just as I thought," General Floyd replied with a decisive

head bob as he turned towards them. "So far, I have only heard accusations, but I have yet to hear an ounce of proof."

Knowing their time was running short, Emmett shifted his gaze towards Colonel Allister.

"What happened to the bodies in the courtyard?"

"Ah, yes," Colonel Allister responded. "Those men were deserters, and their punishments were carried out." He heaved a sigh, pretending to care whether these men truly lived or died. "It is a hard toll on a man's conscience to perform such a grievous act, but I, too, have orders that I must follow."

General Floyd lifted a knowing brow at them, disbelief on his face. "Gentlemen, I believe Colonel Allister has answered all of your questions, and I feel that this matter should drop."

"Wait!" Emmett exclaimed. "What about the tunnel?"

"The tunnel?" Colonel Allister repeated back in confusion.

"What about the tunnel that leads from The Cloven Hoof to the fort?" Emmett questioned.

"There is no such tunnel," Colonel Allister stated. "You are now grasping at straws, Dr. Maddix, and frankly, I feel bad for you. Those tunnels are nothing more than folklore."

Emmett narrowed his eyes. "I can prove the tunnel exists, because I have been in it."

A twinge of fear flashed in Colonel Allister's eyes before he blinked it away. "Impossible. I contend that tunnel does not exist."

General Floyd shot them an exasperated look before his eyes landed on *Hawk*. He grunted, "All right, Dr. Maddix, will you please show me where this alleged tunnel is?"

Turning to exit the room, Emmett heard Colonel Allister say to General Floyd, "Be wary of him. He was a known drunkard when he served on my ship."

Storming out into the hot sun, Emmett walked the path that he had taken just a few days prior. However, his feet faltered when he saw the building. It had multiple storage rooms, running the length of the building, and they all had the same worn, wooden doors. He knew he had one chance to select the right one.

Adrien stopped next to him, his hand shielding his eyes from the glare of the sun. "Which room holds the tunnel?"

"I am not sure," Emmett answered in a hushed voice.

"Not to put pressure on you, but you'd better be right, or we have to come up with a new plan," Adrien expressed, glancing over his shoulder to see Colonel Allister and General Floyd approaching.

"I really want to wipe that smug look off Allister's face," Simeon muttered under his breath.

Emmett walked to the end of the building and slowly walked by each door, trying to determine which one he'd exited before. Finally, he glanced at the ground and smiled. Partial footprints could be seen in the dirt, but these footprints were not made from the tread of military boots.

He opened the door, and his eyes roamed the dimly lit room. It was filled with barrels, but there was no indication of the chests that he had seen previously. He wondered if this was indeed the room that held the passage into the tunnel.

Colonel Allister stood back and huffed, "You are embarrassing yourself, Dr. Maddix. Just end this charade so the general can toss you out and he can resume his tour of the fort."

Ignoring Allister's obnoxious words, Emmett turned towards General Floyd and announced, "It is this one."

Colonel Allister dropped his head for a moment. "You are confused, again. That is where we store the black powder for our muskets."

Undeterred, Simeon walked over, tipped a barrel onto its rim, and rolled it aside. "Do you remember where the door was located?"

Emmett pointed at the back wall. "It was close to the center of that wall."

Stepping into the room, General Floyd grabbed a crowbar and pried off the top of a barrel. "I hate to be the bearer of bad news, but these barrels are full of powder, just as Allister said."

Adrien rolled up his sleeves and grabbed a barrel. He effortlessly moved it to the side and repeated the motion. "Despite Colonel Allister's allegations, Dr. Maddix is a man that I trust with my life. If he says there is a tunnel that leads to The Cloven Hoof in this room, then I believe him."

Over and over, they moved the barrels until the outline of a small, crude door could be seen. When the last barrel was moved, Emmett pulled the door open and saw the familiar, lighted chalk tunnel.

General Floyd walked swiftly to the door and peered deep into the tunnel. Turning back around, he demanded, "Where does that tunnel lead, Allister?"

Colonel Allister gave him a blank stare. "I have heard rumors that chalk tunnels run the length of Gravesend, but this is the first I have seen it," he claimed.

"Do not take me for a fool," General Floyd declared. "You are under arrest, Allister."

Lifting his hand, Colonel Allister signaled three rough-looking, red-coated soldiers. He stepped outside as they ran into the small supply chamber, holding their Brown Besses in front of them.

"Kill them," he ordered before he slammed the door shut.

General Floyd took a step forward, standing tall. With authority in his voice, he announced, "I am General John William Floyd, and I demand you put down your weapons at once."

"We don't answer to ye," one of the soldiers answered gruffly.

"You do," General Floyd confirmed. "You are a soldier in the British Army, and I am your commanding officer."

Another soldier with a wide scar on his chin just smirked. "Well now, I see things a little differently."

The soldiers moved to take aim when Adrien casually turned his head towards Emmett. "I only count three, and there are four of us."

Emmett nodded as he placed his hands on his hips, calculating the exact distance to the pistol that was tucked beneath his waistcoat. "Good point." Addressing the soldiers, he asked, "How are three of you going to kill four seasoned fighters?"

The taller soldier lowered his musket a bit as he spat on the ground next to him. "The way I see it is that us three have guns and ye don't have none."

"Good gracious," Adrien mocked, "your English is atrocious."

"It don't matter, because you four are about to die," one of the other soldiers said.

"I am feeling generous today," Adrien expressed as he started rolling down the sleeves of his white shirt, drawing attention to himself as Simeon carefully retrieved his pistol. "If you put down your muskets now, then I won't kill you."

The taller soldier laughed. "I hope ye are faster than a musket ball."

Once Adrien's sleeves were rolled down, Emmett knew it was his turn to distract the soldiers, allowing his friend time to retrieve his pistol. Reaching out, he placed his hand on General Floyd's shoulder. Addressing the soldiers, he sounded concerned.

"Have you considered that you will be hunted down for killing a general?"

There was a hint of hesitation as the soldiers glanced at each other.

Emmet continued, "Did you know that the military just executed a convicted soldier by placing him in front of a cannon and firing?"

Taking a few steps towards a barrel, Adrien leaned back

against it, drawing the soldiers' attention. They shifted their muskets toward him. This bought Emmett some time to remove his pistol and tuck it against his leg.

"Why are you loyal to Colonel Allister and not your general?" Adrien asked.

"Colonel Allister pays us well," the dirtied soldier admitted. "Plus, we can do as we please in this town, because we rule it."

"Do all the soldiers belong to The Cursed Lot gang?" General Floyd asked.

"Nay," the taller soldier confirmed. "I am sure many suspect, but they don't dare speak up against the colonel."

Simeon shifted his stance, his boots churning in the dirt with an eerie grinding noise. The soldiers' eyes snapped to him. "Did Colonel Allister kill Mr. Jared Rogers?"

"Was he that customs bloke?" the dirtied man asked the soldier with the wide scar. When the man nodded, he pressed on, "Yeah, Allister had him killed."

"Why did you kill him and not the other customs officials?" Simeon demanded.

"He asked too many questions," the soldier with the wide scar answered. "Allister figured out he was a worthless Runner."

"Enough questions. It is time for you to die," the tall soldier stated sharply.

Keeping his hand behind his back, Adrien said slowly, "This is your last warning."

"Shoot them," the dirtied man shouted as they lifted their weapons to firing position.

However, before the soldiers could fully cock their muskets, Adrien, Simeon, and Emmett brought their pistols up and shot them dead, filling the room with a dense, choking cloud of acrid smoke.

Coughing from the smoke, General Floyd kicked the boot of one of the dead soldiers. "What a waste of life." He looked up at the door that led to the courtyard. "Do you suppose Allister left other soldiers to ensure they finished the job?"

"I have no doubt," Adrien confirmed, tucking his spent pistol away and leaning down to retrieve the spare in his boot.

Reaching down, Emmett also grabbed the spare pistol from his boot. But as he turned to Simeon, he was surprised to see no gun in his hand. "Where is your spare pistol?"

Simeon looked at him with a bewildered expression. "How do you fit a pistol in your boot?"

"It is an overcoat pistol," he explained, showing it to him.

Reaching down, Simeon removed a sheathed dagger from his boot. "That just can't be comfortable."

General Floyd cleared his throat, drawing their attention. "I apologize for doubting you," he paused, "for doubting *Hawk*." His tone held remorse. "Your accusations sounded ridiculous and unfounded, but I should have taken proper precautions when we interrogated Allister."

"Thank you for allowing us to prove his treachery," Emmett replied, his alert eyes focused on the door leading out into the fort.

"I will sign an arrest order for Colonel Allister as soon as I get back to my desk," General Floyd assured them as he reached down and picked up one of the Brown Besses. "I just don't know when that will be."

"As much as I would like to discuss Colonel Allister getting his comeuppance, we need to depart before he sends someone to investigate," Adrien stated as he disappeared down the tunnel.

After Simeon followed Adrien into the tunnel, Emmett turned back towards General Floyd. "After you, General."

Sitting next to the window, Martha watched Morgan as he periodically lifted his head from the reeds and used the telescope to peer into her room. In response, she would wave, and he would duck back down.

It had been the same routine for what seemed like hours. At first, she tried to use the letter opener to pry off the nails around the window, but she just ended up with sore and bloodied fingers.

Glancing down at her trousers and filthy shirt, she had no doubt that her father would be furious for her disobedience, but she did not care. She would not submit to her father's will.

Walking to the door, she crouched down and removed two long pins from her hair. Slowly, she started twisting them as she tried to remember how Eliza had demonstrated. To be honest, she had never paid attention to this lesson. It had seemed unlikely that she would ever need this skill.

Hearing boots stomping on the other side, Martha jumped up and ran back towards the window. Ensuring the letter opener was tucked securely in the folds of her trousers, she spun around and tried to calm her racing heart. The door was thrown open, and her father stormed into the room, his eyes narrowing at the sight of her.

"I told you to change."

A tall, middle-aged man with broad shoulders, brown hair, and sharp features walked into the room. He wore no coat or hat but was dressed in a white shirt, a creme waistcoat with brass buttons, grey trousers held up by a pair of braces, and black shoes. He scowled as his eyes landed on her.

"This is your daughter?"

"It is," Lord Waterford replied.

"Why is she wearing men's clothing?" the man rebuked.

Walking over to her satchel on the table, her father picked it up and tossed it at her. "You stupid girl!" he shouted. When she didn't respond, he stepped towards her with his hand back as if preparing to strike her. Rather than duck her head, she met his gaze and tilted her chin defiantly.

"Enough!" the man shouted. "I like her. She has spunk."

The man approached her and grabbed her chin, yanking it down. "I am Colonel Allister, and we are to be wed."

"I think not," she replied defiantly, despite his hand gripping her chin.

Keeping his firm hold on her, his eyes narrowed at her impertinence. "Your father and I made a deal."

"I do not belong to my father."

Releasing her chin forcefully, Colonel Allister nodded. "You are correct. You belong to me now, and soon I will own all your holdings."

"Holdings?" she asked. "I own nothing."

Colonel Allister regarded her with contempt. "Your father bought buildings in Gravesend, and they are under your name. Once we marry, they will belong to me."

"What buildings?"

"The workhouse, the sulphur mill, and a handful of cottages," her father listed. Martha's eyes shifted towards her father, even though Colonel Allister's gaze seemed to bore into hers.

"Why are those in my name?"

"Let's just say that it is a part of your dowry," Colonel Allister answered. "Furthermore, by putting them in your name, your father was able to hide them from his creditors, at least until we get married. Then those properties will belong to me."

"If you release me, then you can have the properties," Martha asserted with a wave of her hand. "I do not need them."

Colonel Allister chuckled dryly. "I think not. I need a respectable wife, and you fit the bill nicely. I heard you danced with the prince regent at your ball. That increases your value to me." His eyes lewdly perused the length of her body. "Eventually, I plan to open gambling dens in London. I will require a wife to help me mingle with the ton, thus obtaining my clientele."

"I will never marry you," she responded with fiery determination.

Colonel Allister clenched his jaw. "You don't have a say in the matter. Your father lost you in a bet at my gambling den."

"I do have a choice," she argued.

He took a step closer and leaned in. "Once we wed, I will inherit your dowry of £25,000, and your father's gambling debts are wiped away." His warm breath was on her cheek, and she scrunched her face, trying not to gag. "After that, I don't need you anymore."

Martha mustered up her strength, knowing her next words may be her last. "I don't care. I refuse to marry you."

Colonel Allister opened his mouth for a moment before he closed it. He turned to Lord Waterford. "You have five minutes to change her mind, or I will do it for you." Walking back through the door, he slammed it shut.

"How could you bet your own daughter?" she asked, her voice aching with the pain of betrayal.

"You were dead to me long ago." His voice was flat, devoid of feeling.

Martha crossed her arms over her chest as she felt the anger building inside of her. "What have I done to displease you? Why do you loathe me so?"

Lord Waterford advanced towards her, stopping mere inches in front of her. His chest was heaving. "I discovered the note that you left on your dressing table only moments after you eloped with Simeon. The ink on the paper hadn't even dried yet."

Martha slowly lowered her hands. "I told you that I loved Simeon and…"

He slapped her hard across the cheek. "You were a coward, and you ran from your obligations!" he exclaimed. "Your mother pleaded that I go after you and save your reputation."

Rubbing her hand over her cheek, Martha replied, "I didn't mean to hurt anyone."

"Well, you did," he declared, "and you deserved your fate, you little strumpet."

"What fate?" she asked, eyeing him with suspicion.

The depth of loathing in his eyes surprised and frightened her. "I followed you to the inn intending to bring you home. But when I saw Simeon depart from a room upstairs, I knew you were ruined. Luckily, the innkeeper noticed me and struck up a conversation. It was decided that we would sell you to a merchant named Wade. He took care of all the details." He scoffed. "I even paid to have the innkeeper killed to ensure you were never found."

"*You* sold me to Mr. Wade?" she cried in outrage. "*You* did that to me?"

"I did nothing that you didn't deserve."

Shoving him hard in the chest, Martha advanced towards him. "You are a horrible, terrible father!" Ignoring his hardened expression, she glared up at him. "Do you know what I had to endure for those years? What I still have to endure?"

He brought his face closer towards hers, his tone menacing. "You deserved that fate."

Reaching into the folds of her trousers, her hand gripped the letter opener. "No one deserved that!"

Lord Waterford's hands grasped her by the throat as he slammed her against the wall. "I tire of your disobedience," he growled. "You will do as I command, or I will kill you."

"Do it and be done with it," she gasped, fighting for air.

For the briefest moment, Martha welcomed death, bringing an end to her horrific memories of the past. But then the image of Emmett came to her mind. An impish smile graced his lips as he held out his hand towards her, waiting patiently for her to accept. Emmett knew her past, knew her shame, and yet, he always accepted her.

Suddenly, it was clear that she had something to live for, something that her heart longed after. How foolish that she did not recognize the signs that she loved him. The way her heart fluttered when she saw him, or the way her knees weakened when he smiled at her. She loved Emmett! She wanted to live, so she could be with him.

Her father's hands tightened around her neck as she pulled out the letter opener. With a burst of strength born of newfound determination, she thrust it deep into his leg.

Yelling in pain, his hands dropped from her throat as he clutched the letter opener. Shoving him to the side, Martha ran towards the door and flung it open, revealing a set of stairs. Racing down them, she saw the front door just ahead. All she needed to do was to run outside, and she was confident that Lord Morgan would save her.

As her hand gripped the door handle, everything went black.

27

THE SUN WAS STARTING TO DIP IN THE SKY AS EMMETT followed Mr. Larson through the long reeds alongside the Thames estuary. Keeping low to the ground, the sound of sheep bleating could be heard around them.

As they came around a knoll, they saw a large group of men in the distance removing barrel after barrel from the cottage. Horse-drawn wagons positioned near the front were being loaded with the contraband. Two horses hitched to a black coach stood near the main entrance.

Roughly counting the men in his head, Emmett stated, "I count about fifty men."

"I count more than sixty," Mr. Larson contended. "Some guards are loitering on the opposite side of the pasture."

The rest of the group caught up to them before Eliza suggested, "It would be best if we waited until the wagons depart before we try to rescue Martha."

Benedict carried Eliza's black longbow in his hand, and a quiver of arrows hung off his shoulder. "I hate to say it, but I agree with Eliza." His eyes shifted towards the cottage. "We can't just leave a trail of bodies."

Wearing men's clothing, Miss Josette proposed, "I can scale the cottage wall and retrieve Martha."

"No," Adrien stated. "You would be visible to the guards."

"I could at least stay in the room and help protect her," Miss Josette offered.

"Too dangerous," Eliza responded. "We just need to wait until the wagons depart."

Simeon's eyes kept darting between Eliza and Josette. "May I ask why women are present on this rescue mission?"

"No, you may not," came Adrien's immediate response.

A ruffle in the reeds caused everyone to reach for their weapons, but they relaxed when they saw Lord Morgan peeking out at them. "I am glad that everyone could make the journey," he remarked as he crouched down next to them.

"What is the status?" Eliza asked.

Morgan pointed towards a window on the second level of the cottage. "Martha is in that room," he shared as he handed Eliza the telescope.

"I see her," Eliza confirmed after she looked through the telescope then passed it to Emmett.

"Is she safe?" Emmett asked, accepting the telescope. He aimed it towards the window and saw Martha standing there.

Morgan huffed. "Her father has slapped her around a few times, but she has spent most of her time standing near the window."

"Perhaps we could go back and ask General Floyd for assistance?" Simeon suggested.

Adrien shook his head. "The general is attempting to sort out who's loyal to the Crown versus who's loyal to Allister. I doubt he has any men to spare right now."

Emmett watched the men loading the wagon, then murmured, "Some of those men are from the workhouse."

Eliza's eyes grew sharp. "We can't kill those men. They are innocent."

Jonathon approached from the rear, staying low to the ground. "What if we just take out the guards?"

"Perhaps," Adrien answered. "However, we can't discount the possibility that some of the men from the workhouse might side with Allister."

Miss Josette's face grew bright. "What if we go through the tunnel from The Cloven Hoof directly into the estate?"

Simeon shook his head. "Emmett and I tried, but we couldn't lift the latch into the cottage. Either it was nailed shut, or a crate is over the opening."

Emmett frowned. "The only way into that house is through the main door."

"Or the windows," Eliza remarked.

Miss Josette brought the telescope up to her eye and turned it towards the window. "Something is happening," she announced.

"What?" they asked in unison.

Keeping the telescope directed towards the room, Miss Josette explained, "Lord Waterford hit Martha, but now she is standing toe-to-toe with him."

"Is she in danger?" Emmett asked, his hand reaching for his pistol.

Scrunching her forehead, Miss Josette continued looking into the telescope. "They disappeared from view..." she paused, "wait... Martha just ran past the window."

Eliza's eyes grew calculating as Benedict handed her the longbow and an arrow. "Martha could be in danger. Let's go get her."

Emmett agreed without hesitation, "I am ready."

Benedict's eyes scanned the cottage. "If we each went in separate directions, we could take out as many guards as possible and buy some time for Miss Josette to scale the wall to assist Martha."

"Why not me?" Eliza asked in an incredulous tone.

Lifting his brow, Benedict responded, "If you were caught,

pray tell, how would you explain why you were wearing men's clothing and carrying a longbow?"

Eliza looked exasperated. "Why would you assume I would get caught?"

"Benedict is right," Adrien confirmed. "You need to stay back."

"Something is happening," Jonathon announced, pointing at the cottage door.

It had been opened, and Colonel Allister walked out with an unconscious Martha flung over his left shoulder. He waited as a footman opened the door of the coach then stepped inside.

After a long moment, Lord Waterford emerged from the cottage, limping severely. Once he'd entered the coach, the footman closed the door and moved back to his position. Slowly, the coach drove around the wagons and made its way up to the road.

Eliza's face grew determined. "New plan. Follow that coach."

BEHIND THE KNOLL NEAR THE CLOVEN HOOF, EMMETT WATCHED as the horses from Colonel Allister's coach were led towards the stable.

Laying on his stomach, Simeon's eyes scanned the pub as he asked, "Why would Allister choose to come back here?"

Adrien shrugged. "He fled the scene after he ordered his men to kill us, so he must not know the general is still alive… or he is just an imbecile."

Miss Josette spoke up from her crouched position, "How are we going to retrieve Martha? There are guards everywhere."

Mr. Larson and Jonathon stayed low as they approached. "We only counted six guards around the perimeter of the pub, but we couldn't see through those dirty windows to get an accurate count of the guards on the inside," Mr. Larson explained, extending the small telescope to Morgan.

Depositing the telescope inside his coat pocket, Morgan's eyes focused on the guard near the side door. "If we take out the perimeter guards, we will need to drag them back into the reeds to avoid arousing suspicion."

Carriages were lining up as patrons flowed into The Cloven Hoof. Emmett turned towards Jonathon and Benedict. "How many guards were inside the pub when you were in there last?"

"I only counted four loitering around the room, but two were posted at the main door," Benedict confirmed.

Jonathon nodded. "That sounds about right."

Benedict looked down at Eliza, who had been unusually quiet. "What are you thinking?"

With calculating eyes, Eliza did not speak for a long moment. Finally, she said, "From this vantage point, I only can take out two guards, but I dare not try to get closer. There isn't a place to stay concealed."

"I agree," Mr. Larson asserted. "A woman dressed in men's clothing and holding a longbow would arouse suspicion."

"I can stay here, or..." Eliza's voice trailed off when she pressed her lips together. "I could scale the wall with Josette and just use my dagger and pistol."

"No," Benedict stated with a shake of his head. "We can't risk your identity being discovered, and we don't know what we are up against. Stay here and provide support for us."

Josette tilted her chin stubbornly. "I can do it. I will scale the wall and look for an opened window."

Eliza did not look as convinced. "That's risky. We don't know who might be in those upstairs rooms. At least at the cottage, we knew which room Martha was being held in."

Morgan moved closer to Josette. "I will go with her and ensure she is protected," he stated. "I have been known to scale walls before."

Loud, boisterous noises drew their attention as the door to the gambling den was opened. "What if Benedict and I continued our ruse as high-stake gamblers?" Jonathon asked.

Benedict huffed. "We were kicked out of the establishment after our last appearance. I doubt they would allow us to simply stroll back in."

"Good point," Jonathon sighed.

Emmett spoke thoughtfully, "I haven't been in The Cloven Hoof before." He turned towards Adrien and Simeon. "Neither have Adrien, Simeon, Morgan, or Mr. Larson."

Adrien glanced down at his white shirt and tugged on it. "But we aren't exactly dressed like gentlemen."

"We might not be dressed like gentlemen, but we most definitely have the air of gentlemen," Emmett confirmed as his voice became more animated.

Frowning, Simeon observed, "You get excited about the most random things, Dr. Maddix."

Emmett reached into his pocket and pulled out his coin purse. "I always carry at least £10 on my person. It may not be a lot of money for a gambling den, but it will get us through the door."

"I don't know," Simeon pressed. "If Allister is in the hall, you could be shot on sight."

"But what if he is not?" Emmett asked with a lifted brow.

"But what if he is?" Simeon inquired.

"Good heavens," Morgan mumbled under his breath. "This is why agents don't work with Bow Street Runners; they are spineless."

Simeon glared at Morgan. "I beg your pardon."

Pointing to The Cloven Hoof, Morgan declared, "We don't have time for this! Martha is somewhere in that building. Her father abducted her and is forcing her to marry Colonel Allister, who is a known traitor to the Crown. I have no doubt that she is fighting to stay alive." His eyes shone with disapproval. "We have to enter that building and save Martha, without having her killed in the process."

"Don't you think I know that?" Simeon defended. "If I thought that was a good plan, I would be the first to volunteer for the job." He turned his gaze towards Emmett. "But you agents keep coming up with horrible plans."

Adrien lifted his brow. "Then, by all means, what is your plan?"

Simeon threw his hands up in the air. "Fine, let's stroll into a gambling den and hope we are not shot on sight."

"Wait, I have a knack for gambling," Morgan admitted, smirking. "And by 'knack', I mean I am really good at cheating at the cards table."

Emmett bobbed his head in approval. "Morgan could create a distraction by placing a large wager, thus drawing Allister to us."

Morgan shifted to face Josette. "Will you be all right to scale the building without me?"

Rolling her eyes at his question, Josette muttered something under her breath too low to be heard.

Jonathon grinned and answered Morgan's question. "She won't be alone. We are all in this together."

"That we are," Benedict responded. "First, Jonathon, Eliza, and I will remove the guards around the perimeter." He turned towards Josette. "After we take them all out, you will go around back and scale the building while we cover you."

Eliza reached out and grabbed Josette's arm. "If no windows are open, you must come back here."

"I understand," Josette responded.

"Mr. Larson, Adrien, Morgan, and I will enter The Cloven Hoof," Emmett added. "Somehow, we will have to eliminate the guards there without causing panic in the room."

Mr. Larson shifted in his crouched position. "If there is even the slightest uproar, Lord Waterford may panic and kill Martha."

"Good point. He is certainly not the best father," Jonathon agreed.

"No, he is not. In fact, he rivals our mother," Eliza stated. "I will stay outside and attempt to determine which men are arrogant gentlemen gambling away their fortunes and which are thugs hired by Allister."

Benedict smirked knowingly at his wife. "Try not to kill the innocent ones."

"I'll try," Eliza replied with a small smile.

Simeon's eyes turned towards the pub. "What happens when we get into The Cloven Hoof?"

Adrien chuckled. "That is when we improvise."

"Worst plan ever," Simeon mumbled under his breath.

28

MARTHA'S HEAD THROBBED AS SHE TRIED TO FOCUS ON THE words she heard around her. Male voices argued near her, but the words seemed jumbled and disconnected. She lifted a hand to rub her forehead but realized that her wrists were bound tightly.

"You are finally awake," her father announced.

Booted steps came closer. An unexpected slap across her face forced her head to bounce against the wall. Bright lights exploded before her eyes. Blinking rapidly, she saw her father and Colonel Allister looking down at her.

Colonel Allister crouched down and met her gaze. "Would you prefer a church wedding, or should we just say our vows now?"

"I will not marry you," she declared. "I would rather die."

"That can be arranged, my dear," he growled before dropping his gaze. "I was hoping you would be more agreeable this time around." He rose and walked back towards a table against the opposite wall. Removing a piece of paper from his coat, he placed it on the table, reached for a quill, and dabbed it in the inkpot. "I am going to just sign our names and be done with it, then."

Her father shook his head in disappointment as he stared at her. "Why aren't you as agreeable as your mother was?"

Martha held her tongue despite the urge to remind her father that he had killed her mother.

Colonel Allister left the paper on the table and placed the quill next to the ink pot. "Your turn, vicar," he said almost jovially.

Standing slowly, her father limped over and bent low over the paper. Tilting his head, he asked, "Should I sign for the witnesses as well?"

Colonel Allister shook his head. "No, we don't want anyone to cry foul over this marriage license, especially since my wife is going to be involved in an accident very soon."

Lord Waterford looked at her with contempt. There was no hint of fatherly compassion in his expression. "Shouldn't we keep her alive until her dowry is deposited?"

"I suppose so," Colonel Allister sighed as he rubbed the back of his neck. Shifting his gaze to her, she saw a gleam of desire in his eyes. "Now that you are my wife," he paused, smirking, "I intend to enjoy my husbandly rights."

Martha shrank back against the wall. "You will do no such thing!" Panicking, her eyes sought out her father with one last hope that he would protect her, but his face was expressionless.

Picking up the license, her father held it out to Colonel Allister. "You need to have two witnesses sign this document before it becomes legal." When Colonel Allister reached for the paper, her father pulled it back. "Just to be clear, this wipes away my debt to you."

"Yes," he confirmed.

Fingering the paper in his hand, her father pressed on, "Plus, we are equal partners as the leaders of The Cursed Lot."

A small sneer appeared on Colonel Allister's face, one that was barely discernable. "Yes, I believe that is what we agreed upon."

Feeling pacified, her father handed the paper to Colonel Allister. A loud knock resonated through the room, and Colonel Allister walked over to answer the door. Opening it wide, Colonel Allister did not seem to care that the man on the other side could see her. "A gentleman has placed a rather large wager, and I came to obtain your approval."

"How large?" Colonel Allister asked.

The man rocked back on his heels. "£10,000."

With a glance at her over his shoulder, Colonel Allister said, "I will be right down." He gave her father a contemptuous look. "This time, can you manage to keep her from escaping?"

"That was hardly my fault."

"That was most definitely your fault, you fool," Colonel Allister grumbled.

"Bah," her father replied, dismissing his comment.

Walking out, Colonel Allister closed the door behind him. Her father turned his heated gaze back to her. "If I were you, I would not aggravate your husband. He will kill you, now that you are of no worth to him."

Martha shook her head slowly. "How could you?"

"This was all your fault…"

"No!" Martha shouted. "It was *not* my fault." Rising awkwardly against the wall, she stood and rested her back against it. "You will not blame me for your failures."

"What failures?" he huffed.

Despite her circumstances, she felt surprisingly calm as she challenged her father. "I may have loved Simeon, but that is not the main reason I eloped with him. I know that now."

"And what was?"

Standing straighter, her voice was defiant. "I was running away from *you*." She pursed her lips. "You have never been a real father to me, and I was tired of living under your oppression."

Waving a hand at her comment, her father dismissed her words. "You are only a woman."

"You do *not* get to discredit me like that!" she exclaimed. "I am more than just my gender. I am a survivor." Her expression changed to one of pity, knowing her father would never change. "I always thought I was a survivor of slavery, but it turns out that I survived *you*."

Her father limped towards her, fury in his expression. "You will not speak to me that way."

"I will." She refused to cower under his venomous gaze. "I will never stop fighting you; I will never stop trying to bring you to justice."

"Justice for what?" her father exploded.

Martha suddenly felt clearer than she had her entire life. "Justice for my mother, and justice for my uncle and cousin."

"They got what they deserved; as did you," her father grunted, showing no signs of remorse.

Martha shook her head. "When I was younger, I didn't understand why you hated me. I would go to the creek and think of all the ways I could please you."

Her father laughed cruelly. "How unfortunate for me that you turned out to be such a disappointment."

Her back stiffened at his cold, unfeeling words. "For these past two years, I have been hiding because of my fears and short-comings. But now I see things as they truly are."

"Which is?"

"I did nothing wrong," she stated firmly. "It was all you! It was your cruelty that led me to run away; it was by your hand that I was sold into slavery. Now, you have bartered me off to Colonel Allister to wipe away your gambling debt."

Furious, her father slapped her cheek hard. "How dare you speak to me in such a horrendous fashion. I am an earl."

Ignoring the throbbing pain in her face, Martha met his gaze, unflinching. "No, you are a murderer and a really lousy father."

There was a knock on the door before it was pushed open. Not bothering to turn around, her father continued to glare at her with hate in his eyes.

A male voice spoke from behind him. "Colonel Allister sent me up to help you guard the young woman."

That voice was oddly familiar. Martha craned her neck to look past her father and saw Mr. Larson standing there with a finger up to his lips. Blinking away her relief at seeing him, she turned her gaze back to her father.

"Go away," her father demanded. "I need to speak to my daughter alone."

"But Allister…"

Lord Waterford spun around and pointed at him. "I said 'go away'."

"As you wish," Mr. Larson acknowledged, turning as if to walk away. As her father turned back to face her, Mr. Larson pulled out his pistol and hit him over the head, rendering him unconscious.

Placing the pistol back into the waistband of his trousers, Mr. Larson pulled a dagger from his boot. Martha put her hands up so he could cut the twine binding them. As the cord dropped to the floor, he gave her a look of admiration.

"I am glad to see you alive, Lady Martha."

Rubbing her sore wrists, Martha just rolled her eyes at his use of her title. "Just Martha, if you don't mind. I am not a lady."

Mr. Larson watched her with pride in his eyes. "You are to me. I have always considered you a lady."

"Thank you." Her expression softened when she saw Mr. Larson blink rapidly for a moment. She could have sworn she saw a light sheen of moisture in his eyes.

Ushering her towards the window, Mr. Larson explained, "We need to get this window open so we can secure your freedom."

Josette's face appeared on the opposite side of the window, and she mouthed the words, "It is locked."

Mr. Larson unlocked the latch and pushed the window out. Before he allowed her to approach the window, he put his head out and asked, "Is it safe for Martha to step out?"

She didn't hear anything, but the answer must have been yes because he held out his hand to help her to sit on the window sill. As she swiveled to swing her legs out, she asked Mr. Larson, "Will you be joining us?"

He grinned. "No, someone has to save your beloved."

Martha started to protest, then realized she had no desire to correct him. Turning her head, she saw Josette next to her with a grin on her lips.

Ignoring them, she started scaling down the wall and was grateful she was only on the second floor.

STANDING BACK AGAINST THE WALL, HIDDEN BY A LARGE GROUP of men, Emmett watched as Colonel Allister descended the stairs and approached Morgan at the faro table. The green, felt-lined table displayed pictures of playing cards and a stack of cards sat in a wooden box.

"I hate faro," Simeon said in a hushed voice next to him.

Emmett's eyes tracked Mr. Larson as he disappeared up the stairs. "I agree. It is purely a game of chance. The player simply bets on whether a certain card will be dealt from the stack. No skill involved."

"I hope Morgan knows what he is doing," Simeon muttered.

Colonel Allister stopped next to Morgan, his eyes perusing

his face and clothing. "I understand you would like to make a bet of £10,000."

"I would," he responded without a hint of intimidation.

Reaching out, Colonel Allister touched his dirty, white shirt, clearly not impressed by Morgan's attire. "That must be a lot of money for the likes of you."

Morgan shrugged. "Honestly, it is just a drop in the bucket."

Eyeing him suspiciously, Colonel Allister asked, "Why haven't I seen you here before?"

"I prefer to gamble in London," Morgan admitted. "Mostly, I frequent the gambling house of Lady Archer."

"Can you prove that you have the funds to make such a high-stakes wager?" Colonel Allister pressed.

"If I lose," he laughed a cocky laugh and boasted, "I can have the money to you before the end of the week." Taking the signet ring off his right hand, Morgan tossed it onto the table. "However, if you require more collateral, this ring will prove that my father is the Marquess of Bath."

Silence filled the room as Morgan revealed his parentage, and Colonel Allister's eyes lit up with greed. Reaching down, he picked up the ring and examined it. Turning his gaze back to Morgan, he informed him, "If you lose, I keep the ring until I get paid."

Morgan gave him an arrogant smile. "That won't be an issue."

Colonel Allister turned to leave, but Morgan placed a hand on his arm. "Leave the ring," he ordered.

Placing the ring in front of Morgan on the table, Colonel Allister claimed, "I was only trying to keep it safe."

Morgan frowned. "And if I win, does this," he hesitated, his eyes roaming the room with disdain, "den... have the funds to pay me?"

Colonel Allister's jaw tightened at Morgan's words. "And I assure *you,* that won't be an issue."

Locking eyes, they stared at each other, neither willing to back down. At that moment, Mr. Larson crept back down the stairs and disappeared into the crowd of patrons.

Suddenly, Morgan grinned and declared, "Let's play!" Turning back to the dealer, he cocked his head and said, "If you don't mind, I would like to ensure the cards are not stacked."

Colonel Allister glared at him. "How dare you presume my dealers cheat!"

Seemingly unaffected by Colonel Allister's presence, Morgan took a moment to admire the cards before he handed them back. "I learned the hard way never to trust anyone when it comes to my money. After all, the dowager countess of Buckinghamshire may have thrown lavish parties, but she used them as a ruse to swindle people out of their money."

Lord Morgan placed his bet, and everyone in the room held their breath as the next card was played. A cheer erupted as the card was turned over. He had won! Morgan pumped his fist in the air and cheered.

Smirking, Morgan turned to Colonel Allister as he put on his signet ring. "I believe you owe me £10,000."

Colonel Allister pressed his lips together hard, the flesh around his mouth turning white. "You must have cheated."

Morgan's brow flew up. "Are you accusing me of cheating at a game of chance?"

"I am," Colonel Allister proclaimed as he placed his hand on the butt of the pistol tucked into his trousers.

Instead of shrinking back, Morgan took a step closer to Colonel Allister. "Interesting," he murmured. "And I am supposed to take the word of a liar and cheat?"

Many of the patrons ran past Morgan to escape the danger now lurking inside The Cloven Hoof. They fled into the night rather than stay and witness what was about to transpire.

"I am neither a liar nor a cheat," Colonel Allister growled as two thugs appeared behind him.

Morgan winced. "I apologize. The word I was looking for was..." he hesitated, before snapping his fingers, "murderer." Glancing over his shoulder, he looked at Emmett, Simeon, Adrien, and Mr. Larson, who had all stepped forward. "Do you have another term for Allister?"

"Disgraceful," Simeon replied.

Emmett offered, "A despicable human being."

Morgan nodded decisively. "I like that much better." Giving Colonel Allister a quick smile, he chortled, "I think we can all agree the leader of The Cursed Lot gang is a horrible, despicable human being."

Colonel Allister's eyes had widened at the appearance of Emmett, Simeon, and Adrien. "What are you doing here?" he asked in disbelief.

Emmett smirked. "We are not dead, if that is what you are asking."

"This might not be the best time to inform you that General Floyd isn't dead either," Simeon said. "Your men failed, and it was quite painful to witness."

"Did you train them?" Adrien asked, feigning concern. "If so, you might want to work on... well, everything."

"No, no, no!" Colonel Allister roared as he pulled out his pistol. "You were all supposed to be dead."

"And yet, we're not," Adrien remarked. "I suggest you give up now, so we don't have to kill you."

Morgan interjected, "May I collect my winnings before we kill him?"

Adrien nodded. "You may collect your winnings, and then we will kill him."

"That sounds like a great plan," Morgan said, rubbing his two hands together.

"Will you two shut up?" Colonel Allister shouted, aiming his pistol at Adrien. "I don't know how you managed to survive, but tonight you will die."

"Oh, that is easy to explain," Adrien started, "we over-powered…"

His voice faded as Colonel Allister cocked his pistol and leveled it at his chest. "I said 'shut up'."

Withdrawing his pistol, Emmett's eyes scanned the hall and counted ten armed guards standing around, waiting to do Colonel Allister's bidding.

"The game is over," he exclaimed. "The general knows that you abused your position as colonel of New Tavern Fort to run a sophisticated smuggling ring."

Colonel Allister shifted the pistol to point at his chest. "You have no proof of these ridiculous accusations. I will simply explain to the general that I was set up by Lord Waterford."

Adrien frowned sadly. "Frankly, I am disappointed in you. Is that the best explanation you can come up with?"

Anger flashed in Colonel Allister's eyes as he considered Adrien. "Why shouldn't I kill you right now?"

"Because your treasonous actions attracted the attention of *Shadow,* who is outside waiting for you to make an appearance," Adrien replied.

Colonel Allister's eyes shot towards the door as Emmett said, "If you are thinking about escaping through your tunnels, I would rethink that option. General Floyd has posted soldiers to guard the entrances."

Colonel Allister's gaze roamed the men until it landed on him. "You think you are so clever, don't you, Dr. Maddix?"

"I do find myself to be quite exceptional…"

Colonel Allister spoke over him. "You are a bloody fool. I have power, wealth and, once again, the girl." He gave him a cruel sneer.

"You are wrong," Emmett replied deliberately. "Martha escaped about, what…" He turned to Mr. Larson, "…about ten minutes ago?"

"Around that," Mr. Larson confirmed, his alert eyes scanning the room.

"Pardon me if I don't believe you." Narrowing his eyes, Colonel Allister barked over his shoulder, "Get Lady Martha from the upstairs room."

"We saw your men unloading the ship's cargo and storing it at the cottage, sulphur mill, and The Cloven Hoof. Why so many locations?" Simeon asked.

"Most of the customs officials accepted bribes, but revenue men were not as easily convinced," Colonel Allister replied. "When certain ships came into port, the customs officials doctored their records to allow for the smuggled goods. We stored the contraband overnight, rotating between the three locations, until we loaded the wagons to drive them to the Crobwell estate where we distributed the goods." His smile grew smug. "If all went well, those items were sold on the streets of London less than thirty-six hours after being taken off the ship."

"Why involve the British Army?" Adrien pressed.

Colonel Allister huffed. "The British Army is made up of criminals. They are forced to decide between joining the military or going to prison. Since most non-commissioned officers at New Tavern Fort are outcasts, it was easy to convince them to join The Cursed Lot and run this pitiful village."

Emmett shook his head. "You were supposed to uphold the law, not abuse it."

Allister's jaw ticked, and the hatred in his eyes grew palpable as he glared at him. "Because of *you*, my commission was terminated in the Royal Navy, so I set my sights on Gravesend. This town has been a smuggler's paradise for centuries. Once I secured my post at New Tavern Fort, I molded this town into the enterprise it is today. I sent press gangs to round up the dissenters, took control of the underground tunnels, and eliminated my competition."

"I would congratulate you on your successful venture, but I

find your methods deplorable, and frankly, evil beyond imagination," Emmett said, his voice filled with contempt.

Before Colonel Allister could respond, the guard came back down the stairs, assisting a limping Lord Waterford. "Lady Martha is gone," the guard announced.

"No!" Colonel Allister bellowed. "She is mine!" His eyes grew wider and more desperate as they roamed the hall, his motions frantic. "Where is she?"

"Somewhere safe," Emmett answered.

Allister leveled the pistol at his chest. "Give her to me."

"Never," he growled.

Cocking his pistol, Allister thundered, "You will not win again!"

Before Emmett could move, Colonel Allister pulled the trigger, just as Simeon shoved him out of the way.

29

At the sound of gunfire, Martha and Josette ran to the front window of The Cloven Hoof. Peering in, they saw everyone standing in a semi-circle, pistols drawn in a tense stand-off. The only exception was Colonel Allister. He was standing in the middle, his mouth moving, his hands gesturing wildly.

Martha's eyes gravitated towards the ground where Simeon lay, a pool of blood under his right shoulder. "We have to help them," she insisted, urgently.

Josette reached behind her and pulled out a pistol, extending it towards her. "Do you know how to shoot this?"

Nodding, Martha accepted the gun and confirmed, "Eliza trained me."

"Good." Josette pulled out another pistol from the front of her trousers. "Let's go save the men."

As they kept low, they were almost to the door when Eliza approached them with her longbow in hand. "You weren't thinking about going in there without me, were you?" she asked with a teasing smile.

Martha grinned. "I knew you would catch up to us." Her

smile faded. "Simeon has been shot, and the men are in a stand-off."

"Where are Benedict and Jonathon?" Josette asked.

"They went around back to secure the perimeter and haven't come back yet," Eliza informed them. "We will need to take out as many of Allister's men as we can before we use up our element of surprise."

Josette nodded her understanding as she started moving towards the open door. Eliza quietly stepped to the other side of the door and peered in, her eyes alert. Nocking an arrow, she pulled back the string and waited as Josette held up three fingers, silently counting down until she fisted her hand.

All three women moved into the doorway, Martha shot her pistol at Colonel Allister, hitting him in the chest. Bringing his hand up to the wound, Colonel Allister turned and ran from the room while chaos erupted around him. The smell of the acrid smoke filled the air around her as Josette shot at another guard.

Arrows whizzed by as Eliza released them in a rapid-fire motion. More pistols rang out as the last of the guards dropped.

As silence fell, Martha looked around the room and saw the gang members' bodies strewn on the floor, many with arrows sticking out of them. After confirming Emmett, Adrien, Morgan, and Mr. Larson were still standing, she ran to Simeon on the floor and saw the pool of blood was growing.

Reaching down to her large shirt, she ripped off a section and dropped down next to him. "Stay with me, Simeon," she pleaded as she pressed the cloth tightly against his wounded shoulder.

Moaning, Simeon rolled his head back and forth. Emmett crouched down next to him. "Move your hand," he ordered. She complied, and he pulled back Simeon's shirt, revealing a red, oozing bullet wound. "We need to take him to the hospital."

Morgan shouted from across the room, "Are you coming, Emmett?"

Martha saw indecision on Emmett's face. Reaching for his

hand, she urged, "Go! Go get Allister. I'll take Simeon to see Sister Mary. She'll know what to do."

Emmett squeezed her hand, and they exchanged a smiling, intimate look that made her heart race. "I will come back," he said, his words holding promise.

"See that you do," she replied, releasing his hand.

As Emmett rose, Simeon reached out and grabbed her arm. With pain-infused words, he whimpered, "I love you, Martha. Don't leave me. I love you."

Martha put her hand around Simeon's and leaned closer to his ear. "I am right here."

Simeon's eyes flickered open as he moaned, "Why don't you love me anymore?"

Brushing a piece of hair from his forehead, she answered, "I will always love you."

Instantly, his body visibly relaxed. Feeling some relief that her words had calmed him, Martha heard Emmett say curtly, "He is losing too much blood. You need to get him to the hospital."

His tone surprised her, and she turned back to look at him. Why was he upset? "Emmett…" she began, but her words were silenced when Josette placed a hand on her shoulder. "Martha, come quickly. It is your father."

After one last glance at her, Emmett turned and ran towards the back door.

Reluctantly, Martha rose and left Simeon, making her way to her father's side. An arrow protruded from his chest, and a large patch of blood saturated his shirt around his right breast. She was tempted to just leave him there. Instead, Martha ripped a section of his shirt and pressed down on his wound, hoping to stop the blood flow.

After a moment, she unbuttoned his waistcoat and yanked his shirt to the side, revealing a bullet wound, as well. Pity that both a bullet and an arrow to the chest did not kill him, she thought.

Martha's eyes roamed the room. She saw Josette crouching

next to Simeon, speaking to him in soothing tones. Eliza was nowhere to be seen, which was for the best. She sighed. How was she going to transport these men to the hospital?

At that moment, Benedict and Jonathon strode into the room, their eyes holding compassion while they moved towards Simeon. Benedict announced, "My wife informed me that we have a wounded Bow Street Runner. We had to commandeer a coach from a simpering lord, but now we can bring Simeon to the hospital in style."

Martha looked down at her father and noticed his face was increasingly pale. If she didn't help him, he would die. "Do you have room in the coach for my father as well?"

"We do," Benedict answered, "if that is what you desire."

"It is," Martha replied, knowing she was extending him the mercy he never showed her. Despite the hatred her father expressed for her, Martha could not step aside and do nothing. She had to act as her conscience dictated.

Rising, she took a moment to ensure there were no other wounded among the bodies. Finding none, her heart mourned for these men and their families. They had chosen a life of smuggling, a life of crime. But at what cost? Their lives. What a horrible debt to be paid, she thought.

EMMETT RAN OUT AFTER LORD MORGAN, ADRIEN, AND MR. Larson as they ran towards their hidden horses. Mounting them without stopping, they kicked them into a run as Mr. Larson shouted, "Allister rode towards the main road."

Using only the light of the moon, they raced their horses down the main road leading out of Gravesend. If Colonel Allister arrived in London before them, it would be nearly impossible to follow him. Too many forks in the road.

Urging his horse to run faster, Emmett tried to keep his mind focused on intercepting Allister, but his mind kept replaying Martha's words to Simeon. He was such a fool! He had fallen in love with her, but she didn't love him in return. She loved Simeon.

He replayed his moments with Martha, knowing his memories were the only thing that he was entitled to keep. He had naïvely imagined that Martha was warming up to him. She had seemed to want to kiss him just as much as he wanted to kiss her. But that must have been his imagination playing tricks on him.

A lone rider's horse was kicking up a lot of dirt just ahead. Riding low in the saddle, Emmett pressed his horse to go even faster. He was just starting to close the distance when Allister's horse suddenly reared.

Emmett heard shouting over the pounding of his horse's hooves as he neared Colonel Allister. In front of the colonel stood several highwaymen with their pistols aimed at him. But they were not just any highwaymen. Gaspard and his gang had arrived.

"Get out of the way!" Allister ordered as he reached for his pistol. He stopped when one of the highwaymen shot his musket in the air as a warning.

Reining in their horses, Emmett reached for his pistol and aimed it at Allister. "It is over," he declared.

"Never!" Allister exclaimed.

"Dr. Maddix?" Gaspard asked. "Is that you?"

"It is," he confirmed. "And the man in front of you is Colonel Allister."

Gaspard cocked his pistol, and his next words were filled with sarcasm. "Gentlemen, it appears that we have caught the leader of The Cursed Lot gang and a distinguished military officer."

Allister pulled back on his reins as his horse grew restless, stamping its hooves. "You have no right to speak about me so disrespectfully." He looked around, searching for an avenue of escape. Panic filled his eyes as he realized he was completely encircled. He was trapped. "I demand that you let me ride past."

"Just give up so we can arrest you and drop you off to the general," Adrien said dryly. "Why are criminals so opposed to being caught?"

"Why don't we just drop him off at Newgate?" Mr. Larson suggested.

Morgan nodded. "Newgate might be a better location before he is court-martialed."

"Either way, he will hang," Adrien pointed out.

"Good point," Morgan replied. "Why not just shoot him now and save all the time and hassle of a trial?"

"Or you can just hand him over to us," Gaspard suggested.

Colonel Allister glared at Gaspard. "You have no dispute with me, highwayman."

Gaspard's eyes narrowed. "Your press gangs shot my son, killed my friends, and ravaged our town. All so you could continue your illegal dealings without opposition."

"I am not the only one smuggling in Gravesend," Colonel Allister proclaimed. "Your town has been an ideal location for smugglers for centuries. I just happened to manage it more efficiently."

"Just because something has been done for centuries, doesn't mean it should continue," Emmett said. "You murdered innocent men and women, took advantage of the poor in your parish, and manipulated the soldiers under your command." He adjusted the reins in his hand. "You will hang for your crimes."

"Like you should have?" Allister sneered. "You shot me in the leg."

"I did, but only because you murdered Eleanora," Emmett responded.

"She was just a whore," he asserted in a cold, emotionless tone.

Every muscle in Emmett's body tensed at his words. "How dare you dishonor Eleanora! She did nothing wrong, but you tried to take advantage of her. When she rebuffed your advances, you killed her."

"She attacked me," Colonel Allister maintained. "Besides, you were the one keeping her as your strumpet."

"I was not!" Emmett exclaimed. "I was trying to protect her by hiding her from *you*." He cocked his pistol. "And it turns out I was right to do so. You are a monster."

"Dr. Maddix," Mr. Larson said, cautiously. "Do not kill him. We will turn him over to the authorities for a fair trial."

"He doesn't deserve a fair trial," Emmett contended, his pistol not wavering in the least.

"No, he doesn't," Adrien confirmed, "but you don't want to kill him in cold blood."

An image of Martha came to his mind, and his anger started melting away. He didn't want to disappoint her, even though she wasn't his. Regardless, he would always love her.

Uncocking the pistol, Emmett pointed it up in the air. "Thank you. I wasn't thinking clearly for a moment."

However, Gaspard was not as easily convinced as he shouted, "You may not want to kill him, but I do not have the same scruples." Reaching up, he grabbed Allister's arm and dragged him off his horse. "Stand up," he ordered.

Colonel Allister rose slowly, maintaining a defiant stare at Gaspard.

"Empty your pockets," Gaspard demanded.

"No," Allister declared. "I do not have to do your bidding."

"You do." Gaspard motioned one of the other highwaymen over and ordered, "Put your pistol to his head, and if he moves… shoot him."

Reaching into Allister's pockets, he pulled out a coin purse and a sheet of folded paper. Depositing the coin purse into his pocket, he said, "Thank you for your donation to help the people of Gravesend."

Unfolding the paper, he shifted it in his hands as he held it up to the moonlight. His eyes grew wide as he read it. Scowling, he walked over and handed it to Emmett.

"What is this?" Emmett asked, accepting the paper. His heart sank when he recognized the special license form. "When did you marry Martha?"

"What?" Morgan, Adrien, and Mr. Larson shouted in unison.

"It is binding," Colonel Allister insisted.

Squinting as his eyes scanned the paper, Emmett stated smugly, "There are no witness signatures, and Lord Waterford signed it as the vicar." He folded it and ripped it into small pieces, watching with pleasure as they blew away in the wind. "This was not a valid marriage."

"What have you done?" Colonel Allister shouted as he started to move but crumbled to the ground when Gaspard hit him over the head with the butt of his pistol.

"I tired of him talking," Gaspard admitted. He walked to his horse and pulled a length of rope out of his saddlebag. Bringing it back, he tied Colonel Allister's hands and legs. "Do you want to do the honors or shall we?"

Emmett shifted his gaze toward the crumpled, defeated form of Allister. "We will deliver him to New Tavern Fort, but we will inform the general of your heroic actions."

Two highwaymen lifted Allister and placed him face-down across the saddle of his horse, tying his wrists and ankles to the stirrups. Gaspard patted the horse's neck. "The town of Gravesend will rest easier tonight knowing that Colonel Allister's reign of terror has ended." He reached for the lead on the horse. "At least, I know I will."

Accepting the lead from Gaspard, Emmett gave his friend a look of appreciation. "Thank you," he said earnestly.

"No, I should be thanking you for saving my boy's life and bringing Colonel Allister to justice," Gaspard expressed.

Emmett smirked. "All in a day's work."

Chuckling, Gaspard asked, "As a doctor?"

"No, my other profession." Emmett chuckled as he kicked his horse into a run, pleasantly acknowledging that this would make the journey exceedingly uncomfortable for Allister.

❦ 30 ❦

MARTHA PLACED A COOL CLOTH AGAINST SIMEON'S FOREHEAD
as he slept on a straw mattress in the hospital. Looking down at
the man she had loved so desperately in her youth, she knew her
heart had shifted regarding him. She did love him, but not like
before. He reminded her of days long past. As much as she
wanted to resent those carefree days, she realized that she would
always look back on them with fondness.

Glancing over at her sleeping father, Martha finally recognized that her past had molded her into a strong and giving
woman; a woman who looked at others with empathy; a woman
who strived to help others, despite their social standing. She was
proud to be the woman she had become.

Her abusive childhood, falling in love in her youth, eloping,
and finally enduring and surviving a prison worse than death
allowed her to find joy in serving other people and easing their
burdens. She had not succumbed to bitterness or hatred. She had
chosen compassion and love. How ironic that she had to experience so much heartache to achieve that purpose.

A soldier stood watch over her father, and he tipped his head
when she made eye contact with him. Martha bent her head in

acknowledgement before turning her attention back to Simeon. He deserved a good life, and she wished him every happiness. If only things had turned out differently. She started to stand, but his hand reached out and grabbed hers.

"Don't go," he pleaded in a raspy voice.

Leaning forward in her seat, she placed her hand over his. "I was just going to ask Sister Mary to prepare some broth for you."

"I don't need broth," Simeon replied. "I just need you."

Holding his hand tighter, Martha smiled down at him. "You have always been so overdramatic."

He attempted to chuckle, but it came out as more of a grunt. "I discovered that it was the best way to get your attention."

Martha laughed. "Do you remember when you covered yourself with mud and leaves and tried to convince me that you were the Thames monster coming to eat me?"

Grinning, Simeon shared, "If I recall, you were screaming like a banshee, and half the village came to see what the commotion was about."

"Didn't your father flog you after you washed off in the river?"

"He did. But it was worth it." Simeon's eyes slowly drifted towards her father. "What will you do now?"

Still holding his hand, Martha sighed. "I hadn't really thought about it, yet. I suppose I will go back to Lady Lansdowne's household and be her companion."

Simeon's eyes were imploring. "Marry me, instead."

Her face softened as she looked at him. "Oh, Simeon. You know I can't do that."

"But I heard you tell me that you loved me," he protested.

"I do," she replied. "However, it is not that simple..." Her words trailed off as she tried to think of the right words.

Closing his eyes for a moment, Simeon's next words verbalized what she had not yet admitted. "Your heart belongs to another."

"It does," she answered honestly. "I am sorry. I never meant to hurt you."

Shifting on the bed, Simeon let out a grunt of pain before saying, "I wish that things could be different. I wish that I could go back in time and pick another inn."

Martha gave him a tender smile. "Life is full of coincidences, but as we get older, we realize that those seemingly random coincidences were when fate interceded on our behalf."

His face grew sorrowful. "We would have been happy together."

Tears came to Martha's eyes as she admitted, "I have no doubt. You were my first love."

"I wish I was your true love," he whispered, blinking away the moisture in his eyes.

Martha brought her free hand up to hold his hand. "For so many years, I had bitterness and contempt for you, but deep down, I knew a part of me would always love you. But now, I long for different things."

"I will always be here for you, Magpie," he insisted. "If you ever change your mind," he paused as his voice hitched, "I will be waiting with open arms."

Martha's lips tightened as she tried to fight back the tears. "To be honest, I am nervous about confessing my feelings to Dr. Maddix."

He gave her a slight shake of his head. "Don't be. He loves you."

"How do you know?"

Simeon's eyes softened, but his voice was soft, almost fragile, as if it would break any minute. "I know because he looks at you the same way I do, with love and admiration in his eyes."

Removing one hand from his, she reached up and brushed

the hair off his forehead. "I want you to be happy, Simeon. You are a good man."

A deep clearing of a throat came from the main door as Martha shifted in her seat to see Emmett looking hesitant. "I came to check on Simeon," he announced before he walked to the opposite side of the bed. "Do you mind if I look at the wound?" he asked Simeon.

"Go ahead," Simeon agreed.

Emmett glanced down at their adjoined hands briefly before he pushed aside Simeon's shirt, revealing the bandaging. Removing it, he examined the wound and seemed satisfied. As he applied clean bandages, he expressed, "Sister Mary did a good job of removing the bullet and cleaning out the wound. That will reduce the chance of infection."

"That's great news." Martha smiled as she released Simeon's hand.

Stepping back from the bed, Emmett said, "I want to thank you for jumping in front of me to take that bullet."

Simeon grunted as he placed his hand to his wound. "You don't need to thank me. Consider it an apology for my boorish behavior this past week."

Grinning, Emmett advised him, "You should take it easy for two weeks, including no fighting or undercover work. Your body needs to rest if you want it to recover."

"Thank you, Dr. Maddix," Simeon said. "I think I would like to go home to recover."

"Really?" Martha asked.

Simeon smirked. "It is time the prodigal son returned home."

Martha laughed. "Your mother will be pleased. I have never seen a mother dote on a child as she did with you."

"That is because your mother wasn't the best example of motherhood," Simeon quipped.

"Good point," she admitted, smiling.

"Martha," Emmett ventured, "may I speak to you for a moment?"

"Of course," she answered as she rose and followed him towards the back room.

As they reached the door, Emmett stepped aside and let her pass before he followed her into the room. He left the door open and stood more than a proper distance away. He smiled at her, but the smile did not reach his eyes.

"I am relieved that Simeon is alive."

Taking a step closer towards him, Martha noticed that his eyes seemed guarded. "Sister Mary did great work."

"I agree," Emmett confirmed. "Sister Mary is better than most physicians that I have come across." He reached back and rubbed the back of his neck, looking uncomfortable. "I thought you might like to know that we destroyed the marriage license we found on Allister."

"Thank you," she expressed. "With all the excitement, I had forgotten that Allister had forged the document."

A long, awkward silence passed between them as they stared at each other. Finally, Martha found the courage to say, "Emmett, I never thanked you for saving my life." Good, that was a great start, she thought.

Emmett's eyes roamed her face and seemed to hold longing. "You don't have to thank me. All I have ever wanted was for you to be happy."

Taking another step closer brought her close enough to touch him. She clasped her hands together, instead. "You have made me immensely happy over these past few weeks. I would never have found the courage to leave Chatswich Manor if it wasn't for you."

"I doubt that," he argued softly. "You are brave and strong and better than I could ever be."

"I disagree. You have also helped heal my anguished soul." She bit her bottom lip and looked up at him through her lashes.

"You were right, I found reasons to fight." *I fought for you*, she thought, wishing she had the strength to actually say those words.

Emmett's hand lifted, but he clenched his fist and brought it back down to his side. "You shouldn't say such kind things to me, Martha."

She furrowed her brow. "Why not?"

His eyes shifted towards Simeon's bed, and his eyes grew sorrowful. "It will inflate my ego," he replied vaguely.

Martha couldn't understand why Emmett was so distant, and it pained her. Gathering her courage, she took another step and tilted her head to look up. As she perused his handsome face, she saw that his jaw was clenched. She wondered why he was so tense, but as she opened her mouth to ask him, he spoke first.

"I plan to accept my cousin Rachel's offer to run their hospital in Rockcliffe."

Her mouth gaped at his unexpected news. "You are moving to Scotland?"

He nodded, pain etched on his face. "Yes, I feel that it is the best thing for me to do right now."

If she were strong, she would have asked, 'What about us?' Instead, she asked, "I thought you enjoyed running the hospital here?"

"I did, but I find I need some time away."

"I will miss you," she said, her eyes lowering to the lapels of his coat.

Raising her eyes, she saw Emmett swallowing slowly. "And I will miss you," he replied with a shaky breath, "but it is best if I go."

"Best for whom?"

"My career," he responded much too quickly.

Her lips tightened as she tried to make sense of what he was telling her. "You have never cared about your career before."

"Things have changed."

"Emmett…" she started but hesitated, looking for the courage to say her next words. "Don't go, please."

His hands rose to rest on her forearms. "I would love to do your bidding, but I have no right." He leaned down and kissed her forehead, his warm lips lingering on her skin. "I wish I could have been the one," he whispered. Before she could react, he dropped his hands and walked out the door.

Tears flowed unheeded down Martha's cheeks as she thought about running after him, begging him to stay and love her. But her feet stayed rooted to the ground, and her mind whirled with confusion. Why was he leaving? Why did he look at her with such longing, yet planned to go to Scotland without her?

What had changed between them? And when had it shifted?

"Is she still looking out the window?" Benedict whispered, concern in his voice.

"Shh! She can hear you," Eliza admonished.

"Should we send for a doctor?"

"I think that may be the problem."

Turning her head from the window, Martha saw Benedict and Eliza standing near the doorway of the drawing room. "I am perfectly well, I assure you." She tried to soften her words with a smile. Addressing Benedict, she asked, "How was your meeting with Lord Beckett?"

"It went well." Benedict gestured towards the settee, encouraging her to sit. "I would like to update you on what was discussed."

Lowering herself down, she prepared herself for the worst.

After Eliza sat down, Benedict walked to the drink tray and

poured himself a drink. "Emmett was at the meeting with Lord Beckett as well, and he inquired after you."

"How nice," she murmured. "I hope you assured him that I was well."

Benedict twirled the drink in his hand as he scrutinized her. "What happened between you two?"

"Nothing of consequence," she replied, blinking quickly, hoping they could not see her eyes fill with tears. "What did Lord Beckett say?"

Glancing with concern at his wife, Benedict took a sip of his drink before sharing, "Your father was found guilty of murder for his brother and nephew, but there was not enough evidence to convict him for your mother's death."

Clasping her hands tighter in her lap, she responded, "I should have testified."

"To be frank, that would not have made a difference," Benedict said, coming around to sit by his wife. "Regardless, your father will be hanged next week for his crimes."

"Do you wish to go?" Eliza asked.

She shook her head. "No, I already made my peace with him."

Benedict's eyes held compassion as he added, "Colonel Allister was court-martialed and sentenced to death for all his crimes in and around Gravesend." He leaned forward and placed his glass on the table. "Furthermore, both Allister and your father were stripped of their titles, which unfortunately removes your title as well. I am sorry."

"Don't be," she assured him. "I never desired a title."

"There's more," Benedict shared. "All of your father's entailed properties reverted back to the Crown, and your father's creditors have laid claim to the properties he bought in Gravesend under your name." He paused and grinned. "Now for the good news, Prinny has decided that you are entitled to the £25,000 that was specified in your uncle's will."

She smiled. "That was most generous. I would like to use some of that money to help support the hospital in Gravesend."

"That is not necessary," Eliza assured her. "We plan to support the hospital, now that we know of the town's dire situation."

"Perhaps I could go and assist Sister Mary as a nurse," Martha mused.

"I was hoping you would stay on as my companion. At least until we sort out why you are behaving so stubbornly," Eliza said.

Martha smiled weakly. "I thought you had fired me."

Eliza dismissed her comment with a wave of her hand. "I never fired you as my friend, and I am worried about you."

"Don't be," she insisted as she rose. "Now, if you will excuse me..."

Benedict spoke over her in a firm tone. "Sit."

Surprised by Benedict's direct order, she obeyed.

His words may have been sharp, but his eyes were full of kindness. "Martha," he began, "like Eliza, I have grown to think of you more than just a friend, more like a sister. Not only are you a godmother to Caroline, but I have enjoyed the laughter and tranquility you have brought to our home." He smiled. "What I am trying to say is that you are a part of our family, and I can't sit back and watch you suffer like this."

"Like what?" she asked, trying to appear brave.

Eliza lifted a brow. "You have been moping around the townhouse all week," she stated. "And we can't help but notice that Emmett has not come calling."

Smoothing out her primrose gown, Martha just sighed. "I cannot help it if Dr. Maddix has no desire to see me." Her heart ached at those words, and the agony of her soul was intense. Why didn't he want her?

"Hmm," Eliza murmured loudly. Tilting her head towards Benedict, she said, "It is a good thing we are both spies."

"Yes, the very best," Benedict agreed, smiling.

"Let's go over what we do know," Eliza encouraged. "Emmett was in love with Martha before we went in and saved the men at The Cloven Hoof."

Martha shook her head sadly. "You are wrong. Emmett does not love me."

Benedict gave her a knowing look. "He referred to you as 'my Martha'."

"Well, if he did have feelings for me, they must have changed," she said softly.

Eliza rolled her eyes. "It doesn't work that way, and especially not that fast," she insisted. "Since arresting Colonel Allister and bringing him back to New Tavern Fort, we have not seen much of Emmett."

"That is because he is planning on running Lord and Lady Downshire's hospital in Rockcliffe," she shared.

"Interesting," Benedict murmured. "Is that why Emmett looked like death when I saw him today at the meeting?"

She furrowed her brows in concern. "He looked bad?"

Benedict nodded. "He has gone back to doctoring in the rookeries and rarely sleeps."

"Oh," she replied as she looked down at her hands. "Dr. Maddix is a very good man."

"The best," Eliza confirmed. "But we," she pointed at Benedict, "don't understand why you two have parted ways."

Martha rose and walked back to the window. As she looked out onto Portman Square, she confessed, "I asked him to stay, begged him even, but he wanted to focus on his career."

"And you believed him?" Eliza asked in surprise.

Resting her head against the wall, Martha tried to hold back her tears. "No, but it was clear that he didn't want me in his life anymore."

Silence filled the room as the tears in her eyes overflowed and ran down her cheeks. She made no effort to wipe them away.

"Can you explain to us exactly what happened after you charged into The Cloven Hoof?" Benedict asked after a few moments.

Martha didn't bother to lift her head as she replied, "Simeon was shot, and I helped tend his wound. Then Josette informed me that my father was shot."

"What about when you told Simeon you loved him?" Josette's voice came from behind her.

"What?" Eliza exclaimed.

Finally lifting her head, Martha turned in surprise. "Simeon was moaning and asking me to stay, so I offered him comfort. That was all."

"No," Josette replied as she walked further into the room. "I heard you say to Simeon that you 'will always love' him, and then I saw the look on Emmett's face."

Benedict lifted his brow. "Now it makes sense. Emmett thinks that you chose Simeon over him. He is being a gentleman and honoring your decision."

"No," Martha rushed to explain. "I do love Simeon, but not in a romantic way. He is my friend and my first love, but I love Emmett." It felt so good to admit that out loud. "I love Emmett," she repeated with more conviction.

Eliza smirked. "Why are you telling us?"

Martha pressed her lips together before asking with great trepidation, "But what if you are wrong?" Her stomach churned at the thought of confessing her love only to discover Emmett didn't really love her at all. "What if Emmett doesn't want me?"

Eliza rose and walked over to her. "Then you will always have a place in our home."

"I know that Emmett loves you," Benedict shared.

"How do you know for sure?" Martha pressed softly.

Benedict stood and joined Eliza, placing his arm around her shoulder. "Because Emmett looks at you the way I look at Eliza."

"You and I share a similar mindset, Martha. We don't trust men. But Dr. Maddix is different," Josette said with a smile. "He is a good man with a kind heart, and he would be a fool to pass on you."

Martha drew a shaky breath. If what her friends said was true, then Emmett still loved her. Looking up at Benedict, she asked, "Do you know where Emmett is now?"

Benedict grinned lopsidedly. "I do, but you will need some assistance getting there."

"Why?" she asked.

"Because he is at a workhouse in St. Giles, and that London district is no place for a lady."

Martha smiled. "It is a good thing that I am not a lady anymore."

Shaking his head, Benedict responded, "You know what I mean. Give me ten minutes to recruit your friends to go along with us."

❧ 31 ❧

EMMETT YAWNED AS HE LED ANOTHER PATIENT OUT OF THE ROOM he was using. He needed a break, but the line of waiting patients at the rundown St. Giles workhouse ran the length of the long hall. He had been working all night and through the day, stopping only to go to the meeting with Lord Beckett and Benedict. It was good to see his friends, and he had tried to be discreet when inquiring after Martha.

Every day, he checked the newspaper for her engagement announcement, but thus far there had been no mention of Martha. Perhaps they'd married by special license.

Never had his heart mourned like it did for Martha. When he last saw her, he desperately wanted to plead for her to love him, but he could not do that to her. She had made her decision, and he had to live with that. He had to live a life without her.

A dirty little boy ran up to him with an apple in his hand. "I'm supposed to ask if ye're hungry." He held out the apple to him.

Emmett crouched down and put his hand up to turn down the offering. "Thank you, but I am not hungry." His stomach growled at that moment, but he didn't want to take this little boy's food. He couldn't imagine how hungry these people must be.

The little boy stepped closer, and Emmett could see his hollowed eyes. "The kind lady brought us lots of food, but she wanted me to bring you this apple." The boy leaned forward and whispered, "She is worried about you."

"Who is this lady?" he asked.

The boy grabbed his hand. "Let me show you." He let the boy lead him to a small room on the first floor. When he walked in and saw Martha, his feet faltered, and he was rendered speechless. She was dressed in a primrose gown with her hair perfectly coifed, but it was the smile on her face that caused him to stare at her. *I must be going mad*, he thought to himself as he heard the little boy run out of the room.

Martha closed the distance between them until she was standing close enough that she had to look up at him. The smile on her face had not dimmed, and she was looking at him with such an intense longing that he found himself transfixed. Finally, he found his voice.

"How are you here?"

"Benedict brought me," she replied.

His eyes could not seem to get enough of her as he basked in her beauty, but his sanity for her safety won out. "It is not safe for you to be here in this workhouse. There are riots all the time because of the lack of food and poor living conditions."

"Then it is a good thing we stopped at the market and brought food with us." She beamed up at him.

He perused her face, bemused by the light sprinkling of freckles on her nose. Why was she torturing him? She was standing so close, but he didn't dare reach out to touch her. Didn't she know that her presence was making him miserable, knowing that she would never be his?

"Perhaps I could come call on you tomorrow..."

"I love you," she rushed out. Eyes wide, she slapped her hand over her mouth and took a step back.

Emmett stood dumbfounded for a moment. When he found his voice, he asked, "Can you repeat that?" He was sure he'd misheard what she had said.

Lowering her hand, she took a few shaky breaths before saying, "I don't know when I started falling in love with you. It could have been when you protected me from those thugs at the inn, or when I danced with you for the first time." Tears filled her eyes as she took a step forward. "All I know is that I love you more than my words can express."

"What about Simeon?" he asked, hoping that he was not dreaming. But if he was, he hoped he would never wake up.

She wiped away tears that were flowing down her cheeks. "I will always love Simeon as I would a friend."

"A friend," he repeated in confusion. "But I heard you say…"

Martha stood on tiptoes and pressed her lips to his, silencing his words. After a moment, she broke the kiss and leaned back. "I have wanted to do that for so long," she admitted shyly.

Emmett grinned impishly. "You always have permission to kiss me."

She lowered her eyes for a moment, then looked up and met his gaze. "I may have loved Simeon in my youth, but I am a different person now. And if I was required to repeat every one of my past trials to experience the love I feel when I am around you, I would do so willingly."

Emmett gently put his hands on her cheeks as his heart raced. "I love you so much," he stated. "I have been miserable this past week thinking about you and Simeon together."

"And I have been miserable at Eliza's townhouse not knowing why you had distanced yourself from me."

He chuckled softly. "If I had known there was even a glimmer of hope for us, I would have never left your side."

"I asked you not to go to Rockcliffe."

Emmett's thumb started rubbing her left cheekbone. "I thought you were asking me to stay and watch you marry Simeon."

"Heavens, no!" she declared forcefully, making him smile. "I wanted to marry *you*."

Martha's eyes grew wide when she realized what she had just said, and her cheeks grew bright pink. Leaning forward, he kissed her cheek before whispering in her ear, "Don't be embarrassed. I feel the same way." He leaned back to look into her eyes. "I dreamt of holding you in my arms, but I never wanted to pressure you or make you uncomfortable in any way."

Her face softened. "That is why I love you so much. You have always allowed me to choose my own path and supported me in my choices. You have always accepted me."

"Now, back to your original comment," he said with a roguish grin. "Do you want to marry, have kids, and live happily ever after?"

Martha's smile vanished. "You should know that I am barren."

"How do you know?"

Martha tried to lower her chin, but he kept his hands firm, willing her to look at him. "In all those years at the brothel, I never once got pregnant," she admitted, her words laced with grief and pain.

Emmett pulled her close and kissed her forehead. "Do you even want children?"

"I have always wanted children," she replied softly.

"Then we will adopt."

She leaned back, the worry still visible in her eyes. "Do you not require an heir?"

He shook his head. "I love you, Martha. You have brought joy back into my life, which has been sorely lacking." His voice hitched, and he took a moment to reign in his emotions. "And I would choose you over anything else, even my own life, because you are my saving grace."

"But what if my past is discovered?" she asked. "When you are an earl..."

He cut her off, revealing honestly, "I love you not in spite of your past but because of it." She started to open her mouth again, and he put his finger over her lips. "Will you stop trying to talk me out of marrying you? It won't work."

As he lowered his finger, she pressed, "I just don't want you to wake up in a few years and realize that marrying me was a mistake."

Tenderly, he assured her, "When I am old and grey, I will still love you desperately, because I have never met a woman as kind-hearted, loving, and brave as you. You may think you are not worthy of me, but you are wrong. I am not now, nor will I ever be, worthy of your love."

His words had the intended effect, because she relaxed into his arms. Finally, he found he had the nerve to say, "I am going to kiss you now."

Her eyes, brimming with love, sought his lips. "I wish you would."

"I love you." His lips brushed gently against hers as he spoke, his voice low and soft.

"I love you, too." Her lips caressed his again.

He held her face gently, not wanting to frighten her, so he was surprised when she brought her hands up his chest and around his neck, pulling him tighter. He chuckled against her lips before deepening the kiss, reveling in the fact that she had chosen him. Dropping his hands from her cheeks, he brought them to her waist and pulled her tight against him.

After a few passionate moments, he rested his forehead against hers. "I can't believe you are finally in my arms and kissing me."

She smiled as her hands started weaving through the back of

his hair, distracting him immensely. "When I agreed to my father's bargain, I never anticipated that I would fall in love with you."

He leaned in, closing the distance between their lips, and kissed her. "Or that you would agree to marry me."

She smiled. "True, I never thought I would marry."

His arms tightened around her waist. "I am so glad you changed your mind."

"Thank you for being patient with me."

Lowering his head, his lips hovered over hers. "If you knew how much I loved you, then you know that I would have waited for you until the day I died."

Pressing her lips against his, Martha showed him how much she loved him, without words. Lost in a passionate moment, his mind barely registered the knock at the open door.

"We finished passing out all the food." That was Eliza's voice.

It was quiet for a moment before Benedict added, "We should leave before it gets too dark outside."

"Did you tell him about the special license yet?" That was Adrien's voice.

Reluctantly, he broke the kiss and leaned back, just slightly. "What special license?"

Benedict grinned. "For my wedding gift to Martha, I went to the Archbishop of Canterbury and requested a special license for you and Martha. However, it cost me a small fortune, since her father had already purchased one for Allister."

"Thank you," he said. "I will reimburse you."

Jonathon walked into the room and laughed. "He must be addled. Didn't you just say that it was a wedding gift?"

"Men don't think clearly when they have just kissed a beautiful woman," Eliza teased.

Turning to face his friends, he tucked Martha against his side. "If it is all right with my fiancée, I think tomorrow is a fine day to be married." Saying the word 'fiancée' made him smile with pleasure.

"Do we have to wait until tomorrow?" she asked sweetly.

His heart soared at her words. "I will marry you whenever your heart desires."

Josette walked in the room and rushed up to Martha. "Wait until tomorrow. Eliza has a surprise for you."

Guessing the surprise, Martha's eyes sparkled. "You do? How did you find the time?"

Eliza gave her a mischievous smile. "I commissioned a wedding gown for you when we first arrived in London. It was obvious to us that you and Emmett were smitten with each other."

"We took bets on when you two would get engaged, but I was off by a week," Adrien admitted.

"So, who won?" Emmett asked.

The group laughed, and Benedict revealed, "Mr. Larson won."

Martha looked up at him and smiled, causing the dreary room to become brighter. "It appears that tomorrow is a perfect day for a wedding."

STANDING IN THE DUKE OF REMINGTON'S LAVISH BALLROOM, Martha couldn't believe that so many people could fit in one enclosed space. The Duchess of Remington insisted on throwing a ball celebrating their wedding. They had been married for just one week, yet somehow the duchess had managed to invite half of London to the ball.

This past week had been a dream. For the first time, they

both were able to sleep through the night, without nightmares plaguing them. It felt amazing to be well-rested in the morning, but it felt even better when she awoke in Emmett's arms.

Hannah approached with a hand on her bulging stomach. "How are you enjoying yourself?"

Smiling at her dear friend, Martha gestured to the crowd. "How did the duchess accomplish this on such short notice?"

Jonathon walked up with a drink in his hand and handed it to his wife. "Isn't it obvious? My father paid everyone to attend."

Eliza laughed as she appeared on Benedict's arm. "Don't listen to Jonathon. He declined my mother's request to host a ball in his honor."

Smiling roguishly at his wife, Jonathon put his arm around her shoulder. "After spending so much time trying to woo Hannah, I just wanted to spend time alone with her."

Adrien laughed from behind. "I am still under the impression that you just wore Hannah down until she felt pity for you." On his arm, Kate waddled next to him.

"Behave, husband," Kate admonished with a smile. She reached out to Martha and embraced her warmly. "It is time for me to retire, but I just wanted to say that you look lovely tonight."

"Thank you," Martha replied, looking down at the beautiful, rose-colored gown with jeweled, embroidered flowers. "Eliza commissions the most beautiful clothes."

Eliza smiled at her compliment before asking, "Where is your husband?"

Martha loved those words and didn't think she would ever tire of being reminded that Emmett was her husband. She had been worried about her wedding night, but Emmett had been patient and tender with her, easing all of her fears.

"Oh dear, we lost her," Hannah replied. "Newlyweds are terrible conversationalists, are they not?"

Jonathon laughed. "To be honest, I am not sure we fared much better."

Emmett approached the group with Luke and Rachel beside him. He leaned down and kissed her cheek. "Did you miss me?" he whispered in her ear.

"Desperately," Martha responded softly.

Rachel reached out and embraced her. "I am so glad that we are related now." She took a step back. "Please say that you will let Emmett run our hospital in Rockcliffe."

Turning her admiring gaze towards her husband, she said, "I will go anywhere that Emmett wants me to go, assuming he is always by my side."

Emmett reached for her hand and brought it up to his lips. "How am I so lucky to have you as my wife?"

She smiled cheekily at him. "If I recall, you asked."

"Best decision of my life," he remarked, returning her smile. "It is time for our first dance."

As he led her towards the chalked dance floor, the Duke and Duchess of Remington met them before they stepped out of the crowd. The full orchestra was warming up in the corner.

Martha curtsied. "Your graces," she said respectfully.

The duke watched her with kindness in his eyes. "What a remarkable journey you have made over these many years."

Martha shifted her gaze towards Emmett as she responded, "It was worth every step."

Taking a moment to look at his duchess with love in his eyes, he returned his gaze back to her. "I wanted to thank you for helping my Eliza and being her friend."

"I owe Eliza my life, your grace," she replied. "She is the reason I am standing here."

The duchess smiled warmly. "I believe that you two were fated to help each other. Together, you've both grown stronger than you thought possible."

"I would like to think so," Martha admitted.

The duchess and duke exchanged another look before the duchess said, "We have heard stories about you both, regarding your bravery and service in Gravesend."

Emmett shifted his stance, looking uncomfortable. "It was our duty to king and country, your graces. Nothing more."

Martha could see respect in their eyes at her husband's comments.

"Prinny told me that he offered you an earldom for your bravery, but you turned it down," the duke observed, giving Emmett a pointed look.

Martha gasped. "Why would you do that?"

Emmett smiled weakly. "At the time, I thought you were engaged to Simeon, and I suggested he be the one awarded the honor for his service."

"You did that for me?" How she loved this man!

His eyes crinkled as he gave her a tender smile. "I would do anything to make you happy."

The duke placed his hand on Emmett's shoulder. "You are a good man, Dr. Maddix. I hope to serve with you one day in the House of Lords."

"Thank you, your grace. If you will excuse us, it's time for me to dance with my wife." Emmett bowed respectfully before escorting her to the middle of the dance floor. Music filled the room, and he led her gracefully in a waltz.

Basking in the nearness of her husband, Martha asked, "Do you regret turning down the earldom?"

"No," he replied. "I am my father's heir and will already inherit an earldom one day." His eyes grew wary. "Do you resent me for passing on the title?"

Martha shook her head, causing her curls to swish back and forth. "Nothing you could ever do would displease me."

He leaned close and whispered, "Remind yourself of that when you find yourself cross with me."

She laughed softly. "To be honest, the only title I ever want is Mrs. Emmett Maddix."

"You are easy to please, my love," he teased.

"Why would I not be?" she asked. "You have given me the greatest gift of all."

"Which is?"

"Unconditional love," she responded. "And to me, that is everything."

With adoring eyes, Emmett stopped dancing and pulled her to him, kissing her right there on the dance floor. Vaguely, she heard cheers and whistles, but her focus was on feeling her husband's arms around her, knowing there was no other place that she would rather be. For in his arms, she was finally home.

EPILOGUE

ONE YEAR LATER.

HEARING HER HUSBAND'S RICH, BARITONE LAUGHTER, MARTHA looked up from her book. The field of purple flowers around her danced in the wind. Their scent brought a smile to her lips. She felt sure their estate in Rockcliffe had the loveliest bell heather field in all of Scotland. Placing her book down, she smiled as Johnny dropped down next to her on the blanket.

"Babies are horrible at playing hide and go seek," Johnny complained. "They don't even try to hide."

"Is that so?" Martha teased as she reached out and ran her hand through his hair. "But you have been such a good cousin to baby Matthew. Your Aunt Rachel and Uncle Luke have told me so."

"I like being a part of such a big, loving family." He grew silent as he lowered his gaze. "Is that wrong of me to say?"

Opening her arms, Johnny leaned into her and rested his head against her chest. "I am so grateful that you are a part of our family," she expressed, brushing her lips against his hair. "And your mother would be so proud of you."

Unexpectedly, Johnny's mother had died from consumption only a few weeks after she had started working for them. Before she passed away, Emmett had promised her that Johnny would lack for nothing and received permission to adopt him into their family. What a blessing Johnny was in their lives!

Emmett walked up, holding his three-month-old nephew, Matthew, in his arms. Smiling at Johnny, he asked, "Why did you stop playing?"

Johnny rolled his eyes. "You standing behind a tree with Matthew is not hiding."

Emmett laughed, but before he could respond, he heard Rachel say, "I have come to get Matthew for his naptime." As she approached, she had a broad smile on her face. Accepting the infant from Emmett, she snuggled him close. "I love being a mother," she said, her eyes full of love.

Emmett dropped down next to Martha on the blanket and kissed her cheek. "How are you faring?" he asked with his usual concern.

"I am perfectly content," she assured him, reaching for his hand.

He offered her a boyish grin. "You always say that."

"Because it's true," she insisted. "You have given me more than I could ever ask for or ever dreamt of."

Leaning in, Emmett kissed her on the lips. "You are easy to please, wife of mine."

"Gross," Johnny groaned loudly as he fell back onto the blanket.

Rachel laughed. "My sentiments exactly." She reached into her pocket and pulled out a letter, extending it towards her. "Eliza sent a messenger to deliver this to you."

Excitement built inside of her as she accepted the letter,

hoping it revealed what she had requested from her friend. "Thank you," she managed to say as she tore open the envelope and opened the letter. Her eyes widened as she read the contents of the note. When she finished, she brought the paper to her chest and closed her eyes, attempting to reign in her growing emotions.

"What is it, Martha?" Emmett asked, reaching for the letter.

Tightening her hold on the paper, she looked up at Rachel. "Would you mind taking Johnny back to the nursery while I speak to Emmett privately?"

Eyeing her with interest, Rachel nodded as she shifted her son in her arms. "I will, assuming you share the contents of that note later."

"I promise," Martha replied as she held out her hand for Emmett to help her rise. Once she was on her feet, she looped her arm through her husband's and led him towards a bench near a cliff overlooking the Urr estuary.

Emmett glanced at her curiously before asking, "Are you going to tell me what was in that letter?"

"Patience, my dear husband," she admonished with a smile.

Once they reached the end of the path, she turned to face him, eager to share her news, but she became distracted by the love shining in his eyes. Even a year later, she never tired of the way Emmett looked at her, as though she was the most precious thing in the world. Instead of revealing the contents of the note, she stood on tiptoes and kissed him.

Emmett wrapped his arms around her waist and deepened the kiss until they both were breathing hard. Breaking the kiss, he pressed his forehead against hers, his arms still wrapped around her. "I would love to continue this later, but I am curious about what news was delivered to you."

"Oh, the note," she breathed as she leaned back. "I almost forgot."

Emmett smiled smugly. "I'm happy to see that you are still affected by my charms."

"I am, hopelessly," she confirmed, returning his smile, "but back to the note."

Martha stepped out of his arms as she unfolded the paper and pressed it against her chest. "At night, I hear you whispering Eleanora's name in your sleep, and I hear the anguish in your voice."

"Most women would be furious if they heard their husband whispering another woman's name in bed," Emmett joked.

"I am not like most women," she challenged.

Emmett leaned in and kissed her. "Thank heavens for that."

She playfully pushed on his chest. "Stop trying to distract me."

Chuckling, Emmett leaned back and watched her with amusement.

"Ever since we were married, I have tried to find the perfect gift for you," Martha explained. "It has taken me some time, but I finally tracked it down with help from a few friends."

Emmett's face was full of love as he started to express, "You didn't need to get..."

"I did," Martha assured him as she handed him the paper.

Watching him closely, she saw a range of emotions cross his face as he read the contents of the letter. Finally, when he finished, he looked at her, his mouth agape. "How?"

Hoping he was not displeased by her efforts, she rushed to explain, "I asked General Floyd to request the records of the men that were impressed by Colonel Allister on that fateful day, and then I asked Lord Beckett to use any connections he had in America."

"Why would you do that?" he asked, his hands still gripping the paper.

"I had to," she replied softly. "That address belongs to Eleanora's mother and her siblings. What you are reading is the response to the letter I wrote to them explaining what happened aboard your ship and how you obtained justice for their daughter."

His eyes widened in disbelief. "Her mother doesn't blame me for Eleanora's death! She expressed gratitude that her daughter wasn't alone in her final days and thanked me for ensuring Colonel Allister received his comeuppance." He spoke slowly, each word filled with wonder. "She even invited us to visit with them in Boston."

Martha nodded. "If you would like to go, then we should..." Her voice stilled as Emmett turned his face towards the horizon. Placing her hand on his sleeve, she asked, "Did I displease you?"

He shook his head before turning back towards her. "I can't believe that you did this for me."

"It was a simple thing," she responded, attempting to downplay the work that had gone into discovering this information.

His hand rose to gently cup her cheek, and his eyes filled with intense love. "I do not deserve you," he murmured in a low voice. "This past year has been the happiest year of my life. Then you go and give me a reason to love you even more." Tears welled up in his eyes as he gazed at her. "And I didn't think that was possible."

"I just hope that I make you as happy as you make me," she replied, placing her hand over his.

A tear dropped down onto his cheek, and she reached up to wipe it away. "Thank you," he said. "I'd assumed that Eleanora's family would despise me. I hadn't even considered apologizing to them."

"I thought you might feel that way," she explained.

"I would like to go to America to meet them."

She smiled. "I assumed you would."

Emmett put his arms around her waist, bringing her close. "How can I ever thank you for your perfect gift?" He smiled at her, his eyes crinkling in the corners. "I could buy you anything your heart desires."

"What my heart wants is not something you can buy," she revealed.

"And what is that?"

"You." She looked at him with longing.

"But you already have me."

"Then, perhaps we could add a little girl to our family?" she asked softly.

Emmett smiled. "Certainly! We could adopt a girl if you would like."

"No, you misunderstood me." Reaching for his hand behind her back, she brought it to rest on her stomach. "We don't need to adopt."

He drew back, his eyes widening in surprise. "You are with child?" She almost laughed at the shock in his voice.

She smiled as joy filled her, a growing bursting joy. "I am."

Picking her up, he swung her around, hugging her tight. "We are going to have a baby!" he exclaimed, his voice echoing off the cliffs.

As he returned her feet to the ground, his eyes filled with tears. "There you go again," he said, his voice hitching, "you just gave me another reason to love you more."

Martha placed her hand on his cheek. "Thank you for saving me," she whispered. "A year ago, I didn't think I had anything to fight for, but I was wrong." She wrapped her arms around his neck. "Now I have a dashingly handsome husband, a son, and a babe on the way."

Pulling his head closer, she whispered against his lips, "You have given me everything. What an extraordinary bargain!"

COMING SOON

The Baron's
Daughter

"Even a lie can become true…
in time."

by

Laura Beers

ABOUT THE AUTHOR

Laura Beers spent most of her childhood with a nose stuck in a book, dreaming of becoming an author. She attended Brigham Young University, eventually earning a Bachelor of Science degree in Construction Management.

Many years later, and with loving encouragement from her family, Laura decided to start writing again. Besides being a full-time homemaker to her three kids, she loves waterskiing, hiking, and drinking Dr. Pepper. Currently, Laura Beers resides in South Carolina.

Made in the USA
Middletown, DE
20 June 2022